GOODNIGHT OPHELIA

BY

PENELOPE FARMER

Copyright © Penelope Farmer 2015

Penelope Farmer has asserted her right under the Copyright, Designs and Patents Act 1988 to be identified as the author of this work.

For Deborah Owen who believed in me through so many years

And for David Macfarland: because

Our histories of past events are somewhat like wrecks upon the sea beach: things are thrown up because they have been entangled in sea-weed: ie facts are preserved which suit the temper or party of a particular historian.
Sir Humphrey Davy

No living creatures known to the writer so closely resemble man in the tendency to wage pitched battles as do ants. Vast numbers of separate species, or of hostile factions of the same species, may he seen massed in combat, which is continued for hours, days, or, in at least one case noted, for over a week. Some of the most extensive battles observed have been fought between neighboring communes of Tetramorium coespitum, a small dark-brown species common to America and Europe.... To be sure, civil wars are, unhappily, not unnatural to human societies, and indeed to social aggregations of humbler creatures.
.... How do these ant warriors recognize friend from foe? How acute and delicate and accurate must be the sense organs seated in the antennae, which [seem to be the] instruments of recognition "He does not carry the odor of my species, my commune, or my caste. Therefore, we will fight!" To a human philosopher meditating upon these things, it seems a small difference on which to divide two such closely related creatures into hostile camps. But mayhap he who counts this for abatement of the common fame of ants for wisdom might find, in the history of human wars, originating causes as insignificant and unreasonable. *From: www.antcolonies.net/howantscarryonwar.html*

To lose one parent… may be regarded as a misfortune; to lose both looks like carelessness. *Oscar Wilde. The Importance of Being Earnest.*

Children begin by loving their parents: after a time they judge them. Rarely, if ever, do they forgive them. *Oscar Wilde: A woman of no importance.*

CHAPTER ONE

There can't be too many people, especially of my age, who discover who they are via Wikipedia. It is preposterous, I think, of course. Sometimes –often - I wish that I had not.

This room I'm lying in offers little by way of diversion, let alone comfort. The last room I'm likely to know, it's a private room in an NHS hospital. Medical aspects have been softened slightly in honour of the fees I pay, but thicker curtains patterned with small pink roses, two pictures on the walls, a digital television set angled jauntily above the bed and bigger than standard ones, can't hide its true nature. The little washbasin in one corner has lofty, institutional taps. The green linoleum of the floor, with its distressing shine, the green of everything, walls, floor, ceiling, even of the low chairs on which my visitors sit, are all too obviously designed to be easy to disinfect on the one hand, to soothe the patient on the other. Still more unmistakeable is the machinery of illness; my special bed with iron bars at head and foot and handles to raise it up and down, to make it shake: the tall stand, stationed alongside my pillows, from which falls the sagging plastic sac draining liquid into my left arm; the morphine pump placed conveniently to hand: the board hooked to the foot of the bed above my feet on which are written my medical notes. The only relief is the sky outside my window. Drifting clouds, an almond tree, a broad window ledge where pigeons sometimes sidle coyly, together or apart, evade medicine, make my world seem just a little bigger. When I am well enough to notice I am grateful.

The pictures do no such thing. Chosen, I daresay, to soothe rather than animate the patient, they, too, look easily wiped. One is of a vase of flowers, another, its surface too smooth for its own good, shows an indeterminate English landscape. When I shut my eyes – as I do most of the time - they are far less vivid to me than the first pictures I remember, in the first room of my life, the night nursery in the house next to the church where I grew up.

'*I remember I remember the house where I was born*' (we were made to learn so much poetry when I was little, some good, some definitely bad) '*the little window where the sun came peeping in at morn.* Etc, etc. But the window by *that* bed – *my* bed - was a large eighteenth century sash one. The sun did not peep through its panes so much as smash against and through them, as shattering to my infant eyes as the church bells were to my infant ears during bell practice every Wednesday from six o'clock to eight. The way it reflected off the glass of those two pictures meant I only saw them properly on cloudy mornings.

One picture was of a girl floating on a stream and holding flowers: a girl with the same name as my mother's. I used to think – maybe I was right - that my mother left it there deliberately so that I would not forget her after she left my father, left me at three years old. In my earliest childhood I confused this picture with the one next to it in which more flowers surrounded a very lively rabbit. The girl - Ophelia - was not the least lively. She lay on her back, her mouth a little open: the flowers she held were live ones: the flowers that floated around her long dress, her feet, looked as dead as she did. This led me to assume – for years, for most of my life – that my mother too had died, not long after her departure.

I'm another Ophelia; nominally I am. I don't feel like one and I rarely admit to my second name. I rarely answer to my first name, Jane, either –J added to O making JO, I've been known as Jo or Joey most of my life. The only time I felt the least like an Ophelia was the day aged eighteen or so that I smoked pot for the first and nearly the last time and lost my virginity to a would-be melancholy, definitely stoned and rather sarcastic poet – or would-be poet - very Hamlet, I thought him, not quite seriously, though not exactly princely. I bled all over his filthy sleeping-bag in a cottage full of mouse droppings somewhere outside Oxford and was sore afterwards in that place I did not know then was called a vagina, any more than I knew what the orgasm I didn't have was called; or even that there was such a thing as an orgasm.

I don't know what happened to *my* Hamlet. Probably he ceased to be melancholy and became an executive of Lever Brothers or a stockbroker or city lawyer – types not quite as fly-by-night, not to say toxic and certainly not as overpaid as they are these days – we know about all *that*, don't we? Nor did I know till I learned through Wikipedia what happened to my mother's Hamlet, the one she met in Paris – the one whom she claimed to see as her Hamlet – her mother's side of her family had been theatrical in years back - and with whom she conceived me. She never saw *her* Hamlet again either. Both of them left Paris before my mother realised that a second Ophelia – me - was growing inside her. Whereupon she was rescued from shame by the man I've always called 'Daddy', her first cousin, who, to the horror of his own mother, married her, in a quick and private ceremony and who, afterwards, brought me up. This man *was* my daddy in most respects, as well as my first cousin once removed, a concept I found puzzling, when I first heard it. How *could* a cousin be removed once, let alone twice?

One housekeeper when I was a child had a little radio on which she listened to Housewife's Choice and Music While you Work. One record often requested on Housewife's Choice was called *Oh Mein Papa,* a soaring tune played on a shimmering yet sickly trumpet, melancholy and tiresome both. After I'd been told around the age of thirteen that the father who reared me wasn't my genetic one, and had taken in, more or less, the fact I had two fathers - it took a while – I always added a letter when the song was announced. *Oh Mein Papas*, I'd think, amused by my own joke, *Oh Mein Papas*. At the same time, the fact I had two fathers defined my childhood as much as the fact I had no mother. The difference was that I could *tell* people I had no mother: their pitying looks gave me a means of getting my own way, with soft hearted adults anyway: it did not always work like that with children. (At my boarding-school when I told my fellows that my mother was dead, the nice ones cried 'oh you poor thing,' the nastier said, 'so even your *mother* didn't like you enough to want to stick around.' This was yet more evidence of how bitchy girls could be. No wonder I've tended to get on better with men.)

What I could not tell my schoolfellows - or anyone who did not know it already – was that I had two fathers. Having two fathers did not fit with the image of the time – the fifties - when everyone was trying to push the war out of mind and consciousness, pretending to children that it hadn't really happened. They succeeded on the surface, pretty much. Forget all those families where Daddy wasn't washing the car or Mummy in a neat little apron taking cakes out of the oven or doing the washing-up, because there was no Daddy – he'd been killed in the war or been replaced by a flighty lover or else, though nominally returned, got drunk or screamed at night or prowled around stupefied. Forget, too, Mummy's previous life doing a man's job in a factory or even

MI5, having flings with pilots about to fall to their deaths in Spitfires. Forget flighty pilots, one-night stands. It was back to normality: the songs on the housekeeper's radio were all about love and marriage, it seemed to me. *'Let him go let him tarry'* went one song, *'let him sink or let him swim… let him go and get another that I hope he will enjoy – I'm going to marry a far nicer boy.*

And this was to be my fate. My father – the one I called 'Daddy' – brought me up for exactly that, to marry the nicer boy and live happily after, the way everyone – every woman had – in that mythical time – it seemed mythical to me as I was growing up – BEFORE THE WAR. So they thought and believed; so they taught nice girls like me – brought up to be 'ladies' - to think and believe.

Hamlet's Ophelia and I did have one thing in common. I may not have fallen in love with any young and melancholy princeling. I might not have gone mad and drowned in a stream surrounded by flowers. But I did have a Polonius for a father; my father and Ophelia's both good but old-fashioned men, rearing motherless daughters as best they could: men who believed in daughters behaving in ladylike ways, having nice thoughts, preparing themselves for marriage by learning how to attract and keep nice boys of good families: men who offered bad –and good - advice at every turn.

'To thine own self be true,' was Polonius' advice to his son and probably to his daughter also. 'Just be yourself, darling, and you'll be fine,' was my father's advice to me before he sent me off, protesting, to those dreary dances where I was supposed to encounter a suitable husband but never got much beyond snogging, damply, the odd tongue-tied and spotty youth who whispered in my ear, along with Frank Sinatra 'You make me feel so young…'

But how could you be true to a self – *what* 'self'? - when you did not know who you were, because no one ever told you? When you've spent most of your life wrapped in deceptions woven by the people you trusted most – by my adoptive father and by the person who was closest to being a surrogate mother, in my case? When everything could suddenly be upturned and overturned, leaving you without a familiar self? When a song you lived in utterly – not a song I'd heard in the fifties admittedly, not till the seventies when I knew perfectly well what it meant in all its sweet tenderness and lewdness - was '*Come rub it on your belly like guava jelly?*' Oh the irony of that.

I've looked for my real father, my real mother all my life; and as soon as I found them, wished that I had not. Oh the irony of *that*.

I only ever saw two pictures of my mother. In the first, taken at my christening, she is holding me and standing besides my father, flanked by godparents I don't remember encountering again: all of them must have thought that taking an oath to protect my virtue was enough – not one was around to defend my virginity eighteen years or so later. My mother looks very pretty and very thin, despite the unbecoming hat she wears at an angle, despite the fox fur round her neck, the narrow dress clinging to her elegant flanks and ending halfway down her calves. I wondered sometimes why my father showed me that picture. Did he do it to remind me I had been christened, to remind me to remain a virgin till I'd netted the appropriate young man and wore his ring on the third finger of my left hand? If so, it was in vain.

The second photo that included my mother turned up years later while I was clearing out my father's desk after he died. It showed my father and a group of what looked like twenty-somethings on a sailing holiday. How I recognised my mother among them I don't know: I'd only ever seen the one picture of her. She looked younger than the rest, not much more than eighteen, meaning that this snap would have been taken less than a year before she conceived me, and rather less than fifteen months before my father so quixotically married her.

At the time, I was more interested in the version of him the picture showed than I was in that of my mother, despite the stack of letters that revealed my father's treachery in full. Grief trumping rage for this moment, I pushed them aside and I let myself be transfixed by the image of my father leaning against the tiller of the boat, his already thinning hair on end, his pipe clamped to the corner of his mouth – at that stage still topped by his little brush moustache – his over-long shorts slipping down over his skinny frame in a way once very familiar to me: he put on weight only in later life. He looked so carefree, so happy – maybe because my mother was of the group: that he'd always adored her was one thing I did know. He looked also, amazingly, *amazingly* young.

This made me mourn him still more, even as my fury with him grew. Can you imagine Polonius looking young?

But of course he had been young, once. Just as both Ophelias and Hamlets come at all ages: the deaths they live through by staying alive much worse often than the ones they succumb to in adolescent fury.

In the country of old age death does not come decked with flowers, does not come with swordfights, stabbings, adolescent melancholy and fury; it comes with bones crumbled, flesh sunk in, piss and shit flowing unchecked, bodies ending like bodies begin in the care of others, their excretions contained by throwaway cloth, and wiped up by carers. It comes with a longing and a dread that have nothing to do with love or madness, but only with the inevitability of death, the brevity of life and an end which Ophelia neither saw nor knew about, the silly girl. All she got was the short story, which did not include the indignity of pain, at least not the kind I'm confronting these days, the kind I must owe genetically – another irony - to the man my mother thought of as Hamlet in the stormy winds of *her* youth.

Long before I fell ill, the conviction that my mother died young – might have died young – comforted me. It left me free to imagine her body remaining as I used to think my own would: old age is not something you foresee in yourself. Just so, I thought, the young and lively flesh in those photographs of my mother would never have marked and shrivelled, she would not have seen her bright and bushy pubes reduced to a scanty grey stubble, or the smooth clear skin of her back covered in the great brown splodges that have appeared on mine.

A previous husband berated me for minding about such signs of age. 'It's what inside your head that matters,' he always said, but alas he wasn't around for long, *his* signs of age did all too thoroughly for him, to my acute grief, and the husband that succeeded him averted his eyes very obviously. I think he did - he's younger than I am. For sure he made love to me in the dark, though that may have been in part because of his own physical deficiencies, starting with his overload of flesh. It's more than possible, too, that he married me for my money, but so what? We have grown fond of one another: better than fond, I think, for which I'm grateful. The fourth man to provide me with a wedding ring - my father could not say I'd failed in my duty to find a husband, though I do not think he envisaged quite so many - he makes daily visits to my death bed, spends far longer than he needs and doesn't wrinkle his nose too obviously at the stink of old age and urine that has me wrinkling my nose, even though it emanates – it must emanate – from myself. Nor do I begrudge him his prospect of my money: I got rich by marriage, among other things, why shouldn't he? And actually, cynicism apart, my calling him as I do *The Husband* ' in inverted commas - it began in part as ironic, in part because it pleased him - has become ever more the point. We do, overtly, like each other very much: we've been husband and wife in every sense apart from begetting children and I don't doubt that he will mourn me. These days I believe that this may be as good as it gets – and better. It's not as if I will ever be able to prove myself wrong.

It is reported – and I will find out for myself soon – that at the moment of death your whole life flashes before you. That's involuntary, if so. What I find myself doing now in my hospital bed, trawling much more slowly through my past, is not. It could be, of course, an attempt to assuage my guilt for a sin I did not know I was committing – that I barely reckoned as a sin, given my innocence - yet which has haunted my life ever since I learned of it.

I am no mythical heroine: I inflate myself by making such comparisons. Yet self-inflation always has helped me confront the questions stamped into me at birth. I imagined myself a lost princess when I was small; later, hearing the term 'Latin Lover' saw my real father as a French version of Rudolf Valentino (my mother had met him in Paris, he must be a Frenchman then). Later still, as a teenager, I imagined one parent at least and possibly both dying a martyr's death at the hands of the Gestapo. I daresay it's the same process that reminds me now – and with which I identify - of those heroes forced to atone painfully for sins against the gods, committed as unwittingly as mine, heroine though I am not. As I daresay it's the same relentless questions that force me to go beyond the mythmaking and tell myself my real story, over and over, at the same time forcing myself to hear. It is as if I am, at once, both Ancient Mariner and wedding guest.

CHAPTER TWO

My elder daughter comes to see me this afternoon, bringing her two youngest children– the two elder ones are both too busy revising for exams, she tells me: I daresay the thought of a hospital visit to their dying grandmother was even less of an attraction. The two she brings – both girls – are a credit to the latest temple to consumption near where they live in West London. The elder wears what looks like leopard patterned ballet shoes, Calvin Klein Jr jeans, a dinky little denim jacket, patterned with small studs, and sidles through my door still plugged into an Ipod headset. When her mother insists she removes it she protests 'I've got Rihanna on, she's like so *cool*', but obeys, very sulkily, sneaking a look at me. The younger one – much younger, my elder daughter's afterthought, I suspect - replaces a pink Gameboy in her Hullo Kitty backpack with much better grace. Her pink t-shirt claims *I'm so cute,* in sequins, on her feet are fluorescent pink crocs covered in what look like brilliant little broaches. All this makes me almost nostalgic for the school uniforms I resisted for my own children throughout the seventies: let alone for the corduroy boy's shorts, passed on from my friend Thomas - and sensible brown Clark's sandals I wore in the late forties when clothes were still on ration. In these days of recession, global warming, it also makes me wonder if my grandchildren's children will view this decade much as my generation – the middle-class part of it at least - saw the decade before the war: as an age of unimaginable plenty; all the sweets you could eat, enough petrol for your parents to drive anywhere they liked, and – to me most astonishing of all - shells from Japan that opened up in water and produced multi-coloured paper flowers.

Though I've propped myself up to be ready for the visit, I make out I am asleep at first, only open my eyes and smile as they came near. The last visiting grandchild – my son's youngest boy - refused to kiss me: I did not blame him one bit. But these two peck my cheek obediently, the younger one saying as she does so 'I love you, grandma' to my dismay and astonishment: how they do throw that word around these days. In my youth we barely admitted we loved our husbands except in the most formal of ways, let alone parents, let alone grandparents. We never hugged them, any more than we hugged our female friends. The rapid brush of mouth on cheek served for all family, for the closest of acquaintances, but nothing more. Some of my generation have – self-consciously in my view – taken to hugging everyone in sight, not something I've ever subscribed to.

This child, though, the darkest-skinned and prettiest of my daughter's good-looking four, is a sweet child: she fits, pretty much, the claim of her t-shirt and I find myself shutting my eyes again and mouthing back, 'I love you too.' It's the drug has got to me, probably, and I'm not sure she hears. When I open my eyes again she has retreated and the high green ceiling looked as remote as ever.

My daughter leans over me now: laying her mouth on my cheek, she says, 'Hi, Mum, how are you?' in a tone which might even be affectionate. I don't respond – the response I feel like making – quite unfairly I know – is to leap up and say meanly, 'I'm not dead yet, bad luck.' It's just as well I'm not strong enough. Pain and morphine have me in their pincer grip that morning. Maybe – probably – I would feel more affectionate if they didn't. As it is I need to take things out on something or someone. It's always been my elder daughter's bad luck to get in the way of me and my problems, and pain and morphine not to say impending death, are worse problems than most. I do my best with my grandchildren: I ask what they've been doing. The youngest one answers, excitedly, 'Daddy got us a Wii': at this even the elder one manifests enthusiasm. 'It's such a fun thing it's so cool. I love it.' I do not know what a "Wii" is. My daughter's explanation – 'it means we can all play stuff together' is not enlightening.

She gives me a kindly look. 'Don't worry, mum. It doesn't matter. It's all got so much more complicated these days.' I nod, weakly, trying to smile; I even try to join in still more. 'What are those things on your shoes?' I ask the little girl. She looks blank for a minute. The bigger girl answers for her. 'They're jibbitz,' she says. 'You collect them. *She* collects them.'

'I've got twenty already. Mummy gives me one every time I get a star at school,' the smaller girl says, beaming

'*Giblets*?' I ask. '*Giblets*? I'm pretty sure she didn't say that but I'm happy for once to play Idiot Ancient. It's helping me forget my discomfort.

My daughter and elder granddaughter speak simultaneously, the first looking indulgent, the second scornful. 'Jib*bitz.*' the mother says. '*Jib*bitz' shouts the child.

'Shall I buy you one?' I ask my younger granddaughter. She nods her head fervently, the beam spreading ever wider. 'Ask your mum to get some money out of my bag,' I say. 'It's in my locker.'

'What do you say to your grandmother?' chides the mother as she heads towards the bedside table. The little girl looks back at me almost startled: she has thanked me in her way and we both know it.

'Thankyou, Grandma, thanks ever so,' she whispers.

She follows her mother round to the far side of the bed. She inspects carefully, in turn, first my drip feed then the morphine zapper lying besides me.

'What are those for?' she asks. I hear my daughter clear her throat – she must be trying to come up with some anodyne explanation. I get in first. I tap the line of the drip. 'It's to make me less thirsty. And *this,*' I say, stroking the zapper, 'this is to stop me hurting,'

'Do you hurt a lot? Is that why you have to be in hospital?'

'Sometimes I hurt, but not when I have this. They're very good in hospital, making things not hurt.'

'I don't want you to be hurting, grandma,' she says mournfully.

'It's alright, darling, when I've got this, I don't.'

I look down at my elder daughter still crouched by the locker, rummaging in my bag, hoping she approves of what I've said. I don't want her to see me as wilfully upsetting her children. She looks up at me and nods. Then nods again. Not much later, returned to upright, holding a five pound note, she says, "I'll bring the change back. They don't cost much. You're tired, mum' she adds, 'and we're late. We'd better be off.'

'Take ten. Don't bother with change,' I say. 'Get as many of things as you like. And something for her sister too.'

The elder child prodded by her mother says thank you in her turn. I don't ask what she will buy with her money. When she kisses me goodbye she whispers in my ear. 'You did say *giblets,* Gran, didn't you? That's cool. Jibbitz are babyish really.'

She steps back, re-orders her denim jacket, grabs her Ipod out of her pocket. 'See you later, Grandma,' she says, passing it from

14

hand to hand as if wondering how soon, decently, she can return to Rihanna. The younger one jigging a little from foot to foot, looks at me concernedly.

'Promise you won't hurt any more, Grandma,' she says.

'I promise,' I say – how I wish I could keep my promise. But a lie in such circumstances counts as a pretty white one, I think, smiling at her, wryly, as they leave, the door thumping to behind them. For a moment I can still see the shape of my daughter through the figured glass: the children are too short to reach it.

CHAPTER THREE

I was born two months before the war started in a village in Kent, close to the Surrey border. My mother ran away when I was three, but my father and I remained in the same village, in that same house next to the church till I left, first, briefly, for Oxford, then London, where I've spent the rest of my life.

It was an end of terrace house, early eighteenth century and beautiful but far from comfortable. There was no heating of any kind other than the old range in the kitchen, replaced by an Aga after the war, and open fires on the floors above. My father never seemed to mind or even to notice the cold: he was surprised when, as an adolescent, I demanded a heater for my room for when the fire was not lit. The floors from top to bottom were made of polished boards up through which the wind sneaked as mercilessly on winter days as they sneaked under every door and between the cracks of every window. Standing alongside what had been the road to London, the house had once been a coaching inn: if you dug up the garden you came across cobblestones – the remains of the old road, my father said. He too had been brought up in the house. His father had passed it onto his one remaining son when he died. My father and mother had moved in straight after their marriage.

Members of his family had been in this village for generations: my grandfather's mother was buried in the churchyard. I was taken to put flowers on her grave sometimes and on that of the baby which she had died having, my grandfather's little brother. He had only survived a week or two - his grave was tiny, lying on the opposite side of the path from his mother's grave and just over the wall from us.

I often reflected on those premature deaths in a pleasantly gloomy way. I thought about death a lot during my childhood; perhaps it was because of the war, perhaps because of dead Ophelia on the wall of my bedroom, perhaps because of my departed, maybe dead mother. Though I did not for one moment imagine my own death let alone see myself dead, it might have explained why I was much more intrigued by the funerals – when I was little I called them 'dead weddings' - than I was by the live ones, preferring the solemn single knell from the church bells as the cortege processed through the church gate and into the church to the merry jumble of the sound that created the appearance of the brides and grooms.

Live weddings during the war, were always austere anyway; bride or groom and sometimes both in uniform, not much in the way of veils and bridesmaids and long white dresses, the bare minimum of flowers. How could such weddings compete with the pomp of the funerals; the coffin with flowers on top, the men in top hats, the sombre people in black walking behind, waiting under the yew tree by the gate? I would sit with my nose so tight pressed against the window that the tip must have turned white for lack of blood. I can feel now the pressure of the cold against my skin, see the misting of the pane with my breath that I had to wipe every now and then, feel the mysterious ache that arrived along with the smell of my own breath. All I had to watch during the funeral service was the waiting hearse –if the body was continuing to the crematorium - and sometimes the village taxi-drivers, thin Mr Jenner and fat Mr Jenner, wearing their dark blue uniforms and caps with shiny peaks, along with black ties for a funeral, standing besides the upright black cars that were almost the only ones I'd ever ridden in. But I would never leave the window before the coffin's procession emerged from the church, whether heading for hearse or graveyard. I was an obstinate little thing and persistent, traits which have remained with me throughout my life.

I didn't of course tell my nanny or my father that I preferred the funerals, let alone that I wondered sometimes if my mother herself might be in one of wooden boxes, wider, mysteriously, at the top end than at the bottom; still less did I dare ask if I could attend so mysterious a ritual. Though I did not know the word 'morbid' I could sense it, know that adults would not think my curiosity very nice, let alone appropriate. But maybe they sensed my inappropriate questions because it must have been about this time my father tried to introduce me to alternative mothers – not a stepmother, he appeared to have no interest in replacing my mother till many years later – but nice suitable women, wives of his friends or colleagues. It was a vain hope on the whole and there were so many of these woman – Mrs This – Mrs That - all similar kinds of people, the kinds that turn up in villages like ours, that they run together in my head. They were sometimes but not always the ones he tried to inflict on me later, when he thought I needed instruction on growing up as a woman, most of whom had only one clear idea of what I should aim for in life – a husband, of course – and gave me a great deal of specific advice about how to achieve this aim, and even more specific advice about how not to, which left me more baffled than anything else, especially when the advice was contradictory.

For now I'll just say this: that I always doubted my mother's advice would have been the same. I assumed her a romantically free spirit, an assumption that did help me to forgive her, a little. Women who achieve the husband and then abandon him the way my mother abandoned hers must have seen, even in those days, that there are other things in life. What these things were I did know a little. My father, for all his conventions and his limitations – an Englishman out of central casting an American friend called him once –not only loved his cousin, my mother, but had just enough imagination to understand why she ran away or at least to have listened to her explanations as to why she was doing so: part of this explanation he passed on to me in due course. He also had enough imagination to hope that by doing so he would make me see that she was not simply abandoning me for myself but because of the kind of life staying would have meant for her. Maybe that was how he comforted himself, too. Yet he did feel abandoned, obviously, and so did I. How could the child I was understand my mother's boredom? Nineteen years old when she married my father and gave birth to me, she was stuck at home thereafter with a husband and baby and increasingly no servants to do the chores she'd never been taught how to do. Servants those days were called up to help the war effort, meaning that while my mother's contemporaries summoned into the world by the demands of war were freed from their female shackles, she was ever more bound to them. The aged Nanny did not cook or shop or wash. Those were my mother's jobs and she had to learn from nothing how to do them, all by herself.

War – whether imminent or arrived war – had a lot to answer for in the lives of my generation: more than most of our children and grandchildren understand. In some respects we were affected vicariously, through the wars' effects on our parents. In others its impact was more direct, for social or generational reasons.

But for war – or rather its imminence – the havoc Hitler was causing long before it broke out, I, for instance, might never have been conceived.

The Husband came to visit me in hospital this morning, bringing carnations, flowers I don't care for and anyway, not caring to mimic my namesake, I prefer my room to be flowerless. But I say nothing. He has brought them with the best of intentions, and even though it's an example of how totally unlike we are, this unlikeness suits us both. If I've never loved him, romantically speaking, I've felt rested within the lack – or seeming lack - of mutual tastes. This worried me when I first met him (through a lonely hearts website I'd signed on to at a bleak moment - how much life has changed in such respects; my parents never had such options nor, in my youth, did I). Yet I've felt much more comfortable watching a football match or some crapulous documentary about cars on Channel Five with this husband than I often felt with my more literary, more musical partners. And I've enjoyed what he does know: he's an academic scientist, not a very high-flying one, teaching biology at one of those universities that used to be polytechnics – hence his relief as marrying into my money - knowing a lot about the habits of ants and muttering loudly whenever some news report on the telly gets science wrong. Professor Growser I call him. Ms Ignorant he calls me. But it's all very fond. And over the past few years I've learned a lot about those busy but bellicose creatures ants – 'animals' he calls them; they remain insects to non-scientific me.

One of the other ways in which we are most different is in my attention to memory – to my past – and his lack of interest in any of his. Previously he used to discourage me when I started reminiscing. But dying gives you dispensations and so these days he lets me talk, and appears to listen, though I think the person chiefly listening to me is myself, trying, endlessly, to separate true memories from false ones - an impossible task of course, as he, ever the realist, points out.

'Memory distorts everything, you must know that,' he chides in his rather rumbling, rather northern voice, shifting his belly in the uncomfortable, slippery, green easy chair. (His paunch was another thing I didn't care for, but am used to by now, in fact had grown almost fond of. It felt comfortable against my back in bed, before I got too ill to share ours. I didn't like beards either; it seemed a cliché in someone in his job. He has one of those too.). His shirt is coming out of his trousers, I notice. He has a hole in one of his ridiculously thick – like something you'd wear with hiking boots – socks – they seem incongruous with the crumpled suit he sports today: he doesn't usually live up to sartorial clichés of provincial academics, rarely wearing corduroy trousers, thick sweaters, hiking boots. He goes to work in a tweed jacket and those grey trousers public school schoolboys wear; and sometimes – often – in this admittedly well-worn suit and a proper shirt, with or without a tie. I hadn't married him for his dress sense, for sure.

'Do ants have memories?' I ask – but then hope he hasn't heard. He's all too likely to tell me, in detail; and right now I don't want to add to my knowledge of natural history. He says nothing, fortunately – he's too busy blowing his nose.

'I hope I'm not getting a cold. Half my students are hawking and sneezing at the moment, I can hardly hear myself think. And most of them don't know to cover their mouths when they cough. They may have fancy haircuts these days and wear what looks like fancy dress, half of them. But they're barbarians, just the same. Always asking silly questions, half of them. Time I retired.'

He was always saying 'time I retired.' But he never did. I daresay it would be different once I died and he had money, even though I couldn't imagine what he'd do with it. He couldn't imagine either, though he claimed he'd find something good.

'Good luck to you,' I'd say. I was grateful for his not pussyfooting round the fact that I would soon be dead. Most people say brightly things like 'next year we can…' and then stop short, fiddling with something awkwardly.

It is a grey drizzly morning in very early spring. The branch of blossom tapping on the window is more dispiriting than pleasant, though no more dispiriting than the gibbet-like thing which holds my drip, the spouted cup on the bedside table, the bowl of grapes I never feel like eating, the invitation of the open box of tissues to clean up everything in sight.

One used tissue is lying, I notice, on the green shining linoleum, the combination of the two almost the most dispiriting thing of all. I find myself wishing I could end my life surrounded by cotton handkerchiefs and wooden floorboards. But I can't.

'God, this place,' my husband says looking around him: if he notes the tissue he makes no attempt to pick it up, the slob. 'It's like something out of a bad novel.'

'How would you know? You never read novels. You're thinking of medical soaps.'

'That's why I don't read novels. I *feel* like a character in a bad novel,' he adds. But then this watery light, shifting around bed and chair, rather greenish, turns us both into creatures struggling under water, make this most factual of men look almost fictional: mythical even, like some kind of shapeless, run-down, protean figure, with no more existence outside this room than I have myself these days. 'Someone in a deathbed scene,' he says. 'At least animals have the sense to go away to die by themselves.'

'Thank you so much for coming,' I reply tartly, blowing an ironic kiss.

When he's gone I drift back to my last memories of my mother, just before she left. They were almost the only ones I can date exactly - it was my third birthday, and she was going to take me to the market in the village, one of the few treats available during the war. That had been a sunny morning too. I'd sat on my pot, looking at my shadow on the wall and thinking how big I looked

'Come on,' my mother was urging. 'We can't go until you've *been.*'

I'm not sure now that she would have cared if I had 'been' or not. But the aged nanny was very keen on what she called "being regular"; my mother might grumble about the nanny, even to me, but she'd never dared go against her.

This time, though, when I had at last released my two miserable turds she'd pushed the nanny away. 'I'll do this,' she said, wiping my bottom with such tenderness, it was as if she knew – she must have known – that it was likely to be for the last time. Which is perhaps why I also remember from the market, later in the morning, that the calf that pressed against the railings near where were standing had excrement running down its backside.

'He's done a big job,' I said loudly. 'But he hasn't got a mummy to wipe his bottom,' I did not know, of course, how soon I would not have one either. This bit I don't remember, but Patty, my mother's best friend in the village who was with us at the time used to remind me of it sometimes. My mother had been embarrassed, apparently.

'You were such a touching little thing,' Patty told me years later, 'And your mother could be so prissy.' Perhaps if she'd known what my mother had done for *me* that morning, she would never have brought the matter up, even though she was one of the few people who did not avoid mentioning my mother. I'd loved her for that, as these days I love my husband for failing to pretend that I'm not dying.

CHAPTER FOUR

These times, I have good mornings and bad ones. Today I'm having a good one. This doesn't mean much by most measures; I'm still terminally ill, doubly incontinent – thank the lord for catheters - suffering from a bed-sore or two, and with the morphine zapper at my side that can be brought to more active life at the touch of a button. At the same time I'm not in much pain, and for once my mind is working reasonably well and so is my sense of taste. I've had a boiled egg for breakfast, an underrated pleasure. Also it is sunny and early April – an April which can't afford to be my cruellest month this year, since it's likely to be one of my last: well it *is* cruel in that sense of course, but this morning let's not dwell on *that*, let's just be grateful – I am grateful – that I'm well protected, will be for ever protected, from its sometimes vicious winds and spattering of rain. And from its dead land breeding too, apart from that almond tree outside my window. Though I did spend a happy few minutes watching a pair of angry cock sparrows dispute something or other: at this moment, still better, the victor is courting his lady love, fluttering his wings and tail and singing musically. I didn't know that sparrows sing musically when courting: how strange I've had to wait seventy years to experience the pleasure of hearing the trills. Best of all, my favourite nurse is on duty this morning. Peter is the only male nurse on this ward, but the one I prefer by far, especially now I've got a room to myself, as a private patient. Peter and I exchange risqué jokes, which at their most risqué would probably pass most of my fellow-patients by, especially the gaga ones. Thank god – it's the only thing I can be thankful for – that I'm dying young enough not to be gaga. Also that I am not dying on a public ward. When I complain about any aspect of my treatment Peter says sharply: 'you should be so lucky. You should have seen the programme about one geriatric ward I saw on the telly last year.'

'I wouldn't be on a geriatric ward,' I said. 'Not with cancer.'

'You think so? You're over seventy. Over sixty-five is geriatric here, disease no matter.'

I do not like to hear the word 'geriatric' applied to myself. But he's right of course, I am 'geriatric', like it or not. But it's what I like about Peter; he tells it straight.

Peter is built like a truck-driver, not exactly bursting out of his nice little white jacket - its difference in length from the doctors' white coats an indication of his more lowly status – but looking as if he might. With his relatively thin legs and relatively small feet, he also looks top-heavy. He has eyes like buttons, a gold earring in one ear, a shaven head, a singe roll of flesh on the back of his collar, graven lines from nose to mouth, a tendency to play with his earring when he's not having to busy himself with catheter, drip or whatever and a wonderful line in camp. I'd swear he was gay – but he has a girlfriend – his fiancée he always calls her - another nurse; they're trying to buy a flat together. He also has a good line in complaints against the system he's working in which is, he complains, riddled, *riddled* with sexism, though not in the usual sense. 'Do l look like a sex-maniac, darling, but that's what they think – that all male nurses want to do is exploit cunt.'

'How do I know you haven't got a hard-on right now?' I ask, not looking in that direction.

'That would be most inappropriate,' he says primly.

'And that was very kind of you. You could have said "most unlikely". Sometimes,' I add wistfully, 'I could think of much better things you could do with mine than shove in a catheter. Well I could have once,' I added, glancing at the swollen belly hiding my genitalia from me, more or less, 'But all good things have their day.'

'Is that your cliché for this morning?' he asks, grasping the frame from which my drip is suspended, and wheeling it a little nearer. He goes back to his rant. 'What about all those male gynaecologists? Does being a doctor stop them being sex-maniacs? It's class distinction that is, and I could tell you some tales, I really could tell you, about gynaecologists. They'd make your hair stand on end.'

'No thanks,' I say. 'I'm past all that. I'm supposed to be thinking about death not erotica.'

'Eros and Thanatos. One and the same thing, dear,' he says. (A philosophic bent lurked in him somewhere, I'd noted this before and wondered what his girlfriend made of it.) 'You didn't sound as

24

if you were past it a moment ago. Weren't you making a lewd suggestion? Or did I miss something?'

'Just a manner of speaking,' I say. 'But why are you a nurse, not a doctor? Couldn't you have been?'

'What, and spend seven years and more training, just to end up being able to shout at nurses?' he says.

'Why are you a nurse then?'

'Because I *like* looking after people: even the likes of you. Why shouldn't I?'

He is serious for once. I believe him. I know in my own body that he likes looking after people. He does it very well. The other nurses – the women – do their job well enough, most of them – and most are kindly. But when they perform such intimate tasks as taking off my dirty nappy – cleaning me up- they don't make me feel as if I am being mothered. Peter does make me feel that way: no need to say that I connect it with my last memory of my mother wiping my bum. Nor is it just that I am grateful for being *able* to shit – morphine gives you dreadful constipation. I just love him for what he does, as himself, in that simple, singular moment, that is all.

At times, in betweenwhiles, I resent it. I did tell him once he must be perverted or something to want to spend his life cleaning up old women's backsides. But he is perfectly capable of being sharp, not to say waspish himself and this time, too, he didn't smile sweetly or purse his lips in a disapproving way, or walk out slamming the door discreetly behind him the way one of the women might. He said. 'Do you think I like cleaning up your shit? It's my job. One of the worst parts. But there you go, old lady.' And then he smiled at me cheekily in such a way I could not but smile back. I refused to let him see it. I just turned my head, my smile, and buried them in the pillow. And he gathered up the dirty nappy, the bowl he'd washed me with, the soap, the towel, and with a disdainful shake of his not very neat belly, his surprisingly neat bum, he departed the room.

Ten minutes later he brought me a cup of tea and fed it to me in a cup with a spout, as lovingly as ever, humming jauntily, very slightly mocking me, 'Oh what a beautiful morning,' as he did so, his gold earring glinting in the light from the window. He smelled of disinfectant and, the smallest bit, of after-shave. He tasted –

everything was smell and taste now: much of the time I found myself confusing them – better than the tea. How strange, I thought, to feel so mothered at long last: but by a man.

CHAPTER FIVE

Everything is normal to a child. Everything that surrounds them, day to day, seems normal, that is, including things far from normal in peacetime terms. Even the nights when the sirens sounded and I was hauled out of bed to sit under the stairs, to nibble on fish-paste sandwiches and sip hot milk – flavoured by Ovaltine if I was lucky –while the bombers flew over towards London and then flew back, sometimes dumping their surplus cargo of explosives all too near us, even those nights seemed normal enough to me: not to say fun. I was disappointed when the war ended, though canny enough not to say so, waving my flag on VE day as enthusiastically as anyone else.

I remember too, but with less pleasure, my father's frequent and mysterious absences: especially when I was old enough to wonder where he was: he only ever said that he was away 'doing his job.'

For my father had something else in common with Polonius apart from being wifeless and the father – the effective father – of a child called Ophelia. He was a working courtier; in this case only nominally of a monarch, more precisely of a government. Meaning that he was a civil servant. Not just any old civil servant: he was a clerk in the House of Commons, which meant that he hadn't been allowed to go into the army when the war started, as he had, passionately, wanted, and his widowed mother who'd lost both her other much older sons in the first war equally passionately had not. I don't know what would have happened to me had he been able to join up. Would my mother have taken me with her when she ran away? Would she even have run away I often wondered? Sometimes I wished he had gone and then felt guilty for wishing that. As it was, as a single father, as opposed to the single mother most mothers were then, their husbands far away, he was allowed a nanny and a housekeeper to look after me and run the house.

When the war ended his job was important to me too. It almost felt sometimes as if the only mother I had was his employer: my father always called it *the mother of parliaments*; this was one of the many myths about my past that I created to mitigate my orphaned state, to help stifle the questions, the uncertainties that have always plagued me.

I spent a lot of time in Westminster as I was growing up, visiting my father at the House, as he always called it, during the sessions in which Parliament sat. In the early days I was escorted by my nanny, thereafter by the ill-tempered ex-governess who replaced her; but from the age of thirteen or so I took myself on the train journey from Sevenoaks to Charing Cross. From there it was a one-stop ride on the District Line to Westminster.

Watching the series *Upstairs, Downstairs* years later, I was reminded of my father and his colleagues. Working alongside their parliamentary masters and mistresses, they too observed their most intimate, private – even sometimes scandalous behaviour: I think my father may once have interrupted one minister fucking a secretary on his desk - I could be making that up. Not that my father was ever going to sell his memoirs. He was as discreet as all civil servants were then, none admitting to, let alone acting on, any preference for one political party or another. Yet he did sometimes, in private, make his views of his masters known. During that period of my late childhood, early adolescence, when to the disapproval of onlookers we'd developed a domestic intimacy more like husband and wife than father and child, he would announce over dinner such things as 'Churchill seemed battier than usual today', or 'George Brown was spectacularly drunk, even for him' or – later – 'I've never seen Richard Crossman so bad-tempered.'

(In particular, though this came later, he made clear from the start his loathing of Margaret Thatcher, whom he'd had the misfortune to escort on a parliamentary jaunt to some independence ceremony or other in some part of Africa. 'Frightful woman,' he'd say 'Quite frightful.' Adding reluctantly, 'But very good looking of course. She'd give us all hell, making a fuss about everything, refusing even to sit with anyone who wasn't what she called 'one of us', then she'd put on her hat, fluff up her hair, step out of the plane and the Africans *loved* her. The ruddy woman.')

My father always did tend to admire blue-eyed blondes, even though his two most adored women, me and my mother, were dark-haired; in my case almost black-haired. My mother, it's true had blue eyes, but mine were very dark. This shows how irrational men are, especially set-in their ways ones like my adopted father.

I am about ten.

Check: the dim stone underpass leading from Westminster underground station, the iron grille behind which waited the policeman we had to encounter first. I'd announce his name airily, before the former governess escorting me could speak – how she glowered then – and the policeman would smile at me not at her, I am glad to say, open the gate and let us through.

Check: New Palace Yard, green and empty but for the odd jackdaw. Then, *check*, the wide stone steps eroded by centuries of feet – Charles I en route to his trial for two - that brought us up into the vaulted spaces of Westminster Hall, where in later years I would sit wearing a hat along with other wives and daughters of House of Commons functionaries hearing De Gaulle orate in language so slow, so orotund, that even I with my schoolgirl French could understand most of it.

Check: the Victorian vaulting, patterned tiles and raised marble statues of past parliamentary luminaries of the Central Lobby; amid them my father whom I ran to hug as the old governess departed (she'd only return when it was my time to leave.)

Check: the much emptier spaces of another lobby, the name of which I forget, at its centre a large model of the old palace of Westminster enclosed in an even larger glass case. I was too old by this time of course to fall for my father's trick – though to please him I'd gone on pretending I had fallen, long after I'd seen right through it: it was one of the significant rituals of my visit. 'Blow' he'd say, 'blow' and so I blew while he surreptitiously pressed the switch on the other side of the case and on came the light inside; the first deception of his I saw through – it took most of my life to see through important parts of the rest.

Check: another part of our ritual: lunch in the Stranger's dining room. 'Am I a stranger?' I'd ask each time. 'Everyone who's not a member of the House or who doesn't work here like me is called a stranger,' my father would reply. Bending down to give me a kiss as he did so he usually added. 'But you're not a stranger to me, you little chump.'

I don't know if that dining room now is the same one that I ate in throughout my childhood. The repairs to wartime damage brought many changes to the building. The dining room I carry in my head still is the restored one, I suspect, in all its fake Gothic splendour.

It had pale wooden panelling, arched, stone-framed windows with coats of arms at their stone centres – I think there were coats of arms but I may have made that up –and curtains and carpet of a vapid green not far-off the colour of the carpet in my grandmother's sitting-room (I say *my* grandmother; I always had to call her 'Granny' anyway – the sniff she gave when I did, her un-grandmotherly reluctance to see me was, I thought, because grandmothers were like that, having no idea as yet that she bore no genetic relationship to me whatever.)

The chairs were green leather with a gold portcullis, the symbol of parliament, stamped on the back. They were slippery to sit on and for a long time my legs were too short to make sitting on them comfortable. 'Stop wriggling Jo,' my father said mildly. And I answered, crossly – but not too crossly - 'I'm not wriggling. Just trying not to fall off.'

'Muggins,' he said fondly. And, then to distract me, 'If you look out of the window, 'you can see the Thames.' Which might have been true for all I knew, but I was much too small then to see out of them. The windows were placed too high up.

'No I can't,' I said.

'So what do you want to have? Tinned pawpaw?' This was his usual joke: tinned paw-paw whatever that was, was always on the menu. And he knew as well as I did that the next part of the ritual was our mutual inspection of the Hors D'oeuvres trolley, a fascinating contraption consisting of three or four layers of little dishes suspended on a frame that could be swung round, allowing us to inspect each layer before choosing what to have: always sardines in my case, followed by roast chicken and ice cream, while my father would opt for anchovies and Russian salad, then chomp his way through such English staples as steak and kidney pie and steamed treacle pudding.

And almost the whole time I would be gazing round the dining-room amazed at how like crows everyone looked in their dark suits, cawing crows too, what with their deep male voices. There were a few women – family members like me, but old, in sensible tweed suits and hats with little broaches pinned to them; and also two female MPs whom my father pointed out to me in whispers as if they were some rare species – which they were, in fact. Both wore armoured hats like the carapaces of beetles and to my memory looked fearsome: one very thin, the other very fat they *were* fearsome. They would have had to be to have invaded this male stronghold with its dark suits, its respectable jowls and bellies, its rumbling voices and outbreaks of haw-haw-hawing. It was a resounding parody of a room, gaunt yet fulsome, resounding but discreet. It smelled of meat. Its habitants smelled of meat. What with all that green upholstery, that brown wood, that talkative population I felt as if was inside some well-furnished cage at feeding time in the zoo.

What I have to remember, now, is that most – in fact all – of the adults I saw round me on that day, like all adults at that time would have experienced the war in one way or another, none of them pleasant; either watching fellow-warriors blown to pieces round them and – or – suffering injury themselves or mouldering in prison camps for years or pulling people out of bombed houses or being bombed out of their own: at the very least they would have had friends and relations who'd experienced such things, and would have lost some of them. They would have looked, horrified, at previously familiar places turned bomb sites, shrank from horror pictures of Belsen, of Auschwitz, of mushroom clouds going up over Nagasaki and Hiroshima, (the latter – Belsen, Nagasaki - matters of which I still knew almost nothing.)

As a child, of course, this did not occur to me. But later, after I'd attended debates in the house, in particular after I'd heard such men as these – and the few women –shouting at each other with real not pretended venom over the Suez crisis, I realised not only that had they had known all this, but that since – given the Malayan crisis –the Korean war – let alone, now, Nasser's defiance – these same people would have been responsible - partly – for making war, and could possibly, later, be responsible, partly responsible, for entering or starting other wars. They were politicians: this was their job. How *could* they appear so pleased with themselves, not to say smug, thought my adolescent self?

What I wasn't aware of, not till much later, was how you can live in the middle of history and let it pass you by: how, much of the time you forget - you have to forget - all about it. I didn't know, let alone understand, such phrases as 'humankind cannot bear much reality.' I didn't know about the walls we place round ourselves; in particular how we place them around our children. Into whose hearts and minds such things leak anyway, one way or another. Hadn't we, or our friends, had fathers or brothers killed, or if not killed, screaming in horror in the middle of the night? Hadn't we heard air-raid warnings, sheltered from the raids under the stairs or in the shelters? Hadn't I myself seen my nursery window shiver noisily, collapse in dangerous glittering shards on the linoleum, when one of the last V2s of the war fell on our village: some of the shards only just missed me. And wouldn't we learn all too soon about Belsen, Horoshima, et al, and not so long after, hadn't I who read newspapers from an early age, seen, lying on a table in the sun, in the bay window of my school common-room, those dread headlines 'H-Bomb exploded': an intimation of doom that echoed ever after through my twentieth century life? Till then, I think, the sheltering had worked. Thereafter I had no such protection: such matters could keep me, too, awake at night. Later, like the crows, I learned to shut them out.

Check: my father himself: sitting across the table from me, smiling at me indulgently from time to time while demolishing his steak and kidney pie, along with the over-cooked vegetables – just how he liked them - that accompanied it. 'Excellent steak and kidney they do here,' he'd say to me, 'You should try it, Jo,' talking to me as usual as if he was taking a wife or some woman friend out to lunch. Some of the crows – the meaty males – shuffled or dawdled or hopped or hustled past on their way out of the dining-room; their shirtfronts white, their ties striped, their faces and hands – but especially their hands – pink and white and bulbous. Some of them I noticed had fat bottoms. Some of them nodded at my father. Between eating and chatting me up, he'd nod back and sometimes when the meaty male had gone, or at least was out of earshot, he'd lean over to me to whisper, 'that was so-and-so', naming some well-known politician of the time. With whom, of course, he would have been, literally, on nodding acquaintance, sitting in committees with him, day in day out, taking notes or whatever he did: his job was vague to me then and not much less vague now.

My father smoked his pipe throughout my childhood. The final ritual of our lunches in the Strangers' Dining Room was always his lighting of it, to go with his cup of coffee. I snuffed him up, loving the suspect familiarity of his smoke, vegetable yet bitterly spicy, not at all like the sourness of cigarette smoke. It was for me the essence of maleness – of him – no less than those other smells I'd seek out more secretly, sometimes, the alien muskiness of the handkerchiefs and ties in his drawer that I'd press to my nose, enjoying what it encountered as much as the sweet silkiness against my skin. When he'd smoked for a while, drunk his coffee, tamped the pipe out and put it back in his pocket, he teased me for a minute- by now I was impatient to go, urging 'Hurry up Daddy,' not wanting to miss the next bit of the ritual. For a long moment he looked at me across the table, smiling fondly, indulgently and stroking his upper lip with its long-departed moustache – my father always did cling to his habits well after their origin had gone – before climbing to his feet. 'Time to report for duty, Corporal Worralls,' he said. 'Ay ay, Cap'n Biggles,' I answered mixing up my armed services a bit, not quite accidentally. Even as a child I knew how to send such things up, though careful not to do so in such a wholesale, let alone vicious way it could upset my father.

Check finally; return to the central lobby; the Speaker's procession. We were not late, of course. We never were. The crude shout 'Hats off, strangers!' had only just begun to echo from the high vaulting of the central lobby as we hurried in. The sound made me shiver as usual, pleasurably. If I'd been wearing a hat – sometimes I had a school felt one on, or in the summer a straw hat with flowers round the crown – I'd pretend to take it off and he would hiss – 'So you're a boy then today, Jo' – which had become another of our private jokes, not funny really, but it always evoked one of my father's sillier laughs. The men around us now did take their hats off, if they were wearing them; not many were. The policemen tucked their helmets under one arm and stood to attention like soldiers. Next came the clatter of feet, the near gallop of the procession toward us, led by a brisk man in britches, tailcoat and buckled shoes closely followed by a particular friend of my father's, the Sergeant at arms, still more dolled up – besides the britches and shoes he wore a robe, had a ruffled jabot down his front which made him look like a frilled lizard: after years in the army, he was a thin, permanently tanned, rather wrinkled man. He carried the mace over one shoulder and was followed by the speaker himself in his long robe and wig. I liked the Sergeant-at-Arms and when I was little tried to make him smile, shouting 'Hullo Uncle Jim': in vain, his eyes remained firmly to the front. By this visit, I had given up, though I did smile, not very enthusiastically, at the Sergeant-at-Arms' wife who happened to be alongside us that day: she had bent down in her patronising way and smiled at me. She was one of the women to whom my father delegated my female guidance, and I didn't appreciate either that or her one bit.

She especially failed in her duty towards me now. When the clatter of feet had died away and the policemen had replaced their helmets, when the wax-work-still lobby had come back to life, she turned to my father and said. 'So how's your little orphan then?' rather sharply - I'd just trodden on her toes (she wore open-toed sandals on stockinged feet, the stockings turning her toes into a row of little corpses.) I hadn't meant to stand on them, though I would have done had I thought of it, had managed to invent some way of making it look accidental. Fond as I was of her husband who used to try and teach me to bowl a cricket ball over arm like boys – not that I was particularly keen on playing cricket, yet I did appreciate his lack of discrimination - I really did not like the Sergeant-at-Arms' wife.

I could not believe what I'd just heard. 'I'm not an orphan,' I protested. 'Orphans don't have any parents…. And…' I gestured towards my father. The Sergeant-at-Arms' wife – I was supposed to call her Aunt Anne but I did my best not to call her anything - turned a little pink and said hurriedly 'Of course not. I meant that figuratively, Freddie,' she added to my father. I didn't know what figurative meant, but he obviously did because he nodded, then said 'How are you, Anne?' not sounding entirely pleased. 'I never saw you in the dining-room.'

'Oh no,' she answered. 'We've got a big do on tonight, that's why I've come up to town today. I've just nipped in to bring Jim's dinner jacket. I had a bite of lunch in Peter Jones and now I'm off to Fortnum's – the usual merry round.'

It did not sound the least merry to me.

I was too busy reflecting on that word 'orphan' to notice how the conversation went on. 'Orphan' was a word I associated with Oliver Twist in the comic strip version in one of the comics I contrived to read – my father banned comics so contrivance it had to be – or with poor girls in night dresses living in cruel children's homes, or with little match girls dying of cold, or, nearer my own class in life – one I was well aware of even then, given the insistence of my mentors - such unfortunates as Mary in *The Secret Garden*. 'Orphan' was not a word I associated with people living at home with someone they called 'Daddy' the way I did, even if I was motherless.

Puzzling as this was, it did not take up more time of my time than it had to, not then. So many mysteries are dumped on children by their unwitting elders: more mysteries than usual in my case, because of my father's forgetting of my age during our intimate, almost spousal, dinners together, passing on confidences that went right over my head. I did wonder for a while if I'd been misinformed about my origins. I even began inserting the word 'orphan' into my very commonplace fantasy, deciding that it confirmed I really *was* the daughter of deposed foreign royalty and as a true princess would come into my own one day. But the wonder faded; as time went on, the word 'orphan' came to seem like one of my inventions, one of the stories I made up to elucidate my father's mysterious tales. It remained close to me on the one hand, remote on the other.

CHAPTER SIX

I discarded the picture of Ophelia that used to hang in my bedroom, long ago. Ophelia might be my mother's name and – less directly – mine, but I could not see either of us in the figure carried by the stream, with no direction of her own: I'd come to hate that picture: I wish it wouldn't hang about my memory the way it does. Not even my having come across, many years later, Peter Blake's version of Ophelia banished that drifting – sinister – soppy – Ophelia entirely. I wish it had.

Peter Blake's Ophelia was/is quite a different figure, one to which I related much more from the moment I encountered her; more than I care to, if I'm honest. She is no more cheerful that the other Ophelia but she is much more human, less like a dryad or water nymph. Younger too, almost a child, she stands upright, on her own feet, nose red, daisies in her tangled hair, flimsy blouse torn open on one side, revealing a perfect little breast, all ready for the surgeon's knife; oh yes, I can relate to that. She holds out the stalks of dead flowers, her mouth very slightly open makes you feel, even shape the questions lurking, waiting to come out – the very same questions that I have asked – but only in my head - for most of my life. Where's my mother? Who's my father? Who am I?

(Where *was* Ophelia's mother by the way? Does the play ever say? I have no copy here so cannot look it up, and my Husband is unlikely to know - literature is not his thing- 'his cricket bag' as my father would have said.)

My son has been to see me this evening: of my three children he's the one who visits most regularly. One of my two daughters does not visit at all; but then she lives in Australia. She will, I suspect, fly over for the funeral: my middle child always was punctilious, just the way I've always been, about my work, even about my children, up to a point. This means she won't have to face me again, alive. We do talk on the telephone sometimes but she always has an excuse for not visiting my deathbed. When she does come, she might ask to see the corpse, but I doubt it, she'd be more likely to curse than kiss my cold brow, I think, at my sourest. Actually I am being unfair; before she left for Australia I got on

36

much better with than her than with her sister. She may even kiss me in genuine sorrow she may even regret these halting conversations. Myself, I would be beyond regretting, but I am not beyond regretting now, not entirely. And I can't help feeling how different things are these days between my son, my afterthought and me, than it is with either daughter: how much less forced.

Or maybe I just find it easier to make an effort around my son. Or maybe he finds it easier to make an effort round me than either of my daughters. He comes in several nights a week as if, for all the frequent and understandable irritation I evoke in him –isn't it the role of aging parents to irritate their adult children? –*he* is going to miss me.

I have always assumed myself lacking in maternal feeling, in some if not all respects. How could I know how to be a mother, my only memory of motherhood the touch of loo paper on my bum? Leaving aside their new-born babyhood, which moved me in ways I found surprising, I saw myself as rearing my children dutifully, the best I could, but no more. I assumed they thought the same: that they saw no reason to be grateful to me. It was a wonder now that they still bothered to come and see me – or phoned in Aussie daughter's case –that they seemed concerned at my condition. Was that a matter of duty too? I thought it must be.

My son was reared as dutifully as the rest of them. As a child – unlike the others – he'd rail at me for 'not being a proper mother' - though when asked, he could never explain what 'a proper mother' was. On the other hand it was he who had roused in me the real moment of maternal feeling I remember once they'd ceased to be newborn. It was the moment I experienced – I thought so – my one true epiphany; when I actually felt – did not have to make myself manufacture - a waft of pure motherly love. And maybe, in some atavistic way, he remembered.

He can't have been more than four or five months old, and I was lying in bed one morning when his father carried him in for his feed. The moment he saw me the little scrap broke into a huge smile, beaming all over his face, reaching out his arms, and something stirred in me: it really did. And perhaps I did continue to love him, truly, in my frozen way. It helped that he was himself a loving little boy, ignoring my physical detachment, snuggling up against me, putting his arms up when I put him to bed – 'kiss kiss' he'd say, even when he was very small, 'kiss kiss.' And I would kiss him, awkwardly. And I was and am grateful – truly – that this one child would not let me simply put on an act.

Even as he grew up and turned more physically remote the way boys do, he would not let me forget my maternal duty. He had a wild temper and if he felt I was not giving him his due he would scream, yet again, about my not being a proper mother etc, a view I could only concur with. Once he was so angry with me he brought out a box he'd been constructing and painting to give me for my birthday and broke it in front of my eyes, throwing it to the ground and stamping on it, a memory which makes tears start to my eyes even now: he was hurting himself more than anyone. In this way he forced me to understand him. And understanding meant that at such moments my reluctant heart was forced to ache: it aches again, now, as I tell it.

Memory resists chronology – mine does. My head addled by morphine and illness it wanders where it likes, much stronger than the vague attempts of mind and will to order it. Tonight, for instance, after my son's visit, it drags me from my orderly trawl through my childhood, hurls me forward in time to our basement kitchen, circa 1969/70, sitting at the long white table, acquired from Habitat and already looking shabby, accompanied by my two friends and a bottle of whisky. The remains of a children's tea – fish fingers and peas - is scattered around us, the children themselves are rioting at the sitting-room end of the room (we are the generation of what an Observer comic strip calls 'the Knockers-Through': true to stereotype, we'd duly knocked through.) The only child missing is my son, the baby of the group, being put to bed upstairs by the current au-pair girl, a farmer's daughter from somewhere near Biarritz, who is supposed to talk French to the children, but is keener on improving her English. I will shortly have to go upstairs myself and read the child his story. Meantime, my friends and I make discreet merry with the whisky bottle - not too merry: one of them, living too far away to walk, has to drive home and I have to spend my evening once the children are all in bed and we've eaten, editing an ill-written, painful but enthralling account of a veteran's experience of the Korean war, so

I'll need a clear head (this will not please my husband who likes us to spend our evenings à deux, having a leisurely dinner and then watching some suitably intellectual telly programme or listening to music.) It will not please him either, that there is no sign of dinner. I am laughing uproariously at a story told by the friend married to an American and recounted in a cod American accent, vaguely hoping he will be late and equally vaguely casting my mind round what's in the fridge when I hear the rattle of the basement lock and he appears, his head still bent from negotiating the low door. He is wearing his dark grey city overcoat, carrying his briefcase and an umbrella and his copy of the Financial Times. My friends do not notice him and continue laughing. Only when the children start shouting 'Daddy' Daddy' and rush towards him, do they look round, startled, and then fall silent. Still clutching newspaper, briefcase, umbrella, his head still a little bent, he hugs the children awkwardly, then advances on the kitchen, ignoring the attempts of my friends to greet him: he does not like them and they do not like him, largely because he makes his feelings clear. He towers over us for a moment, darkly. Only then does he dump down paper, umbrella, briefcase amid the clutter on the table, shoving away cups, plates as he does so. 'Is there to be no dinner then? And shouldn't you be putting the baby to bed?' he asks, staring at me relentlessly.

    My friends, having swilled, hastily, the remains of their drinks, are gathering up handbags, summoning children. 'Heavens is that really the time,' they say, indicating the large kitchen clock which has been in full view throughout, 'heavens we must get home – 'Ted – or Fred' or whatever their husbands' names were (it's a long time ago now, one of them died in her early thirties, the other was whisked off to Albuquerque by her American husband, who could not stand the English climate and against all our best intentions we lost touch) 'Ted or Fred will be wondering where we are. What are *we* going to have for dinner? Help!' And off they go. My husband, meanwhile, still in his overcoat, not a button undone, is whisking the glasses out of the way then clearing the rest of the table, with heavy sighs. He nods goodbye to my friends, just, but I don't think they even see him.

    'Let's get a Chinese,' I say as I start persuading the two girls that it's time for bed.

'Let's get a Chinese,' he echoes ironically. 'It doesn't sound as if we have much choice.'

Though that was a fairly sample scene, of the time, I am being unfair to him. Leaving aside the fact that our marriage was already beginning to fall apart, he was always tired at this end of the day. In particular he'd made clear, often, that he did not like to find anyone around when he arrived home, wanted the children preferably bathed and ready for bed, so he could sit on their beds and read to them and be generally fatherly in an effort-free kind of way; above all he wanted dinner on the stove or in the oven, ready to place on the table when he came down. Despite relatively advanced views on childrearing and parenthood, he was traditional in such ways.

'But you can't expect me not to see my friends, can you?'

'You've got all day for them. Why do they have to be here at bedtime? Let alone dinnertime? Please,' he adds, advancing on the dishwasher with a handful of plates and cups. Afterwards he goes to the baize notice board, ruffles up the random notices and jottings pinned to it.

'What are you looking for?'

'The takeaway menu. I'll order something and one of us can pick it up when you've got the children ready.'

'I'll go,' I say. I need to placate him before telling him of my plans for the evening.

'If you're still fit to drive,' he says, glancing at the whisky bottle.

'Of course I'm fit to drive.'

He unbuttons his coat, sits down at the table with the menu and a glass and starts on the whisky himself.

'Have I driven you to drink?' I ask kindly, as he looks down the menu. 'Don't order chicken with cashews, we've have it every time and it's getting boring,' I add over my shoulder, leading the children to the stairs, 'Let's try the Szechuan one instead. Or the Chinese mushrooms.'

'Will do.' he says.

'Are you going to read to me, Daddy?' asks the youngest, lagging behind.

'Of course, sweetie, I'll be up.'

Peace restored, for now, he picks up the phone. I'll keep my need to return to editing till later. He'll have work himself with any luck: he does, sometimes.

CHAPTER SEVEN

My mind is still deep in those marital years when Peter comes in to tend me the next morning.

'We all married so young in my day. Not like you – isn't your fiancée over thirty already, didn't you say? We'd all finished having children in our mid twenties, just about. But you're going to have teenagers when you're sixty if you're not careful.'

Peter finds this subject all too personal. 'Who says we're going to have children. We're got to get married first.'

'And when are you going to get married?'

'Mind your own business, Madam. I am not contracted to answer personal questions.'

'Nor you are,' I say humbly, humbly for me anyway. (It really is none of my business. But still it intrigues me the way, these days, people so drag their feet so over such matters. But of course they can, legitimately, have sex without marriage, unlike us.) 'Just contracted to ask them.'

I add. 'We were girls of our generation. That's how we were expected to do it. Get married, breed young. Live, love, die in a day, like mayflies.'

'In which case you're a bit past your sell-by date by now, aren't you, dear?' he says.

'Ooh, manners,' I say. 'Now who's making personal remarks?'

'You love it,' he says. 'You love it.'

I'm thinking meantime, but I don't say, that it wasn't just that we were expected to marry young, or youngish, or simply that we needed sex. It was also the fact that there wasn't a great deal else for us to do, at least not interesting stuff, not unless we were particularly strong-minded and able, not to say committed. ('How about taking a secretarial course, Miss X?' Or 'it sounds like you would make a good teacher, Miss Y.' And of course we could always go off and be nurses, if we didn't mind washing old people's bottoms –as Peter was doing for me, now.)

The lack of alternatives did not entirely apply to me. Fallen by chance into the publishing industry, I was beginning to move over from the secretarial side and encouraged to do some editing when I got married and we started our family. I refused to give up my job then, consenting only to going part-time, and to working from home, when possible, through the earliest years. This was one of many arguments I had with the father of my children: it did not help that his mother disapproved deeply of my part-time motherhood and passed on her views to him. As she had left him and his siblings to be brought up by nannies before the war and had sent them all to boarding-school at the first possible moment after it, I don't think even my husband found her disapproval persuasive. What did persuade him was the work of John Bowlby that I had, foolishly, brought into the house and which he read from cover to cover, unlike me.

Did I not know that for babies, small children to be deprived of their mother's continual presence would damage them for life? No, I did not. What cared I for traumatised baby monkeys, for cloth mothers, for wire mothers? I cared about my children as I did, as I could, and that was that, whatever guilt I was left with.

Though not sharing joblessness with my fellows, I did share some of the other, less overt motives for our precipitate marriages. Many of my contemporaries were looking for fathers, certainly, if not in the same way. One of those two best friends – both of whom I'd met during my time in Oxford – had grown up alone with her mother till she was seven; her father was in a Japanese prisoner-of-war camp and did not return home till a year after the war ended. He seemed a stranger to her then and never became much less of one. He also screamed at night in his sleep and died not much later. This was an extreme case of course, but my other best friend had not known her father very well, either, though both, probably, were better off than a friend, much older than us, who had been a impertinent teenager when her father reappeared, had found herself suffering his hungry looks, his roving hands and worse.

Knowing all this about my friends, though, I knew rather more of them than they knew of me. They did not know about the paternal pieces missing from my family jigsaw, for instance, only that my mother had run off. They were also far too discreet to ask even jokily if I knew what had become of her: 'jokey' the one way we knew to approach such difficult issues. We were all more reticent then; we did not discuss our sex-lives, or not in any detail. Having been in Oxford with me at the time, both friends knew about the love of my life, but only in outline, and they'd never known when, exactly, I'd lost my virginity, any more than I knew exactly when they had lost theirs, or even if, like me, they had done so before they were married. Nor did we describe our experience of childbirth; most of us didn't. (One neighbour of mine called Virginia Something, we cynical three re-named Vagina Something because of her misbegotten tendency to describe her most recent labour, contractions, forceps deliveries, inductions, the lot, to unfortunate – usually male -neighbours at dinner-parties.)

But why this man, this marriage? I was, I admit, on the rebound from my great love, the love of my life. Maybe, too, I was influenced by my first date with this husband-to-be – a trainee banker: he took me to the opera, a production of *Rigoletto*: my very first experience of opera on stage. The idiocy, the passion, the totality of what I saw at Covent Garden, framed by red velvet and gold braid, reminded me of my great love in the way that nothing else had done since, or ever would again (except possibly the final scene of a production of *King Lear* seen years later with another husband and also featuring a father and a dead daughter.) The anguish of the jester, Rigoletto, for the daughter he'd had killed not knowing it was his daughter, even brought me to tears, a rare event. My escort put his arm round me. Perhaps my tears were what made him fall in love with me. Perhaps his delight at my response – put in ways I now see were patronising – 'how could I bring you to something which could upset you so,' he murmured, first hugging me, then later when I wept a little more, kissing away my tears - helped me fall in love, somewhat, with him. And maybe I fell in love with him too because I assumed, wrongly, that he felt as deeply as I did about what we'd seen (as I continued to feel, up to a point: all my life since it's only opera that has let me acknowledge the passion I keep hidden inside me, even from myself.)

That was one mistake. A second was my being beguiled – not to say misled - by the unexpected passion this otherwise unashamed highbrow showed when talking about banking. My third was letting myself be beguiled as much as my suitor's beauty: long and lank, curly-headed (he resisted this) he had dark eyes a little sunk into his head and high cheekbones like an English Nureyev.

Unfortunately, this was the only way he resembled a Russian dancer; he did not use his body well, in bed or out, unlike my great love, his opposite, who had not only been stocky but also much older and only beautiful, most likely, to me.

He wasn't such a bad man, this first husband; honourable in most things, he was everything my father could have wanted for me; the public school and Oxford educated son of a solicitor, in a profession likely to make money. He didn't deserve me for sure. But then I didn't deserve him either. Nor do I find it the least surprising that I never again attached myself to anyone like him. I did not need to: one effect of the Second World War – and, in England, the 1944 education act it engendered - was the way it shuffled up classes and nations, leading women from my generation to meet and involve themselves with men from other worlds than their own. My mother's adventure with her Latin Lover, or her resistance hero (I continued to assume that he was French, and said whenever asked, 'Oh yes, I'm half-French,' indicating my olive skin, my dark hair etc) was a rarity in her day. In mine they became much more of the norm. I knew one woman in Oxford who even married an Indian and went to live in Delhi. I don't know how my father – my adoptive father – would have responded to that.

On the other hand –and it was years later, by which time attitudes had shifted – he had barely raised an eyebrow, or not in front of me, when my elder daughter married the son of a tribal king from somewhere in Southern Africa. It helped, probably, that this princeling's mother was the daughter of an English earl who'd fallen in love with her African prince while he was being educated in England. It might have helped too that the lady had abandoned her husband when she discovered she was to be only his second, junior, wife and brought her son back to England, to his grandparents, who sent him to Eton, Exeter University – where he met my daughter - and finally Oxford, for an MA in law: from there he had became a successful barrister and as senior legal advisor to the Tory party seemed likely to end up in the lords in his own right. Both he and my daughter had more in common with my daughter's father – and with my adopted one - than I ever did. As my daughter also took after her father, physically, they made an exceptionally handsome couple, turning heads wherever they went.

This marriage was her one and only unconventional action. At the same time, given how impeccably correct and upper class her husband was and is – and the grandson of an earl at that - it seemed at the same time one of her most predictable and conventional actions, far more predictable in our family terms than Aussie daughter's marriage to the son of a Durham miner she met at university in Newcastle. Seeing her, him, their four beautiful half-caste children together, it amazed me that her father and I could, possibly, have engendered this.

I realised, of course, that motherhood would affect my work badly. At the same time I had lacks and losses in my life to make up for. Very soon after our wedding – too soon - I acceded to my husband's pleading and agreed to leave out the Dutch cap with which, at last, as a respectable married woman, I had been fitted by the Family Planning clinic. I became pregnant at once. This was when I first discovered that my spouse undertook all new activities with the same enthusiasm he'd shown for banking. I did not enjoy this half as much when the activity involved me: my astonishment and even dismay at his approach to fatherhood was the one thing my mother-in-law and I had in common. She was quite as horrified as I was at his desire to be present at the birth. *I* did not want to be present at the birth. A system called Twilight Sleep had allowed middle-class women who could afford it to drowse through the whole process, my mother-in-law said: it sounded exactly what I wanted: alas it had been discredited even before her son, my husband, was born, she'd added regretfully. Given that I, too, would be obliged to be present throughout the disagreeable process I was grateful to one of my two friends for telling me about an enlightened obstetrician who'd initiated classes in childbirth, and whose hospitals offered an experience much less authoritarian and altogether more enlightened than most hospitals did then. She'd only mentioned in passing that husbands were encouraged to attend such births: assuming my husband would be equally appalled at the idea that did not worry me.

I should have been worried; as I should have been worried that husbands were expected to attended some of the sessions in which we ever larger-bellied females were made to lie on the floor and learn to pant rhythmically to the coming and going of still imaginary contractions to help control our reactions to potential pain. Some husbands resisted this. Mine not only insisted on coming with me, he read the cyclostyled pamphlets on offer much more thoroughly than I did, and, even worse, started showering me with books that told me far more than I wanted to know about what I would have to undergo. Thank goodness the birth gurus had not yet caught on to the idea that alcohol was bad for expectant mothers: I could at least comfort myself with a glass of wine, or of whisky, better still.

Just how obsessed he was – just how much distance there was between us – had first become apparent, when the Cuba crisis erupted, four months before my baby was due, a week after I'd attended my first birthing class and brought the first leaflets home. We were doomed, I thought. As for my baby: even if it got born it would be better if it hadn't been. Listening to the radio, hour by hour – we didn't yet have a television set – reading the newspapers end to end, I could think of nothing else. Nor, though we continued to have meetings, edit copy, take directives, could anyone else in my office –my friends there anyway. Even while making sick jokes about the effects of radiation sickness, even while mentioning what wonderful material this would be for books, we assumed, tacitly, there would be no more books. To me it was the inevitable outcome of the headline I'd seen aged fourteen '*H-Bomb exploded.*' Each night I'd lie awake appalled at the still feathery movements of my doomed baby inside me, then fall asleep to dream of Armageddon.

The father of the child would have none of it. When I expressed my fears he told me not to be so neurotic – 'no one's going to drop nuclear bombs, even Khrushchev wouldn't be so stupid as to let it get that far – as for Kennedy…' - when I told him of the atmosphere in my office he said that it showed how immature and hysterical publishers were, how not in the real world. When I suggested it might be better if our baby wasn't born he looked at me in horror – 'how can you say such a thing?' –and continued to immerse himself in books about childbirth and parenthood. (His first major – possibly his only real rebellion against his parents and upbringing - was to repudiate all his mother's ideas about babies being fed at fixed intervals then banished to the bottom of the garden; our baby was going to be indulged from the start – fed on demand, I suppose, I said gloomily – never left to cry and so forth; all of which was going to cause me far more trouble than it would cause him.)

Our breathing classes were held in a bleak hall the opposite side of the Strand from the hospital itself. Maybe it was a church hall: I don't remember exactly. All I do remember is that it was very, *very* cold. This was February during one of the worst winters in memory. Snow lay on the ground throughout, even in London. The teacher brought in paraffin heaters, convection heaters, everything she could; but it didn't help much. I went to the classes wearing ski-socks, boots, mittens, woolly hats, all of us did. They made us look the more ridiculous, lying on the floor, bellies upward, grunting and groaning, urged on by a teacher – I think she wore a tracksuit of sorts under her layers of wool - 'Come *on*, mummy, try harder, buck up!' I don't remember much about the hall: only that there was a squadron of plastic chairs stacked up at the back and one or two tables. There might have been a tatty travel poster tacked to a sidewall inviting us to the sunny Caribbean (some hope) and I might or might not have invented the low dais on which the teacher stood between faded velvet curtains. But I do certainly remember the hardness of the barely polished boards on which we lay, little improved by the thin foam mats we had to fetch from a pile by the plastic chairs at the beginning of the class. As I remember the satisfaction and amusement with which all of us women sat ourselves down on plastic chairs, fetched and placed for us by our husbands halfway through their first session - 'come on chaps, show you are gentlemen and not just good for stud!' - and watched them forced to stretch themselves on the floor the way we had been expected to.

I don't know if this was normal practice; I suspect not. Our teacher was particularly fervent and uninhibited –perhaps she had to be given the conventional attitudes of the time among maternity wards and the obstetricians in charge of them. She referred to our husbands as willing stallions. When told of any other pregnancies she enquired 'are they with us too?' But then this was a generally strange, almost apocalyptic time, the streets lined with piles of ever dirtier and ever more frozen snow, roofs, trees, street lights, laced with frost and hung with icicles, traffic hushed to a minimum in rutted streets, pedestrians slipping and sliding on icy pavements;

we pregnant women should not have been allowed out. But the fervour of converts to the new system – whether the fervour was our own or that of our teacher or as in my case, of our husbands – the scorn of our teacher when any of us were too chicken to turn up, kept us coming; I suppose that was what kept us coming. It was far easier for me than some: I only had to trek from my office, wondering as I did so if this winter would ever end; if my baby would find itself frozen inside me for life.

The fathers were a mixed bunch. Not too many of them city men like my husband in his city suit, all looked ridiculous lying there, not to say self-conscious. I was not the only wife to start giggling. At the same time we were delighted to find them no better than we were at getting the exercises, the breathing right, to see them wriggling with embarrassment when the teacher shouted ever more stridently – 'Come on, daddy, how are you going to help mummy if you can't do better than that.' Or 'aren't you interested in her getting through contractions' – or 'don't you want your babies born easily and naturally?' Adding 'who put them in there then? I assume all of you had something to do with the process. Or is mummy having a virgin birth?'

Such outspokenness was unusual at the time; my husband, pale as ever, looked distinctly uncomfortable; this was not how he'd expected to hear himself called 'daddy' for the first time. I think he winced. The more so because of all the men he was the least able, the most clumsy, heaving and groaning quite out of time with everybody else, his long limbs jangled and jumbled anyhow. It was he on whom the teacher placed her hands most frequently, lying them on his belly far too close to his genitals for his comfort, I suspect – not that near of course, but near enough - shouting 'Breathe, daddy, *breathe*, where are your lungs, daddy, keep time, one – two- three – that's better – what's the matter with you. Breathe.'

My neighbour and I giggled together. She was my friend there, the only woman who shared my cynicism. "Bring on the Pethedine,' she would murmur as we lay on the floor, side by side. 'Hark at her,' she said now, nodding at our ever more frenetic teacher, her ample breasts jigging up and down as she demonstrated her methods over and over again. 'She'll forget herself any minute and demand they learn to look after their pelvic floors so as to add to mummy's pleasure. Some hope.'

I was beyond hysterical with laughter: I was hysterical with terrifying questions. What was I doing here? How had I got myself involved in all of this? What was I doing with this pale and lanky man – I did not find him so beautiful any more. If I did feel some affection for him how could I love him, really love him, as I ought to love? I had my mother's Latin lover in mind perhaps; I had my own inevitably lost love making me ache and ache for what? –an unattainable something that my rational unromantic self despised as belonging to romantic women's fiction, the kind I had no desire to edit? How absurd was *that*. But how I ached. At the same time I was overcome with terror. What was I of all people doing bringing a baby into such a dangerous world, the uncertainties of which I knew better than most? Who was I exactly? It was not a matter of simple genetics. These days, knowing your origins is seen as important, but no one realised then how many diseases had a genetic basis. Nor was it envy, the kind I might have felt when I heard my pregnant fellows talking about their mothers coming to help them after their babies' birth. Having barely known a mother, I did not know how to miss one. What I felt was much more existential, even ontological: a lack in my very being. How could I look in a mirror and know exactly who I was? How could my baby know exactly who *it* was?

My thinking then, submerged within my terror, can't have been as clear as that or even clear at all. But I think, looking back, that this was the essence of it: as it was the unstated essence, barely recognised even by me, of the furious row that erupted that night, starting with me laughing at my husband in the birthing-class. He did not like being laughed at: the ridiculousness of the class could not invalidate his belief in the system we had embarked on, as I'd rather hoped it might. 'You can have the baby instead of me if you like, daddy,' I heard myself saying sourly. 'You're much more keen on all this than I am.'

'Don't be silly,' he said. 'This is going to be the most important day of your life.' I groaned. Things went on from there. It ended with him going to sleep on our not very big sofa acquired like most of our furniture from a junk shop; young bankers were not paid then the way they are these days. It was not just the shortness of the sofa compared to his long body that made this a major sacrifice. Our two roomed, unheated flat grew ice inside the windows overnight and had led to many anxious discussions – mostly initiated by him – on how we were going to keep our baby warm. We had imported enough heaters to make the bedroom tolerable, but this did not yet apply to the sitting-room. I think he arranged himself on the sofa fully clothed, head and feet overlapping- its arms at either end, with every garment, every jacket and coat he owned on top of the blankets he'd snatched from the so-called airing-cupboard – it, too, was unheated. I meanwhile shivered alone in our double bed, less from cold – it was cold without him in all senses – than from a desolation that reached down into depths of me and that I feared would never be assuaged.

We made things up after that disastrous night: we had to. My baby three weeks late, I never re-encountered my birthing class friend. My husband and I agonised alone through that final, interminable waiting time, which meant that by the time I went into hospital the snow had receded; snowdrops were being sold on street outside. The arrival of the baby too– not, thank god, in front of him: I had an emergency caesarean, what a waste of all that heaving and panting – stopped our quarrels for a while. Though we were both exhausted by the broken nights, I did not suffer seriously from post-natal depression and to the extent I did my husband was sympathetic, having read the books. Our baby, her head not having been pushed out of shape by the birth canal was especially good-looking and also, for her first six months, exceptionally peaceful, though this was not to last. It felt good, too, that, unlike books, a baby could not be re-edited, that all I had to do was service her; which I did, not unwillingly, though I continued to fit in such service with my work; I was disciplined and organised even in those days.

'I told you you'd feel differently once the baby came,' my husband said smugly, coming across me gazing with awe at my infant, not long after her birth. I spat at him. 'What do you mean, how do you know what I feel?' Maybe his slight smile was a little superior, but maybe I was, just a bit, unfair. For I do think that, possibly, my giving birth to our child had made us somewhat closer: there's nothing in the world like shared parenthood I can honestly say. Until my insistence on going back to work pulled us apart again we were almost happy.

CHAPTER EIGHT

My son came again tonight. He's very faithful and even loving. I wonder about him; about how little I know of his life outside this room.

He still has a temper, I suspect. I daresay his wife sees it sometimes. (He's always kept me apart from his marriage– in a rather apologetic way – as if he fears I might infect it somehow; so I don't know for sure.) But what I get mostly is irritability. 'Oh god, Mum,' he groans, his face closing up: meaning I go on too much –I don't know why I find myself so garrulous these days, especially around him. Of course he puts up with it sometimes – the privilege of the dying, I suppose; it's amazing what your nearest and dearest will tolerate from you then. Also it makes for something to talk about when I'm feeling well enough, a way of fulfilling the exhausting duty of those visited in hospital to entertain their visitors. I am, too, aware that some of the things I have to tell will die otherwise, along with me.

He looked tired tonight, I'd thought. He kissed me then sank down onto the green plastic leather of one of the chairs with a heavy sigh, laid his newspaper besides him, then got up again, reached over my life lines, took a tissue from the box on my bed-side table, blew his nose, looked round for a bin and not seeing it stuffed the tissue in his trouser pocket. He was still wearing his suit – he'd come straight from work. But he took off his jacket now, hung it as carefully over the back of his chair as if covering the shoulders of another person, and loosened his tie; actions I watched with tenderness: they contained all the life that would soon no longer be mine.

Contained, too, life that had never been mine, though it belonged to me. My younger daughter had taken as much after my mother's side of the family as the elder took after their father's. My son – it was obvious to me now – he looked unlike any of them – favoured his grandfather's: with his thick hair, his black eyes, his much more defined, much stronger features: he did not remind me of anyone I knew well – except himself – and except, ever more, of my real father. He was over forty already. He'd thickened a bit round the middle.

53

We sat in silence for a while. Rooting around for something other than enquiries about his family – this had seemed a sensitive subject lately -I found myself retiring into a past much easier to think about than the more recent one that had occupied me since his last visit. My son had always been interested in my wartime childhood: his two elder sisters had raided my memory when required to do so for school projects, but that was all. If the subject came up at other times, if I was asked about the day, late in the war, when the rocket had fallen near our house and the windows of my nursery had been blown in just as I was being rushed in through the door they would sigh heavily and start chanting, in unison, 'How-the alarm -went -you-had-to-run-in- from-playing-in -your -sandpit -and -how -the -window -fell -in –how- you -nearly -got hurt- but didn't –but-some-other-girl was ('Peggy' I'd interject here;) –and-how-the-taxi-driver-said – 'there was I caught on the ma'ogany' and- someone –really -was –killed- and- Mr Churchill –stood –on-the-green- and –made a v-sign, blah blah blah, boring boring boring.'

('But scary,' my son had always protested here: he always was more sensitive to what people might have felt. He still seems to be.)

He'd been a war-gamer as a boy. He spent his days painting tiny soldiers, then refighting battles across an enormous board in the corner of his bedroom, sometimes eighteenth or nineteenth century battles, Marengo or Waterloo or Alma in the Crimea, at other times first or second war battles: the Somme – a thankless battle he did not persist in - or Arnhem; whatever.

Sometimes I'd say to him: "don't you understand that war is for real, not a game, that people get hurt? I've told you about your great-uncles killed at the Somme or your father's godfather killed at Dunkirk.'

He looked at me as if I was crazy. 'Of course I know the difference. This is just a game; or a puzzle, or like working out a theorem in maths. But that's all.' And then sometimes he'd add reflectively; 'I suppose there always will be wars. It's a pity.'
I should have known better, I suppose. It was clear that his interest in moving miniature soldiers across miniature battlefields - and even in changing some historical outcomes - did not translate into any desire to see wars erupt for real, let alone fight in them

himself. He never got into fights in the school playground despite his uncertain temper. His teachers told me, approvingly, that sometimes he did his best to break up those of other boys, or even to prevent them altogether. Later, at public school, he refused to join the military corps.

We continued sitting in silence. My son blew his nose again and reached over me for another tissue. I almost said 'I hope you're not getting a cold. That's the last thing I need.' But I stopped myself in time. Instead I heard myself saying, 'your grandfather never really got over the two wars. When he was ninety he was still crying for his two dead brothers. When I asked him what he thought of the Gulf war he just said he'd seen too many wars.'

My son sighed. 'I suppose he had. Look at all his books. You passed the children's ones on to me, don't you remember? Henty: heroic boys going to war, boring stuff.'

'I didn't know you ever read them.'

'They were all the same. Dead boring, except for some of the history.'

'Clearing out your grandfather's desk, I found stories he'd written Henty style. He'd even done little drawings in the margins. He always wanted to go into the army. He would have done but for his mother.'

'Grandfather *drawing*? I don't believe it. When I asked him to draw me a horse once he said he'd never been able to draw. What was his mother like?'

'Old.' I said. 'She didn't like me. I wasn't her real granddaughter. But you know all that.'

'Yes,' he said.

It was almost dark outside now. I asked him to turn off the main light, because it hurt my eyes. The two of us cocooned within the circle of light thrown by my bedside light, the room seemed much less institutional: the high ceiling's disappearance into dark created an intimacy that increased the tenderness and the pain, at least for me.

I asked for a drink. He came over and fed me lovingly from my little cup with the spout, as if he was the parent and I was the child. For a while longer we sat in companionable silence. At last he said: 'I suppose I'd better be going.' And then he said again. 'Even my childhood feels a long time ago now.'

'Not as long as mine does,' I said. 'Let alone his.'

Before he left, he kissed me again then held my hand in a way that moved me, and I gripped his hard. We didn't say another word. But as the door sighed to, I thought about my un-grandmother, dressed in black from head to foot in all the few years I'd known her, thinking much more sympathetically these days how hard it must have been for her; her two elder sons killed without producing grandchildren, and the one dumped on by her youngest son no genetic relation; no wonder she declined to acknowledge me. She drank black tea out of chipped crown Derby cups with tarnished gold rims, their blue and white livid and deathly; her house smelt of mothballs and doom. As a child, of course, even as a young woman, I didn't understand the pain that shrouded both her and my father, but I think I did feel it living in our house as well as in hers; a kind of deep, crepuscular melancholy, turning up as a waft of sadness or depression here, a bolt of terror there, appearing as unexpected words on a page when I sat down to write a school essay or a diary entry or, later, in my edit of some bellicose text. It was as though a veil of grief had been thrown across my childhood.

I thought of the shelves in our house, lined by rows of thick, jacketless volumes: my father always took the jackets off his books; he said it made them look untidy. Churchill's *History of the Great War* took up half one shelf, followed, as the volumes appeared in turn, by his *History of the Second World War*. Then there were the accounts of the generals, like Montgomery, biographies of others, British or German, Haig, Alanbrook, Rommel, accounts of Dunkirk, or D day, *The Dambusters* and so forth, then the memoirs – the men who'd escaped from prison camps, (*The Wooden Horse, Colditz*) the heroic spies tortured by the Gestapo, sent to Belsen or Ravensbruck or worse (*Odette, The White Rabbit.*) I didn't read the histories, or campaign accounts, only the memoirs, the escapes, the spy stories: meaning I knew more than was good for me about Gestapo methods of interrogation.

(On a top shelf that I didn't investigate until adolescence, there were one or two books that had my mother's name inside them. A tattered copy of *Alice in Wonderland*, an even tattier copy of Grimm's fairytales and a much better tended copy of *1914*, the poems of Rupert Brooke with a soupy portrait of him as its frontispiece. This had been given to my mother for her sixteenth birthday; she'd written the date under her name and added the page number of the poem that dripped on about 'some corner of a foreign field being for ever England'. There were also a couple of novels in French bound in those dreary yellow paper covers that bound all French books till quite recently. Had my father given them to her, I wondered? But if so he had not inscribed them.)

CHAPTER NINE

As I tell myself, often, I am not merely re-living my own life in this haphazard way. All of our bodies, all our life stories are small histories of the times we live in. This is not a solipsistic statement. It does not mean – or say – that we – any of us - are at the centre of everything. But whether we like it, or not, whether we make sense of it, or not, we wear our times both in our memories and on our bodies. Not till we get old, though, till we become aware that our little life will be rounded all to soon by that long feared sleep, do we begin to have some idea where we come from, where we fit in: and sometimes not even then.

There are days when my memory goes nowhere coherent, when I can barely tell waking from sleep or sleep from waking. Buoyed up by pain – or sometimes – too rarely – by relief from it, I drift in a dream of thought and fragments of memory, some bright, some dark, and some quite indifferent. At the same time I am tormented by the feeling that there is something else to say. But what exactly I don't know let alone how to say it. I don't know even if it is worth saying. Not least because people like me coming from where I came from – particularly women coming from where I come from, no matter where we've gone next – have spent the last half century learning to be embarrassed about it, to laugh at the narrowness of our horizons, the gentility of our concerns, the chintzy ease of our little lives, to assume bit by bit that our particular square of ivory – set on an island that for all its glorious – and inglorious – past is no more truly significant these days than a Canary island no one has ever heard of - is of no interest or relevance to anyone except ourselves and sometimes not even to ourselves.

So how dare I have the temerity to think that somewhere lurking in me there is something worth saying - if only to myself?

I do dare repeat this. That the elusive theme I'm seeking connects most definitely to the way the lives of my generation, whatever part of it we come from, were led within the shadows of wars: the kind the twentieth century invented and which weighed on our parents both metaphorically and actually in ways which could not but affect us, their children, far more than we knew.

I think I even dare suggest that there might still be something interesting – and still relevant – to be said about the anachronistic English upper middle class among which I grew up. For our parents and our grandparents started and entered the wars, after all, with a naive, yet admirable decency that did not allow them to make much sense of the often vile mayhem that surrounded them, approaching it in the most simplistic and inadequate of terms: good and evil, honour and duty. Take my father, for instance: quite a wise man in his way – he saw too much of the foolishness of great men not to be canny. At the same time he gasped faintly in the waters of so much reality, right out of his depth: seeing, for instance, that idiotic Suez stand against General Nasser as a necessary– and honourable - defence not only of British territory but of British - and imperial –honour. One of my few serious fights with him was about that. Yet my father's views on the Suez venture were shared by people across the country very far from being upper-class dinosaurs like him. All of whom would, most likely, have been as horrified by the evils done in the name of Empire that have surfaced since, as I am now.

My father was a man, you could say, somewhere between Lord Jim and Bertie Wooster, with a bit of a Home Counties Pooter thrown in. Who tried like most of his contemporaries to educate their children – someone else's child in his case – for a world that barely existed any more or was, at least, rapidly disappearing. A world where gentleman were gentleman, ladies were ladies, and the lower orders bantered with them politely and still sometimes doffed their caps – or if they did not do so were called by my father in his most unreconstructed state 'the revolting classes' or the 'hoi polloi' in an intended-to-be funny accent: a world in which I never felt quite at home. Yet despite that, I was what I was, where I was, where I could not but belong whether I liked it or not, crying 'England for St George' when asked to – or at least when I was very young – and assuming that the mere fact of being English made you luckier *than* if not – quite - superior *to* anyone else in the world. And though I rebelled against all that as I grew up, the rebellion remained inside my head or was carried out in places where I could not be seen, like that cottage outside Oxford. A seemingly quiescent teenager, I never spoke– let alone shouted – my growing disagreement to or at my father, never fought with him the way I saw many of my contemporaries fighting with their parents. How *could* I rebel, openly, against my father? He was all I had, as I was all he had. What I did instead was learn to hide, to be deadpan. I learned deadpan particularly well – sometimes in ways that could be and was interpreted as insolence by people like Aunt Anne, but always in ways subtle enough to give them or her no obvious reason to object.

Deadpan was a skill I've continued to find useful throughout my life, both professionally and privately. It helped, for instance, in negotiating publishing contracts. I still employ deadpan even now, lying in my hospital bed. I did it last night after the Husband and I had watched a television programme on the little television set suspended above my bed: a programme which may or may not have triggered some of these reflections; or at least focussed reflections I'd been having.

It showed a very busy, loud and extremely annoying Russian woman, a self-made business millionaire, who runs an agency business in London, liaising between English public schools and Arab sheiks and Russian mafia moguls as desperate to send their sons to the said schools, as the schools were desperate to attract their lovely money. The Russian woman, accordingly, arranged for the boys to be taught such un-Russian and un-Arab skills as polo and ballroom dancing, along with instruction on formal table manners and how to chat politely to the headmasters, plus a host of other equally useful or useless skills. Including, of course, fluency in the English language

My husband, as a northern grammar school boy and proud of it, was astounded by Arab and Russian attention to such frivolous and expensive niceties, let alone their seeming desperation to acquire the social skills of a Britishness that he himself considers anachronistic, not to say a joke. He grew very indignant. I, to his irritation, did not. 'Haven't you got a view on this; you with all your aristocratic connections,' he asked several times. I shook my head. 'What aristocratic connections?'

'Your father sounded posh enough to me. 'I'm so *orfully* glad to meet you. Was there a *frightful* queue at the Hindhead traffic lights?' he mimicked.

This husband had only met my father once, just before he died. He was in a care home in West Sussex by then, close to where he'd spent the his last independent years of life, alongside my stepmother till she died, and hard by his favourite golf club. Alternating between his bed and a wheelchair he was very deaf, incontinent, shrunken, ghostly, enthused by little except by international golf on television, the odd good English cricket result and by his great-grandchildren – my grandchildren - several of whom he hadn't met, and to whom technically he was but slightly related, but all of whose photographs sat on a shelf beside his bed. 'Could you imagine a prettier bunch of little girls or nicer-looking boys?' he'd ask, every time I visited. Adding wistfully, of the third eldest girl, whom he'd never seen -she lived in Australia: 'she does look so *awfully* like your mother.'

He was so depressed by this time he did not often bother to put in his always-temperamental hearing aid. In honour of this new son-in-law he did try it that day, but after an excruciating series of whistles gave up – 'I'm afraid I am so very feak and weeble these days,' he said - *feak and weeble* a joke spoonerism he'd used ever since I can remember. Much as it used to irritate me in younger days, it now just made me feel sad; growing ever sadder as I listened to him conducting polite enquiries about our journey– he might have been at a cocktail party – about the traffic lights at Hindhead, the 'hideous' A3 – about his great-grandchildren, about a dramatic win against New Zealand by the English test cricket team which he'd watched only the week before.

Once, wistfully, he waved out of his window and said, 'you can see the Chanctonbury Ring from there on clear days. Have you ever walked up to the Chanctonbury Ring?'

'No,' said my husband, his territory more Kinderscout than South Downs.

'I walked up it twice in a day once. Your – her' – he waved at me – 'mother wasn't up, so I went up with everybody else in the house party, but when she woke she said she wanted to go so I walked up again. But I was a young man then, it wasn't too hard.' He indicated me again. 'You should know that your future wife does look awfully like her mother. She's got darker eyes and hair that's all. But her mouth is exactly the same shape.'

'Golden lads and lasses must like chimney sweepers come to dust,' I thought, wondering 'why chimney sweepers?' as, with an ache, I tried and failed to replace the image before me of my father's shrunken body with the lively young pipe-smoking version I'd only ever seen in photos. Thinking too how strange it was that the older my father became the more it was as if my mother had never left, as if she had remained part of his whole life. Maybe she had done in every sense that mattered to him; even while he was making sure she would never be part of mine.

The husband went into the bathroom and shut the door. My father beckoned me over.

'What's this one? Number four?' he asked in a stage whisper. There was nothing wrong with my father's memory or ability to count, even then.

'Yes,' I said. He could have heard that. He did.

'Well try not to let this one go, darling. You're not getting any younger, you won't keep attracting them much longer.'

My money will, I thought. But did not say.

The present husband had come back into the room by then, so heard my father's last words. He smirked in as much as he could ever be said to smirk. My father turned his monologue to cricket once more. And not long after, evening sliding in, we left him to his television, his bed, his photographs of the little girls. 'Goodbye Corporal Worralls,' he said to my astonishment as I bent over him– this was a game that had not survived my childhood; or so I thought. 'Goodbye Squadron Leader Biggles,' I said, into his ear, kissing the vacant skin of his cheek. I wanted to cry. I think I did cry a bit, though not so anyone could see,

Driving back up the 'hideous' A3, my husband said, 'Your dad sure did like cricket, didn't he?'

'He sure did,' I said. After a minute I added, to relieve my sadness and also my rage – rage that arrived too late to be expressed, to him. 'Did I ever tell you about the documentary on the Tory party he was asked to take part in.'

'You did,' he said. 'Once or twice.'

'I didn't see most of it. He didn't think I'd be interested, drat him, he didn't tell me the programme was on. All he said to me was 'they took me to a cricket match and then sat me with my back to it. How was I supposed to watch?'

'If they took me to a cricket match,' said my husband 'I wouldn't care if they sat me with my back to it: I'd rather they did.'

That was the last time I saw my old father – my adopted father - alive, though I spoke to him on the telephone a time or two, not that he seemed able to hear a word I said. Next time I saw him he was laid out dead on his hospital bed, looking no more alive or dead than he had then, so waxy that he seemed less withered, if anything. They'd taken his teeth out. His mouth was sunk in. How cold he felt, when I kissed him, weeping, yet whispering in his ear what I had never been able to whisper during his life time: 'why didn't you tell me? Why *didn't* you?' And that was a whole week or so before I cleared out his desk drawers and found the letters from my mother that he'd never passed on.

CHAPTER TEN

One of my tactics for dealing with pain – apart from morphine – and there's some pain for which only that will do, and even that isn't always enough – is to go inside my head and start walking the streets of the many places I've lived in. Or rather *start* trying to walk the streets. These days, the place where I always end up, the only one I seem able to remember, totally – almost totally - is the town – the village – in which I grew up.

We take such places for granted when we're young and living there. I don't know at what point most of us begin to realise that what we've always assumed to be normal life has turned into social history: something you understand all the more when you notice your children's eyes glazing over as you try to tell them how it was. Grandchildren are more interested sometimes, but only sometimes. 'The olden days,' mine call the times before they were born, my times and their parents' equally.

My father having moved from that village when I got married and he felt able at last to take another wife – even then I did not know if he was divorced or a widower and did not ask - I never realised how entirely my old world had passed until I went back there years later and felt as felt as out of time as Rip Van Winkle. Of course the village was changing even as I grew up: the bakery on the corner opposite closed, and the milkman exchanged his pony trap for a hissing electric float. But I did not see the closing of all the other familiar shops, the replacement of useful ones like grocers and ironmongers by wine bars and antique or charity shops, the filling up of any empty space with houses. The market field where every second Monday I had watched sheep and cattle milling about in their metal pens, eyed by farmers dressed in old tweed and battered hats, and with the thick Kentish accents that don't exist any more - the market which holds my last memories of my mother – is now a Barrett Homes estate. By the time I got back to the village the deed – the deeds- were done.

In my head now I banish the changes. I am walking out of our front door with its polished handle and doorknocker, with the pointed portico over the door, painted green like the door itself. I'm coming down the steps, well whitened by the daily woman – my father called her the 'charlady' -who came in three days a week. (Does anyone whiten a doorstep now? I don't know: I've certainly never whitened any doorstep of mine.) To my left is the church, opposite our door, on the left side of the green, is the house with the advertisement for Hovis in its window that I prefer to remember as the baker's shop rather than the private house it soon became. Directly over the road from me the village green reaches away to my right, ending in the flourish provided by the statue of some famous general who used to live in the village, and who stands, one leg forward, ready for action, waving his sword in the air. (That statue has been joined these days by another, of Winston Churchill sitting in his armchair: the phallic activism of the heroic general opposed to the mental – almost female strife given the squat image – engaged in by dear Winston, the local hero. But mentally I banish this.)

To my immediate right, the big green door of our garage cuts off what used to be the road to London: all the stage coaches would have had to rattle through that arch en route from country to city. On the far side of the garage is the house lived in by Mrs Green, a widow with her hair in a bun and a very red nose, meaning she probably likes her beer or even her gin, not that I knew about such things then. Her son, Bert Green, is the butcher's boy, a useful neighbour to have in the time of meat rationing – sometimes he slipped us the odd bit of, probably illegal, pig. Mrs Green has friendly conversations with both my father and the housekeeper over the shared garden fence and my father gives her eggs from our chickens; her space of land is too small for keeping chickens as well as growing vegetables. She keeps rabbits in a hutch, though, and, in exchange, allows my father the odd one.

Further along is the sweet shop above which lives, its owner, nice Mrs Cosgrave. The sweet shop is one of the few shops that still exists today, turned in part newsagent, with porno magazines arranged along a top shelf: what *would* nice Mrs C think of that? Beyond stands a house lived in by the local greengrocer and his family. Beyond that a little pub and beyond the pub another shop or two.

And so it all was; an almost comically typical village of its time, with its pubs – on Saturday mornings after paying the bills my father used to take me into the George and Dragon and buy me a fizzy lemonade while he took his pint of bitter and talked local gossip and cricket with whoever else was in the there: with its greengrocer, ironmonger, haberdasher, its two teashops, its two grocers: the smart one patronised by the middle classes, the other, *The International Stores* by what my father called the 'hoi polloi' which in this case included him: among his many idiosyncrasies was his refusal to use the up-market grocer. 'Ridiculous prices,' he'd say, puffing on his pipe, 'and the stuff there's no better. The International will do us just fine. And I always like talking to Peggy.' (Peggy was the wounded V2 heroine who served behind the grocery counter.)

I didn't appreciate his idiosyncrasies then the way I do now, though I ought to have done, considering the way he'd taken on my mother against everyone's advice – and to the never-diminishing disapproval of his own mother. But that was how my father was: wholly predictable, on the one hand, unpredictable – or wayward his mother would say – on the other.

On our side of the Green the road ran straight. On the other side it ran downhill. This fact amused me: it seemed as perverse –as idiosyncratic - as my father. On the far side of that road, from the green, lived my mother's best friend in the village in a cottage converted into a mansion: she came from a rich family: 'stinking rich,' my father said. I spent a lot of time in her house, with his approval and to my pleasure – there was a stream at the bottom of the garden in which I used to float, pretending to live up to my name – Ophelia –as in the picture on my wall. But unlike that stream, it wasn't pretty. There were no flowers and a lot of duckweed and much more fun than playing Ophelia was catching sticklebacks and minnows in jam jars alongside the best friend's son. Much more fun also was the best friend, the only one of the female mentors chosen by my father whom I actually liked and listened to; some of her advice was, I suspect, far from what he was hoping for when he sent me across the green.

There were things in that village that I did not take in at the time: children don't for instance, notice buildings much, or think they don't: they certainly do not observe with any interest the quality of its brickwork or building styles. But this was Kent, land of Wealden clay, and something, somehow, of the care, the decoration, the general excellence of its brickwork went in, quite as much, maybe even more than the sweet sweep and rise of the chalk downs to the north of us, where sometimes in early summertime, magically, I encountered cowslips. The stepped brick mouldings under the highest eaves for instance, the tile hung tops to some buildings, the windows framed in stone or different-coloured or differently aligned brick, the geometric patterns - diamonds and squares picked out in grey against the red brick of the building which housed the ironmonger's and haberdasher's shops, with their slanted doors: (saws, nails and screwdrivers purveyed by Mr and metal-haired Miss Evendon on one side, confronting rows of knicker-drawers and sewing necessities offered by the Misses Luckin – one sweet-looking but sour, the other witchlike and jolly -on the other; not dissimilar, it occurs to me, to the way the statues of the active and the armchair generals, symbols of quite different kinds of war, now confront each other on the Green.)

My mental feet take me even farther tonight, right through the village, to the duck pond and the brewery. They take me, too, not quite willingly, to the place I only discovered years later, as a Christmas postman. As a child I must have been aware, vaguely, that such a place existed. I often saw its inhabitants going about the village: in my head now I see a skinny lank-haired woman in a ragged skirt followed always by two or three dirty children with dribbling noses. She pushed a broken-down pram in which sat not a baby but miscellaneous objects she must have begged from somewhere; a legless chair, perhaps, torn clothes, cracked crockery, a box of cereal, a hunk of wood. She would have come from the complex of rank, dark, crumbling houses tucked away somewhere beyond the duck pond and grouped round a littered and filthy courtyard. All of the houses ran with damp, were decorated if decorated at all by faded pages torn from old newspapers and magazines. How many other dark places and secrets did this village contain without my ever suspecting them? I wonder.

This group of slum-dwellers – now, I think, they'd be called 'the under-class – and or 'scroungers'– sat at the very bottom of the village hierarchy. For there was a hierarchy, of course: class in other words. What seems odd to me now, though, is this: that despite such overt, totally accepted social distinctions, where, except for the local window-cleaner, a Socialist radical who tried and failed to get himself elected to the parish council, everyone appeared to know their place, we all lived hugger mugger, side by side, butcher's boy next to civil servant. Whereas now, officially classless, we mostly don't. The middle-classes have taken over both big and little houses on the Green. The rest – my father's hoi polloi – live in the newer houses, on the council or private estates where houses are either for rent or a good deal cheaper.

My father could be unpredictable in matters of hierarchy as in everything else. When buying cheese and bacon in the International Stores, for instance, instead of the fancier grocery: when walking down the street with Mrs Green, red nose and all, and buying her a drink in the little pub along the road – though not the George and Dragon; *never* The George and Dragon. Before I was old enough to eat with him in the evenings, he used to eat supper in the kitchen with the housekeeper sometimes, much to the scandal of my Nanny – 'It's not right,' she'd scold while she was putting me to bed, and I'd look back blankly not knowing what she meant – sometimes he'd even help with the washing-up. All of which left me the more astonished not to say baffled by the fracas that occurred when I asked to join the Brownies: what could the *Brownies* have to do with class?

The daily woman – the charlady – who came in when was about eight or so, lived in another house on the Green and had a little girl about my age called Maureen and we used to play together in the garden. Maureen went to the village school, a building that looked a bit like a church to me; it lay well down the London Road beyond the Post Office, a school I was obviously not sent to; state schooling then was not for the middle classes, the way it was for my children, at least at primary level. Though that school can't have been worse than the truly terrible little dame school I went to two villages along the North Downs, in Surrey, at least I was not going to pick up what my father would have called an 'accent' – that is any accent that did not sound like his.

Maureen had a collection of satin hair ribbons in different shades of pink that I deeply envied. My nanny also envied her curly blond hair on my behalf but I did not, perfectly happy with my dark-brown and unfashionably dead straight locks, even if I did wish they were contained by a pink satin ribbon rather than a plain green one. Otherwise we were dressed much the same –her pleated skirt and my corduroy shorts from the best friend's son both, obviously, hand-me-downs. Clothes rationing still applying we all wore what we could, just as we ate what we could. Whatever else war is or isn't – this also goes for the long aftermath of war - it's a great leveller. Not that Maureen appreciated the shorts much; 'why are you wearing boy's shorts?' she'd ask. And 'Your hair-ribbon's falling off.' It was in Maureen I first encountered a bitchy little girl.

Still she was a useful playmate, and since we only ever played during the holidays and at weekends, I was unlikely to pick up her 'accent' or she mine. She did what I wanted, mostly, despite the bitchery: though she would have preferred to play at doll's tea parties with the cups and buckets in the sandpit, she put up with my wanting to make sandcastles with them instead and when I was tired of that, she could usually be persuaded to hide behind the chestnut tree while I looked for her, or vice versa. She was also a useful listener to the stories I used to make up about myself. About my being a princess for instance, and how one day someone would come and fetch me and take me to my castle.

'Princesses have curly golden hair,' objected Maureen, touching her hair ribbon, smugly. 'Not straight black hair like yours'.

'Snow White had black hair in the film,' I said.

'*Proper* black hair,' said Maureen. 'And curly. You've got hair like string.'

'And you've got hair like a mop,' I said.

'*Haven't* I? A beautiful golden mop, my mum says.' Maureen burst into song – she had a goodly selection of those. '*Buttons and bows,*' and '*If I knew you were coming I'd have baked a cake*'. Songs, that reluctantly, enviously, I'd find myself joining in with – I liked songs like that – even though all I could offer was a very out of tune '*Run Rabbit Run*' which my nanny used to sing to me sometimes. The radio didn't go on for music in our house, at that time – *Oh Mein Papa* came later - only for comedy programmes like ITMA. Once – learning bitchery in my turn – I heard myself saying in a funny accent 'Can I do you now sir,' adding, 'that's what your mummy should say to my Dad when she comes.'

Maureen didn't seem to notice my bitchery.' She could, couldn't she?' she said. 'We listen to ITMA too.'

Once – but only once - I made up a story about my mother: about how she'd gone to London to help win the war and been killed by a bomb straightaway and that's why she never came back.

'That's funny,' Maureen said. 'I heard my mum saying she'd run off. That's what I heard.'

I didn't say anything, overcome by my usual sense of guilt: it was my fault, I thought that my mother had run away – she hadn't run away from my father, the way he so kindly said. She'd run away from me because I was so horrible.

I burst into tears then and when they came to find me, said, 'Maureen pinched me.' And then feeling guilty about that said, 'No she didn't.'

'That's enough anyway,' my nanny said. 'Go and find your mummy, Maureen. It's time for your lunch, Joey. You come along.'

It was Maureen, though, who put me onto the Brownies. She came wearing her uniform one day – except because of clothes rationing she didn't have the full uniform, merely a brown scarf round her neck held together by a mysterious but fascinating thing called a woggle, and a brown beret with a badge. She told me all about her Brownie pack that met in the hall of the village school, about the Brownie toadstool and Brown Owl – in this case the Vicar's unmarried eldest daughter – about Elves and Pixies and Gnomes. 'I am an Elf,' she said. 'We have to walk round the toadstool saying, 'we are the little Elves, helping others not ourselves.' And we can do badges. I'm doing the sewing badge. Brown Owl is showing me how to hem a hanky.'

Though I did not fancy hemming a hanky, I did desperately want a woggle.

'You could be a Brownie too,' Maureen said. 'You could always ask Brown Owl. She's always saying she wants….' Maureen fished around for the word and then came up with one that was and wasn't quite 'recruits.' I didn't know the word recruit either, but I knew what she meant, so I said. 'I'll have to ask Daddy first. But I'm sure he'll let me if she will.' It seemed simple enough to me. The village school was only just down the road: I could walk there by myself, no trouble to anyone.

But my father did not seem to think it was a simple matter at all. Nor did Maureen's mother who scolded her for giving me the idea, or so Maureen told me, resentfully, next time we played together (I was being Hardy at the time and she was being poor beaten-up Stan Laurel. That might have added to the resentment.)

'Why can't I go to Brownies in the village school,' I kept arguing. 'Why can't I?'

'Because only the village children go those Brownies. It wouldn't be appropriate,' my father said.

'But why can't I? You play cricket with Maureen's daddy and all the other village people. What's the difference?'

'Because it is different. And you can't.' My father was tired that night. He'd had a long day at work, longer than usual. His mouth, his jaw were set in an obstinate geometry that I learned to know well over the years, but didn't need to take much notice of, not then.

'But why can't I?' I whined. I could and did whine, but to my nanny more often than him, because I felt so guilty about driving my mother away and because we so needed each other, he and I.

'That's enough, Jo,' he said sharply, slamming down his whisky glass and then picking it up again and looking at as if to check he hadn't broken it. He took another rueful swig.

'Then if I can't go there why can't I go to one near my school? Janice Hunter goes to Brownies there.' (I'd done my research by this time.)

'Because there's no one to take you and there isn't enough petrol anyway.'

'Why can't I go on the bus? Everyone is going to go to Brownies except me,' I said, forcing myself into tears. Remembering something I'd read recently – I was already beginning to read way above my age level, precocious brat that I was - I added. 'You're blighting my life.'

My father burst out laughing at this. 'Where did you get *that* from?' Then he turned serious again. 'You can't go on the bus. It's enough, Jo. You're tired and it's your bedtime. In the morning you'll be bright as a button. And you'll've forgotten all about this.'

But I didn't forget. For a while I really did feel my life was blighted by not being allowed to join the Brownies, even though I knew that the Brown Owl of the pack Janice Hunter went to near our school was fat Miss Groomless – never was a name more accurate we used to snigger as we neared puberty and knew a bit more about these things – who taught the second class to the bottom and who wouldn't have looked or sounded any better in her Brown Owl uniform than she did in the tweed coat and skirt she wore to school winter and summer. And even though I already suspected that I was more than likely to suffer the fate of a very naughty – and to me very admirable - girl called Susan Haywood, who'd been thrown out of the pack for vandalising the Brownie toadstool. VANDALISING THE BROWNIE TOADSTOOL. What *fun*.

Maureen and I stopped playing together not so long after the Brownie business. But not before she had added some more songs to her repertoire; "l*et him go let him tarry*,' I remember, was one of them.

'Why are all your songs about getting boyfriends and getting married?' I asked Maureen once. She looked at me in astonishment. Even if she could not make up stories about her past she could and did make them up about her future, something that I never dared do. 'Because that's what I'm going to do when I grow up: get married of course,' she said. As this was something that was constantly enjoined on me, class made no difference here.

But Maureen, unlike me again, also had ideas of what she was going to do before she got there. All her singing was practice: she didn't merely sing she performed, holding her skirt out, twirling about, making cute faces between the lines. She did seem to sing very well too, I thought, not that I was any judge; I could hear she sang in tune though, if very loudly. Sometimes her mum put her head out of the kitchen window and shouted at her to pipe down.

'I want to be like Judy Garland when I grow up,' she said. 'Or maybe just Dinah Shore.' But the nearest she ever got to that – I daresay her golden curls helped – was being Carnival Queen one year and riding on a float wearing a lacy pink dress and a cardboard crown covered in glass diamonds. I saw her picture in the paper, but didn't see the float itself; I was away at boarding school by then and bank holidays were for the hoi polloi and not for me. The last time I'd seen Maureen in the flesh she'd left school and gone to work in the International Stores alongside V2 Peggy. I saw her there one day when I was sent in to buy a pound of sugar. She was wearing a blue overall, her hair was not held back by ribbons any more but by Kirby grips – I had a neat brown slide in place of *my* hair-ribbon - and as she weighed out my sugar and poured it expertly from the scales into the blue sugar-paper bag she didn't look at me at all, and when she had to speak to me she said 'Miss.'

Peggy was called away then to the other side of the shop and Maureen said 'Psst, Jo,' Putting her finger to her lips she reached down into the tin of broken biscuits and shoved a handful my way which I had to shovel into my pocket as best I could, terrified that Peggy would turn round and accuse me of stealing. Luckily she did not.

I didn't eat the biscuits either. They were all crumbs by the time I got home and I emptied them onto the lawn for the birds, more annoyed with Maureen than anything; she could have got both of us into trouble. Though I did not understand then why I was annoyed rather than grateful at her taking such a risk on my behalf, I understand better now. I think she did it as more a statement of power than generosity: I can even applaud her for showing so much spirit.

I wonder if Maureen is still alive. I suspect she's formidable matriarch if so, and that these days, without our parents looking over our shoulders, we'd meet on more equal terms, if still with nothing much in common except our shared past; at least I hope we would.

CHAPTER ELEVEN

Jenny arrives in my room today, peering bashfully around the door first to see if she would be welcome. Her seeming bashfulness is the only thing that continues to annoy me about her: she is not at all bashful in reality. I would never have let her get so close to me had she been.

'God, Jen,' I groan. 'Spare me the act.'

She arrives at the bed and kisses me on the cheek, briskly.

'You love it really, gives you the chance to slate me,' she says, unwrapping a tiny bunch of violets which she proceeds to arrange in a glass on the table at the end of my bed, but not before giving me the chance to look at them more closely. They are perfect, their purple so rich and full they remind me, inexplicably, of deep water: they make me want to cry. I don't reject them the way I reject - politely for the most part – other gifts of flowers. I do not want to die surrounded by them, like Ophelia.

'Not for much longer,' I say.

'Enjoy it while you can then,' she says, her face more doleful than her voice, as she sits down on one of my fake leather chairs. She will miss me I know: I am the nearest thing she has to a mother. She fell out with her own as a teenager and has barely spoken to her since. I can't quite say she is the nearest thing I have to a daughter, but on bad days it has sometimes it has felt like that, though this is not so much my real daughters' fault as mine.

('It's because you and I don't have all that mother/daughter baggage behind us,' Jenny said once and of course she is right. But other people manage to negotiate the baggage somehow; why are we – my daughters and I - so bad at it? You could say the same of Jenny and her mother. Why are they?)

Jenny was my ex-publishing assistant. Arriving in the firm, the way I started in publishing, as a secretary, she was one of the few who managed from the beginning to negotiate my eruptive temper. Most of my staff considered me a monster: like my predecessor, my own boss, I was famous for making my secretaries cry. Not that I cared: I got results, just the way he had got results from me.

She doesn't exactly look like a monster-slayer, Jenny. The apparent timidity with which she entered the room today is typical. But the timidity, bashfulness whatever you like to call it –

enhanced by dark, lightly protuberant eyes that hood themselves and look sideways at you at any first encounter - belies a capacity to stand up for herself, tearfully or otherwise: as I discovered the very first time she hovered awkwardly in the doorway of my office.

'What's the matter with you,' I said, noting as I did so how tall she was, her head bending as if she was used to having to bend it in order to avoid hitting it on lintels or even ceilings. 'Either stay out or come in.'

'I think I'm supposed to come in,' she said, in a soft voice that was slightly but not obtrusively Northern.

'Oh for God's sake…'

She still hovered, her eyes wide open now and gazing at me directly. She was narrow on top and much broader at the bottom I noted: her horizontally striped trousers did not flatter her in the least.

'Do you always speak to your secretaries like that?' she enquired, in what appeared to be dispassionate interest. 'Am I supposed to cry? I can if that would make you feel any better.'

'Or you could just get out?' I suggested.

'OK,' she agreed, benignly, meekly, turning to go.

'For god's sake, girl, just come in and sit down,' I said.

And so things began. And went on going, bit by bit. It took a time for us to trust each other, considerably longer for me to learn anything much about her: she was almost as taciturn that way as I was myself. What I learned much sooner was that though she was not the most efficient secretary I ever had she was capable of becoming a good, even brilliant editorial assistant and in due course editor: as she did.

'How's the office,' I ask, wearily from my sick bed – by now Jenny is the editorial director of my old firm, arriving at that position at an even younger age than I had.

'Difficult,' she said. 'You know how it is, the salesmen rule. But you don't really want to hear about that do you?'

'Probably not,' I say. 'It wasn't like that when I started, as you know. Is everyone wearing suits round the office these days?'

She laughed. 'Only some of the moneymen. It sounded much more fun in your day. I'd love to have encountered Gloria.' (Gloria had been the resident office dragon.)

'No you wouldn't,' I said. 'You would not.' Even though by this time I could feel nostalgia for Gloria, there was still no affection there. I assumed she would be dead by now, like my first boss whom I had loved; it was just as well, seeing what had become of their beloved firm.

We sat in silence for a few minutes. I was wincing with pain.

'Are you feeling bad?' Jen asked at last.

'What do you think?'

'Shall I go?'

'No, please stay.' I held out my hand, she moved the chair up closer to the bed and took it and we sat there like that till the Husband turned up and she slipped away.

'Nice woman,' the Husband said.

'Yes.' I wanted to cry. I did, a little. I added, after a long silence. 'We had fathers in common, neither of them believing in educating women. He was a top trade unionist in Sheffield, you would think he'd have known better.'

'Chauvinist organisations, unions,' he said, thoughtfully. And then he added, in a tone of astonishment, 'She's what, thirty years younger than you? And her father still doesn't believe in educating girls? Surely it all changed by the time she grew up.'

'No,' I said, 'it didn't. It hasn't. How can you be so naïve.' I remembered something Jenny had told me when she was working as an editor alongside me, about something her father had said when she he didn't think she was in earshot. It was in response to a question from a friend of his about what his daughter did. *'She says she's an editor. But I'm not quite sure what that means. I just know she reads a lot, but she never did much except read anyway. It's just as well she's found a job that pays her to do it.'* She had added then, to me. 'As far as dad is concerned, someone writes a book and then someone else prints it. He doesn't understand all the stuff in between.'

I felt too tired to pass this on to the Husband. I didn't. I fell asleep

My friendships with women are rare and have been for most of my life. I have been unlucky, partly. Losing, so early, the two friends of my youth, the ones I drank whisky with across our kitchen tables, was one thing. I never managed to replace them. I was too busy was the excuse I allowed myself. Most likely, quite as much, I was afraid I'd lose any new friends the way I'd lost the old ones, and before them, more significantly still, my mother. I'd begun to realise, too, that I was in general more comfortable around men, starting with my father and going on with my first boss, the man who'd made a publisher out of me, all those years ago. (That's a part of my life I'd like to remember again in more detail some time but not yet.)

CHAPTER TWELVE

As an adult, I understood much better why the quasi matrimonial relationship between my father and me was viewed with such disapproval by his female acquaintances, not least by my mother's best friend across the road, whom I loved and the wife of the Sergeant-at- Arms whom I did not. I wonder what they would have thought if they had heard him inveighing – to me - against his political masters, the way he sometimes did: in particular the Tory ones. Once I said – innocently – I was still young enough to be innocent then – 'you like Labour people much better than the Conservatives. 'Why don't we vote for them?' (I was still too young to vote myself, of course. But I had gone around sticking up notices saying 'Vote Conservative' before the last election.)

My father harrumphed at this and did not answer. And I see now, as I could not then, that the Tories were his tribe, he had to vote for them. (Not that he would have seen it quite like that; most likely he wouldn't even have understood what 'tribal' meant, in relation to him.)

Another of his tribes was his House of Commons colleagues; not surprisingly given that they were all privy to matters they could not talk about outside: every one of them would have had to sign the Official Secrets Act. It was this tribal camaraderie I think that made my father see the Sergeant-at-Arms' wife a possible mentor for me, part of his determination to see that in due course I made a good – and happy - marriage. Though he may have understood the circumstances that drove my mother away, he could not have imagined that women might want to reject marriage in general, the way it was constituted then. Given how forgiving he was of my mother, this took me by surprise.

One of the bonuses of working in the House of Commons was the extraordinarily long holidays. Officials in those days free throughout every parliamentary recess, my father was at home a good deal more than most.

He kept himself busy of course, helping the part time gardener grow vegetables, getting elected to the parish council as an independent member, serving on this committee or that, playing cricket in the summer, golf and bridge all the year round. At the same time he accepted with alacrity the invitations that came from the Sergeant-at-arms' wife for us to stay with them for a week or two in my school holidays, at their house not far from the Sussex coast. I don't think his motive was just my further education, let alone any wish to be relieved of my company. It was as much that it enabled him to go golfing with the Sergeant-at-Arms, still better enabled him to go sailing, something he enjoyed even more. Sometimes the sergeant-at-arms' wife and I were invited to join him and the Sergeant-at-Arms on the boat. Mostly we were not, which meant that I spent a lot of time – much more than I liked – in her company. 'My honorary daughter,' she'd introduce me with a fond smile when anyone came to call, or when we met anyone while shopping in her village. That was not how I saw it.

I don't know what I disliked most about staying with the Sergeant–at-Arms and his wife. I disliked *everything*: starting with her making me call them 'Aunt Anne' and 'Uncle Jim.'

'But they're not my uncle and aunt.' I'd protest to my father.

'It doesn't do any harm,' my father said. 'Go along with it.'

'It does me harm,' I said darkly. 'It does *me* harm.'

But he just laughed in his usual, maddening, indulgent way. And that was that.

I didn't like Anne's house, its gloomy Edwardian spaces all dark wood and thick green carpet, with frowning diamond-paned windows that never let in enough light. I didn't like her leather sofas, too wide for me to sit on comfortably and slippery besides (though I did like the big leather pouffe shaped like a pig, and sometimes badgered my father to get us one like it: they cost a fortune in Harrods,' he protested.) I didn't like her shiny velvet curtains, or the uncomfortably big and high bed in which I had to sleep. I didn't like her gloomy kitchen with its formidable red tiles, wooden draining-boards and dark green walls, where she tried, not very efficiently, to teach me wifely skills; skills I suspected she let the housekeeper perform when I was not around. I hated her dogs, four black Labradors that slobbered over me and looked, I thought, like black slugs: she called them the 'Wagger Boys,' which was even worse. I hated her headscarves and tweed skirts, the socks she wore over stockings on her thick legs to go walking, the stout walking-shoes into which she put socks, stockings, etc, the hooked walking sticks for pulling down the bramble branches too high for her to reach. It always did seem to be the summer holidays when we stayed with her: we always did seem to be going out to pick blackberries, an uncomfortably prickly occupation.

Mostly I was set to pick berries from the lowest part of the bushes. 'You have to bend right down,' Aunt Anne would scold me. 'Look at the ones down there; you're missing all the best ones. Look at your basket, it isn't even half full.' But sometimes if she'd pulled down a particularly inelastic branch that threatened to swing back up again unless she kept two hands on her walking stick, she'd make me pick the fruit off that, ignoring my protests that she should leave some fruit for the birds.

'You Silly Billy,' she'd say. 'You *Silly* Billy. There's more than enough berries for them.' And she'd sweep her hand round all the other far too prickly bushes –there were rosehips, sloes, things I didn't know the name of but which were obviously inedible – by her - because otherwise I would have been made to pick them too. Once, I remember she protested so vehemently that she lost purchase on the branch and it swung right up and out of reach, scratching my face as it did so. 'Oh dear, now you *are* a wounded soldier,' Aunt Anne sighed, not adding that it was my fault for being a Silly Billy, though the look on her face said just that.

When she wasn't ordering me to pick ever harder, or shouting at one or other of the Wagger Boys for daring to suggest with excited yelps and much quivering of its fat slug bottom that there was a rabbit not far off, she'd would be offering little snippets of advice. Such as:

'Men like being flattered. Good flatterers get the best husbands.' Or 'Never go out without putting on lipstick. Of course you're too young for lipstick now but do remember that when you're older. Men don't like scruffy women. You must always be well turned out.'

When we arrived home with our full baskets I'd have to help her make jam or blackberry-and-apple something, suffering yet more advice meanwhile on how to get a husband, though not so much about how to keep one, which may or may not have explained how many I managed to lose. I despised her advice, but enough sank in to cause me a few – if passing - difficulties later when I embarked on the search for myself; my even wanting to embark on such a search makes me realise now how deeply I had been infected by all this. Hating - and despising – every last bit of it, I even despised my father when he and the Sergeant-at-arms appeared, beaming, wind-blown and sunburnt after their day on the water, making short work of whatever inevitably meaty treat had been prepared with my unwilling help: cooked meat was bad enough, raw uncooked meat still worse ('don't be such a juggins,' my un-Aunt Anne would say bracingly when I demurred at being asked to help roll the bloody chunks in flour on her big wooden table - 'it's just meat, it won't hurt you'). The men said things like 'you girls seemed to have had a useful day' as they devoured the beef stew, the blackberry-and-apple whatever. And I do have to admit that my father seemed to enjoy these days out – the whole visit – as much as I ever saw him enjoy anything: this makes my grumbles seem churlish now. It felt churlish even then. In an attempt to make me more tolerant, my father had told me that Anne lost her only child – a little girl – soon after birth and had never been able to have another: a fact that reminded me uncomfortably of the baby in the grave over the wall at home, and of my dead great-grandmother. But my great-grandmother was long dead, I didn't have to put up with her in real life, the way I had to put with the awful – UGLY I told myself -Aunt Anne with her deep voice and unedifying chortle and her endless patter of unwanted advice. 'Well I wish she wouldn't try to make up for dead baby with me,' I'd say meanly. Though next time I saw her, I did, at first, try to receive her advice a little more graciously.

   At the same time I couldn't help thinking – as meanly as ever – that her childlessness was just as well for the children – in particular the female ones: imagine having Aunt Anne for a mother: having her as a mentor was bad enough.

CHAPTER THIRTEEN

I have more time than I want to think now. My mind is the only part of myself that is able – that continues to take exercise – when I'm awake that is; judging by my dreams it is pretty active even when I'm asleep, no doubt a result of all the drugs they're pumping into me. Doesn't morphine induce hallucinations? How strange that it's being locked here, within my blocked, uncontrollable body, that allows me to range farther beyond myself than I've ever managed - dared – to before.

I wonder if it has something to do with the weighty twentieth century history that the Husband made me read, just before I got ill. He'd handed it to me with some kind of loaded comment – something about its possible effects on the way I saw the past that I was – as he put it – always going on about: 'Your bloody childhood. Etc, etc, etc.' (Admittedly I surprise myself these days; I never used to talk about that past.) He doesn't remember *his* childhood, or claims he doesn't. He can't remember much about stuff that came later either. It would get in the way of what he's doing now, he says, which, to him, is all that matters. His capacity to remember formulas and arguments is astonishing to me: no less astonishing than his incapacity to remember such things as his grandmother's Christian name. Let alone her maiden name. Let alone the names and faces of his teachers or school friends or anything like that. *Trivial stuff*, he claims. Why should I stuff my brain with all of that?

In the hands of the historians, views of the past can be overturned at any time. But history does have its clear parameters. And most of those twentieth century ones I had lived through, and the ones I hadn't lived through, that came before my time, my father and my mother had lived through. So why had I made so little sense of them? Submerged by daily life – essays to be written, meals to be cooked, love to be enjoyed, mourned or regretted, nappies to be washed, meetings to be attended, manuscripts to be edited –I had only ever observed history in passing, except when it converged on my life - all our lives - in ways I could not but notice: like the day the V2 exploded in our village, or the day I saw the headline in the paper about the H-Bomb. Or on those days of such history-turning events as Kennedy's assassination and onwards up to and beyond 9/11, the times when history drags you into itself willy-nilly, making you spend weeks scouring the media for the reason for it all and even then not beginning to understood it really.

I thought of the meat men, the pink and white dark-suited crow men, chomping up their roast beef and steak-and-kidney pie in the House of Commons dining room as though the war had never happened; as though they mightn't be responsible for starting new ones. There was still little affection in my memory of them. But at least I understood better their seeming oblivion. My sixties were not swinging or rebellious but full of babies: my first husband's idiosyncrasies and our seething disagreements are at least as strong now as my memory of the Cuban crisis. During my first pregnancy I trembled through the latter: the first month of my second (much too close to the first: my husband had read something about having children close to each other making them bond better) saw me weeping over the dead Kennedy. I carried my third, unwanted but in the end favourite child, my son, through the Summer of Love hardly noticing it was happening – or the '68 youth revolts the following year, not long after he was born, come to that: I was too busy trying simultaneously to rear my child, give my other children and my husband some attention, and calm down my pissed-off boss. I had my first adulterous affair during the three day week, and despite the agonies of my divorce, around 1976, the seventies in general seemed less the age of catastrophe that I read they were than one freer, naughtier, full of my children of course, but also seeing the arrival of lovers, especially my second most favourite one – another who did not, could not turn into a husband. All of which remains far more vivid to me than the Yom Kippur war or the military putsch in Chile or even the winter of discontent. My eighties were Margaret Thatcher for sure and the miners' strike and monetarism, but appositely, for me, as vividly, was the decade of the rich second husband, expensive cars and hotels and also my greatest successes in my publishing job: with ever more wars to be written about and no one yet tired of reading about them – Vietnam! – Angola! –Lebanon! – Grenada, even Grenada! – all made landings on my desk. This husband's departure with the sexy widow in the next chateau – she was younger than me and could have his baby, something that seemed and still seems reasonable enough, if painful at the time - blighted things for a while, considerably, but I did not have much time to grieve. My children mostly gone, I was working harder than ever: the way the publishing world was going, I had to. I merged the administrative departments of my firm with those of two other houses, later on, in the early nineties, agreed to move all our offices into a more corporate building. Still later in the decade, the abolition of the National Book Agreement, and the arrival of discounted books having the effect on sales that we'd predicted, we were taken over by a large American house and though Jen survived - I made sure of that - my life in the firm was over.

Just before the takeover I married for the third time: to a long-known, very successful literary agent who'd always adored me and whom I too found I loved, in my way. His sudden and unexpected death, followed all too closely by my unsought golden handshake might have left me rich but in all other respects seemed the end of history – *mine* - though not in the way everyone else meant - the collapse of the Soviet system, the end of apartheid, and the rise of Islamic terrorism, etc, etc, etc. But *was* it the end of history - mine or anyone else's? In one word: no. History as always just went on a-going. The truest thing ever said about it, by Walter Benjamin, I think, was that the angel of history moves forwards with its face looking backwards all the time. (When I mentioned this great thought to the Husband, lately, he merely snorted. It even drove him out of my room to have a cigarette. I do wish he didn't smoke.)

It is evening now. My son has been and gone: he looked tired and depressed and I worried about him as far as I am capable of worrying about such things in my final days. There's nothing I can do so what's the point? Yet I ache for him just the same and wish that my ever-speedier decline wasn't there to make him sadder. Not that I said anything. At the best of times it's hard to subvert lifetime patterns of communication with your nearest and dearest, and this is not only not the best of times, it doesn't appear to belong in real time any longer.

'Got the paper on you?' I'd asked. When he opened his bag I saw there was a paperback thriller alongside the copy of the Times, his files, his laptop. 'What's this? Escape literature?" He grinned. 'It's in my genes isn't it? How else did you ever chill out, except with crap like this?'

'Good crap,' I said primly. 'Well-written. More than can be said for the Times.'

'Oh god, mum, do you never give up?'

'Do you want me to?' He handed over the Times. I let it fall

But that was an hour ago. I have slept a little and calmed down more. The final Husband and I sit together now, in the peaceable way we have arrived at these days. He is reading the Guardian, making a mess of the pages the way he always does and commenting out loud from time to time, but without any apparent interest in my taking in let alone responding to what he says. He has a small glass of single malt alongside him: the bottle was a gift to me – my favourite tipple – but alas I cannot stomach it any longer: I have to enjoy it vicariously, through him. 'Breathe it over me' I say once and he does, touching my shoulder very sweetly before lumbering back to his chair. He has the sports section of the paper on his lap now: the section I never bothered with except when tennis was on – he, on the other hand, is as passionate about the sports he likes – particularly Rugby –League - as my father used to be about his favourites, especially cricket.

Though I haven't watched live sport since I grew up, as a child I did accompany my father to various events: athletics, Rugby (Union, of course), cricket. I used to watch him play cricket for various teams, too. I even used to caddy for him at golf. My pretending to be enthusiastic was the only way I knew how to make up to him for not being a son. In such areas I was sure he'd have preferred me to be a boy.

'Green gold and purple,' I recite out loud now.

My non-sequiturs always have baffled this husband. 'I don't know what you're talking about,' he says.

'My father's MCC tie. The colours.'

'I still don't know what you're talking about.'

'Cricket. Lords. Marylebone County Cricket Club. Oh, never mind.' I realise that I've got it wrong anyway. MCC colours were red and yellow. Green gold and purple was the Eton Ramblers. This is information I do not divulge. My family's patrician origins give this grammar school boy too many chances to tease. There's almost nothing in my background that he can't make comedy out of - alas I can't do northern well enough to make comedy out of his. Once I dared mention the one atavistic belief that has survived the erosion of all those other beliefs of superiority I was brought up with, social and national: the belief that Surrey – where I went to school – was a county infinitely inferior to its neighbour, Kent - in which I was born. He had looked at me in incomprehension. From his Northern perspective the Home Counties were all indistinguishable Tory heartlands and all equally a joke.

'Women are banned from the MCC,' I say now. 'Well they were. When Dad was its oldest member he voted in favour of letting women in. He said it would stir them up a bit and about time too.'

'I'm a Wigan Warrior myself. Would he have wanted to let me in?'

'I doubt it,' I say, adding, meanly. 'My father played cricket too. And golf. He didn't just watch. Not until he was old.'

'Rugby League is more dangerous than golf. I've only ever *watched* rugby league, me.'

'That's what I mean.' I say, looking pointedly at his paunch.

'Och and him such a fine wee fellow too.' His cod accent something between Irish and Scots, he is smiling at me cheerfully and patting his belly with affection.

I look him back at him just as affectionately. Not so long ago I'd have continued in this mode, him going along with it willingly, until I pushed it so far that we quarrelled. But I am too tired now. And, besides, overcome by sudden grief; the memory of the sweet curve of his belly against my back in our bed at night contains everything I am losing – have already lost. I can't even ask him to lie down on this bed and remind me because it would hurt too much.

I am hurting already. I press the friendly button of my morphine pump, close my eyes and lie back, groaning, hoping the pain will ease. And once again find myself thinking about my father. As the thoughts surface and fade, fade and surface, I home in – try to home in – on what has puzzled me most of my life – why I, so intransigent towards almost everything and everybody else always tried so desperately to please the man who brought me up as his daughter.

Had I feared that like my mother he would go away? There *was* that: of course. But I think it was as much, if not more, to do with something I can name now if not then: our mutual – shared - fragility. And, too, with the feeling that I owed something to him for exposing himself to such fragility, something that was beyond the simple fact of paternity, something more willed and for which I could only be grateful, even without knowing what, exactly, I had to be grateful for.

CHAPTER FOURTEEN

Growing up with war meant taking for granted air-raids, bomb sites, ration books, siren suits, gas masks– how I loved my Mickey Mouse gas mask – meant being as familiar with the names of Churchill and Hitler as I was with those of Mrs Green and Leslie next door, of Mrs Cosgrove at the sweetshop. But it did not mean I understood what war meant. I wasn't startled into that till I was nearly thirteen, about to go to boarding school, when my father took us across the channel and we drove from one side of the France to the other, to the banks of the Rhine, the German frontier.

The final act of the production of Verdi's Rigoletto that, years on, saw my first date with my first husband, showed a solitary building to the right of the stage inside which a murderer lurked: the moment the curtain rose to reveal its dangerously friendly window I was reminded of arriving at that town by the Rhine. It had been late and getting dark - my father always kept going far too long: ahead of us at last we'd seen our rectangle of light, offering, we hoped, not very hopefully, supper and even beds for the night.

Where were all the other buildings, I wondered? Hadn't there been a sign with a name on it, wasn't this supposed to be a town? The building with the lit window looked like a solitary tooth sticking up in an otherwise empty mouth. It may have been a town once: but, to my memory, I woke in the morning and looked around at a more or less flattened one. Only two or three very stark, utilitarian buildings like the one we were staying in replaced the ruins. I didn't need to be told by my father that war had done this. What had happened to all the people in the town, I wondered? This, too, I didn't ask.

That was the early fifties: a time when not many English chose to drive across Europe for their holidays. Apart from too many signs of war and a great lack of tourist facilities, there were strict limits to the amount of currency you could take. People like us who could afford holidays retreated to places like Frinton or Bognor Regis or Ireland at the furthest. But not my father. Neither his far from reliable cars deterred him, nor the shortage of cash. The first car in which we ventured across the channel was a pre-war

Wolseley that had belonged to my grandmother and which I loved because in those days, long before Health and Safety, it had running boards you could ride on. The second was a stodgier thing, a black Morris Oxford, only slightly more reliable. Neither of those vehicles liked climbing mountain passes.

One reason for these travels – apart from the fact my father loved travelling his whole life and had driven all over Europe before the war: in my flat somewhere is a great stack of albums filled with fading and not exactly skilful snaps taken on such holidays –was that my father loved mountains: he'd been a climber in his late teens and early twenties. He had foresworn all such risks since I was born, limiting his climbing to the motoring kind that too often left us halted part of the way up some high pass, the engine boiling, steam spitting out from under the bonnet. We had to wait until the radiator had cooled and he could re-fill it with fresh water before setting out again: on the highest passes we endured this ritual at least twice. He seemed to regard it as a challenge, part of the adventure rather than a nuisance. I wasn't so sure. I'd stay in the back of the car reading my book, hoping that no one would pass to see my father standing against a background of snow-covered peaks dressed in his holiday gear of long woollen socks, over-long, over-wide khaki shorts and a faded aertex shirt topped by a battered panama hat, and leaning against his spitting car, patting it as proudly and tenderly as if he was patting his dog.

There were more reasons for these trips, though, than my father's love of mountains. The most significant probably was his ambivalent relationship towards Germany: some of this was in relation to me, for reasons I could not understand, but not all of it, by any means.

On the one hand as he once said, very sadly, towards the end of his life, 'I can't really like the Germans. They killed my brothers during the first war and my friends during the second.' On the other hand, partly because of the mountains, he loved south Germany and Austria. So much so that when, during his climbing days, he was faced with the prospect of civil service entrance exams, he chose not to improve his French but the German he'd picked up climbing - to the baffled fury of his mother, who could not forgive the Germans for the slaughter of her two elder sons, and who, in any case, regarded all trips to what she called

ABROAD - even no further than to Calais –as inadvisable at any time. (For some reason she seemed to exempt Switzerland. Maybe the cuckoo clocks reassured her; or maybe she confused Switzerland with Scotland.)

That time he'd stayed with friends of one of his fellow climbers, a Munich family, who had a summer-house up in the Bavarian mountains, quite near Hitler's retreat; not that Hitler at the time of my father's stay was anything more than a provincial leader, despised, not to say hated by his rather aristocratic hosts, the elders of whom were forced to flee to Argentina when Hitler annexed Austria. Naturally he hadn't heard from these friends since war broke out. On the small chance of finding them he'd sent a letter to their old Munich address and to his surprise had received a reply from the youngest daughter of the family. 'We didn't think you'd want to know us any more after what our country has done,' she wrote.

My father wrote again: *of course I want to know you still*. A week or two later came another letter, inviting him and me to stay with the daughter's family: she was married now, she said, with two sons. She and her husband had a farm in the Bavarian Alps where they spent most of the year. These days she did not care to be in Munich.

And so there was I, language-less, apart from two phrases my father had insisted on teaching me before we set out: '*ich kann kein Deutsch.*' And '*Ich verstehe nicht*' and faced with two equally English-less and baffled boys in worn lederhosen – twins, it turned out, Walter and Nikolaus, more or less my age- who were put to entertaining me while my father and our hostess made up for lost time and years of officially being enemies. Halfway up a green slope, backed by the inevitable snow-capped peaks, their house looked like any Swiss chalet, except that this wasn't Switzerland and as far as I could see lacked all forms of amusement apart from farm work ('no thanks,' I said, or rather, '*Nein, danke,*' when invited to milk a cow) or going for long walks up impossibly steep slopes pursued by the maddening tinkle of cow and goat bells, and then being forced to run – yes, run – back down these same impossibly steep slopes, zigzagging wildly, in danger of turning one if not both ankles at all times: the boys had instructed me in the gesture-backed pidgin language that we contrived between us, that this was the only safe way to descend. It did not seem very safe to me. I have never liked heights, and the one thing I enjoyed about these hikes were the flowers that proliferated the higher we went – the precise brilliance of gentians especially delighted me – on which I could feast my eyes. It was a good excuse, that, to rest my breath. Just the same I did find those flowers amazing: the contrast between their tiny detail and the vast panoramas below filled me with a delightful dizziness. Lying in bed now I can still see the flowers: I can almost smell their blue. It's the only thing about that country I remember with affection, and the only reason I went on more than one of those desperate hikes before I rebelled and insisted on staying behind and reading on the wooden balcony in the front of the house. The slope dropped away there, too, but the carved wooden railings kept vertigo at bay.

   I do not think it was just physical vertigo. There was something about this place where all colours seemed, if not primary, far too primitive and bright - greens, blues, whites, the brown of wood, the red of geraniums, the mixed blue green of pinewoods -that disturbed me deeply. I would look for reassurance, often, to the far end of the balcony where my father sat in deep conversation with the twins' mother.

   Though she wore plaits wrapped round her head and the local dirndl dress, this lady conformed to no other stereotype of German womanhood: to my memory she was witty, cynical and not the least concerned, not to say careless, about what her family was up to - all I remember of her husband is that he spent most of the time outside, working on the farm. When I ran out of reading matter I sat and dreamed and listened, picking up the odd mysterious phrase. They spoke in English much of the time; despite my father's efforts, his friend's English was much better than his half-remembered German. I had the impression that he confided rather more in her than in his English friends, even in my mother's best friend. Maybe this friend was more sympathetic than any of them. Maybe, once, years ago, he'd been a little in love with her. Maybe her wartime suffering, of which he later told me a little, added a depth of understanding that my father's English women friends lacked. Or maybe he was just that much farther from home. I think he talked about my mother and, presumably, my parentage. Once I heard him say mysteriously– I think I heard him say - 'She should really learn some German.' I certainly heard his friend reply after a long and maybe startled pause: 'I'm sure she's learning some from the boys already.' (She was wrong about that.)

A moment later, I heard her add, even more mysteriously. 'Silence is bad for families. Isn't it about time you told her?' Told me what, I wondered. Or maybe I had misheard her. I thought I must have done.

'No,' my father said.

'Yes,' she answered: and again: 'Yes.'

A lot of children might have been fazed by the hand-to-mouth way in which my father and I lived throughout these trips, the unreliability of his vehicles, the daily uncertainties about where we were going to stay, what we were going to eat, whether our money would hold out. But I wasn't fazed, or not often. I enjoyed all – or almost all - of it. Our shortage of cash, unfortunately, obliged my father and I to share a room – in those days before Lolita and Humbert Humbert no one seemed to worry about fathers and daughters sharing rooms. Sometimes, to our mutual horror, we were obliged to share a bed, kept apart by a big bolster down the middle. One night, not long after we had left my father's friends, arriving in a particularly close, deep valley between mountains, I had, still worse, to share a bed with our hostess, a woman on whose door we had knocked in desperation as darkness fell. In this case no bolster separated us. Beneath the shared, bulbous, goose-down eiderdown – in the mountains, I'd encountered the now ubiquitous duvet for the first time – I lay all night, stiff with fear that my lustily snoring hostess was going to roll over onto me. Once or twice she did, asphyxiating me with a reek of mould, dried lavender, fire, cooking, old wood, old woman, within which I felt smothered, cramped and utterly alone. Everything in that house was cramped, I remember. It was crammed with carved wooden thises and thats, with stoves, china figures, cushions, plates, bowls, painted trays, tortured Christs on crucifixes, pictures of serious saints. It was all so dark, *dark* - sinister even. And though I did fall asleep at last, I dreamed uneasy dreams and woke in the morning hearing in my head once more the mysterious and disturbing phrase I'd heard –I thought I'd heard -'Isn't it about time you told her?'

At some level my father might have heard what I was thinking. I might even have asked my question, whispering it out loud, hardly knowing that I did. I do know that he had seemed pre-occupied from the moment we'd restarted our travels. The next day, as we were starting the ascent from yet another deep valley between mountains, I emerged from my book – I was a little tired of all the driving now – to hear him say, irritably. 'Doesn't it make you feel sick, reading in the car?'

'No,' I said. I was about to return to my page when he reached over me and flipped the book shut, something so unlike him, I looked up, not only indignantly, almost in shock, to find him staring at the road straight ahead of us, as if nothing had happened. 'What did you do that for?' I asked, crossly.

'I think there's something you ought to know, Jo,' he said stiffly. 'You're almost thirteen, quite old enough for the truth.'

We had begun the ascent; yet the road still lay in shadow, terrorised by mountains.

'Know what? Know *what*?'

The road became steeper. Painfully, manipulating the lever more clumsily than usual, my father was changing gear. Painfully, the engine took on a new note.

'What?' I said again; beginning, distractedly, to look for the page in the book I'd lost.

'Put that away will you?' He was still clutching the gearstick, still staring at the road ahead.

'What?' I asked again, more alarmed now than cross. And ever more alarmed when he rapped out, flatly, staccato, the plainest statement he'd ever given me or ever would – I had to strain to hear it, against the panting of the engine.

'I'm only your adopted father; don't you see; not your real one. Your mother... made me your father when you were born.'

'What do you mean? *Made* me your father?' I glanced at him, surreptitiously, hoping for reassurance. But the expression on his face, the way his head hunched into his shoulders, forced me to fear for the first time, wretchedly, that there could be no reassurance. On up we climbed – it wasn't as long as many climbs he'd inflicted on the old Morris but it seemed to be objecting even more than usual, as if heated still more by what had been said. A telltale puff of steam erupted from the bonnet: then another and another – 'Damn,' my father said, and braked, jerkily, alongside the road. 'Damn, damn, damn.'

He climbed out into the shadow of the hills. I stayed in the car, fingering my book, longing to return to the certainties it offered. But my father having swung open the bonnet and propped it up, letting out a still more furious rush of steam and the smell of hot oil, burned metal, had come back to the car, leaned over me, turned the handle and wound down the window. Then he walked round to my side, and putting his hand on the lip of the window, tapping it from time to time, began talking as if a cork had come out of some mental bottle and he had to say what he needed, then and there, while the engine was cooling down.

Had he leaned into the car, looked me in the face, I think I would have covered my ears. But having to strain to hear what he was saying, to the mountains it appeared rather than to me, forced me to listen, in some strange way. I don't know how much, exactly, I took in. I don't even know how much he told me that time of my mother's return from Paris and their hasty marriage: our conversation has been subsumed into one or two other conversations, when I was somewhat older. It could not have helped that I was still so innocent I barely understood that you did not have to be married to have babies. I do remember, acutely, the relentless rat-a-tat of his voice, the distressing baldness of what he said: and also the shock of it - my terror and yes, my rage. I remember weeping and asking: angrily. 'Then who is my father?' And when I received no answer from him, then or ever, crying out, 'I don't want another father. You are my real one.' For I loved my father – *this* father: I knew I loved him, most of the time. It might occur to me later that having two fathers - '*oh Mein Papas*' had its advantages, but for now all I wanted was him, singly: 'oh *Mein Papa*,' I chanted to myself as I watched him take out his bottle of water, fill the radiator, close the bonnet and come back to the car. 'Oh Mein Papa.' He started the car. We drove on. Not another word was said then or for quite a while; years even.

I tried to go back to my book. I don't think that I succeeded.

I still have a photograph taken on that trip- it must have been two or three days later and we must have persuaded another, rare, tourist to snap the pair of us on my father's little Kodak camera.

Though the photo is blurred and in black and white I can still remember the colour behind us and beneath our feet. After climbing yet another pass we were standing on the Rhone glacier itself, he with his arm parked rather awkwardly round my shoulders, both of us wearing National Health spectacles, mine pink and supposed to correct my tendency to squint, his round black wire ones. I wore the coat and skirt made of the tweed he'd bought for me on last year's trip to Ireland and had made up by a tailor there; the skirt was a kilt, the jacket slightly sporty, like a hacking jacket. My plaits fell straight, either side of my ears. Above Clarks' sandals, my socks reached to my knees, folded over invisible elastic garters. My father had forsworn his holiday shorts for that chilly place: he wore long trousers and a sweater with leather patches on the elbows. We both grinned madly at the camera while behind us a deep crevasse reached away into shades of ice ever deeper, greener, ever darker blue, yet translucent at the same time. We had walked a little way into that crevasse. I remember the colour deepening as we went yet losing none of its icy luminance. The cold, too, had grown ever more intense. But now we stood safely outside in the open air, grinning away, half-masking the entrance that led into those frozen depths, while close in front of us, right under our feet, another kind of depth and distance fell away.

CHAPTER FIFTEEN

I seem to be in remission again at the moment: to my and everyone's surprise. Not that I can move from here, given my level of helplessness. I'd decided, too, a while back, that I did not want to die at home, surrounded by my own things: I've never clung to this surrounding or that, or to the objects in them. Given the endless shifts of my life I hadn't expected or wanted them to stay the same - did not trust them, you could say. How smugly they announced: look at me, I'm going to outlast you. The plain and indifferent walls of this room, the plain indifferent metal of bars and legs seemed, altogether, more trustworthy. And there was this too: fond as I was of my present husband, I did not rate his qualities as nurse and carer; had I been an animal in a pen it might have been different matter, Maybe I was wrong, maybe his rough and readiness was just what I needed to prevent my ever less lived or comfortable life from spiralling beyond its bearable limits. But the limits were bearable at the moment and they looked after me well here at the moment: they even entertained me sometimes. At least my friend, Nurse Peter, did.

'Seems I'm going to be around a bit longer,' I said to him once at this time. 'Tough titty.'

'I'll survive,' he said. 'I've known worse.'

'What a hard life you have.' I said. 'So how long do you think you're going to have put up with me, the way this thing is going?'

He looked at me, meanly, even while tenderly washing my withered remaining breast. 'Not so long, I suspect. Don't get your hopes up, darling.'

'I think you're supposed to be jollying me along, not depressing me,' I said.

'Do you want me to tell you lies? I do a good uplifting lie, me, if that's what you want.'

'No. I don't want lies,' I said. And then, with a sudden rush of bleakness: 'Mostly I don't.'

'That's my girl,' he said. 'That's why I love you, darling.'

'Will you miss me then?' I said.

'There'll be others,' he said. 'Maybe: or maybe not. I don't find many I can enjoy being rude to. But you know how it is: people come and go.'

'Go, mostly,' I said.

'Yes, go. Of course.'

He patted my cheek more sweetly than ever. 'It's a hard life,' he said. 'But I hope you had a good one, mostly. Better than this bit, anyway.'

'Mostly,' I said.

'Well I'd better be getting on. It's the end of my shift and I've got a date.'

'With your fiancée?' I asked.

'Who else? Do you think I have a whole harem? I should be so lucky.' He picked up his basin and cloths and soap, made a note on my chart, adjusted my drip, filled my water jug, patted, thoughtfully, a bunch of grapes in the bowl alongside it and tip-tupped quietly out of the room.

'Try and sleep for a bit, dear,' he said, before the door clumped to behind him. 'Try to sleep.'

He could be a puzzle sometimes, Peter, and equally, on bad days, an irritation. 'Why are you such a cliché,' I'd asked him once when he was being especially chirpy.

'And just what do you mean by that exactly, dear?' he asked, giving me a look that could have been either amused or furious.

'All your camping about,' I said.

'And what about *your* cliché? Foul-mouthed old woman, boasting of her sexy past? You think I haven't seen it all before?' he said. 'You get every cliché in the book doing this job.'

I was annoyed in my turn. But I wasn't going to show it. I could have reported him, I suppose, to his superiors, for being rude. But what was the point?

'What clichés do you like best?" I asked, coldly. I was overwhelmed suddenly with memories of what he'd called 'my sexy past. Did I boast? Maybe. Yet conquest had never been the point of it exactly. Comfort seeking was more like it and not necessarily sexual comfort. Not that I was going to tell Peter. We weren't that close, after all, hardly close at all, both of us performing most of the time, putting on our acts. In this final place how else were to make our -my - reality bearable?

'Wouldn't you like to know,' he said. 'Wouldn't you like to know?' And then - it seemed a non-sequiter but maybe it wasn't – he said. 'I've told my fiancée all about you. She said she'd like to meet you sometime.'

'Bring her on,' I said. 'But don't leave it too long, unless she merely wants to inspect the corpse.'

'I'll tell her,' he said, his deadpan as efficient as mine.

'Damn you,' I said. And he went out smiling a small smile directed more or at himself – or his fiancée perhaps - than at me.

I did sleep for a while. When I woke up it was dark and the Husband was sitting in the low green chair to my right, doing the Sudoku in his Guardian, the light of the one, lit lamp falling directly on his page. I turned my head and watched his shadowed profile for several minutes before he realised I was awake.

Younger than me he might have been, but he was beginning to show his age. His beard had ever more threads of white in it; his hair, too, more grizzled, his likeness to a badger increased by the day. I hadn't seen him as a badger before. But so he was: almost an old man already. Yes.

His pen moved so quickly as he frowned over the puzzle – the hardest version of it of course. He was solving it much more quickly than I was solving my puzzle. My puzzle, now, being him, this room, this low light, this life – nasty brutish and short as it was. Good old Thomas Hobbes, I thought. Good old Thomas Hobbes. But then why did this body, this near-dying body of mine, and this not-so-near dying body of his and his grief or not grief at my dying and my grief or not grief at the same thing, why did they bring this sudden over-powering sense of terror and loss, so intense that not even a Peter could have laughed, jollied, teased me out of it? Cynicism wasn't needed here. But I didn't know what was.

The Husband looked up at last. 'Alright?' he asked, seeing at last that I was awake.

'Possibly.' I said. 'What gives with you?' I asked.

'The usual. The ex banging on at me over something or other, Mr C banging on the door three times, looking worse than ever, stinking like a ferret and complaining about a dripping tap. And then claiming he couldn't get his stove to work. And then I had social services calling me, saying he wouldn't let them in. And what was I going to do about it? They don't want to have to stretcher him out again. I think next time it happens they won't let him come back there. They'll put him in a care home.'

'About time,' I said. 'But what a fate: poor old boy.'

But I wasn't that much interested in Mr C. I was never going to have to deal with such problems any more and after all, they like everything else, like me, were ephemeral. I am not one of those people like the ones you read of in obituaries who continue to do good works till they draw their last breath. I merely have the sense that it's pointless, that in the end everyone travels into the dark, just the same.

Some of them go into the dark, though, at the beginning; and maybe that's what the good workers are on about. Such things make me feel the wearier though and the wearier still when I think of Mr C whose war began and never did come to any end that anyone could possibly want for him.

Mr C was/is our tenant: a statutory tenant living in the bottom of our house, about whom the more unscrupulous estate agents were for ever sending us letters, claiming they could get him out by one foul means or another; not that they ever called them foul; in this as everything else estate agents do good euphemism. We were too outraged even to consider it. Nuisance as Mr C was, banging on our doors at all hours about this, that and the other (his knocking was particularly thunderous not to say doom-laden: it made us jump every single time) he did not deserve this final betrayal. His life had given him more than enough of them and the only thing it had left him with was his home.

We knew some or even most of his story; partly from our predecessors in the house, nice people who'd begged us to let him stay, partly from Mr C himself, partly from his older sister, a retired bank-manager's wife who visited him every now and then from somewhere in Surrey and always came up afterwards to thank us for being nice to him and for not trying to get him out. Our predecessors had warned us against her, said she was an ogre, but we just found her distressed and grateful.

Mr C was, after all, her little brother. And now she had to see him turned into this.

Mr C had been 19 when the war broke out in 1939, had been called up immediately and having endured his basic training been sent to France, from which he escaped shortly after via the horrors of Dunquerque. I say escaped: but it was only his body escaped. He'd suffered very badly from what was then called shellshock and spent years in a mental hospital somewhere, crazy as a loon, until, some time after the war, some bright spark of a doctor – a psychiatrist - came up with the bright, fashionable idea – but haven't all – or most - psychiatrists then and now been full of bright fashionable ideas that will banish unhappiness for ever? – that he could solve Mr C's problems by excising a large chunk of his brain. Much calmer as a result of this treatment he was discharged from hospital and sent home for his ageing mother to tend; in due course, he was even able to tend his ageing mother, something he did very well, within his limits, according to his sister, the bank-manager's wife.

But that didn't mean he was normal: far from it. Trapped in a time warp of ideas, of his past life, contained between rigid tramlines of doing and being, he was un-manned entirely by the smallest shift in his routines.

We knew many of these routines almost as well as he did; what days and times he set out shopping pulling a wicker basket on wheels; what day he did his washing and then hung out his sad clothes and ever more ragged cloths in the little patch of land alongside the house, that he called his garden. We knew – how could we *not* know given the crack of doom delivered by door knocker that proceeded it – what time each week he paid his rent – along with a request each time to lower it, even though we knew, he must have known, that the social services paid it, that less rent could not make slightest difference to him. Some other routines we didn't know so well -we'd see him set out at certain times each week, but never knew the reason. Till one year, at Christmas, he told us about one of them.

I don't know whether we did him a favour by asking him up for a drink. It was a lot to do with my guilty conscience – a rare enough thing in me, a guilty conscience, but for some reason this man roused it in me more than most. I could not stand him; the sight, let alone the smell of him gave me the heebie-jeebies, even though I knew it was none of his fault. My husband was much kinder and more skilful: he said Mr C reminded of his grandfather, an army sergeant whom he very dimly remembered, and who had been badly gassed in the first war and turned into a bad-tempered old sod, never doing another day's work, and hated by his whole family till the day he died. 'Happy memories then', I said, and 'Cheers,' and left all negotiations to him.

But that didn't relieve my guilt. It led to the suggestion that we invite Mr C up for a Christmas drink, settling him down in the sitting-room on the ground floor of the house: it had been part of Mr C and his mother's flat before the other statutory tenants had been moved on by the developer and obstinate Mr C re-located to the basement, ten years or so before our time.

Mr C sat gingerly on the edge of the sofa and sipped at a half-pint tankard of beer. He pointed at the corner of the room, by the window.

'My mother died there,' he said.

I had an unsettling image of the bed – maybe the same thankless iron bed on which Mr C now slept downstairs, folding up the bedclothes each day as precisely as if he was still a young soldier in barracks.

'Another beer?' the Husband asked hastily now, though Mr C's tankard was still almost half-full.

'No, thank you. I only take a half-pint.'

'Well you don't have to stick to that here,' my husband said.

Mr C went on. 'I take a half-pint every Thursday lunchtime. At twelve o'clock. I get on the bus and go down to Putney Bridge to the Duke's Head on the other side of the bridge. We were in camp on the Fulham side, my mates and me. But we walked across the river to the Duke's Head for our pint, my mates and me, walked across the bridge. But I never had more than half a pint, even in those days. I never had a strong head.'

It was the longest, most coherent speech we ever heard him give. Maybe it even surprised him. He swallowed the rest of his beer at a gulp and said: 'it's my suppertime. It's waiting.' And he left.

Nasty brutish – if not so short – Mr C was getting on for ninety now - did not begin to cover it. No, it did not.

'What else is new?' I asked the Husband, at last.

He shrugged. 'Your daughter rang from Oz to ask how you were. I told her you were well enough to talk, so she'll ring you here.'

I groaned. 'That's all I need.'

'What a bitch you can be sometimes,' he said fondly. 'Do you feel well enough for a drink?'

Meaning could he have one. Both of us knew that alcohol – the pleasure of alcohol – was yet another thing I had lost.

After he'd gone – and too late for me – as efficient as my younger daughter was in most respects she never was good at getting her timings right and time differences for some reason were always beyond her; her mild dyslexia might have been one reason for that– my Australian daughter rang. We had our usual stilted conversation. This distressed me for once – maybe it was the time of night – and I had the impression she picked up the distress and became distressed in her turn. Her efficient tone slipped a bit: she always *had* used efficiency, my younger daughter, to cover her fury with me – as so I supposed it was. At the same time, she'd been more willing than the older one to express what she felt; she'd slammed doors, shouted at me, dropped out of school for a while, taken drugs and so forth – her father considered this all my fault; it probably was; likewise her two children with the Durham miner's son without benefit of marriage, though in fact this had upset his chapel-going parents more than it had upset either him or me: we were just grateful to see her settled. Her transformation into a successful – and married - Australian businesswoman and housewife, surprised us both. Maybe it was only at such a distance she could have put herself together. And maybe she had lost something in the process – this possibility had not occurred to me till I heard her voice just now. It reminded me what I'd almost forgotten that despite the storms and the fury I had always been closer to her than to elder daughter. That she, of my three children, was the one I'd understood best.

'I wish I wasn't so far away, mum,' I heard her say now. And to my equal astonishment heard myself answer meekly, thinking of my surrogate daughter, Jen, wishing it was as easy between my real daughters and me; 'And so do I wish you weren't.'

That was too much probably, for both of us. Middle child reverted to her usual briskness. 'I really can't come yet you know.

It's the Easter show. The kids would kill me. And there's a lot going on at work.'

CHAPTER SIXTEEN

My nanny left when I was ten or so, to be replaced by the bad-tempered ex-governess. For a while the meals à deux with my father ceased.

But I did not forget what he had told me during them and during our holidays about his younger life 'before the war', 'gadding about on the continent', and, going further back, about his mother, my un-grandmother who so disapproved of me, but whom he said had been a good old soul really, helpful to everyone. About the two older half-brothers whom she mourned and whom he still did, especially the younger one who had been like a father to him, his real father a grandfatherly figure mostly.

Yet in all this, he never said a single word about my mother's past, though he had known her for most of her childhood, not to mention married her.

No one would ever tell me about my mother. The only thing that reconciled me to the arrival of the bad-tempered ex-governess was that she had been my mother's governess for at least six years of her childhood and judging by the friendly nickname my mother had given her – Ollybird – her real name was Miss Oliver-Brown – they'd had been fond of each other. In which case, I thought, she must have been much nicer to my mother than she ever was to me: every time I begged the ex-governess for stories about my mother she, too, refused me, buttoning up her button mouth and looking more disapproving than ever.

In retrospect I feel sorry for her. She was one of those spinsters whom my father so desperately wanted me not to become. There were a lot of them around in my young day: women very far from being the independent 'single women' we see them as now. Even the term 'single women' suggests an element of choice. Whereas 'spinsters' were women who had none: who purely and simply had not found a husband: not necessarily because they weren't desirable or wife material, or averse to men (there were some lesbians around, no doubt, not that I knew anything about such things then: my innocence seems breathtaking). Yet in the eyes of the world they were unwanted women. Full stop.

Many of these women had lost fiancés in one or other of the two wars. Those who'd lost – or not found them – due to the second war were not quite so badly off. My mother's friends had discovered the pleasures of freedom, of a sex life untrammelled by wedding rings, and the kinds of work not previously available to women: some of them weren't in a hurry to forego all this once the war was over, even when the men returned and took back their jobs.

The bereaved fiancées of the First World War were different; fewer of their men returned. All children of my generation were educated by some of them – mostly the poorer kind, who, forced to support themselves, had gone into one of the very few options open: teaching.

This seems reasonable to me, looking back, and why my father and his like should regard these women with such horror – at least regarded with horror the idea their daughters should suffer similar fates – I do not know. I understand still less why the second dirtiest word in relation to our future was the word 'teacher'. One reason he resisted my going to university was that I might end up as one – what was there for educated women to do even then *except* teach? – No jobs on offer in Shell, or Leverhulme or any investment bank for us. 'Once a teacher always a teacher,' my father said.

'Why do you let them teach *me* then if you think they're so frightful?' I asked him once, during one of meals together, times when he let me get away with comments he might otherwise have designated as 'cheek.' But he looked away, attended to his pipe and couldn't give me an answer.

Ollybird didn't teach me schoolwork, even though she had taught my mother. But she was certainly a spinster and not an amiable one, unlike the splendid ones – my father called them 'splendid' – who rode around on upright bicycles with baskets front and back and more or less ran our village. They of course had money of their own, did not need to work the way Ollybird always had to, her fiancé killed alongside theirs. I can feel sorry for her now – a bit – but I certainly did not feel sorry for her then. Whatever she'd been like in my mother's childhood, by the time she reached me her life had soured her. I can imagine, now, that she might once have been a pretty girl. But by that time the sweetness of her blue eyes, round face, rosy cheeks, was belied by a button mouth and little gold-rimmed spectacles that never dared to glint the way gold should. I was always being sent to bed early – to my indignation my father went along with this – given lines to write, having my sweets confiscated, told that I was rude and should apologise – but then I *was* rude to her - very. She reminded me of a particularly uncomfortable cushion, squashy on the outside, but stuffed with what felt like bricks.

'I don't think Ollybird likes me much,' I said to my father, who just answered, fondly, 'Don't be such a juggins, she loved your mother and your mother loved her, why shouldn't she like you?' And when I tried to explain I couldn't. And when finally I wailed 'I hate her,' he said sharply –this was rare for him – 'Behave yourself, Jo,' and that was that.

'I don't think Ollybird likes me,' was something I also said, plaintively, to Patty, my mother's former best friend.

She was more sympathetic: she said 'Hmm' and I think did try to intercede with my father. But he still would not want to hear one word against Ollybird, from either Patty or me: he told me off again, quite severely –' your mother loved Ollybird' - 'well I don't,' I thought. Things growing worse and worse, I cried at night and banged my head against the pillow in frustration because what else could I do? *Your mother loved Ollybird.*' Was that why he would not listen, why he wanted the hateful woman to go on looking after me and living in his house, destroying his precious intimacy with me, just *because* my mother loved her?

Even Patty who did not seem to like her much either –she called my minder 'Woollybird' –grew tired of my moans. She urged tolerance; 'your mother was really fond of Woollybird you know,' she said. And then, more thoughtfully: 'times change. People change as they get older. Women like her have had hard lives.'

I had no intention of feeling sorry for my tormenter. 'I think she was always horrible,' I said. 'Maybe she was a witch bewitching mummy so she thought she was nice. But she doesn't need *me* to like her.'

Patty laughed. 'You're much too fond of fairytales, darling,' she said, 'though they certainly make a change from Thomas the Tank Engine.' She didn't often make it so clear that, given her houseful of boys, she saw me in a daughterly light.

By this time Ollybird had begun to talk to me about my mother a little. But not to tell me anything I wanted to hear. 'You're as lazy as your mother,' she said once. And, another time, 'don't you dare to cheek me; I had enough of that from your mother.' Or, once, worse still – her comments grew ever more open as time went on - 'the way you behave I can see you growing up to be just like your mother.'

'And what would that be like?' I asked meekly. But she told me even more furiously not to be cheeky and pinned her mouth tight shut. This did not stop her saying more to other people. I heard her in the kitchen once, having elevenses with the daily woman, the *Music while you Work* theme going on in the background as Ollybird said - 'The flighty little thing. Leaving her own child. Who'd have believed it?'

Angry as I might have been about my mother's desertion, I was not having anyone else say such things. I burst into the kitchen yelling 'How dare you? How dare you talk about my mother like that?'

Ollybird's face went red, I noticed with satisfaction. She locked her button mouth, tightly.

The kitchen clock ticked. The daily-woman rattled her spoon against her saucer and then stirred her tea yet again. The radio segued straight from the signature tune of Music While you Work into 'Oh What a beautiful morning.' The daily woman too was rather red in the face I noticed, though whether from embarrassment or amusement how could I tell. But I do remember her starting to sing along to the music. After a minute I joined in. 'Oh what a beautiful morning' we carolled while Ollybird, looking flummoxed for once, stared from one to the other and after a moment got to her feet, grabbed me by the arm and marched me out of the kitchen and up two flights of stairs, all the way to my room.

I told Patty about this, next time I saw her. 'Hmm,' she said in a way that made me dare embroider the situation a little, if not much. I did not need to: Ollybird had done for herself, was *hoist on her own petard* not that I then knew this quote from Hamlet. All I'd had to say to my father, almost weeping – I suspected that tears would help my case – was 'She's always saying nasty things about mummy.'

'What things?' he asked sternly. I told him. Patty and later, when questioned, the daily - who didn't like Ollybird much either, the way she was ordered about – both backed me up. Within two days Ollybird's bag was packed. She had gone.

'Your dad is such a romantic fool,' Patty said to me once years later. This was something I knew by then too: it was the Ollybird incident, probably, first began to bring home to me just how much my father still loved my mother: how he was even less willing than me to hear a word against her, even if the words came from her abandoned child; me. And even if it didn't stop him thwarting her, as he did, deceiving me so bitterly in the process.

My father did not replace Ollybird. I was soon to go to boarding school in any case and Patty said I could stay in her house till then, when necessary. I think she liked this as a balance to her three sons. I also think the fact that I was my mother's child mattered to her. She was one of the only mentors offered me by my father who I really liked: as in really, really, *really* liked.

Given that she was not always as virtuous as she should have been – not that I knew that till later – it was surprising that my father trusted her so: but I know he did. He'd never objected to my going across the green to muck around in the stream at the bottom of their garden with her sons, thereafter checking on the owl, glaring at me from his cage. As well he might: owls didn't belong in cages I thought, even then, though this one had been injured and rescued by a local gamekeeper, one of Patty's husband's patients, who had given him to Patty to take care of while he recovered. She called the owl Oswald, of course. She also had a tame – relatively tame badger for a while from the same source: for a self-confessed townie, Patty was surprisingly fond of animals.

Sometimes my father went visiting the doctor's house with me. He seemed to love that family, almost as much as I did. As I grew up we passed many riotous evenings, sometimes just with Patty's family, sometimes with other families, playing games like Racing Demon on Patty's faux-Sheraton dining-table, protected by a baize cloth. And on more Sundays than I can count we went over for Sunday lunch. My father would drink several glasses of her wine and become far more jolly than usual, despite – maybe because of – Patty's constant teasing – 'what's the gossip Freddy, how many state secrets have you got for us today?' and 'are those your gardening trousers? - Isn't it about time you got them cleaned' –

pointing at a pair which looked perfectly sanitary to me if a little old and shabby. Even in wartime and after it when things grew ever more austere, there was very little that looked old let alone shabby in Patty's house.

She also, sometimes, amazingly, teased my father about his adoration for my mother – though in the kindest, gentlest of ways - for some peculiar reason he seemed to find this comforting. Certainly it was the only place apart from our house in which my mother's name was ever mentioned.

Patty was a tallish pink-cheeked woman, not thin but well-rounded, her weight going up and down all the time, according to whatever diet she was on. I swear she had two different wardrobes for her fat and her thin selves; the thin one was silkier, the fat more woollen and concealing, but both of them elegant: she was always elegant, even when she was what she called 'slopping about' in trousers – 'slacks' she called them – and a loose sweater. She smoked black Russian cigarettes – goodness knows where she got them from – in a long holder and when she wasn't teasing my father she was teasing her husband, a silent man, who sat at the other end of the table and smiled either sweetly or irritably, according to whether she was being kind to him or not. She was also very rich; or her father was. 'A spoiled not so little rich girl.' she called herself 'and thank god for that. For being rich I mean', she added. 'How boring life would be if I wasn't. What couldn't I get up to?' When most other women of the time were buried in domesticity she always seemed to have a bevy of old retainers cooking, cleaning doing her laundry, standing in queues for fish or meat on her behalf. One of them, Violet, the cook, Patty would lend to my father sometimes on the housekeeper's day off. An evil-tempered and rather deaf old woman, she always wore a light blue overall and looked, I thought, not unlike the equally ill-tempered corgi, Jezebel, on whom mysteriously – to me – Patty doted. And though she'd cook exactly the same sort of meal in our house as she'd cook over at Patty's it never tasted quite the same. Patty seemed to season everything about her and make them taste better. She certainly made things taste better to me, a lot of the time.

Not that she always so benign. Over the years I learned to feel sorry for her placid – mostly placid – husband whom she claimed to betray all over the place. 'Poor old Reggie wasn't much interested in getting it up,' she said to me years later, after she'd helped me out in ways which left her talking to me much more openly than before. 'God knows how I ever managed to conceive the boys. Can you blame me for taking other lovers?' She even had a flat in London: for such goings on, I presumed. She offered it to me as a base once, but I declined: I didn't think my father would have approved, fond of her as he was. And anyway I would have found it complicated. What was I supposed to do when she had one of her lovers in? She was well into her forties by then, but the lovers still kept coming – so she said, though these days I wonder how much of this amorous hype was pure fiction. Then I was surprised - in a pleasurable way – that life could go on so long.

She also had a ferocious temper. She used to spank her boys with a hairbrush when they misbehaved. 'Did it hurt?' I'd ask Thomas, in curiosity and almost envy – 'what does it feel like to be spanked? – I used to lie in bed imagining it almost pleasurably, despite the grimaces with which he answered me, the rueful way in which he tapped his bottom. 'Someone's got to do it she'd say to my father. 'They're boys aren't they and Reggie never would.'

(It could be that the curiosity these spanking episodes engendered lay behind my one experiment in S and M with a squash-player who practised the odd stroke on my backside with one of his rackets. 'Oh,' I heard myself saying. And. 'Wow' and 'Ooh' and 'Ouch.' And 'That's enough.' Afterwards he stroked my bum tenderly and said, 'you're going to have some fine bruises. Would you like to return the compliment?'

I shook my head violently. I didn't like his way of putting it, nor the flushed look on his face, between greed and salaciousness and glee; nor was I attracted by the idea of him turning *his* bum up for my attentions. 'What am I doing here?' I wondered. And I got dressed and left as soon as I could, ignoring all the frantic phone calls of the next few days – thank god for there were no mobiles then, no texts. Nor was I drawn into such activities again even when the suggestion came from nicer men. Sex seemed complicated enough without that.)

Goodness knows why my father saw Patty as an appropriate mentor for his daughter; he must have had at least some inkling of how she was; or maybe he didn't. Maybe he thought she was just a flirt – he enjoyed flirting with her, I noticed, when I was old enough to notice such things. The advice I got from her was the opposite of all those urgings to chastity imposed on me by everybody else. When I was sixteen she asked if I was still a virgin and when I confessed, confusedly, that I was, said 'Well don't leave it too long, darling, I lost my virginity when I was fifteen and I've never missed it for one moment.'

(On the other hand it was Patty, sadly, who gave me the worst advice I got from any mentor; that I should never on any account chase men, because men didn't like it. Though she backed this up with some very funny stories about one or two single women in our village who, according to her, had so chased, this seemed to me, even then, advice likely to inhibit not to say blight the social efforts of many girls – not that I would let it inhibit me; I was too close to my father to be self-conscious round males of any age. But I felt sorry for those who were.)

Maybe my father trusted Patty because she had loved my mother. And because I knew that too, I sometimes asked Patty about her. But even she would never say much, though she did sometimes come out, seemingly inadvertently, with such things as 'how your mother would have laughed,' or 'your mother would really have approved of that' – and once, very abruptly. 'I do miss your mother sometimes. But no more than you, I daresay.' Adding, ' sorry darling. I shouldn't have said that, should I?' 'Yes you should,' I said, more grateful for this than I understood, let alone knew how to say.

I loved her probably more than I loved anyone except my father. This made it still harder in the end.

I wasn't feeling so good yesterday evening. Jen put her head round the door, late, but I waved her away, grateful to think she wouldn't feel rejected the way my real daughters might have done, things so much more complicated around them.

The night that followed was particularly restless, my morphine pump more in heavy use. Not that it seems to help much: not enough anyway. Peter will have to give me another enema: little as I can eat my gut is uncomfortable and tight. When I did manage to fall asleep, I dreamed about Berlin, about my visit there in early 1990, a few months after the wall came down, its trashed remains plastered with posters and graffiti still visible everywhere between what had been the two Berlins and was still two Berlins in every sense that counted; one full of flashing neon, gaudy commercials, ritzy glass buildings, the other dour, lightless, concrete, scarcely a billboard in sight.

And then there were the stolid little Trabi cars running around - or rather lumbering -everywhere, all the more clumsy and stolid-looking compared to the Fiats, the Mercedes and Audis that had joined them. Remembering the Trabis, my father suddenly came to mind; stolid, out of date, naïve in various respects, still soldiering on with his out-of-date views, his out-of-date financially disastrous decency, doing his job as Englishman and father, as retired civil servant and aficionado of golf and cricket. My lovely dinosaur father with his knightly ideas about women, still fighting his dragons – not capitalist ones in his case, at least not capitalism as he knew it then, which he believed in– we're not talking twenty-first century global capitalism here. My father as Trabi would do very well, I thought. Angry as I had been with him for the last few years, my mourning for him still weighty enough but even more painful in consequence, I lay in bed with my morphine pump and my drip, my special pillows, trapped within plastic lines and machinery and within my own cancer-trashed body, loving him as totally and painfully and irritably as ever.

CHAPTER SEVENTEEN

I am still bad-tempered this morning, and not just because I am in pain. When I moan at Peter one time too many that he's being clumsy while washing me, he says: 'Sometimes I think your mammy did not spank you enough.'

'She never spanked me at all,' I say. 'She walked out when I was three.'

He's reached my midriff by now. But I feel him stop now, and when I look at him he is holding the washcloth close to him, so close that a large damp patch is spreading on his white nurse's jacket. His eyes are far away, gazing beyond me at the empty green wall.

'Penny for them,' I say. He jumps.

'Fancy,' he says, "Where was I?' He starts sponging me again, rather too hard this time.

'Careful,' I say, but less irritably than I before. 'You're getting at my lumps.' (I have little red lumps all over me these days, lumps about which I fee quite proprietorial in a rather perverse way as if I am the tumours now and they are me. Perhaps I'm just saying; Cancer *is* me. OK.' But that's not quite what I'm saying, exactly. Never mind. My head is so fuzzy these days it takes off into places where I can't follow it, nor do I want to.)

'Beg pardon,' he says and turns gentler; particularly gentle, humming what sounds almost like a cradle song – I cannot place it – as he does so. I wonder about his mother. But I do not ask. That Peter's past is dangerous territory is something I discovered one morning after yet another night spent walking my head round my father's village.

Peter had been washing my calves that time when I asked him if he, too, remembered the place in which he grew up.

'I don't care to think about it,' he said, dropping my right leg abruptly

I ignored the warning in his voice. Rage swelled up suddenly: rage not at him but at my fate.

'Why not?' I asked viciously. 'Did you have an abused childhood? Were you bullied? What? Give us the 'misery memoir, Peter. After all I know the upbeat ending – I've seen you here.' I

113

said more fondly. But Peter wasn't having any of it. He pursed his lips again.

'I had a perfectly happy childhood, thank you. But like I said, I don't care to talk about that,' he said. 'I think you heard me, madam. Is that all?'

'Yes,' I said.

We have no such problems this morning. But he has almost finished with me, is turning away from the bed when he fishes in his tunic, and holds something out to me.

'Did you see this?'

'What?' I am too weary even to turn my head.

'This.' He puts into my hand an envelope with my name on it in Jen's handwriting. 'Your friend Jen gave it to Staff last night. She said you didn't look too much like company. Staff forgot about it till now."

'Thank you,' I say.

I open it when he's gone to find a postcard; on one side Jen's familiar scribble, on the other publicity for a book to be published by my old company. At the top is the one thing has not changed: the firm's familiar name and logo. The greater part of my life had been spent working for that name; seeing it here, now, in my alien bed, drags me back into that other life, to a past that would look, I thought, to Jen's juniors and maybe to Jen herself more foreign than most: the publishing business that I started in. Compared to the publishing business now it appears as Trabi-like as my old dad.

When I started in publishing, Americans publishers visiting London offices were amazed, even enchanted by what they found; 'it's all so old world', they'd say. Not till the late sixties when I went to New York for the first time and saw that their offices looked like offices, reached via lifts like polished metal boxes lined with mirrors and made by firms such as Otis – a name that always made me think of the gloomy song about the woman who is sent to the electric chair for shooting her lover– '*Miss Otis regrets she is unable to lunch today.*'- did I begin to understand why.

I loved my un-office-like office, though. It was the place in which I felt most at home, far more than in the marital one. The work I did there – especially as it became more and more editorial – seemed to give me back to myself. The anxieties engendered by

114

the pressures of the work, in which I like everybody else always felt I was falling behind, by the antagonism of the dragon receptionist cum telephonist Gloria – definitely not chosen for her charm and beauty as American receptionists were - by the tantrums of my boss, notorious for making secretaries cry, were not the least existential, nor related to my uncertain identities: they did not keep me awake at night, let alone terrify me, the way my duties as wife and parent did.

As with most London publishers, our business had been long established in what used to be a private house, two Victorian houses run together in this case, with not one but two narrow and creaky stairs covered in pot-holed linoleum, winding up round corners so tight they made it impossible for two people to pass. The entrance office, Gloria's domain, was equally tacky and dark.

Though I never came to love the legendary Gloria, I enjoy her in retrospect and even then I enjoyed her legendry status among New York publishers and writers. She had brilliantly hennaed hair, wore flowered prints in summer on garments that looked more like cleaners' overalls than normal dresses, and, through the winter, home-made sweaters, garishly striped. In the few gaps between feeding plugs expertly in and out of the switchboard, fielding calls and passing them on, packing or unpacking books on the counter, greeting often startled visitors and seeing them either in or in some cases smartly out, admonishing passing staff and feeding her beloved, the office cat, she could be seen placidly knitting yet another sweater in ever more surprising colours.

Gloria was probably the least glamorous appendage of unglamorous premises: this did not stop her and all of it appearing glamorous enough to me, if only at first. Early on I had to stand back on the stairs for Graham Greene: another time I shrank before Philip Larkin. Once I even found myself sharing the lift with Leonard Woolf, a good friend of the senior editor: this can't have been long before he died.

Our office was alone of its kind in having a lift of any sort. It was no glitzy steel box; more like a goods lift, with double trellised doors, it creaked and groaned upwards very slowly and reluctantly and had been known to stick between floors. On the upper floors the corridors were narrow, made narrower by heaps of books on either side. One wall was lined with little cubbyhole offices:

through dirty glass, editors, copy-editors, secretaries, accountants could be seen bent over typewriters, piles of paper on their desks. Only the head of the firm had a proper, private office, panelled, low ceilinged, with a faded, worn but probably rather good turkey-carpet; it was as full of his pipe smoke as it was of manuscripts and books.

At first the place seemed infinite; it took me a long time to locate any office I was sent to find. And though I soon found my way about, I never quite lost the feeling that the lift could go on creaking up indefinitely, to floors long unvisited in which a wicked godmother might sit with a spinning wheel waiting for some sleeping beauty –one of the inefficient and upper-class young secretaries and publicity girls who floated in and out, prepared to take the miserly salary offered just for the chance of meeting Ian Fleming or Alan Sillitoe or Ted Hughes or whoever, while they filled the gap between school and marriage. Or alternatively where some ever more aged copy-editors would sit like Bartleby refusing to write and gradually mouldering away till they dissolved into a mouldy and evil-smelling dust of paper, wood, leather, like something out of Edgar Allen Poe.

I of course, started like one of those secretaries, not even a very good one: I, too, got shouted at by the cantankerous boss. On the other hand, the education given me by the love of my life during the weeks we were together - the sharpening of my thinking processes, the purpose and direction he'd insisted on in my reading - began now to take effect. The boss listened when I made the odd editorial suggestion. He started giving me jobs that involved copy-editing; in a little while he was handing me manuscripts to comment on. It probably helped that I was good-looking, even though he was not someone whose hands roved where they shouldn't. Reputed to have not only a wife but a long-term relationship with an aging female poet from another firm, he did not flirt except in the most kindly way with female staff - when he was not bellowing at them. Undeterred by the bellows, I enjoyed his eccentricity, enjoyed his not being in any recognisable way a businessman, let alone a corporate man, like some of his American counterparts.

I was not his only admirer. Gloria, 'her downstairs' as he always called her, revered, not to say hero-worshipped him, partly perhaps because, as a distantly descended cousin of the firm's original founder, he was the one director left who bore its name. When it became clear I was his favourite, that he might even be grooming me to take over his job in due course, she turned more hostile than ever, a hostility that reached its zenith during my first pregnancy.

'Here comes our office mountain,' she'd announce, glaring at my stomach in its discreet green maternity dress. She was not the least appeased by our boss sanctioning my pregnant presence; not that he approved of my infant either. 'What did you have to do that for, you silly bitch?' he'd enquired when I told him, first scratching his ear then knocking out his pipe in a distracted kind of way; it was still alight. 'You were getting on so well here I was all set to make you my official assistant.'

He of course like most people had assumed I would resign at once. When I told him that I intended to continue working, though I would have to go part-time for a while, and might need to work from home sometimes, he looked thoughtful. 'I'm not sure we can accommodate that,' he said. 'This is supposed to be a business.' (It was the first time I'd heard him acknowledge the firm was a business in any way whatever.) 'Well I suppose if we must: if you insist on going ahead with it. You're not liable to miscarry are you?' he asked hopefully. From anyone else that would have been outrageous, but the way he said it, like an elderly child enquiring after sweets, disarmed me. 'You *are* joking?' I asked, sternly. 'Partly joking,' he said. 'Well never mind. I suppose women must have children. I just wish they wouldn't have them here.'

'Men are responsible for the babies too,' I said.

'Ah but we leave them to our wives.'

'Why's that do you think?' I asked.

'What about your husband?'

'He knows I want to work.'

'Don't bring the brat into the office then. It isn't a crèche,' he said, again waving a hand and in doing so knocking to the floor the magnum opus of his most important non-fiction author which scattered all over the turkey-carpet and had both of us on our knees putting it back together, collating the pages with difficulty.

'This bloody book's even longer than the last one. And now I suppose I've got to read the damn thing,' he groaned when the manuscript was back on his desk: for a publisher, he seemed to find reading an awful chore. 'Well I suppose you could copy-edit this at home in due course. It will be a relief to have it out of my sight.'

I did find myself editing it at home a few months later, spread all over my kitchen table. But I did, too, need to bring the baby into the office once or twice in the early months, at moments of emergency, important meetings, for instance, that the boss insisted I attend. I even put up, mostly, with Gloria's loudly expressed disapproval at the sight of my Moses basket.

'Are you turning the place into a nursery now?' she asked the head of the firm, to my face. 'It's a bear garden as it is–' she cast a hand round at the toppling heaps of boxes, the piles of paper, the milling employees, even the cat, 'It only needs a bawling baby and we'll all be in the bin. Is that what you want, to put me in the bin? Who's going to run the place then, may I ask?'

He laughed, as he always did – 'Come off it, Gloria, you're indestructible you can handle anything. And the brat's not going to be left to you to mind anyway.'

'I should think not.' She sniffed and turned to the switchboard, which was beginning to buzz, shoving in a plug so hard it looked likely to break. 'It's bad enough having the cat under my feet all day.' Her voice changed to the gravelly sweetness with which she always answered the telephone. 'Good *morning*: X and X publishers. Can I help you?' The head of the firm and I looked at each other and headed for the lift.

It was fortunate my baby was so placid. She slept soundly through most meetings, her basket stashed in a discreet corner. When she needed feeding I removed her to the ladies, while my boss conducted business that did not need my presence. And though he too grumbled loudly about the whole thing, 'Bloody babies don't belong in offices, what are you thinking of?' he enjoyed, I think, the look of astonishment on the faces of visiting editors, executives, lawyers, even authors: all of it added to his reputation as a maverick – a successful one at that. (Throughout the years he was running it the firm did very well, for all his seeming lack of interest in the business side of things.)

But if he was a pioneer, in a way, in the matter of the baby – or babies- all three of my children appeared at the office at least once in their early months -then so, oddly enough, was I.

I have to admit that though I attended the odd demonstration I never had time to be a serious feminist: I was too busy rearing my family, doing my job, trying to hold together my ever more fractious and difficult marriage. But in the matter of bringing my babies to the office you could say I did, inadvertently, set something of a precedent, as my boss frequently pointed out.

I was grateful to him for this. In my way I loved him, the work I did for him ever more my solace and safety. Though he never enquired about my family life, he was the only person in years I told – some time later when we'd grown ever closer and I'd drunk too much sherry in his office before heading to the opera with my husband - about my uncertain parentage.

'I suppose being French explains the way you look,' he said as if such a confession was all the same to him. 'And very nice it is too. Your husband's a lucky man.' He followed that statement with a sharp glance and re-filled my sherry glass. 'I'm not sure he always realises he is,' I said.

That was the very night I got pregnant again with my youngest child; the sherry, probably, was as much to blame as the opera – Cosi Fan Tutte, one of my husband's favourite if not mine (I prefer my opera, unlike my life, to be far from rococo, more raw and red) yet even that released me from my usual tight control, in this case of contraception. It could be my husband exploited it on purpose: maybe he was hoping another baby would restore our marriage to the way it had seemed to be after the births of our older children. But if he'd had any such hope, consciously or unconsciously it was to no avail. Even before the birth, our marriage had reverted to slipping away from him, from me, from us.

The new pregnancy did not in the short term help my relationship with my boss either.

'How many more brats are you going to drop?' he enquired. 'Isn't it time you got yourself sterilised. Three children are more than enough.'

'You are unspeakable,' I said. 'I'm thinking of resigning.'

'Aren't I?' he said cheerfully. And then about as ardently as he was capable of said 'Please don't.'

He called his secretary in even before I left the room. As I closed the door I heard him shouting at her, not long after his 'Get out' echoed right down the corridor and she rushed out sobbing as his secretaries often did. She won't last long, I thought. (She did not.) For a moment, as often, I felt sorry for his wife – maybe if she knew about the poet mistress she was grateful that it kept him out of her way for much of the time. Or maybe they suited each other in some weird way. I didn't know: I had very little idea of how marriage worked in those days. All I knew of this wife came from seeing her once a year at the office Christmas party – did he keep her in a box meantime I wondered, and bring her out and dust her down for this occasion? A rather wispy but elegant woman who looked as if she was miles away, peering vaguely around the room, she in fact remembered all our names and faces and knew what cliché to offer each of us when she did the rounds of her husband's staff. I saw Gloria, dressed in something with ribbons that made her look like an ungainly Christmas parcel, almost curtseying when it came to her turn, an abasement not seen at any other time, as if the boss's wife was actually the queen: but then she was, I think, something vaguely aristocratic. Everyone came to those jolly, extremely bibulous parties, from the man who worked in the packing room to our almost Nobel Prize authors. Even the poetess mistress came, I was told, but I did not know her, even by sight, and if she was there, she kept her distance. It all seemed very odd to me.

CHAPTER EIGHTEEN

Only some memories arrive in my head complete. Others come and go in vivid flashes. It's to do with the morphine, I daresay. The image I woke to this morning was another complete one; of the basement kitchen in my father's house with its Rayburn stove – aged even then - with its scrubbed wooden table taking up a large part of the floor space, with its chipped porcelain sink and wooden draining boards: this was a kitchen more like those in Upstairs Downstairs than a kitchen of today. I am sitting at the table cradling a mug of cocoa – my old Peter Rabbit mug, too babyish for me now, but I still like it - from which I'm sipping very slowly; cocoa is a treat, much nicer than Ovaltine, supposed to be better for me. Opposite Patty and our new daily woman, cradling cups of tea, sit with their heads together. The cups are the blue and gold Crown Derby ones inherited from my grandmother – or un-grandmother – she is dead by this time – both of them cracked, the brown-stained cracks held together with little steel claws. Now they would be regarded as unsanitary, but then their continued use was a virtuous economy that never did anyone any harm, so far as I know. My father drank his breakfast tea out of an identical, equally cracked but much bigger cup every morning of his life until my stepmother came along, grimaced and threw all the cups away, Crown Derby or not. Patty and the daily are giggling like children, occasionally glancing at me. This is something I am not supposed to hear or at least understand.

Patty often sat at our kitchen table. In the days of this particular daily woman – another of my female mentors, if an unofficial one - she sits there particularly often. They appear to be great friends. Patty calls her the Merry Widow, and from all the talk I can see just how merry she is. She's a woman with blond hair worn-out by many perms and dyed too probably, though I wouldn't have recognised that then, a mouth full of crooked teeth, patched with gold that she displays whenever she laughs - which is often - and a big wart on one cheek. None of these seeming drawbacks do anything to make her less attractive, judging by the fact - a fact provided by her - that she has three boyfriends at the very least, whom she designates as 'my friend,' 'my boyfriend' and 'my gentleman friend.' She is, definitely, a very merry widow. Probably she'd been a merry wife too. She said once in my hearing that 'Mr Watts' – she always called her dead husband 'Mr Watts' had told her she laughed too much.

'Can you laugh too much?' I asked puzzled.

She winked at me and laughed some more. 'For sure you can laugh too much,' she said, shaking her head and putting a finger to her lips. 'For sure you can laugh too much, duck. You just take care when it comes to your turn.' Mysterious advice that I took to heart and remembered years later when inclined to laugh too much at the father of my children: a mistake. Mrs W had been right, I thought.

I think it was the apparently rather risqué conversations between Mrs W and Patty that gave me my first inklings that Patty's life might not have been as proper as it ought to be – or so she wanted you to think. Not that she'd have let anything out, directly. She was the doctor's wife after all and had a position to keep up, laugh at it as she did. And Mrs Watts was, surely, a gossip, why else did she and Patty have their heads so close together so often and why were their conversations interpolated with such raucous laughter, during which every one of Mrs Watt's gold teeth winked as merrily as she did, while Patty's teeth – very white for that time compared to those of most of her contemporaries, all of them exposed to British dentistry – were equally in evidence and while I laughed in collusion on the other side of the table, even when I had no clue as to what they were laughing about.

I'm grateful for this memory, still. I smile to myself, lying in my hospital bed.

And of course I wasn't quite as innocent as they thought: not that I thought of my knowing as lack of innocence. What happened to me when I was young, in the potting shed, was simply part of what I was. The fact I had no context into which to fit this bizarre experience left me confused rather than knowing: feeling more than ever that grown-ups were an odd bunch.

Perhaps one flash of memory triggers another, or at least pulls it up the way a fisherman pulls up one fish from the sea, which pulls up another, which pulls up another from way down in the deep.

On my next waking I get this: FLASH. Mr Tremlett. Gardener. Garden Man. A lock of reddish hair, falling across a bald skull. An armchair. A smell of damp earth and of creosote.

Throughout my childhood, my father did as much of the gardening as he could. It wasn't just what he called 'a hobby ' – something I as far as I know I've never had, or wouldn't have called 'a hobby' for sure. At that time, during wartime and post-wartime rationing, growing vegetables and keeping chickens made the difference between half-starving – if in a healthy way – and eating well. Every moment my father could spare he spent outside, digging, weeding, planting: I think he even enjoyed it.

I enjoyed watching him. My father knew how to use his body, unlike my future husband, unlike many of his class and time, not that I knew that then: he moved his arms and legs as easily and as rhythmically as any of the other men digging in other gardens along the row. He'd be brown by the end of every summer. His old khaki shorts hung off his skinny backside. In the middle of his bare back hung a small knot of extraneous skin that he never bothered to have removed; sometimes I'd creep up behind him unseen and pull it –'Ouch,' he'd cry, jumping round, 'Ruddy hell, you little chump. Don't do that. It hurts.' But then he'd bend and kiss me, his sweaty face against mine and I would stroke his equally sweaty, and reddened bald patch, and notice the damp rivulets on his sides and belly and love the smell of it. The only time my father ever smacked me – or tried to – he missed – was the time I followed behind while he was planting cabbages and in a fiendish mixture of glee, terror and curiosity pulled up each plant in turn; when he reached the end of the row, he turned round to see all the infant cabbages he'd anchored in the soil lying neatly on top of it, whiskery roots in the air.

I was about four then, probably. The gardener would already have been working for him once a week, to do what my father had no time for. He arrived when I was three, not long after my mother left, when everybody around was urging different kinds of help on my bereft father, including this gardener.

A little ferrety man, long-nosed, with a half bald head, reddish hair – what was left of it – and surprisingly white but freckled skin for someone who worked outside his whole life, he wasn't an old man – though old enough to me - but he might have been too old to have been called up. A limp from an old injury, one leg shorter than the   other, might equally have explained his exemption.

He took to me at once. He'd bring me sweets and little toys he'd whittled out of wood. He called me 'Sweetheart,' and I called him 'Garden Man', following him around the garden while he was working, listening to stories he'd tell me about the plants: he always had stories about the different kinds of flowers and vegetables.   Though I cannot remember any of them now, I do remember him saying; 'say Good Morning, Mr Robin,' when a robin redbreast turned up as our resident one often did, in the hope of worms being dug up. The gardener – his real name was Mr Tremlett – said the robin came because he liked me so much. 'Look at the way, he cocks 'is little 'ead, 'e's saying 'ullo, sweet'eart that's what 'e is.' All very harmless and predictable stuff I suppose. Certainly everyone thought our relationship delightful. 'Look at them together! Isn't it *so* sweet? *Bless* them' Etc.

But some things weren't so sweet, let alone harmless, even if I didn't quite realise that at the time. Such stories are commonplace, these days: the closeting together of a small girl and a middle-aged man would arouse instant suspicion, innocent or not. But I doubt then if my father knew that paedophilia existed; certainly he would never have heard the word. I must have been forty before *I* did. And as these things go what Mr T did was not too bad. I don't seem to shiver with terror and disgust when I think of his potting shed: unless the hectic vividness of the memory is significant in some way. As I awake this afternoon, there it is - *flash* - the shelves laden with old flowerpots of different sizes, in tottering heaps, the rolls of green string, the dusty jars and bottles of various mysterious substances, the clothes pegs – why clothes pegs? – I don't know, but there they always were. I can almost smell the musty, oily, tarry smell of everything. I can see, I can list, the rakes and hoes and spades and forks leaning against the boarded wooden-walls, the bundles of pea-sticks, all different sizes, the red shards of broken pots, the thin wire prongs of the hay rake - why do I see that rake most clearly of everything? –As I do. And all of it higgledy-piggledy: Mr Tremlett, garden man was not a tidy gardener, so my father often complained tidying-up after him, 'But my word doesn't he have green fingers,' he'd add looking at all the flourishing plants outside.

'His fingers aren't green. They're brown,' I'd protest. Which I had reason to know, given how brown they looked against the little white, wrinkly – *thing* – I didn't know its name – that he'd fish out of his pants at least once during each session in the shed.

He never tried to touch me; my role was simply to look at and admire what he presented; that white worm in his brown fingers, the fingernails rimmed black with earth. Did it redden and enlarge itself? I don't know. Such details do not emerge from my private flashorama, though I do remember wondering if my father had one of those things too. Perhaps Mr Tremlett's face went rather red in the course of things. Perhaps it didn't. The only aspect of these events that gives me any feeling of disgust – I feel it now, visualising it - was the old armchair squeezed into a corner, on which my garden man would sit to eat his sandwich with its thin, very thin slice of cheese inside, or maybe an even thinner slice of fatty ham. The chair was covered in patterned velvet so old and frayed that the colour had faded to nothing, the pattern almost rubbed away. On the arms of the chair where he rested his forearms and his hands were big greasy stains, dark and unsavoury. Once and once only, he tried to pull me into his lap – 'come 'ere, little sweet'eart, 'ow about a cuddle,' he crooned in the Kentish accent that does not exist any longer, is long gone, along with Garden Man, I daresay: (he'd be well over a century now, a hundred and ten, even a hundred and twenty.) But I wasn't having any of it: being shown his nameless white worm was one thing: sitting on his lap was quite another, much as I liked – thought I liked him. Or maybe I didn't quite like him. I can feel again, now, the violent shaking of my head. I am shaking it again now, in sympathy.

As these things go I got off lightly – and innocently this time. I was very young, and what he showed me was not much different to the glimpses I got later of my friend Thomas' penis when we were playing Doctors and Nurses, something we indulged in at one point, largely because it was our only access (apart from my glimpses of Mr T's similar thing) to the bodies of the opposite sex– him with his all male siblings, me with my lack of any. *My* bottom was much tidier than his, I thought, that's all. And anyway Mr

Tremlett had stopped showing me *his* bottom, well before I was five. Maybe he feared I'd tell someone, despite the finger he'd put to his lips saying 'our little secret, sweet'eart,' once he'd put his wrinkly thing away and given me another barley sugar or acid drop.

He continued to work for my father for some time. Long after he had ceased inviting me into his potting shed, he used to come into the kitchen to have a cup of tea with the current daily woman, and we'd all pore together over her Daily Mirror. I remember those sessions as much if not more than I remember the ones in the potting shed, associating him equally with the cartoon strips, Garth and Jane and the Ruggles family. The Ruggles family had noses that descended straight from their heads without a dip. Mr Tremlett had a Ruggles nose I thought, preferring to concentrate on that part of his anatomy. I always averted my eyes very carefully from his fly.

He did not put me off penises in general. Maybe he should have put me off, maybe I would have behaved better if he had. On the other hand he did make me wary of ageing men round little girls. When the father of my children and I were living in our first house together, the harmless old man next door developed an equally charming friendship with our eldest daughter, then aged three, which *I* insisted was conducted in the garden, within my sight - my husband, despite being leered at in the showers at his public school as the pretty boy he was, appeared innocent about such things.

My poor father I think now, sadly, lying on my deathbed: my poor old dad. All those things he tried to protect me from – especially anything that would damage my innocence and, later on, my virginity. But he couldn't protect me from the world of bombs - from the V2 which broke my nursery window: or from the lorry which nearly knocked me down when I was ten, riding my bike across the road to Patty's house – that was something else he never knew about. He couldn't – didn't – protect me from that dirty old man. Any more than he could, finally, years later, protect me from the truth about my mother and my real father, hard as he tried, let alone, now, protect me from my cancer: from my immanent death. How could he have done? He did not know about the gene that has led to it. It did not come from him. And I am glad – really - he did not live long enough to see its worst effects on me.

CHAPTER NINETEEN

The fact that I have flirted with fatal illness on and off over the years is something I preferred not to tell my father when he was alive. Even middle-aged I was still his little girl: he'd have fussed and demanded to see my doctor, and since I got off lightly on the whole and up till lately did not lose my hair, there was nothing obvious to show that I was ill, or had been. The flirtation went on for more than fifteen years. Which said, you'd think, wouldn't you, that after all this time I'd have grown so used to looking death in the face that I would have learned to accept the idea of dying. Yet even now, even knowing that death is all too near, even though at times I feel resigned – I think I feel resigned - sometimes I feel scared – how ridiculous this sounds, now – almost to death.

I cannot bear to think I'll not see the sparrows or even the sidling pigeons outside any more: I cannot bear to think of the world going on without me, while I've gone into the dark the way we all sooner or later go into that dark. I cannot bear the prospect of nothingness – the prospect fills me with terror. And no, I do not believe in an afterlife – the way it's predicted doesn't appeal to me much, anyway: who wants to stand around dressed in white among angels and harps, let alone writhe naked among, devils with pitchforks - I'd most likely attract the attention of the latter rather than the former. I was brought up to go to church and have a slight envy of the spiritually inclined, even though I do not understand what drives them. I was not only baptised, of course: I have the evidence of that in the photo of my infant self in a long white robe held by my mother, wearing that slanted hat with brim and feather: I was also confirmed as a matter of course into the Anglican Church, a church which my father attended all the days of his life and which mattered to him greatly, if in a cultural, tribal rather than a strictly spiritual way.

My attitude in general to these matters could be defined, I daresay, by my reaction to the eager young curate who instructed my group in our spiritual duty in the weeks leading up to the confirmation ceremony.

Let's make this clear. I wasn't wholly cynical about the business. It was in my genes to believe, more or less. The grandmother shared by my mother and my adopted father, was a clergyman's daughter: she and all of her family were descended from generations of clergyman, going back to Huguenot divines from France who'd fled to England at the end of the seventeenth century, to escape persecution. I did truly wonder if, I *hoped* that, the touch of the Bishop's hands on my head, let alone taking my first communion would lead to the Holy Spirit sitting on or in my head in some way or other: preferably not in the form of a dove – there was a dovecot at my school and I knew what doves were prone to. Just the same the curate's injunction as to how we should approach the communion service was not merely a matter of not presuming 'to come to this thy table trusting in our own righteousness' but of literally crawling there in abject guilt for our spiritual vileness: 'Hang on, I'm not that bad,' I thought, bemusedly. Shortly after, he was enjoining us over and over 'to take Jesus into our hearts'. To which my instant reaction was; I will bloody well not (bloody at that time was about the worst swear-word I knew), I will NOT. My heart belongs to me.'

Stiff-necked pride, I daresay they – the clergy – would call it. (And not just the clergy, some husbands/lovers have muttered similar things.) But humble as I may be elsewhere – or maybe not - stiff-necked pride of that kind I am happy to have, am happy to go *on* having, so long as I'm conscious: not for so long now. All of which has left me envying the religious sometimes, but really not understanding such literal spirituality at all, meaning I have no option but to see death as a final blotting out, rather than an entry into eternal glory or eternal pain. Someone suggested to me once – I've never forgotten this – that to be truly adult is to accept the finality of death. In which case I am not yet adult, not even now, to judge from the terror that overcomes me from time to time.

Last night, for instance, my husband put his head round the door to find me screaming in the arms of a big bosomy Jamaican night nurse, wailing, 'I don't want to die. I don't want to die.' He retreated at once, looking horrified. 'I'll go and have my fag,' I heard him say, through my wails. And for once I did not want him, I knew he could do nothing for me, not at this moment. Even my dear nurse Peter could not have helped in this moment: I was an infant crying in the night, crying for a mother, crying out for light.

Oh the comfort of that massive Jamaican bosom on which I, old woman as I am, was sobbing, almost screaming. 'I DON'T WANT

TO DIE.' 'Course you don't want to, darling, who does,' she said. 'You be quiet, child, I'm here'. She was stroking me now. And then she said – I'm sure she shouldn't have said it, these days medical staff are not supposed to impose their religion on you in any way– suppose I'd been a Buddhist or a Muslim? – 'and when you die the Lord Jesus will be waiting there for you, I promise, darling. *Upsidaisy. Hush* now.'

Believing it not at all, I still found that expression comforting. I found *her* comforting, the twenty even thirty-year younger mother on whose bosom I was laying my aged, still partly chemo-bald, infant head. My terror eased, died away altogether. I lay quietly, her arms still round me, grateful, so grateful, that she did not shift an inch to move me, though they must have been aching dreadfully by then.

In due course the Husband reappeared, opening the door very gingerly, looking as if he feared what he might find. He also looked sheepish and smelt of beer. I was tucked up and tidy by this time –as far as I could be in either head or body – and tending to fall asleep.

'Thank Christ,' he said, which was heartless, but just what I expected and also needed, without a doubt. ' I really can't cope with stuff like that.' he said.

'You're drunk. Do you think *I* can?'

'I'm not. Though could you blame me?'

'Now who's feeling sorry for himself? And I thought it was me had the better reason.'

'I'll miss you,' he said, though not managing to do more than take my hand and drop it.

'I'll miss you if I was going to be in any position to,' I said. 'But I doubt it.'

'The grave's a fine and private place -' he said.

'Hark at you. Has grief driven you to literature, at last?' I said.

'It's what you quoted me the other day.'

'Did I?' I think I fell asleep then, hearing him groan. When I woke again, he was gone, though the room still smelled a little of the pub. The Jamaican night nurse put her head round the door at that moment.

'You be alright then, darling?'

'No. I'll never be that. But better,' I said, giving myself a morphine jolt even so, just for the hell of it.

CHAPTER TWENTY

The key thing I now know about the dying is not they are dying: but they are still very much part of life.

Again: there is the strange fact that no matter how sick you are your hair keeps on growing: mine is returning fast now despite all the rough treatment. And as for my finger and toenails they are as rampant and active as ever: I'm told they will keep growing for a while after I'm dead.

Again: take smells: some of those that emanate from me these days relate to my illness, are less smell than stink. But some smells are as they ever were, if I bother to investigate.

This morning before the nurse appeared I reached my left hand – the one without the drip - below my swollen gut, inserted my fingers beneath the synthetic material that fields my uncontrollable excretions, and inserted them into that once powerful little slit of mine. Then, avoiding the line of the catheter plugged into my urethra, I set them to exploring my genitals. Afterwards I put my fingers to my nostrils. And there it was: the same old lovely sexual smell of me at a time when eroticism seems unthinkable, when the energy necessary to achieve orgasm feels as unachievable as the energy needed to send a rocket to the moon.

I always have liked the smell of my cunt, ever since I first sniffed it on my fingers as a very small child, after giving myself sensations of whose nature I know nothing, only how nice they felt. All of it a long time before I heard any of the words - 'clitoris', 'vagina', 'masturbation', 'orgasm' - let alone knew what they meant. Even now, to my astonishment, I felt, touching myself, the faintest of faint – but unmistakable – stir of that same pleasure. I feel it again now, as I sniff my fingers for one last hungry time.

Eros and Thanatos: Here we go again: Eros and Thanatos - actually they are words far too fancy for the reality of that smell and the reality of my present condition. Greek and Latin yields – should yield – I thought - to Anglo-Saxon here: let's just call it fucking and death.

But how can I encompass the sadness this engenders at the same time? I had known so much pleasure over the years, alone or in company: soon it would be no more: it *was* no more in every sense that mattered. Mostly I hurt too much. Death is beginning to trump all.

Bloody death. Terrible death. And, suddenly, I am overwhelmed by this thought: that all my - our -major apocalyptic fears about the world generally, contained in words like 'nuclear winter', 'peak oil', 'global warming', fears about dirty bombs, suicide bombers, the lurking of death in backpacks, the turn of a wheel, a clap of thunder, bird flu, gene mutation, meteor hit, are not simply about wholesale general extinction, but belong much closer to home.

We are animals, after all, dedicated to survival, programmed to look out for death and danger. Even if we banish both, the way we sometimes imagine that we can, we still start at shadows, have nightmares in the dark, fear moths, spiders, outside places, hamburgers, transgenic foods, morbid obesity, our very moles, lumps, wrinkles, as reminders, harbingers of what we all come to in the end; of what I'm coming to, soon.

Has there ever been a time when the more general fears – whatever you call them - the wrath of God, Armageddon, black hole - have not been at base, less about the fear of general extinction than about the fear of personal – *my* - extinction? Because you can, you think, avert apocalypse: by good behaviour, belief in this God or that, marching against the politicians' bombs, using low-electricity light bulbs. Does this mean that at some level we imagine that by such means we can avoid our own?

Even now I cannot avoid my own, local catastrophe, it does not mean I don't fear those general ones. I fear them for my children, grandchildren and the whole wide world. But that too is not particularly selfless and generous, that too relates to my personal survival. As long as they – my children, my grandchildren the world - survive, I will live on somehow, even after I'm dead and buried. But if everything and everyone disappears into some big black hole, there will be nothing of me left. Zilch. That is the terrifying thought.

(Unless Jesus – the ~Messiah – Allah –the virgins – the angels - live of course. But how can I, how can anyone seriously trust that, nice as it would be? – Well some think it might be nice – I don't go for the virgins myself.)

Smell was all the sex I knew about till I was at least twelve or maybe even thirteen– I didn't recognise my experience in the potting shed with Mr Tremlett as having anything to do with sex. My father, looking the other way, gave me a book that told me a lot about insects and rabbits but did not seem to have much to do with me. Patty, designated to tell me about periods – she called it *The Curse* – was far more straightforward, but equally baffling. That's never going to happen to me, I thought, never. But of course it did. I was at boarding school by then under the aegis of my final mentor, its headmistress, a woman who liked sherry and Benson and Hedges cigarettes, fags which she smoked, like Patty did her Sobranies, in a very long holder.

I doubt if my father would have cared for my headmistress's instructions on life either, had he known what they consisted of. It was a small school and every night she came round and kissed every one of her pupils good night. When you were older and one of her favourites – I *was* one – she kissed you a mite too firmly on the lips: indeed very firmly, and sometimes for up to thirty seconds – or so it felt. Innocent as I was, the import of this escaped me entirely until some time after I'd left school, when I learned to my astonishment that my headmistress was rumoured to have been in a long-term lesbian relationship with her maid, a woman who looked after her clothes and her flat and was always upholstered within a fearsome green dress, topped by a small white frilly apron. I'm still not sure whether I believe this story. And I hadn't at all minded the kisses: they made me feel loved, especially when, latterly, they came with a hug that made me feel mothered besides.

The sole piece of verbal instruction I received from this source, though it did not seem much like that, came a year or so after I left her school. My father by then was a very good friend of hers – she got on particularly well with single fathers. He sent me to see her, following a report from my landlady in Oxford that I was coming in late at night and she thought I might be getting up to no good. In fact she knew I was getting up to no good. The episode in the mouse-dropping cottage had somehow leaked out. (In those days, when 'lock up your daughter' attitudes were still in fashion, landladies did not just see themselves as landladies but also as in loco parentis. They kept ears well to the ground: and sometimes beneath it. She must have picked up on my terror that I might be pregnant, even though I had confided this to no one, except, via the darkest of dark hints, to my then one and only and just in passing female friend.)

My ex-headmistress sat me down in her room and asked 'sherry, darling?' 'Yes please,' I said. It was a large sherry. I think I got a little drunk.

We talked about everything for a while except my sex-life – about the school, her sixth form, her teachers, what my contemporaries were doing. At last she said, abruptly.

'I hear you have a boyfriend, darling.'

'I had one,' I said.

'And I hear…'

'Yes,' I said. I giggled. Which was as much as an admission as I need make.

'And how is it, darling?'

'Lovely,' I said. Even though it hadn't been, even though the episode had never been repeated.

'I'm glad,' she said. 'Not that I would know: I never did it myself. Another sherry, darling?'

We talked about school a bit more, about Oxford, about my father and then I left. She retired a year or so later and fell in a swimming pool one night, after a few too many sherries probably. I was both sad and not sad about her death, concluding, then as now, that for such a woman to be found floating dead in a swimming pool was as suitably bizarre an end as any.

I had not told my father about this conversation. But when I heard about her death I did tell Patty and we both laughed like anything. I always could tell Patty anything and thank goodness, given what she did for me, in due course.

When I say I went to Oxford, I did not mean I went to the university. My headmistress had persuaded my father – much against his beliefs and instincts – that I should be allowed to try. 'Don't waste her brain,' she told him – and in a weak moment – perhaps this was due to too much of her excellent sherry – Tio Pepe – he had agreed to let me take Oxford and Cambridge entrance. And to my surprise, if not theirs, I was accepted at one of the Oxford women's colleges.

But I turned the place down in the end. I always was contrary: and maybe in some ways it was out of yet more desire to please my father (I knew that proud of me as he was, he was still not happy about it; like most men of his background and generation he regarded a university degree as the means for getting a good job and so wasted on women, whose only object in life was, should be, to be good wives and mothers. 'You'll just go off and get married then what will have been the point?' he'd said to me once, looking baffled.). It was also – more obviously to me – because of the two teachers I knew at the school who had been to Oxford; dowdy old women I thought, with spectacles on chains and flat shoes. I did not want to end up like them. Nor did I like either of the other Oxbridge successes: one a thick-legged girl from Newcastle who wanted to be an engineer, and the other a mathematician, a very jolly and spectacled young woman, not at all girl-like and with an unbecoming thatch of curly hair. The thought of spending three years in the company of women like that, old or young, did not appeal to me. So I turned the place down, though I did not demur when my father suggested an Oxford secretarial college, because it would give me access to one aspect of Oxford that did appeal to me: the surplus of men.

In my conversation with the headmistress, over a year later, she asked me if I regretted my decision.

'No,' I said. 'I get most of the advantages without having to write the essays. And secretarial stuff is much more useful. I always *could* have ended up teaching of course.' I looked at her sideways. Smiling faintly she took a sip of sherry rather than that bait. After a minute she did say distantly, with the smallest of sighs, pursing her lipsticked mouth.

'And we could always do with the odd Oxbridge educated graduate here.'

For what, I thought? My school turned out – it might not have been her intention, but certainly it was the parents' intention - wives, cooks, secretaries mostly. Over-educated women were known to put men – potential husbands – off.

The headmistress sighed, put up her spectacles and looked me straight in the eye.

'What does your father feel about it?' she asked.

'I don't think he minds. He was afraid,' – I hesitated – smirked a bit – but continued to let her hold my gaze, 'he was afraid I *might* turn into a teacher. What else could I do with a degree?'

She flourished her cigarette holder. 'Ah - a teacher: like me. I was engaged once, of course. But my fiancé insisted I would have to give up teaching and that was the end of that.'

'I don't think he'd mind if I was like *you*. Provided I didn't take him to the opera.' (This referred to a trip to Glyndebourne to which she had treated him.)

'I didn't think that had gone down too well. He fell asleep,' she said.

'He did tell me afterwards he thought he'd now 'done' Glyndebourne. I hope he didn't snore.'

'Not very loudly,' she said. 'But I hadn't thought of inviting him again'.

When I left she kissed me lightly on the cheek. No more lips now. Perhaps she only reserved that for pupils. Or maybe she assumed I might be more worldly wise these days and might take it in the wrong way.

Not so long after, it occurred to me - with relief – that, to judge from this meeting, my headmistress might not have disapproved of my great love, unlike my other mentors, other than Patty. (Aunt Anne would have disapproved especially. Good, I thought.)

The secretarial college started its term in late September somewhat before the Oxford term began. At the beginning of September my father and I went away on a fortnight's holiday. It was not the usual motoring trip. I think he, like me, saw this holiday as valedictory in some way: I was close to my entrance to at least nominal adulthood and from now on things could never be the same. We went to a small resort on the Italian coast near Viareggio – a horrible place - but our place was much smaller and more exclusive. For him it was quite an extravagance: currency restrictions had been lifted by now. Apart from the odd excursion, to Florence one day and Pisa another, we divided our time between the beach and the resort's very good restaurants. Somewhere I have – I had – a picture of myself on the hotel beach, which he must have taken. I am lying on my front, wearing a conical-shaped sunhat with a wide brim, and with my hair in little plaits, reading a book. I even remember what the book was: Graham Greene's *Brighton Rock*, about a world and people I found as distasteful as I found them fascinating: I did not even *want* to know they existed. Nor was I the least attracted by Catholic notions of sin and death that underpinned the story. On the other hand I admired Pinkie's sheer cheek, not to say amorality –not to say chutzpah – not a word I knew, though I have learned it since and in such respects wished I could be like him, in a non-criminal version, and without the murders and the bad end thrown in. Had my father read *Brighton Rock,* I wondered, looking up at him in his deckchair, reading a hardback copy of one of Churchill's histories: much too big a book for the beach? I doubted it. Dickensian lowlife was more his line. That was something he could dare to believe in. I was not so sure about Pinky and his lot.

In the evenings over dinner, we talked. It was the first and only time he talked to me at length about my mother. Perhaps he thought it was his last chance.

What an amazingly pretty, not to say beautiful, young woman, she was, he said. But of course I knew that. Her beauty had come across even in that christening photograph of her dressed in that slinky dress – horrible I thought it as a child –that slanted hat, and, slung round her neck, the sinister fox-fur. The fox's grinning little face bared its teeth within an inch of my infant self, wrapped in a white woollen shawl, the elaborate lace of the family christening robe trailing below. I'm not sure that new birth and taxidermy were appropriate juxtapositions, but I don't suppose anyone noticed at the time. It was long ago, before the war, and as we are always being told, they did things differently then. All my father said was that her outfit was considered fashionable but then he would, wouldn't he? He'd been besotted.

Over our dinners – antipasto – prawns or grilled aubergine or whatever – followed by a primo piatto– pasta or rice –followed by the secondo piatto - meat or more likely fish, followed by cake, or ice-cream and fruit - he told me about his having seen my mother first at *her* christening. He himself had been ten years old.

She was, he said, pretty even as a baby. Prettier than me I wanted to ask. He hadn't thought much of babies, aged ten, but even then he had noticed how pretty she was. Everybody said so.

Her mother was not, had never been, a well woman: she suffered from her nerves my father said, while her husband was much older and in the navy and away at sea a lot. As a result my mother had spent much of her childhood being shuffled round the families of various cousins. She hadn't come to my father's family: he too was like an only child, so much younger than his brothers that there was no nursery for her to join. But she did go to other cousins, a large family with children ranging from twenty-year olds to toddlers for whom one more child was scarcely a burden, given the scores of nannies and nursery maids employed to look after them all. My father had also been seconded to that family at some time in most years and so had watched my mother growing-up, watched over her growing-up you could say the way he talked about it. 'Growing prettier by the minute,' he'd add. And I knew it wasn't just my father had thought that - everyone, including Patty, said my mother was beautiful. 'You're quite like her,' they'd sometimes add, doubtfully; and I knew that was true too at the same time as knowing I was much too foursquare and beaky to be beautiful in the same way. Eventually, once I came to know that I could and did attract people – how I could attract people – I didn't care if I was or not.

'But of course,' my father assured me several times on that holiday. 'Of course I saw her as like a sister in those days. I never for one moment imagined she'd grow up to marry me. She'd find someone much more interesting and handsome, someone who wasn't like a brother to her.'

But this hadn't stopped him adoring her more by the year. And still more when she grew into beautiful adolescence: my mother never seemed to have suffered from spots and puppy fat the way most of us do as teenagers. And as for her figure -look at that picture of her after my christening, the silk dress revealed everything, including the fact that, shortly after childbirth, her body showed no sign of it whatever. I might not have existed, you could say. As, of course, for her, I only did exist for those nine months of her unwanted pregnancy, those three years of my life, before she ran off.

'And then one year she came on a Broads holiday with me and my friends. That was an accident, really. It was just after she left school and before she went to Paris to be finished and learn

French. Her mother had been going to take her to the Riviera that summer, but she got ill, as usual, and when my then girlfriend fell out of my trip I suggested your mother came instead. Of course all the girls slept on one boat and the boys on the other so it was quite proper and your grandmother said I would be a perfectly good chaperone, she did not have a moment's worry that your mother would not be safe in my hands, even though she would be the youngest girl by several years. But I think she was just relieved to have your mother off her hands so she could concentrate on being ill as usual. To give her her due, she died only a year or two later, just before you were born, so maybe she really was ill this time. She'd had rheumatic fever as a child and did have a very bad heart.'

'Well, to cut a long story very short' (and it was a long story by my father's usually taciturn standards – he had drunk quite a lot of Chianti and by now moved on to grappa) 'there your mother was, being very charming and all the young men fell in love with her and all the girls of course were jealous. But I don't think your mother noticed any of it, she was so artless and innocent.'

(At this I raise, now, if not then, a metaphorical eyebrow. I somehow doubt the artlessness: not that I have much evidence for my doubt, except perhaps the fact that, given her mother's frequent indispositions and her father's equally frequent absences even after his naval career had come to an end, my mother had grown up surrounded by much older cousins. Innocence did not seem likely to be attached too closely to such a childhood. It took place in the twenties and early thirties after all, an era much more louche than the fifties in which I was grew up, especially in London where my mother and her parents lived and where her mother, when well enough, had been part, according to my father, of what he called, disapprovingly, 'the cocktail set'. My mother was not a country bumpkin for sure: unlike my father who always called himself just that.)

'And then she went to Paris. And you know how she came back.'

'Expecting me?' I said firmly, not sparing him. I had had a fair amount to drink too. Though he kept a watchful eye on me, he considered me old enough to drink a whole glass of wine or even two, now that I had left school.

'Yes. Expecting you. She came to me so tearfully, I don't know why she came to me, but she did. I asked if the man would marry her: that would be the decent thing. But she shook her head and said absolutely not, looking more beautiful than ever. And so of course I said *I'd* marry her, and bring you up as my daughter. And I wanted to say this, darling, before you left home, I wanted you to know that not for one moment have I ever regretted accepting you as my daughter, Not for one moment. I couldn't have loved you more if I had been your real father.'

His voice almost broke, to my embarrassment. I had never seen or heard him like this, nor did I want to.

'Did she say who *was* my real father?' I asked, brutally.

We were sitting on a terrace by the beach, a terrace roofed with vines and looking out over the sea, on which the moon made a long pathway. Some people moved around the beach carrying little lights. Behind us, in the restaurant proper, a three-piece band was playing a medley of Puccini arias – even though I hadn't yet seen an opera, my headmistress had given me a good grounding in such music: unlike my father I had taken to it well. But it was all too conventionally romantic to be tolerable just now and having to sit listening to my father bare his soul – for so I called it, cruelly and critically - was more than I could stand. But I had to stand it. I loved him, didn't I? All I could do was punish him in what way I could, without silencing him, totally. He *was* giving me information I'd wanted and needed my whole life. I just couldn't bear its coming so wrapped in emotion. Punishment might also be a way of eliciting still more information, if I asked the right, bald question in exactly the right way.

I took a finally swig of Chianti, tipped coffee from my cup onto a little heap of sugar on the saucer and then scooped up some coffee-flavoured sugar and tasted it thoughtfully.

'*Did* she say who my real father was?' I asked again.

Someone on the beach started playing a guitar. Someone else started to sing. I felt as if I could step on to the moon path reaching across the water and waft myself away, carrying my knowledge of my paternity with me, if only it was vouchsafed.

My father shook his head. I could have sworn that there were real tears in his eyes.

'And what about my mother: Did she really die?' I asked. I knew a lot of people had died in the London bombings as I also knew – the only thing I knew – that that was where she had gone.

'She is dead to us,' was all he would say, shaking his head. It could have meant anything. But actually it meant deception, though I still didn't know this then.

Then he said. 'Of course everyone was against our marriage: my mother, even her mother. Both our fathers were dead by then. Everyone thought I was quite mad. And of course it was quite mad, in that respect, sometimes I thought so myself. And I've often wondered over the years if I really did the right thing. But it brought me your mother for a little while. And it brought me you. And you must remember how things were just then. Your mother confessed her condition to me just after the Munich crisis, when Neville Chamberlain came back smiling and said 'peace in our time.' He nodded reminiscently here. 'Even smiling, Chamberlain looked as if there was a bad smell under his nose,' he added.

'So?' I asked, feeling cross now. At this moment of all moments I did not want one of my father's political reminiscences. I reverted to deadpan, as usual. 'So?' I repeated a little more loudly.

'Everyone thought there would be war just the same. Everyone was a little jumpy. It did not seem a good moment for your mother to be alone with such a problem,'

I did not much like being described as a problem either.

'Perhaps my real father would have married her, but for the coming war,' I said brightly. 'She could have gone back to Paris and told him about it.'

My father shook his head and took out his pipe here.

'Was he her Hamlet?' I persisted.

'What are you talking about, Jo?' He sounded startled.

'Her name was Ophelia too.'

'Oh *that*,' he said. 'Oh *that*. It was her idea to call *you* Ophelia. I was rather against it, myself. But she said there had been actors on her side of the family. I'm not sure she ever saw the play.'

'How do you know for sure he wouldn't have married her, my real father, but for the war?' I insisted. But my father just looked at me and shook my head.

At this moment I knew I ought to feel particularly grateful to him for coming to my mother's rescue the way he did. But I did not feel grateful, thinking that had my mad mother – the true romantic – stuck around she would have managed all this so much better.

'You do know how much I love you, darling,' my father said abruptly now. His eyes were still brimming with tears

I could not bear any more. My father had really gone mad now I thought, showing himself to me so openly, so embarrassingly– it's only now I realise how my going to Oxford, my growing up, was opening him, he felt, to loss and loneliness. Italy was the worst place for us to have come in such circumstances: we'd have done better to go to Morocco and get dysentery. We'd couldn't have got drunk in Morocco anyway, could we, it was most likely dry, being a Muslim country, even if it hadn't been the wine would have been undrinkable; not Chianti or grappa, that's for sure.

I leapt to my feet, 'I have to go to the lav,' I said. 'And afterwards I want to go down onto the beach. Do you mind?'

'Of course not, darling: but don't go down for long, and don't do anything I wouldn't. And please knock on my door later so I know you're back.' He wiped his mouth on his napkin. He placed his spoon more neatly alongside his coffee cup. He waved me a little goodbye. He *was* actually crying, I think, by now. And I think it must have been the drink and grief made him acquiesce so easily to my going down to the beach, alone, at night, to where the frustrated young men lurked – this was the age when Italians did, literally, still lock up their daughters and they had to make do with tourist girls. But of course, at that age, I was quite as alarmed by the predatory young men as my father was; I did not stay on the beach longer than was necessary to run down to the edge of the sea, take my shoes off and dip my feet in the water, at the exact point where the moonlight lay.

I looked back. On the terrace I could see the lonely figure of my father, still sitting there, holding his glass of grappa. And I saw a waiter come and my father signing for the meal. And then, as I started running back up the beach towards him, carrying my sandals in one hand, I saw him get stiffly to his feet and start walking towards the back of the terrace. He was barely fifty, yet I seemed to see in him the beginnings of the old man.

That evening's conversation was never mentioned again. No more questions were asked, no more answers vouchsafed. That is how it was between my father and me, apart from that night and apart from during his extreme old age.

During my own crisis a while later I did mention it briefly to Patty, though, wondering if she could tell me more about what had happened. She looked at me for a moment. Then she said. 'Your father didn't tell you probably. But he was expecting to have to go to war in due course. He thought he would be killed like his brothers. And then your mother would not only have been made respectable by him, she would have been free to find someone nearer her own age and much more suitable. But of course he wasn't allowed to go to war and there they were.'

I don't know what I thought, hearing this. Except maybe that my father was even more of a fool than I'd suspected. But the next moment, thinking how glad I was that he hadn't gone to war and got killed, I could have wept myself at the very idea of it, which quite drove away my fury at his idiocy.

CHAPTER TWENTY-ONE

I am still in remission these days: but also in increasing pain. This does not mean that my terror of dying abates entirely, far from it, but it does mean I have some rather more ambivalent feelings than I had before the pain struck.

The Husband finds me weeping again one evening, and as usual takes himself off, though he returns more quickly than sometimes and for once not smelling of beer.

'Thank goodness,' he says, grinning in his lovely, heartless way, 'I really can't cope with that.' He bends over me and kisses me on the cheek then takes his usual seat on the slippery green faux-leather of the chair besides the bed. We sit in silence for a while. 'You never know,' I say, at last: 'there might even come a day when I'll tell you I don't want to wake up in the morning? What will you do then?'

He looks at my morphine zapper. 'I don't suppose they make that strong enough to kill you. They're too scared of being charged with murder these days. Do you want me to put a pillow over your face?'

'Not if you had to spend the rest of your life in prison,' I say. I mean it.

'Maybe we should get you home,' he says thoughtfully. 'It might be a bit easier there. It's probably too late to get you to Switzerland.'

'Would you mind looking after me at home? Would they let you?' I ask.

He grimaces. Smiles. 'No to the first: probably. No to the second probably too. No.'

'Bloody hell,' I say. 'Just let me die for god's sake. Why won't they? The buggers. They don't think of us they're just scared for their own careers.'

'That's not what you were saying earlier.'

'No,' I say.

'There's Question Time on now on the box – they've hauled in some little BNP turd again, do you want to watch?'

'Why not,' I say; thankful at the change of subject; thankful, too, in spite of everything I could still be interested in such things, on his behalf and everyone else's, if not mine. I wasn't dead yet, was

I? The Husband sits on the bed – as near as he can get without hurting me – holding my hand. And we look up at the television set angled above the bed and watch the turd in question yet again claiming Churchill, the wartime army, all the wartime heroes for his own: even though the turd and most of his followers were too young to have known any such a war. Which does not stop them in any way, sixty years on, from expropriating the old myths: history looking backwards as always. Just how weird,' my husband says – he picks up current colloquialisms from his students and uses them, quite shamelessly – if with a small hint of irony, a little sideways grin – 'Get sorted,' he says and 'cool' and so forth: and now 'Just how *weird*, is that.'

'Weird means all too tolerable. Disgusting more like,' I say, yawning. Too exhausted suddenly to care.

We do not see the end of the programme. My Australian daughter calls – it's already morning for her - to find out how I am. She's retreated since our last conversation. When I tell her I'm still in remission she sounds almost exasperated - *I can't believe you're still alive*, sort of thing. I daresay I'm being uncharitable; perhaps I am just depressed at our failure to turn such exchanges round. I listen silently as she says that the Easter holidays are almost over, that the Sydney Easter Fair is over too, that there is a window in which it might be easier for her to get away, but that it wouldn't last long. Does that mean she wants to see me alive, I wonder, or is she merely hoping to fit a dutiful visit for my funeral into her convenient 'window?' I could weep for both of us. I don't. It feels easier not to care and I've had enough practice in that.

My father drove me to Oxford for the start of my first secretarial term. It did not feel like his driving me back to school. There was no uniform in my suitcase and I took a box full of stuff for my room - books and some posters, mostly, one poster showing a moody looking Juliet Greco, another from the Gauguin exhibition at the Royal Academy: my mad headmistress had carted me off to this along with her other favourites some time during my final year. (She'd been inclined to spur of the moment abductions of this kind, to the annoyance of the teachers whose lessons we were supposed to be attending and the equal annoyance of my unfortunate fellows who were not her favourites. Teachers are not supposed to behave like that as I knew even then. But I was happy enough to go along with such privilege, just as I would, now, accept any offer of a rare cure to my disease, whether generally available or not: some hope.)

I did not pack in my box the teddy bears or china animals, the grinning family photographs that most contemporaries went in for in those days and probably still do. Though I did take the trio of green glass balls held in a net that might have belonged to my mother, though I only knew for sure that they had stood on a shelf in my room for as long as I could remember – as they have stood somewhere in any dwelling of mine ever since. My father did not know how the trio had arrived on that shelf either; he said they were designed to keep fishing-nets afloat. In a sense they've kept me afloat instead, helping to connect me to that equally adrift entity: myself.

Once he'd established me in my room with my suitcase and my boxes, he took me out to lunch at the Mitre - his usual sort of food, a roast and all that, though I had a grilled trout and both of us finished up with treacle tart; this last chosen by me as a comforting bulwark against a prospect of my new life that was filling me with sudden panic. Afterwards he conducted me round his old college – New College; nostalgia I thought that was and a bit of pride: 'my college,' etc, etc. But it turned out not quite so simple.

There were few students about. The secretarial college term started considerably earlier than the university one. There were some of those figures I learned to identify instantly as Oxford academics – shabby professorial types with flying hair, younger ones in corduroy - very pink and white, or greyish in some cases, and underground-looking, many of them, as if they spent most of their lives in dim libraries and normal light set them blinking. They made me thankful I was not attending the university myself. Why should I want to be surrounded, taught by, ageing men who looked as if they'd had to be dug up from somewhere, and by younger men in cords about to be buried themselves? Give me a nice randy teddy boy any day, I thought, thinking of Graham Greene's Pinky. (This was not quite true: had a randy teddy boy approached me I'd have run away fast. One of Juliette Greco's boyfriends would be much more like it: that was probably the attraction of the would-be

Hamlet who took my virginity; he looked like a male version of her, dark fringe and all.)

But that was almost a year ahead. Today, my father marched me round quads and gardens and made me peer up staircases on which he had once lived during his Oxford days – 'not on the *actual* stairs, juggins,' he said when I pretended not to know that it meant he had a room off the staircase; this would have been a tease had the whole thing not suddenly bored me. Dutiful but distant I admired the quads, the green lawns, the cloisters, the gardens. I felt ashamed to be so irritated by my father's enthusiasm, but so I was. Still more remote from me seemed the ante-chapel into which he led me thereafter, the wall of beautifully inscribed names at which he pointed; two of them he said belonged to his half-brothers, half step cousins to me, more removed, in cousin terms, even than him. As removed, it felt, as the carved figure of Lazarus emerging from his shroud nearby, his head bent at such an angle – broken-looking -it seemed impossible he could have risen from the dead.

That dissonant, pitiable figure drew me more, though, than the names, inscribed so tastefully by Eric Gill whose work I recognised even then: (my father did not seem to; maybe he did not even know about Eric Gill, something that added to the faint sense of superiority I felt that day, shameful as it was, watching him search through that interminable scroll of dead names.)

My father did not weep so easily these days as he did later. But still I thought I saw tears in his eyes and was more irritated than ever. His brothers meant nothing to me then; I think it was the first time I'd taken in their surname – it was not the same as my father's – let alone their Christian names. 'Jack, that's what he was always called,' my father said pointing at the first name: James whatever, he was inscribed in Gill's beautiful, irrelevant script, 'we never called him James. He was killed on the Somme.' He looked for the second name. And then he really did cry a little because for quite a while he couldn't find it, couldn't locate the second brother, the one he'd especially loved; the names were not in any alphabetical order. 'Typical,' I thought, sourly. 'Why ever not?' And then there he was 'Henry' – 'we called *him* Harry always. He died in a German prison camp of septicaemia. My mother took me out on the village green to tell him he wouldn't come back, most likely. I lay down on the path and wouldn't get up for ten minutes. I was only eight.' I tried to look sad. But I didn't feel sad for Harry, only for my father. Even though the sheer number of names did get to me a little, this James or Jack, this Henry or Harry weren't related to me, after all, except by marriage. I felt more affected by Lazarus, with his desperate neck: with his shrouded limbs. Did he really come back to life, out of *that*? Could anyone?

Not that I showed my feelings. Even in my irritation, I did not want to hurt my father, and as usual – still more than usual - deadpan came to my rescue. I nodded as respectfully as I could. I put out my hand; I did not quite touch his. I did not want to touch his, at that moment he felt as creepy as the Lazarus felt, as pitiable: but I made it look as if I'd thought of it. This was the best that I could do.

From here, this all looks so very hard-hearted. But I was still an adolescent, and to adolescents parents' pain is an embarrassment. You must also realise how little I knew about the first war then, about its mud, its pointless brutality and squalor. It wasn't till the sixties that the television series appeared that made me conscious, for the first time, of its true awfulness. I'm not talking about the sense I'd always had, without quite knowing it, of the way it weighed on my parents' let alone my grandparents' generation, and so, indirectly, weighed on me. I'm saying that only then, watching the black-and-white soldiers wind their way through those sodden and horrible trenches, fling themselves across no-man's land, falling in mid-run, to lie in pools of water and mud, could I have wondered how my father felt, knowing that among those figures might have been his own brothers: in particular the one who he said had been more like a father to him than his real father.

Only a few years later I was editing books about that war myself. And at about the same time my father showed me a letter he'd come across, that had been written by his younger brother to their mother, before he went to war. He'd labelled the envelope 'to be read in the case of my death.' A clumsy way of putting it that seemed to me and the letter was worse, all desperate heroics: – 'don't cry for me, I will be dying in glory to save my country' etc, etc– so naïve, so idiotic, so sad, I wanted both to laugh and cry. But my father thought it was a wonderful letter, redolent of what was best about England and the English. And I hid my smile, yet again, and told him yes, it was a wonderful letter: what a splendid

149

young man his brother must have been (brought up on Boy's Own and Henty books, I whispered to myself, in my superior way).

It did not take me long to start liking Oxford, as Oxford: and to realise that not all academics belonged in some collegiate grave, like premature versions of Lazarus. I knew that some of them were wild enough, not to say randy – in those days making a pass at your pupils was perfectly acceptable and quite often accepted by the pupils too. Not that I *was* one of their pupils. But given the prejudice of that generation of male undergraduates – many of them - against clever women, a prejudice that made them pursue girls who weren't in the university, attending a secretarial college did me no harm at all. Nor did my brain turn out to be a disadvantage: being pretty and witty, both, got me forgiven very quickly, and I had all the attention I wanted: some of my admirers even encouraged the intellectual aspirations that began to emerge in me in such a climate. They stole gowns so that I could attend university lectures: which is how, skipping the secretarial classes I should have been attending, I came to hear the likes of Lord David Cecil talking about Jane Austen – whose work I didn't rate much then, but I did like Lord D – Hugh Trevor Roper and Christopher Hill arguing different causes for the English Civil War – Professor Edgar Wind enthralling the packed seats of the Oxford Playhouse by complicating the work of Raphael beyond comprehension and belief. But my favourite above all was Isaiah Berlin, giving, at breakneck speed, three different versions per lecture of the views of nineteenth century revolutionaries like Bakunin of whom I'd never heard, but now longed to hear more, borne along on the tide of Isaiah's breathy enthusiasm.

I was still relieved at not having to write the essays. Yet I also began to think that I'd made a mistake in rejecting university; I persuaded my father to let me return to Oxford, the following year, to a crammers this time to finish my A levels and attempt Oxford entrance by that route. And so it was – at another lecture, but to a college philosophy society this time – that I encountered my second lover: the love of my life. An episode that very soon I must make myself confront.

CHAPTER TWENTY-TWO

Another evening. And yet another. How many more, I wonder? The pain has eased a little. My son comes over earlier than usual – too early, Nurse Peter is tending to me, and the curtain on the little window in the door closed, telling visitors not to enter. My son barges in anyway just as Peter is washing my feet, separating each toe gently yet precisely then applying his warm cloth. He is concentrating so hard that he jumps when the door opens. He turns, cloth in hand and tells my son very crossly and authoritatively to wait outside until he's finished. My son looks embarrassed and scuttles out.

Through this exchange Peter has sounded quite different; there is no trace of camp in his voice. Does he just put that on? Does he add the equally camp flouncing about, as an act for his patients? Do I put on an act, too, of the dying but still so *feisty* (how I hate that word) old woman? Perhaps I do put on such an act. It's the only way to bear what's going on. Even if Peter and I don't know the first thing about each other outside this place we are acquainted to the core here and that's comforting in some indefinable way.

I tease Peter now. 'Ooh,' I say, 'Doesn't he sound masterful?' But for once Peter is not willing to play such games. He goes back to my feet and washes the toes a little less gently.

'Is that your son?' he asks. 'Hasn't he any manners. Can't he read? There is a notice.'

'He was probably distracted,' I say. 'It's hard for him coming here.' Saying it, I remember my own visits to my dying old dad and realise perhaps for the first time just how stressful my son must find visiting me.

Peter is not willing to be convinced. He's pulling the bedclothes up now. 'Or perhaps you didn't teach him enough manners.'

I object to this. 'I'm not sure it's the time or place to criticise my childcare,' I say coldly.

When Peter does not respond – he's adjusting my catheter again – I add, 'Bringing children up is the hardest thing in the world. As you may find out.'

Peter still says nothing. He tucks me in now, harder than is quite comfortable. He neither looks nor sounds apologetic but he does adjust the covers quite lovingly and gently when I complain. Then he gathers up his bits and pieces, jerks back the curtain on the door window and goes out, looking back as he does so to say 'I'm on early shift tomorrow. I'll see you then. Sleep well.'

'I'll try,' I say. Most likely he doesn't hear.

'Funny-looking bloke: and bossy.' my son says when he comes back and settles himself down. He looks tired. 'Do you mind having a male nurse?

'I prefer him,' I say. 'Usually I do. I ask for him. Are you alright?'

'Just overworked as usual.'

'You still shouldn't have barged in like that.'

'Sorry. I didn't see the sign.'

'Your eldest rang,' he added then, after a brief pause. He always did call his elder sister 'your eldest' in that ironic way. They had never got on – the least intelligent of my children my elder daughter was also the one most like their father and most unlike me. She not only blamed and went on blaming me for my break-up with him, she demanded to go and live with her father and his new wife after our divorce. But he – or they - wouldn't have it. Such further rejection – she always accused me of rejecting her in non-specific ways– soured things even more between us: rather than being angry with her father she blamed me for this too. The way she'd thrown herself into housework and full-time motherhood, I'd always taken -in part – as a reproach.

'What did she want?' I ask.

'She wanted to know if you were in a fit state for the kids to see. I think she wants to bring them in again.'

'Why didn't she ring me?' I ask.

'You know her. Why is she always so difficult?'

At my attempts to defend her, reminding him of her father's rejection and so forth, he just sighs and says, ironically, 'Yeah, well, double whammy, the poor bitch.'

'You've got to get on with her once I'm dead. You're joint executors of my will. What did you tell her?'

'I said you're still alive, you wouldn't give your grandchildren nightmares any more than you did last time they came. Why do you keep talking about dying?' he suddenly bursts out.

'Because I am dying. And there's not a lot I can do about it,' I say soberly. 'Doesn't this whole room tell you that anyway?'

'That doesn't mean you have to rub it in.'

'And, as a matter of interest, why don't you bring your own boys in to see me again?' (I'd nearly said 'to see their dying grandmother,' but checked myself, just in time.)

'You know Mercedes. Her phobias. She thinks cancer is catching.'

'She isn't like most Spanish then. They look after their relations in hospital.' (It's not only my elder daughter and I have widened our family gene pool.)

'Mercedes as you know isn't that sort of Spanish,' my son says gloomily. It always feels odd to me to have a daughter-in-law who sounds like an expensive car. Indeed in some ways it feels almost odder to have a Spanish daughter-in-law than to have a son-in-law who is the son of an African King –of the two she appears more foreign. My son met his wife when she was in London to improve her English, working in a café, and ended up marrying her because she got pregnant: being Catholic she refused to have an abortion. He was, is, decent like that. Besides Mercedes was, is, very beautiful and the marriage seemed to work well enough at the start. I am not so sure now. But maybe his stress is more to do with me: maybe what weighs on him is seeing me so ill and helpless and in pain, though I try to hide the worst of it from my family.

I am tired, so tired. Maybe it would be good, I think, to cease just now, with no pain. At this moment, briefly, there is almost no pain. But instead I fall asleep. When I wake again, much later, my son has gone, the only sign of him the wrapping of a Mars bar on the chair on which he sat. I do wonder, in passing, what he sees in something so old-hat and so unhealthy – I'd saved up to buy Mars Bars myself - from Mrs Cosgrave's - all those years ago. At same time I gaze at the gilded paper fondly, as if it had wrapped him.

I only ever had two Jewish lovers. The second I met through my job; he was an exiled Israeli, an embittered journalist, who had taken part in the Yom Kippur war and written such diatribes against Israel and its policy thereafter, that he'd been forced to flee. In England he'd married an Englishwoman he did not much like purely in order to get himself residency and a work permit. All facts which she, with romantic notions about Jewishness in general and Israelis in particular, ignored, until it was too late for her to draw back. Now they lived detached and resentful lives in a flat in Enfield, while he taught history at a local comprehensive school and in his spare time wrote histories of Israel, its founding, its subsequent progress, its treatment of its Arab minorities. One of these landed on my desk: followed not long after by the man himself, his grey hair flowing out from beneath a little tweed hat, his eyes bitter, mournful, set deep and dark in a prematurely lined face. It was not a bad book this one, less of a diatribe than the others and, following on the election of the first right-wing government in Israel, I thought some of the implications he discussed might find an audience among middle eastern specialists. It helped that he could also write.

  My marriage to the father of my children had only recently ended. I was lonely and missing sex. Perhaps, too, Yitsaak's very Jewishness attracted me, no less than it had attracted his wretched wife: I'd been thinking longingly and painfully of my first Jewish lover. And perhaps I was attracted by the little tweed hat, as well as by his mournfulness, ignoring the bitter and dangerous edge that made his eyes withdraw so deep into their sockets, that sharpened his nose and voice. When he told me his age, my guess out by more than a decade I found he was younger than my first Jewish love, by quite a bit.

  I took him out to lunch to discuss his book. We drank a bottle of wine between us and afterwards he made a pass at me: I did not resist. We ended up renting a room in a hotel for the afternoon, an outcome that seemed sleazy even then – it wasn't a salubrious hotel. What this made quite clear was how desperate I was for sex. When we lay on the rather lumpy bed afterwards, he said. 'I think you must be Jewish. Are you sure you're not?' Each time he raised it this question, which he did at every meeting, I denied it: denied it even more vehemently after hearing the fates of many members of his Lithuanian family during the holocaust – the parts of it that had not emigrated to Israel like his parents, or anywhere else for that matter. There were enough problems in my family past: why should I want to add anything so much more appalling? My father was French I explained, not adding that I did not know him. Apart from which I swore that my antecedents were pure Anglo-Saxon – give or take the odd bit of French, Spanish, Scottish: my family like most English families was a bit of a mixture – every time the matter came up.

This lover's whole conversation it seemed to me consisted of horror-stories: in which someone – German – Polish – Israeli - was doing something unspeakable to someone – or some group – or some multitude of others.

The affair culminated one winter afternoon on Hampstead Heath, near where I was living at the time in a borrowed flat, while I tried to sort out new arrangements as a single parent. After we had walked about for a while in a melancholy way, he told me he wanted to confess some appalling things *he'd* done in the wars he'd taken part in as an Israeli solder. It was foggy that day, you couldn't see more than one tree ahead in the scrubby grove where we ended up; drops of water hung from branches, it was like a scene from a Fellini film I thought as, astonished, I watched him throw himself down onto a fallen branch, cover his eyes with both hands and burst into tears, a preliminary to his confession. It would take a long time, he wept, would I mind listening to him, he had to let it all out at last?

I did mind. Mother confessor was not how I saw myself; I was also increasingly uncomfortable with Yitzaak's almost vicious anti-Israeli stance, his persecution complex. At one time he told me that Mossad had him in their sights, something I did not believe: by now I knew all too well what a self-dramatist he was. That did make the sex very interesting sometimes, but it didn't presage a good long-term relationship: fortunately this wasn't on offer. I also knew he was duplicitous - hearing how he talked about his wife, I was not going to fall for any of it. But he took great offence at my unwillingness to listen to him, especially when he'd let me see him weep and we did not meet again after that day. Though I missed the sex, I really did not like him very much, I realised, and I handed the book to someone else to edit, which I daresay added to his persecution complex, a complex that now included me as deceiving bitch, not to say anti-Semitic villainess.

From then on I avoided anyone who could remind me of my great love. In particular I avoided anyone Jewish: this had nothing to do with anti-Semitism but everything to do with my own confused history.

My great love then: what can I say about that? About him? Reluctant as I am, I must face it all again. The Ancient Mariner could not get away without telling every part of his story, any more than his listener can avoid hearing every part: and nor can I.

Let's start with the obvious bit: that my love was quite a bit younger than my father, but quite a bit older than me.

(Which sets me to thinking not only about him, but also about my father – the one who brought me up – altogether an easier subject. Thus I keep seeing, even hearing, even smelling, all the those things that I particularly associated with him; from the silky run of his handkerchiefs through my fingers in the little dressing-room just off his bedroom (does anyone have a dressing-room these days I wonder?) to the stropping of his razor, which sounded through the house like the call of some demented bird, when he had finished shaving. Clearly he used a cutthroat one, unlike any of my husbands or lovers; but I don't think I ever saw the thing itself. My father was always coy about his toilet: raid his handkerchief drawer as I might, I never dared look into the little bathroom cabinet where he stowed his medicines, his shaving stuff. In any case, I think he kept it locked.

There were other things about my father I took for granted as a child, but became ever more irritated by as I grew up: the speed with which he ate, cleaning his plate, almost before I'd got to mine: the way he put a little heap of salt on the rim and dipped every forkful into it before putting it in his mouth. 'Dad,' I used to protest, 'why don't you taste the food first – there might be enough salt already?' But he never took any notice. Any more than he took any notice of my protests when he ladled sugar onto whatever pudding I set in front of him. It wasn't good for him of course: but given that he lived into his nineties, unlike my real father, it didn't, seemingly, do him that much harm. The ailment that is killing me at a much younger age did not come from his and my mother's side of the family, a notably long-lived one. Though I now know what family to blame, the knowledge came far to late to save me; some kind of punishment, I suppose.

The affair itself now: it started in a seamy enough, not to say all too commonplace way: professor seduces student. Well, kind of. I wasn't his student and he wasn't a professor at this university. But

156

he had taken a sabbatical from the university of California, having been awarded a visiting professorship, entailing a series of public lectures, under the auspices of Isaiah Berlin, who, I think, was a friend of his - both were, in very different ways, historians of political thought, as well as exiles, of a sort: they'd both escaped Hitler, for sure. When I heard that the visiting professor was as good a lecturer as Berlin and maybe better, I persuaded a friend who belonged to the college philosophical society that had invited the eminent visitor to give another, private lecture (a male friend, of course, but not boyfriend exactly; I didn't fancy him in the slightest though I think he may have fancied me) to sneak me in.

I've forgotten which college lecture room was commandeered for the evening. Nor can I remember what I thought, exactly, when I first saw the visiting professor. I know I didn't see him as old – or even wonder what age he was. He was one of those ageless men, not very tall, not fat, but sturdy, with a head of thick black hair, showing not a hint of grey. His eyes as far as I could see – he wore thick spectacles – were very dark: his eyebrows bushy and curiously peaked like the gables of a house – or like a circumflex on a letter of the alphabet. His features, quite without English diffusiveness, were very decided, as if carved. His nose was not especially big, nor hooked, but announced itself clearly. His voice was neither deep nor high, his accent ranged between American and German. He smiled a lot while he was speaking, to himself rather than his listeners, it seemed to me. I don't remember a word of what he said. I daresay he mentioned Hobbes and Machiavelli, the two bookends, as it were, of his political thought, but I can't be sure even of that. I do know that I was dazzled and that a question instantly came to me – what exactly is also gone from my memory - I doubt if it mattered much. But I did eventually manage to ask this question and he looked across at me and smiled and said. 'That's much too complicated to answer briefly, my dear. Why don't you come and talk to me about it afterwards?'

His English might have been idiomatic, despite his distinctive accent. But his request was predictable not to say cheesy. How many lecturers had I observed leering at pretty girls during question time after their lectures and saying just that, as if pretty girls were one perk of the job and included in the payment.

I would have scowled and shaken my head had anyone else made the suggestion. I can't claim never to have been flattered by such things when I was as young as that and still reluctant to appear too keen. But I was also no fool: I was not easily deceived by men, let alone by myself.

I scowled that time. But I didn't shake my head, or only slightly. And when he came down off the platform afterward I joined the cluster of people round him, though making sure to lurk at the back ready to flee on the instant, not sure if I wanted to be there or not.

At first he didn't appear to notice my presence, which may have reassured or equally may have disappointed me. He answered one query or another, greeted this person as an old friend with a very un-English – at that time – hug, touched that one on the shoulder, patted another's back, kissed one woman on the cheek, a second on both cheeks, shook hands with someone introduced to him by one or other of these. I watched with interest the way he worked his pack – laughing out loud there, giving a wink here, his kinked eyebrows raised till they were more like circumflexes than ever. He charmed everyone, seemingly – or most people, at least - with a performance – for it was a performance – that fascinated me. I'm not sure whether I liked him for it. Probably I liked him less: even while fascinated the more.

I was distracted after a while by the boy who'd smuggled me in. I was talking to him and a friend of his, my back to the crowd round the professor, when I felt a touch on my shoulder and turned to find the professor himself, not exactly smiling, just raising those eyebrows at me. I could see his eyes now behind the thick spectacles. They were very deep and dark – the most attractive thing about him. He was not exactly handsome at close quarters, this man, a bit froglike to be precise. But his eyes were beautiful, I noted: not knowing that I was never to see him with such clarity and distance again.

'Your question?' he was asking, encouragingly.

'My question?' I'd almost forgotten it by now: my hands curling and uncurling at my sides, my cheeks heating, I felt too hot in my polo-necked sweater. But somehow I pulled myself together, dredged up the question, stammered it out. He actually looked interested. Maybe he was just pretending. 'How much have you read in this area?' he asked.

'Not much,' I said.

'Ah well. Innocence sometimes produces the best questions. No preconceptions, you see,' he said turning to his neighbour. 'This young lady has observed something clearly that most of us are too well-read to be aware of.'

I still couldn't be sure he wasn't mocking me. I *was* sure I was being patronised. I scowled I think. And he laughed into my face and then proceeded to answer the question as if it was indeed serious. Though I can't remember the answer –if it was one- I do remembering thinking it was more like a rephrasing of my question than an answer.

'You're just asking my question in another way,' I dared accuse him.

'It's the questions that matter more,' he said. It seemed to me even then something of a cliché, though I've realised as I've grown older that it is true just the same. Yet this doesn't stop me wanting answers even now.

Some of those with him were murmuring in his ear. He was looking at this watch. 'I have to go to dinner. But I don't think we've quite finished this discussion,' he said. 'Do you have a phone number?'

'No,' I said. And then: 'Yes. There's a phone at my digs we're allowed to use.'

He had a diary out, was extracting a little gold pencil. 'Give it me,' he said. So I did. When I'd finished and he'd written the number down – adding the name 'Jo', when he'd demanded and got it - he replaced the little pen in the binding of the diary, opened his jacket, carefully, almost pedantically, replaced them in the inner pocket, patting it then to see they were safely stowed. His left hand stayed on his lapel for a minute, while he glanced – merely glanced - straight into my eyes. Then he moved the hand down, picked up mine and kissed it, only briefly, though he continued to hold it a moment longer, gazing down it with an expression impossible to gauge. 'Ah what a hand,' he said. 'You have a hand, young woman, that reminds me of the Virgin Mary.'

It was shocking somehow. It didn't sound like a compliment in the least. I gasped, and then he was gone, and I was left looking after him my mouth open, my cheeks ever more aflame.

'Wow', said my friend laughing. 'You'd better watch out. He's known for breakfasting on virgins, that one. Well he looks as if he is.'

'I'm not a virgin,' I said. And I walked away, hot all over, furious suddenly, barely needing the coat I threw on though it was cold outside, one of the first cold nights of autumn. Then, the heat fading, I started to shiver and went on shivering all the way home to North Oxford: if you could call my digs, my room there, home, with its lofty ceiling, mean gas meter and meaner gas fire, with its flaking walls which my posters could not cover enough to hide their condition. This year I had added a Salvador Dali that I hated but could not take my eyes off: the one of the crucified floating Christ, head downwards, hurtling out of the canvas towards me and making me feel quite dizzy. But the landlady was a don's widow, droopy-haired and droopy-bosomed whose only concern was that her tenants were nice to her equally droopy, hair-shedding dog, did not complain about her boring food and paid their rent on time. In other words, despite the assumptions of my father about respectable dons' widows, she did not see herself as in loco parentis like my last year's landlady: she handed out keys to us all and imposed no curfew times. This would turn out useful over the next few weeks: I don't think I could have spent them the way I did had I lived in the same place as the year before.

I wasn't sure if the professor would ring or not. But the phone-call came at breakfast. We heard it from the dining-room, and one of my fellow lodgers answered, hoping it would be her boyfriend: I did not expect it to be for me.

'A man,' she said, in a disappointed voice, 'For Jo. With a funny accent.'

I turned away hoping they could not see my face – everyone was looking at me curiously - and hurried out to the freezing hall with its tiled floor. The pay phone was attached to the wall by the front door. Close enough to get all the draughts coming from under and over, it did not invite long conversations, and nor did we have one now.

'Yes?' I said. I heard my voice shaking, to my annoyance.

'Do you eat lunch?' asked the voice with the funny accent.

'When I can afford it. We're only on part board here.'

'You can afford it today. Do you know the Elizabeth?'

'Yes,' I said astonished. 'But I've never been there.' The Elizabeth was the one really expensive restaurant in Oxford, the one only those with very rich boyfriends ever got invited to.

'Then that's where you're going. See you at one o'clock.'

'That *is* Professor Rubenstein?' I asked, astonished.

'Who else? How many admirers do you have, little girl?'

I was so annoyed by this, I was ready to say I was busy at lunchtime, but before I could get the words out, he'd put the phone down. Wasn't he so bloody pleased with himself? I thought. The *bastard.* Serves him right if I stood him up. But of course I had no intention of doing that. I even went back into the dining room looking smug, or so my fellow lodgers told me when I refused to tell them who the man with the funny accent was.

It was the best meal I had ever eaten: I'd learned to recognise and like good food on my trips round Europe with my father, even though he merely ate rather than honoured food the way it is honoured now; let alone the way it was honoured here. My host seemed to enjoy the meal as much as I did. I'd let him order for me – is there anything you don't eat?' he asked. 'Oysters,' I said. 'No oysters then. Snails?' I gulped. I had never eaten snails either. But at least they came cooked. "Why not?" I said doubtfully. The arrival of the things in their shells, swimming in garlic butter, alarmed me just the same. 'However do you eat them?' I asked.

'Like this,' he said. Leaning across the table, he picked up the two-pronged fork that sat alongside the earthenware dish holding the half-dozen striped snail shells, seized one and extracted the little rubbery thing from inside. 'Open your mouth,' he said. Obediently – stunned – I did so. And began chewing, still doubtfully. He put one of his own snails in his mouth now. Then he picked up the shell and emptied its garlicky, buttery contents straight into his mouth. 'Go on,' he urged me. I did the same with my shell. And so it was, at once, I got the point of snails; the wondrous point. It wasn't long before I'd devoured my entire plateful, emptying each shell as I had the first and swabbing out the remains of the butter with my sliced baguette. How my father would have hated it, I thought. Despite our European trips, he still had not come to terms with the taste of garlic. For a moment, briefly, I despised him. Not least because he would have been horrified at the very idea of spending so much money on food: – I'd seen the prices on the menu. That this man was obviously much richer than my father was not the point. I even found myself, ashamedly wishing that *he* was my father instead – or perhaps not this man, no, not this one, definitely – but someone like him. Someone who did not only buy me such heavenly food, but who also did not say, with a fond and maddening smile when I tried to stammer out ideas of one kind and another, 'darling you're being much too highbrow for me.'

For this man I wasn't highbrow enough: barely highbrow at all. Over our drinks in the bar next door he'd already quizzed me about what I was doing in Oxford. Seemingly astonished that I wasn't yet an undergraduate, he asked what I was thinking of studying and when I said PPE or history, asked what I'd been reading.

I reeled off a mad list of books I'd picked up lately; Eliot's poetry, Teilhard de Chardin – fed me by a priest who was a friend of one of my housemates and didn't like my scepticism: Churchill's histories of England, novels by George Moore and Charles Williams, social histories by G.M Trevelyan, Tawney's Religion and the Rise of Capitalism, a volume of McCauley's history, Bertram Russells' History of Philosophy, Thomas a Kempis, Kierkegaard, John Smith's History of Virginia, Wuthering Heights, Jane Eyre so and so forth, a very eclectic list. I was omnivorous those days and read almost anything that came to hand, a lot of it from my father's shelves, more not from those– I hadn't found my particular passion Gormenghast there, nor Hobbes' Leviathan, some of which I had read, but only because I liked the prose. I did not mention Nancy Mitford or Elizabeth Bowen, let alone other writers I *had* encountered on my father's shelves - Dennis Wheatley and Agatha Christie, for instance. I did not think that this was what my escort, whom I was just about managing to call 'Nathan' by now – or 'Nate' - meant by my 'reading'.

Nathan – Nate - looked astonished by all of this. "You seemed to have read a lot,' he said. 'But none of them the right things. Except for Hobbes; whose point you appear to have missed.'

'What makes a book the right thing?' I asked.

'There needs to be some pattern some shape to your reading. I can't find any pattern here.'

'Is it your aim to educate me?' I asked. 'Or what?'

'You little English girls are something else,' he said. 'So polite. So pert. So ignorant. So innocent.'

'Not that innocent,' I said, angrily thinking of my deflowering; the episode had not yet been repeated with my Byronic young man or anyone else.

'No?' He raised an eyebrow. But before I could complain how patronising he was, we were summoned to our table. And the snails came on, and the bottle of white wine – 'Sancerre', he said 'the best': something I had to take his word for. And after the snails guinea fowl arrived, coated in a divine creamy sauce, with tiny, sweet haricot verts swimming in yet more butter laid decoratively alongside, and with sauté potatoes in a separate dish. This was followed by crêpes suzettes which had to be ordered for two and meant a big performance besides our table: lavish pourings on of brandy and Grand Marnier, the little burner emitting small blue flames inciting much bigger, blue and yellow, alcoholic flames in the pan that held our crepes.

From beginning to end of the meal I adored its choreography: the dance by men in tailcoats and bow ties, napkins hung from arms that bore dishes and bottles and plates and glasses our way. I adored watching our guinea-fowl carved with a deft and dancing silver knife, watching the haricots verts fanned out so precisely on our plates. The crêpes were the climax of the performance. It was so delightful, so absurd I wanted to applaud. I think I *did* applaud as they were set down reverently before us, swimming in their alcoholic bath. Their production both absurd and extravagant, I didn't any longer care a fig, I thought, about what it cost. I was this man's or anyone's, body and soul - wasn't I? He was filling my glass with a sweet wine now – 'Baume de Venise,' he said.

'Baume de Venise? *Really*?' I said. "While sitting at ease with my Baume de Venise…" I quoted dreamily. I was one up on him here: my escort had never before encountered Hilaire Belloc. I started to recite Harriet and the Matches, but gave up very quickly because I couldn't remember beyond the first few lines and because those I did remember seemed to baffle my companion.

I took another sip of the heavenly Baume de Venise, reminded suddenly of something my father sang sometimes, always out of tune. It was a Flanders and Swan song involving a young girl,

Madeira wine and a lascivious middle-aged man. 'Have some Madeira, m'dear,' I said and giggled. Reciting – but only in my head, I didn't want to add ideas to the ones in this man's head even if a version of them might be there already - 'The very next morning she woke up in bed with a beard in her ear-hole that tickled and said 'have some Madeira, my'dear.' Did my father see that song as a useful warning to me, I wondered? Or could he not imagine that his virtuous – he imagined – daughter would ever find herself in such a situation, sitting in an expensive restaurant across the table from a man nearly twice her age, whose intentions were probably not – how I hoped they were not by now – entirely innocent? Even if he didn't have a beard.

My companion might have read my thoughts: the way he'd begun exploring my face, his eyes as if like tongues, licking it from top to bottom. I shivered. After a moment of holding his eyes in mine, I looked away.

'Do you keep a young woman in every port?' I heard myself asking.

'Aren't you cynical, little English girl. Answer no, not exactly. But I was thinking that retiring to All Souls now wasn't altogether appropriate.'

'Probably not,' I said. 'I thought it only admitted men anyway.'

'Female guests are permitted.' he said almost primly. 'But that is not quite the point. Meet me for lunch tomorrow and I think I might have been able to solve the problem.'

'What problem?' I sighed.

He did not answer me this time. He just stared at me steadily, wiping his mouth with his napkin as he did so. If this was a seduction, it was not the least how I would have imagined it.

'How come you're not fat,' I said, 'If you always eat in places like this?' The coffee had arrived by now and along with it chocolate truffles.

'I do not always eat like this. And I do not usually drink at lunchtime, little girl.'

'Stop calling me little girl.'

'Young woman then.'

'My name is Jo,' I said.

'Jo,' he said, spinning out the word so that it sounded almost multi-syllabled and exotic.

'OK. Where do we go for lunch tomorrow?'

We went to Brown's in Oxford market: Haute Cuisine to greasy spoon in a twenty-four hour jump. Did he think I was just as easy? I dared – dare - think it wasn't quite like that. He ate shepherd's pie and overcooked cabbage off a chipped formica table with every sign of enjoyment – admittedly it looked good; if you like basic English food it always was good at Brown's. I ordered egg and chips but felt much too apprehensive – almost nauseous - to eat much of it. I could barely swallow even my cup of strong tea, though I ladled in sugar, something I never did normally; it was as if I was suffering from shock. Did I mind that my companion showed no sign of apprehension? -he even reached for my chips when he saw I wasn't eating them: I don't think I did mind. Afterwards I found it funny. 'Be my guest,' I said, handing over the bottle of ketchup. He drank tea too: there wasn't anything stronger on offer. Which was why I went to bed with the love of my life stone-cold sober, that first time: as was he. And in the Randolph Hotel no less: my about-to-be lover had taken a room there, he said, for the rest of his stay in Oxford. I blushed, I think, as he headed confidently for the mahogany reception desk while I, attempting to be invisible, stared in amazement at the staircase reaching up behind the desk, past arched gothic windows that made me think, for a moment, of the gothic windows of the House of Commons, and of my anything but gothic father: a thought that, very hastily, I pushed aside.

'I'll still have to live in All Souls officially,' my lover added, staring intently at the polished wooden wall of the lift in which we stood, still not touching, on the way up to our room. This was the only sign of awkwardness I saw in him throughout his wooing, if wooing it was. I saw no such uncertainty once we were naked, embarking on our first full sexual encounter in the lofty and fearsomely canopied four-poster bed.

'You do have hands like the Virgin Mary,' he said afterwards. He took my left hand to his mouth, kissing it much more fervently than he had that first time; even nibbling my fingers. I had to pull them away.

'Excuse me, that's *my* hand,' I protested. 'And I'm not the least virginal.'

'I had noticed, my dear. But that wasn't exactly what I meant.'
'What did you mean?'
Something about you English girls.'
'Your hair is just the colour of mine,' I said idly. 'A bit darker: perhaps.'
'Which is good. I can say it's my daughter visiting,' he said. 'If they enquire. In this hotel I don't think they ask too many questions.'
'Are we incestuous now on top of everything else? Oh what fun. Such sinfulness.'
'My first English lover was a virgin it so happens,' he said.
'Who was that then?'
'Many years ago,' he said lightly. 'Not that anything or anyone who could bother you. Besides it was not only long ago, but in another country.'
'And "is the wench dead"?'
'That I wouldn't know.'
'Gone and forgotten like all your lovers I suppose,' I said, lightly, but feeling bitter already on my own behalf and beset suddenly by a wave of terror and loss so intense it terrified me. It did not go away even when he said, very seriously.
'Gone. But not forgotten. What do you think I'm like?'
'I don't *know* what you're like,' I wailed. 'How could I know? Apart from the fact that you're randy old man,' I added, advancing my hand hesitantly towards his randy part, wanting to stir him up again but not yet used to making free with anyone's private parts apart from my own. But I did want to stir him up again, not out of my own lust, I felt none at this moment: more an attempt to banish the sudden bleakness I felt.
'Not so old: only just over forty,' he said, looking at my hand then placing it firmly where it wanted to go.

CHAPTER TWENTY-THREE

Maybe my weakness has its uses. It is a long time since the memory of my great love has seemed so sweet. What happened immediately afterwards soured things a little, of course. But it wasn't until I'd unravelled the thread leading from the Wikipedia entry to the heart of our private labyrinth, to the lies embedded in my youth, that my feelings became too complicated and difficult, my anger and remorse too intense, to allow such memories in.

But I am too tired for anger now, let alone the rest. Memory, turned blessedly and unwontedly kind, has allowed - given me back, briefly -the sweetness of those few weeks. A sweetness tinged with sadness and irony, of course: but by this time, for me, so much experience has been and gone that few memories come purely sweet.

Jenny is visiting me again this evening. I'm grateful. The Husband has a faculty meeting and having said I wouldn't mind his absence – I really thought I wouldn't mind - I find myself lonely in the unforgiving light of a gloomy spring evening.

'You must be psychic, knowing I needed you,' I tell her. Thinking with astonishment that there's scarcely been anyone in my life to whom I could have admitted such a thing.

She knows me well enough to mock, gently, an expression of such weakness. 'Oh no, you don't,' she says. 'You just wanted the TLS I've brought in.' I don't have the heart to tell her that the dense copy of most Times Literary Supplement reviews is beyond me these days. Some things she doesn't know about me any more and that is just as well.

As she settles herself down, I find myself wondering about her: about *her* loves. I know she was married once to an ex-public school lawyer whom she'd met at university in Bristol. Which of them – she the daughter of a militant trade union leader, he the son of an honourable someone or other – thought themselves slumming by embracing such a union, I don't know. I do know that the marriage was brief and had produced no children.

Over the years I've known Jen, the odd Nick or Matthew or Tom or Ed have swum into our conversations – 'Nick and I did this' –

'Matt and I did that' – but none of them seemed to be around for long and good friends as we are her love life is not something we've discussed much, any more than we've discussed mine. We are different generations after all and I am no Patty to let hints and suggestions of such aspects of my life leak out before my juniors.

So I don't know why I find myself saying now 'I've been dreaming about the love of my life.' Immediately I wish I hadn't said it. There's so much else I cannot say.

She looks startled. 'So?' she says after a minute. 'So.' And then. 'I'm not sure if I've ever had a great love. Maybe I never will. It's not that I don't like sex.'

What dying does to you, I think to myself wryly here. The word sex has never featured in any conversation of ours before, except as a passing joke.

'Good,' I say. 'I'm glad you like it. Sex. It's good – it was good for me. Once.'

'Who was your great love?' she asks me, to my surprise. I would not have expected her to be so blunt.

'He was much older than me. I was still a student,' I say. 'You know how it is. We fucked in the Randolph Hotel. But it wasn't just about seduction. He really was the love of my life. Among other things.' It sounds so corny, not to say cheesy, even as I say it, that I can hardly believe this myself and I'm sure she can't. Yet in all my desperate questionings these days about this love affair, it's a relief to admit it again, even briefly, as something so simple and sweet. A look of scepticism crosses her face, as well it might. But she knows me well enough not to question what I've said, let alone laugh at it. She does say: 'people do fall in love with their professors. Someone at uni with me fell in love with hers. I think they ended up married.'

'He wasn't my teacher,' I say. 'And he was married already.' We sit looking at each other in silence. And after a while, perhaps she feels she owes me an amorous confession, she tells me about her latest but greatest love who is trying to persuade her to live with him in New Zealand.

'Don't fall for that.' I say.

'And give up my job?' she says. 'You must be joking.' But then she adds a little mournfully. 'It is a pity he has to go so far away. This one. It really is.'

I told Jenny no lies, but she did get a very economical version of the truth. The love affair of my life was indeed conducted mainly within the walls of the Randolph Hotel and on that four-poster complete with gothic roundels and William Morris hangings. The Randolph's gothic everything – windows – ironwork – arches – fireplaces, the top of their surround kinked slightly like my lover's eyebrows –continued to remind me, whether I liked it or not – I didn't on the whole - of my father, because of the other Victorian gothic buildings, the Houses of Parliament, his place of work. I told my lover this: about my father: about my childhood, my absconded mother. I did not tell him – and don't know quite why not – that this father was not my genetic one.   Maybe it seemed like one betrayal too many.

In return – or was it in return? –he told me something of his past, much of it far more desperate than I ever cared to know. I could only be grateful it wasn't my history: what a curious thought. At the same time I was glad he did tell me; how could I have borne not to know about him? I wanted to know everything, including whether or not he was married. Inevitably, he was married. He had children too, but he did not tell me – I did not ask – their names. We left this whole subject for the moment, anyway, though inevitably it hung over us – at least it hung over me: certainly it influenced the decision I would take in due course.

He'd been making me read Machiavelli: he asked me whom I thought Machiavelli was writing for; for the prince, to tell him how to run his office, or for the prince's subjects, warning them not to trust their ruler? 'So is this telling me how to run my life, or are you just warning me what a devious bastard you are?' I asked. 'All that stuff about only *seeming* to be kind and good. You married man: seducer of young women, you. I suppose you'll never warn me either where the swift cruel stroke is coming from.'

I determined at that moment, I think, that in this case any swift cruel stroke was going to come from me. Some such would have to, in the end. 'After all you are *married*.' I heard myself wailing. But I did not tell him yet what conclusion that fact was leading me to.

I was even laughing at the time. Half-laughing. He did not laugh. 'Most men of my age are married,' he said sombrely. 'Unless they are homosexual.' I grew still more sombre myself now, envisaging pain and loss. Throughout this time of extraordinary pleasure, not to say ecstasy, there were many such bleak, black moments, coming from I don't know where, some generated by me, some by him, some by both of us. I rolled away from him now, wanting to cry. I think I did cry a little, something I never did with any other lover, my whole life after. That was his effect on me. Or maybe it was just that I was so young and cried more easily then.

'"A prince should only keep his word when it suits his purpose,"' I heard myself moaning. And then - 'did you make me read this book just to make me distrust you?'

'No.' he said. 'It's a book you should read anyway. And it also does no harm for you to learn not to trust anybody.'

A lesson I should have taken to heart, I think now, bitterly, lying on my deathbed, a span or two away from my final husband and lover. Why did it never occur me to include my father among those I should distrust, for instance? Though maybe I should have been no more or less unhappy, no more or less devastated by the truth, had I done so.

The precious sweetness I felt yesterday, remembering Nate, has abandoned me again. I wished, fervently, I had said nothing to Jenny. All this reversion to my Gothic love affair (for so I saw it as I gazed up at the dark canopy of our bed, at the fluted uprights made out of equally dark wood - sometimes I teased Nate by calling him my Dracula, whereupon he'd pretend to bite me) fills me with bitterness today. It is making me even more bad-tempered than the pain; maybe that's because the two pains, physical and emotional, seem one.

I suppose it was bound to turn like that, approaching the dangerous heart of what I've felt the need to relive. Over the past few weeks, memory, re-living the earlier past, has seemed not just what, as both Mariner and Wedding Guest, I'm bound to do, but also the best if not the only means to divert me from the painful reality of my ebbing life. But these memories, hard as I try to retreat from them, precious as they once were and seemed to be again yesterday, now have the opposite effect. Maybe the conversation with Jen – her sceptical look - has unsettled me. For how can I gauge the worth of what happened any longer, how can I know what it means now I know the truth? Bliss - or blissful pain -has turned to torture. Try as I might, I control nothing any more; the morphine takes my head where it will, ever more vividly: little flashes of memory, sensual, environmental, mental, come crowding in, twisting themselves into nightmare. And my only redress is to rage, rage against it, against everyone. Today I have even fallen out with Nurse Peter, snapping at him when he tries to turn me, telling me to leave my catheter alone, telling him he's a sadist, out to cause me pain.

He clamps his mouth and continues with his work anyway. Saying not a word more, he flounces out without any of his usual tender flourishes, which is as well, probably, because I think they would merely have annoyed – no, worse – upset me horribly. I prefer his refusal to show pity, understanding: it has even calmed me, briefly. Now I look across at the Husband, sitting in the ever more depressing sludge green armchair, the pages of the Guardian as usual scrumpled all round him and rage yet again. I'd shout if I could but don't have the strength. I *hiss*, 'Why for fuck's sake do you always have to make such a fucking mess?'

'Does it matter?' he says – not adding 'any more' but he might just as well have done.

'I'm not dead yet. When I am dead, you can do just as you like. But not till then,'

'OK,' he says mildly, and began trying to put the pages straight, making such a hopeless job of this, it infuriates me still more.

'Just take the thing and get out,' I say, and he does. And afterwards I wail, all by myself: from pain, bodily and mental – little of it – or only a little – to do with him.

Nate had a job to do in Oxford, of course and many people who wanted to see him. It limited the time we would spend in our room together - as did the two days I spent nursing a slight cold; he turned out something of a hypochondriac apart from anything else. 'I've too much to do to catch your bugs,' he said, almost querulously. 'Suit yourself,' I answered crossly. He didn't like it when my period started either. For almost a week he would only cuddle me: and when that was over the few days left to us seemed all too short, making my grief at our parting even more intense.

During our whole affair, I think, we only spent three or four nights in his room at the Randolph; mostly we made love in the afternoon. One of those afternoons was in All Souls itself, in the narrow bachelor bed with which they'd provided him, not comfortable at all. It was far from being the best encounter sexually, but probably the funniest. We found it impossible to keep from giggling.

'More Gothickry,' `I said afterwards.

'The real thing here,' he said. 'A bit too real for me I have to admit.'

'Then you should be grateful to me for keeping you away from it so much.'

'Oh but I am,' he said. 'I am.'

He had taken his glasses off, as usual. I gazed into his endless dark eyes, so deep and melancholy and beautiful, the lashes unfairly long for a mere man; I could not drag my own eyes away from them.

'Don't,' he said. 'It is all too much.'

I climbed on top of him, gazed down at those eyes still but from farther away.

'You look like the crucified Christ,' I said.

'But then he was a Jew, just like me.'

'So I've been told.'

It was Nate's Jewishness that troubled me, as a matter of fact, almost as much as his married status, his unimaginable wife, his even less imaginable children, going to school in their mid-western town, a place I could not imagine – did not want to imagine either.

Not *because* of his Jewishness as such. I wasn't the least anti-Semitic, I don't think I knew anything of English anti-Semitism then, even if I had, without realising it, absorbed some of the casual language. I'd had Jewish friends at school and not thought anything of it. He was, for me, a man like anybody else. But what did trouble me as he recounted his past was what he'd brought with him from his early life in Berlin, the city that became, as he grew up, Hitler's capital: that brutality, that pain and prejudice. Not to mention what happened afterwards, during the war, to most of his kind. All this came trailing behind him as he spoke, bringing with it every bit of the horror story that Hitler's war involved: the pedantically organised horror that extinguished much of my lover's family and many of his childhood friends. The horror that hard as it tried, had, thank god, failed to extinguish him.

'The Nazis didn't kill my mother,' he said. 'She died of cancer which may not be anti-Semitic, but is the other scourge of my family: of the women mostly. Breast cancer. She died with all of us around her bed, in the Jewish hospital. We Jews were allowed a hospital, at least. My father was the medical director: unlike other Jewish doctors he kept his job. And I'm glad my mother died before the worst got going, before Kristallnacht and all the rest of it. Even so she saw more clearly than my father did. Before she died she begged him to send us away. Which was why I went to study in Paris, pursuing Sartre, and then to Cambridge because at close quarters I did not think much of French philosophy, after all. It was also the reason my little sister was sent to England on one of the last of the Kinder transports. But my father wouldn't leave. He was a Germanophile, he loved Beethoven, Heine, all the German poets and philosophers, he was passionate about Goethe. He would not allow himself to think that Germans as a whole would allow anything so bad as things turned out. Didn't they allow him and other Jews their hospital, after all? So the Nazis got him, along with a lot of my cousins, my uncles, my aunts, and both my grandparents. He died in Auschwitz alongside the rest of them. Crucified by the myth of the master race, the superior Aryan. A myth as fake as the Gothic arches here,' he said, nodding at the window on the far side of the room.

'I'm an Aryan myself,' I said in a subdued voice. 'Aren't I? How can you love me?'

'Why do you drag it back to yourself, little solipsist? My little black-haired Anglo-Saxon,' he said tenderly. 'My little goy; my shiksa.'

'Is your wife Jewish?'

He looked away and shifted from me a little. This was not, I knew, a permitted subject. But it did not stop me asking.

'Yes,' he said.

'From Berlin too?'

'No,' he said. 'She's an American.'

'Why not an Englishwoman then? Or a Frenchwoman? From when you were in Paris?'

'I was very young then,' he said. 'And I was not in Paris long. Of course I had encounters, I used to pick up girls in the café I went to on the Left Bank. I was a lusty young man and lonely and worried about my family. It was all very natural.'

'My mother was in Paris before the war,' I said. 'That was where she got pregnant. With a Frenchman I think, judging by the way I look.'

'What a shame,' he said. 'She could have met me otherwise. I could have been your father. Was she beautiful, your mother?'

'What an incestuous idea,' I said. 'What fun.'

He frowned. 'Not fun. But interesting.'

'I suppose so,' I said. 'She was very beautiful, yes. My mother. I don't look the least like her. And anyway I think I'd rather have you as a lover than a father. Were you ever tempted to marry an Englishwoman? When you were in England?'

'Why should I have wanted to marry an Englishwoman? Your English government interned me in 1940. Before they decided I was harmless and let me out again, they interned me alongside Nazis, would you believe. No, I did not consider marrying an Englishwoman. Or staying in England once I got my degree. I did some work for your secret services after they let me out, I can't tell you what it was, even now, and as soon as the war was over, as soon as I'd established that my father was dead I gathered up my sister, put the Atlantic between us and Europe, sent her to college in New York State and finished my own education at Columbia. Do you blame me, little girl?'

'Don't call me little girl,' I said, viciously.

'If you like,' he said. While darkness – mental darkness – black as my hair – as his – and blacker - filled our room.

I turned my back on him then. Lying against him, I felt his warmth still, if warmth it was, not the reflection of the hell fire he knew about.

What did I know? What did I know about anything? My mother had run away from me, I had hidden under the stairs against bombs and heard the bombers flying overhead, I'd seen Hitler on VE day burned in effigy while I ate fishpaste sandwiches. I quivered at my innocence, my bland Englishness, the easiness of everything, as the worst of that war came back and enveloped our room. A shame not the least relieved when he said: 'Why do you always talk as if it's

174

some kind of scourge to be English and young and female? You silly brat. Can't you see how I envy you, how that's one reason I love you.' It was the first and only time he ever used the word 'love' but I was too upset just then to notice. 'I live in a land too young to have attics and cellars but that's what I like. In my once country the attics are too ruined and the cellars too dark. But in yours they just speak history. You can live in your bedroom and your sitting room and not feel disturbed by their presence or absence.'

'You mean we can afford to be smug?' I said. 'Even though we were slavers and colonialists, and did terrible enough things in our time?'

'Why do you always twist what I say?'

'Aren't you busy teaching me to think like that, to distrust everyone?'

'That's something else you are distorting. Perhaps we had better leave. Did you not say you had an essay to write?' (Throughout all this, crazily, he would not let me neglect my work, or not more than I was bound to: asking for details of this essay, that reading list. I should have been grateful, I suppose, that sex wasn't all he was teaching me. Maybe I was.)

'OK,' I said, for once almost glad of the prospect of being without him for a while. 'But I'd like a bath first. I stink.'

'Such a heavenly stink.'

'Who's being a solipsist now?' I said more kindly. 'The heavenly stink is all of you, isn't it?' (Solipsism was a word I'd learned from him, and berated myself with ever since. This hiding in my memory is solipsistic I think sometimes, as I lie dying. But then dying *is* the ultimate solipsism: there is no one else inside yours, except for you.)

The bath sweetened, not to say softened us that day. He shared it with me, of course, even then. I lay in front of him, his balls, his limp cock sagging into my buttocks, his chest hair against my back as he soaped my belly, my genitals, tenderly, carefully, my hair, damp at more than the ends, falling across his chest and shoulders. It could have led to more lovemaking: would have done had we not been so weary by now, the pair of us. Still he towelled me down so sweetly afterwards and I in my turn towelled him. When we were dry, more or less, he removed the towels from both of us and turned me round to the mirror over the washbasin. He was standing behind me, I was pressed against him the same way we had been in the bath, though horizontal then and vertical now. Again his hands were cupping my breasts, one of which is no more, the other not at all like the one he was holding; sagging not to say shrivelled. 'Yuk' I suspect, my grandchildren would say, the way children do these days. *Then* he just said 'lovely', rolling one nipple gently between the first finger and thumb of his right hand. It was very broad, his hand. It looked enormous and dark against my narrow chest, my white skin.

I don't think I have described my lover; not his nakedness, that is. He was astonishingly hairy – more than once I told him it felt like making love with a bear. (Japanese women were fascinated by his hairiness he told me another time. 'Like I said, you've a woman in every port,' I complained, a little put out.) He was also thickset; not overweight at all, but top heavy; broad shouldered, short-legged. His body reminded me, a little, of the statuesque figures painted by Picasso in his pink period: all broad, classical plasticity. Except that his body was altogether more urgent, sweaty, *hairy*. Except that, apart from moments like this he was never still or statuesque; he never stopped moving - mentally as well as physically, his hands and features shifting all the time when he spoke. He was the most active man I ever came across. Thinking about him now I wonder if it was because he did not dare be still.

His cock – I could not see it in the mirror then, only feel it rising half-heartedly against my back - was especially thick and dark; much thicker and darker than any cock I came across thereafter.

'I think a beard would suit you,' I heard myself saying now, to his face in the mirror.

'You do?' he said to my mirrored face. "Then I'll start to grow one,'

'But I'll never see it,' I said. It was the first time we had so much as mentioned what would happen once he left Oxford, but as I spoke, I knew that this was true. The moment of renewed happiness instantly turned back into yet another of our bleak moments, the kind that alternated with moments of equally intense ecstasy when I floated everywhere, mentally and physically. All my life thereafter, the bi-polar, manic depressiveness of love was something I did my best to avoid, succeeding mostly if not entirely: love, I'd decided, was too intense; it wore you out. (Maybe, then, it was being an adolescent partly wore me out. Doesn't adolescence set everyone swinging crazily between high and low? But it was not just that. Nate, too, sometimes seemed quite as worn-out by our high and low. And not just because when he wasn't fucking me he was working very hard, as I knew.)

'Maybe you won't,' he said. 'Maybe you will.' He touched, reflectively, the dark shadow round his jaw - even when he was newly shaved, it was still there. Watching his face, I reached up to touch the shadow in my turn, relishing the slight prickliness beneath my fingers.

'Do you strop your razor in the mornings the way my dad does?' I asked.

'He uses a cutthroat? Still?'

'Don't most people?'

'Mine is an electric razor,' he said.

In the bright face of the mirror we looked like two black-haired dark-eyed dolls fitted together, designed to fit together, two of a set, in world where nothing else existed. I did not recognise him – only his likeness. I did not recognise myself – only mine. The sight terrified me: I felt as if I was looking at phantoms. No worse, I was seeing something I never wanted to see. Never.

I wriggled; I squirmed– I was as if fighting my way out of his embrace, 'No' I said. And louder. 'NO! Not knowing what I was saying no to.

'No?'

'NO.'

'That sounds like an ultimatum.'

'Does it? It is then.'

I was fumbling for my clothes, hauling on my Marks and Spencer knickers. (I've never been into what people call 'lingerie' as such. And I didn't need to be with him. He wasn't interested in knickers, only in hauling them off.)

'You don't smell of me any more,' I said, trying suddenly, for my sake rather than his, to make things seem less hectic and strange. 'I don't smell of you any more. That's the problem with baths.'

He reached out for me as if he intended to remedy that complaint, but only half-heartedly, it seemed to me. I shook his hand off, trying to make the rejection more kindly than before.

'I really do have an essay to write,' I said.

All those weeks I had been beset by the words of a psalm that was the favourite of my naughty headmistress; she often had us singing it during assembly at school, and they rang through my head now to the point of blasphemous obsession. The psalm – 139 - returns to me on my deathbed, the phrases jumbled, misquoted, I don't doubt, and none of them having – or at least they should not have had -anything to do with the profane kind of love of which they keep endlessly reminding me. Oh but they do.

'Oh lord thou has searched me out and known me – thou hast fashioned me behind and before,' I'd say to my lover as we lay in bed. 'Thou knowest my down-sitting and uprising; thou understandest my thoughts long before.' (In all the hyperbole only the latter words felt like over-statement: – he – this lord – mine - did not understand my thoughts, before or after, not really, any more than I understood his.)

'If I take the wings of the morning – or descend to the uttermost parts of the sea – even there also shall thy hand lead me –if I say surely the darkness shall cover me – to thee darkness and light are both alike.' That was the last of it I remembered – or mis-remembered - at the time and it seemed to fit absolutely the extremes of sadness and ecstasy between which I – and to an extent we – kept swinging.

Lately I asked my Husband to bring a copy of the Book of Common Prayer to the hospital; I think he had a problem with finding one: but this was and is his problem not mine. As is the fact that he probably thinks this really does mean my end is near.

I open the book anyway and make him bring me my reading glasses. The psalm is there. Of course. And all the words I've quoted too, if not, as I feared, in exactly the right order. And there are other words too that I had quite forgotten: '*Thou has possessed my reins, Thou has covered me in my mother's womb.*'

Was it just all sex really that created this agony and ecstasy: that created this space in my life, a space quite unlike, quite beyond anything I ever felt ever again. Was it 'Love of my life?' Or just 'Sex of my life.' How could I tell, I thought, remembering Jen's sceptical face? I know I've never found anything to compare it with directly. Those sessions in the Randolph four-poster – and out of it – had little to do with the painful penetration on a dirty sleeping bag, the summer before. And despite some good times, nothing in retrospect has seemed like it since. This man, without a doubt, gave me my full sexual education and took me beyond school or university into the full delights of experience, a process that much as it delighted me, sometimes astonished me too, sometimes almost appalled me, prudish little English girl that I still was. But oh the sensations: oh the total, unmistakeable if often messy ecstasy.

    Was it just about sex for him? How could I know? I knew him a good deal less than I knew myself – hardly at all in fact - and I cannot even answer for myself, especially now, given the implications that have become so very clear.

    'Sex is like eating snails,' I said to him once. 'Little chewy bits and then the heavenly butter, the garlic in your mouth and down your throat.' He looked taken aback at first. And then he roared with laughter. And always after – often anyway – the invitation to go to bed tended to involve the mention of the word 'snails'.

    One thing was certain; after this I was never shy of any man's body, never again.

    The fusty smell of his armpits.

The way he'd say, without preamble, let's fuck. Or want another fuck Jo? Using the word 'fuck' naturally, in exactly its proper meaning.

    (That did give me the odd, shocked frisson: my father told me off for using words as harmless as 'fart'. Though I did hear him say 'bugger' once when he thought I wasn't in earshot - not that I knew what 'bugger' meant - I never heard him say 'fuck', in any sense. I heard the word first – together with its meaning – at boarding school, from an American girl, far more knowing than any of my nice English friends. I did not understand all the mechanics straight off: my friend was vague on detail and I was too appalled to press her. What I did get was that this was not a word to be used in polite company, if at all. The way Nate threw it about so tenderly and so casually took me aback. Given the tenderness, though, it wasn't long before my shock flew straight out of the Randolph's arched Gothic window and never flew back in. Once or twice I even managed to say 'fuck' - in the literal sense - myself.)

His sweat running down me indistinguishable from mine.

The grating of his stubble upon my cheek,

The taste of his cock – this, of course, one of the chewy bits. Very gently chewy.

The moment of entry, feeling myself taken up and filled.

And this – the sweetest comment about sexual love that I've ever been given by a lover: he held me very gently at the end of one of our most intense sessions, and said, very softly: 'making love to you is at the same time so exciting – and so peaceful.' Though I don't think I appreciated at the time how perfect that was, I came to understand it thereafter. Nor have I ever repeated the words to any other lover, no matter how loved. I hope – I dare suspect - but how can I know? –that my professor, too, had kept this observation for me.

All these things keep coming back to me in my morphine-filled half-life and there's nothing I can do about it except groan and press my little morphine trigger.
I should not, must not, think any of this. It is obscene. It is whether I like it or not. It brings out the yellow flags and waves them – 'unclean, unclean.'

The last time we were together, he made me walk all the way upstairs, from the bottom of the Randolph to the top. I saw every little arched windows with their stone supports, with their little pieces of coloured glass, reminding me of the windows in the Stranger's dining-room: I noted every curlicue of the iron railings under each wooden balustrade, the carved finials topping newel posts at each turn of a landing. I thought of my father; of the war-making-and-ending politicians who surrounded him. I thought of Berlin and Wagner and concentration camps. I gasped at the pressure of my lover on my arm knowing what we'd do to one another in the course of saying goodbye.

Now in my head, almost, I hear the ominous notes of Gotterdammerung. Everything, all of us, going up in flames. Oh God you idiot woman, it's hysteria to think like that. But why not? Damn it I'm dying after all. I can be as hysterical as I like. The flames of hell are approaching – how lucky I don't believe in an after life. The flames are here already, anyway, fleshly. Come, morphine zapper, come. You're all that I have left.

It took me years to see that Nate was a man just like any other. Sex – wondrous perfect sex – does so distort your thinking: particularly when you never see the man again.

Though I did see him, once, years later; I hid at the back of a lecture room at the LSE while he delivered a public lecture. But I doubt he'd have recognised me, any more than I really recognised him. The eyebrows bristled so by now so that they'd lost their shape, the dark eyes were faded and sunk into their sockets, the lids more significant from a distance than the eyes. His skin was yellow. His belly sagged. He was already suffering from the illness that killed him. But he did not evoke in me the least tenderness, only respect for his lecturing skills, for what he had to say, though I'm ashamed to admit that as usual I do not remember a word of it (what I do remember is that his accent, that strange mix of German, English and American remained the very accent in which he used to ask me, tenderly, if I'd like another fuck.)

Up till that final encounter I'd kept him in some sense a mythical being, no less mythical than a latter day Zeus. When Zeus descended in human form on some poor Semele or other he seemed just as sweaty, hairy, heavy, juicy, I daresay, as my lover seemed to me through those few weeks he spent invading my willing body.

Not that I got that many erupting male juices, not from this lover. He was careful to use what my generation called *French Letters*, a much sexier term it seems to me than the more medical 'condom' of today. It only slipped off the once – but it was not long after my period had finished, and knowing that he said, not to worry, I should be alright. So I didn't think anything of it, till later.

He did once squeeze the contents of one floppy rubber tube onto my belly. He held his fingers to my nose so I could smell for myself what it was like, and then, very tenderly, he rubbed the rest across my flesh, like body lotion; an action I remembered with a bitter pang, hearing years later Bob Marley's song, *Guava Jelly*. 'Come rub it on your belly…' – thinking of my lover getting there first. A pity it didn't smell like guava jelly though. It wasn't a scent I've ever cared for much. It was like the scent that comes off a certain kind of tree – lime trees I think – in early summer, a scent that though it disgusted me in some ways, also reminded me of that unutterably tender moment: of my great love.

So we said goodbye. And it was I who insisted that this was the end of it: that, given the circumstances, we should never try to make contact again. When he protested – as he did - I went into deadpan mode, the first and only time I ever did with him. *No, I could not bear snatched moments during one or other visit. I did not want to be the girl in this particular port, assuming he had others elsewhere -I was cynical enough still to assume he had. I wanted to remember all this as perfect, did not want it going on, all too messily. He had a wife didn't he and children who needed him. He should stick with that.*

He tried to argue with me still, calling me all sorts of names in the process. He argued with me for a long time, but not for long enough, I thought, suspicious about everything. I said my fervent goodbyes in our gothic bedroom underneath the gold and green William Morris canopy and that was it, my steadfastness surprising even me: but I could not have cried even had wanted to. He said that my lack of tears may have meant, perhaps, that I wasn't the little girl he'd l assumed, not any longer, even though my hands still looked, to him, as if they belonged to the Virgin Mary.

'How many other men will they mislead?' he asked.

'That will be none of your business,' I said. 'But I promise not to say to anyone that making love with them is like eating snails.'

'I suppose that's a comfort.'

'If you like,' I said. But it did not comfort me.

And then he was gone.

I thought of him endlessly of course. I did cry then. I grieved. But it all died down in due course, as it was bound to. Had things been the way they are now, I daresay I would not have been able to resist Googling him, to find out how and where he was. But I didn't have such an option then and I'm glad: this was one itch didn't need more scratching than I could help. Had I been less ignorant of his doings maybe I would not have been able to separate myself as fully as I did, surrounding myself with protections of one kind and another, protections that included in the beginning work for exams, exams I passed brilliantly by my standards.

I did not after all embark on a degree. Fleeing Oxford, I took the job in publishing, as a secretary, in theory, but actually as not much more than a typist at first, the job from which I made my meteoric – pretty meteoric - rise. I completed the process by getting married just as my father had always hoped, marriage my ultimate protection, my insurance against the wild swings of illicit love, not to say passion, past and, future. And no, I wasn't in any way 'wise beyond my years'. (It was the way the somewhat startled Nate described me the first time I turned down his suggestions for our keeping in touch: a phrase he qualified, a little later, by calling me an obstinate little nebbish, which didn't wound the way it was most likely meant to, because I didn't know what a nebbish was.) I was just plain terrified: not to say obstinate. I wanted to protect myself forever against the pain of being left by someone I loved and whom I thought loved me. Occasional meetings with such a person was not an option - what would be the point of mere smidgens of pleasure in exchange for a great deal of pain? (I always had been good at deferring or resisting treats; in my youth, in the days of rationing, that was mainly to do with chocolate. I wanted all or nothing even then.)

My rebound of a marriage, to the husband with beautiful cheekbones, proved, I daresay, that I was a good deal less grown-up than I'd thought. I of all people should have known better than to think that, for me, this was the best possible form of protection: look at my mother. Perhaps at heart I was still the little girl my lover claimed when he wasn't accusing me of being too grown-up for my own – or his - good: or when he wasn't calling me a nebbish – or even a word he came up with later, a little 'schnook'.

CHAPTER TWENTY-FOUR

I am alone in here just now and as comfortable as I ever am or can be. The blossom outside the window has gone – the tree is in light leaf now, the clouds slipping quietly past: benign clouds today: unlike my disease. Two pigeons sit in the sun, edging towards each other then edging away. Some kind of ritual I suppose, the kind of rituals that I remember in human terms but which have gone for me forever – not that this feels much loss any more; unlike everything else.

I turn my head, see the green plastic 'easy' chair, and am overcome suddenly by the memory of another chair, my father's battered leather one, one of those chairs that like a pair of old boots had developed its own personality, with its sagging arms, splayed legs, awkward castors, wings that embraced you. A faded red velvet cushion edged in frayed pink braid sat on it always, its clothing, dented more often than not by my father's back. As a child I saw the whole thing as animal, a creature that could get up and walk, that could even speak. My father was so attached to it that it went with him to his nursing home, though the carers did insist on a clean new linen cover. God knows where the chair is now - on some dump probably.

I loved the smell of that chair, between leather and tobacco: it was, to me, my father's smell. I used to creep up behind it and kiss his bald patch over and over until he reached up, grabbed me and put me on his lap – at least he did when I was little enough to hold. Thinking of this now, my anger abates, I tell myself fiercely, yet peaceably too, lovingly, that this man– no, *he* –this man is far too impersonal a term - was my real father, no matter what. What did genes have to do with it? Nothing. And for a moment my feelings emerge from the great black hole into which like light in the universe everything I knew, every certainty I believed in, had for a while been irrevocably sucked: overturning all my sense, my rationality, my disbelief.

In that moment of peace I fall asleep. And when I wake, late, I find The Husband inhabiting the impersonal green chair, reading his paper, tidily for once – he is still on the front page - and I am not angry with him either, reaching out my hand the moment he notices my eyes are open, that I am looking at him. He rises, takes it, leans, kisses my dry lips and then, very gently moistens them for me, the way he has learned to do.

'OK?' he asks.

'Better than yesterday,' I say. 'You know.'

So, long ago I said goodbye to my love and I grieved, mightily. But I also drowned, more happily in erotic memory, evoking each embrace, caress and willing entry, one after another, night after night. Did I wish I hadn't despatched him so forthrightly? Of course I did; sometimes I wanted to call him back, keeping under my pillow the number he had insisted on giving me, despite my protests, and which I had sworn to tear up and throw away, but still couldn't quite manage to. It was just as well mobile phones did not exist in those days for he'd given me a London number too – a message on that would always get to him, he said, even back home in the States. He would answer as soon, as best he could. But all I had then was the pay phone in the hall of my digs, making resistance that much easier.

Had he been able to find me I sometimes wondered, would it have been a different matter? Maybe not. But he could not have found me. I had never told him my surname. I'd not even told him that Jo was a nickname; or that it was short for Jane Ophelia. He made the assumption once that it was short for Josephine (this was after I'd said I identified with Jo in Little Women, the author of which was connected to Emerson, a philosopher whom Nate did not admire) and for some reason I'd let that pass. If I had told him about the 'Ophelia' might a connection have been made? Maybe? Or maybe not. Most likely not. Once he'd said. 'An English girlfriend told me I was like her Hamlet. It put me off her rather.'

'You're too old now.' I said, more reluctant than ever to announce my real names. 'Did you see your father's ghost? Did you drive your Ophelia mad? What put you off?'

'I don't think I drove her mad. She was much too English, that one, far too English to believe she was an Ophelia at heart.'

'Just like me,' I said: adding, for some reason, 'Ophelia? Goodnight. Bloody well goodnight.'

As time went on, erotic memory began to be subsumed by something else: something that did have me on the brink of using that number, payphone or not. Somehow I held off till I was due home for Christmas. An hour after arriving at the house alongside the church, I slipped across the Green to find Patty.

'What's up?' she asked, after embracing me – she was holding me away from her now, looking straight into my face; I daresay she could feel me trembling too.

I hardly knew how to start – we were so reticent in those days such things, such words were hard to get out, even to someone as unshockable as Patty.

'I haven't had the curse. For two months,' I managed at last. 'And I feel sick; quite a lot.'

'Oh dear,' she said. 'I see. What can you have been up to? Well I did advise you not to keep your virginity too long. But that didn't mean not taking precautions.'

'We *did*,' I said, my voice rising indignantly. 'But the thing slipped off. I'd only just finished my curse then, he said it should be alright. I didn't chase him by the way,' I added, angrily. 'It was rather the other way about.'

'I'm glad to hear it,' said Patty, equally sharply: at this point, such sharpness was a relief. 'Well I suppose the first thing is to find out if you are pregnant or just so anxious that your curse stopped. It can happen. I know. It happened to me once or twice when I was your age.'

I had I realised taken one step into a deeper intimacy with her; never so open with me before, she was talking as one woman to another - *oh dear the perils we women face, engaging in illicit sex* - rather than as an older woman advising an honorary daughter, the way it had always been before. At that moment this wasn't something I appreciated, even if I noticed it. I merely grabbed at the vain hope that my lack of bleeding was for neurotic rather than physiological reasons. But I knew it wasn't.

'But if you *are* pregnant, what do you want?' Patty continued. 'Do you want to keep it – after all your mother kept *you*.'

I closed my eyes, feeling faint at the possibility. 'But my father married her.' I said. 'There's no one wants to marry me. Or that I want to marry, come to that.' Which was a lie: I'd have married Nate at once, had he not been married already.

'What about the father?' Patty was asking.

I shook my head, numbly. 'Not possible,' I said. 'Out of the question.' I almost shrieked at this point.

Patty looked at me, shaking her head. 'Well there's always adoption... on the other hand - you *could* keep it. I'd help. Your father would, I'm sure. He helped your mother.'

'And marry him too, like her? What would the neighbours think?' I said primly. Not that I cared. But I thought *he* might, sooner or later.

'To hell with that,' said Patty. 'But let's find out where you are before making any decisions.'

I was numb by now. In voicing my fears I had not expected such immediate practical discussion. In my head I'd kept everything vague, ignoring the far from vague operations of my body, hoping that what they were telling me would evaporate in due course. And now here I was talking about giving birth, raising a child. Or not raising a child: or not giving birth. How could it have come to this? And how could Patty be so cool and collected, so sensible about it all?

She had a gynaecologist in Harley Street. Of course she did. Patty *would* have gynaecologist in Harley Street I thought, sourly, angrier with her by the minute: I had expected her to reassure me, not plunge me into a world of probabilities rather than possibilities, all of them involving medical personnel. I was even more angry – if not horrified – when she hinted that this gynaecologist had access to services quite illegal in those days, yet available dangerously to the poor, in back streets, and less dangerously to rich women, like Patty, in discreet clinics meant nominally for conditions other than unwanted pregnancy. I barely knew what abortion was then and when she did make clear what she was getting at, the idea disgusted me.

No, I thought; and again no, no, no, when the gynaecologist himself raised the issue, having established that I was indeed pregnant; getting on for three months, he said. Meaning that the decision would have to be made very soon.

Patty took me away to consider the matter. And at first she seemed sympathetic to my horror at the prospect of doing away with the little thing growing inside me, the offspring of my lover and myself. 'I'll help you,' she said. 'Or there's always adoption; if you must.'

I didn't want that either. And in my state of emotional and hormonal disturbance, feeling more nauseous than ever, I was sufficiently besides myself to confess to Patty not only that my lover was married but who he was. 'I want his baby so much,' I wailed. 'But I don't want it either? What am I to do?'

Patty fell silent for a minute: very silent. 'You have a lot to think about,' she said, at last.

After a while she added. 'I don't know. 'Maybe on reflection an abortion *would* be the best idea. For you and the baby. Maybe,' she said - this seemed like an attempt to shore up her argument – 'Maybe it *would* be better for your father and the baby and you.'

'Would it?' I said, both appalled and broken-hearted, realising how desperately I needed Patty's support for whatever I did.

'Probably,' she said. And hugged me almost as desperately as I'd hugged her, shaking her head.

'Life,' she said. 'What a bugger. I'm so sorry, darling.'

And then she said. 'I'll pay for it all of course. Your father need never know.'

What a blessing it was I think now, cynically -what a blessing it is – was – to have had a rich friend. Suppose I hadn't? Whatever then? What would my life have been like? Patty had not appeared to put pressure on me. Yet, subtly, carefully, she did. In due course, barely knowing how I had arrived there, I'd found myself, anaesthetized on a surgical table having a legal – supposedly- D and C, another medical term I'd encountered for the first time, which just happened, also, to encounter and remove a viable foetus. I emerged, pale, weeping and bleeding, very sore in cunt and belly. But that was that. Patty explained to my father that I'd confessed a menstrual problem; that she had taken me to see her own gynaecologist who'd recommended this procedure – the D and C so called. He accepted every word of the story. 'All women's stuff,' he said, smiling at me benignly –patronisingly, I thought, but was far too weak to protest. 'Not my cricket bag at all. What a good thing you can talk to Patty. I'll leave it to you and her.'

It helped that Patty was a doctor's wife, I think, and that my father was a man who believed in doctors: he assumed of course that Patty would have sought advice from her husband; (though of course she had not; this doctor kept clear of Patty's doings, as always.) He even tried to insist on paying for what he called 'the procedure', but Patty wouldn't hear of it, and diverted him very efficiently – she knew him well – by threatening to go into gynaecological detail. 'She's a rich woman,' he said to me later, 'if she wants to be so generous….. You're a kind of daughter to her after all – it isn't as if she has a daughter of her own'. What an innocent he was. Perhaps I realised then exactly how innocent: I held it against him, just a little.

I was grateful to Patty: very grateful: I supposed I was. It removed my immediate problems, and not just ones involving the baby. But once it was all over I saw as little of her as I decently could - for a while anyway. I spent much time in my room weeping, and even tore up, ruthlessly, the piece of paper with telephone number on it, handed to me by Nate. My father was very nice to me; 'I expect you do feel very *feak* and *weeble* after something like that,' he said. It was the expression that irritated me deeply by then, but I was feeling far too weak even to groan. 'I'm fine,' I lied. 'I've just got a lot of work to do.'

In January I went back to the crammers in Oxford, worked as hard as I knew how, ceasing all my other Oxford activities – especially attending professorial lectures - and a few months later got my excellent exam results, I moved to a flat share in London with an acquaintance from my secretarial course, who also put me on to the publishing job. And that was that. Yet nothing was quite the same after, not even my friendship with Patty, close as we'd become and would remain on and off throughout her life. Under her ministrations much of my innocence vanished, you could say, if by no means all of it.

And maybe, despite everything mine was, in a way, an immaculate conception. Maybe Nate's gibe about the Virgin Mary had been accurate enough: maybe throughout our affair, raunchy as it sometimes was, I remained, at heart, as innocent as my hands. But I am not sure what took the place of this now departed innocence. There was cynicism, of course, of a sort, but cynicism was not the exact word for it. Had I been wholly cynical I might have taken the job I did, but I would never have married less than two years later or given birth to my three children.

'Wouldn't it be better for the children if you were a fulltime mother, just for a bit?' my dad asked then, like everybody else. 'No,' I said, busy arranging for yet another au pair girl so that I could go to the office. He said no more on that subject: I saw he did not know how to go on with it. But I'm sure he regarded this as the main reason none of my marriages lasted. After the breakup of the first one, he asked once, very sadly. 'What did I do wrong?' 'Nothing, dad,' I said. 'It's the world that goes wrong not you.'

He shook his head, but did not pursue the matter: he had other concerns than me, those days, to my relief. Once he'd seen me safely settled – or so he thought –he'd gone off and found a wife of his own. A brisk widow with two daughters I avoided meeting her if I could: she was fifteen years younger than him and he expected her to outlive him. Unfortunately, having nursed him through heart trouble and bowel cancer she dropped dead herself when he was eighty-five and she not much over seventy. One of his stepdaughters lived nearby and kept an eye on him thereafter: this relieved my conscience about being too busy to visit him as often as I should. In the end, of course, he'd had to go into the home he hated, growing ever more feeble – *'feak and weeble'* – he'd moan, *'feak and weeble'* - while surrounded by what he called 'old ducks' most of them far younger than him. 'What have I done to set up home with a whole lot of old ducks,' he'd moan, too deaf by then to hear what the old ducks talked about at mealtimes, which did not help. (I suppose, these days, *I'm* what he'd have called an old duck. Never mind.)

Up till the bout of pneumonia which left him too frail to look after himself, he'd still been able to drive his car, was reasonably independent. He used to lunch at the golf club where he'd played for twenty years. The younger members – post-Thatcher type bankers and stockbrokers all, I daresay, or company executives, it was that kind of home-counties club – called him I was told once, 'Stuffy.' Sure my father could be stuffy: I should know. But what could self-satisfied animals like them, stuffed to the eyes with unmerited bonuses, what could they know about an old bloke as decent – as honourable - as he was? Fuck the lot.

CHAPTER TWENTY-FIVE

My son comes frequently at the moment: not quite every day, but every other day at least. He sits, keeping me company, almost as quietly and peacefully as the Husband: I could even think I am keeping him company too. I wonder what's going on his marital life, but, of course, I do not ask.

I look at him with love – it's as if for the first time in my life, truly maternal feelings are emerging, that even those I felt when he was little could not have matched. This is ironic. It is not him needs the mothering now – or maybe he does? –it is me. I accept drinks from my son, let him moisten my lips, even help shift my position in the medical bed. Yet, if I welcome my maternal feelings, I don't welcome the guilt and pity they engender; relating to my inability – common to everyone of course, but I have never felt it so sharply before – to protect my child from the pain of seeing what is happening to me now – and much worse to prevent such things happening to him. (I don't mean the effect on him of our damaged gene. There is only a small risk of its affecting males as directly as it affects women: as it has affected me. If he carries the mutation, as he might or might not, he could pass it on to his children, but luckily he has two sons and no daughters.)

Does my dying evoke his future dying in him? I don't of course ask: even though, at night, enclosed within the magic circle of the room's dimmed lights, we talk more intimately than ever before. The distant hospital clatter increases our sense of closeness: I have the impression my son feels our closeness no less.

Once he asks, startling me dreadfully. 'Why did you have children, Ma? I never had the impression you liked children very much.'

'I liked you,' I say. Love is still a word I find hard to speak aloud, even where I feel it.

'Yes,' he answers. 'Sometimes you did. But why did you?'

'It was what we did then,' I say. 'There wasn't much on offer for girls of my generation. Your grandfather never asked what I wanted to do when I grew up; all he ever said was "when you are grown up and married and have children of your own." I suppose I'd have felt I'd failed if I hadn't.'

'And do you regret that?'

'Are you asking me if I regret you? Certainly not,' I say quite violently. 'Certainly not.'

Because I didn't. And I suppose, hard as I'd found it to mother them beyond babyhood, I didn't regret his sisters either. What they got out of this – of me - I cannot be quite so sure.

'Do *you* regret having children?' I asked him.

'Of course not. Though they're little buggers. I think Jake might be trying out weed, he's in a wild lot at school and what am I supposed to do about that? His mother's freaking out. I told him I'd tried the stuff a bit at Jake's age but she says it's stronger now and I suppose she's right? What do you think?'

'Not a lot,' I say. 'One thing I learned having children is you can't control what happens to them. You can try and affect what happens to them, but trying to control their lives just makes things worse. If they're going to hell they'll do it their own way, no matter what you do. Sometimes I can't imagine why you lot all turned out OK: conventional even. I don't think that was anything much to do with me. Or with your father come to that.'

'Aren't you helpful.' he says. 'Were you always so cynical? You sound as if you wished we hadn't been so straight.'

'You call that cynical? I call it just knowing your parental limits. Sorry, son.'

'Don't call me son!' He is laughing. And laughing looks so like his real grandfather suddenly, it wears me out.

Yet for all I see in him, my so awkwardly loved son, how little I know him. What makes people say God, their creator, knows them? '*Oh Lord thou hast searched me out and known me... thou knowest my thoughts long before*?'... What bollocks. It's the same with us, programmed to give birth no less indiscriminately; how can I fathom the spaces inside my son? I know he can be as tetchy, not to say as short-fused as his father. I know he is prone to melancholy: that at the same time he is as guarded as I am. I know the perversely puritanical streak that he appears to have inherited from someone to whom he is only distantly related, my adoptive father (I bought him an absurdly expensive sweater once because I loved it and when he discovered the price, he told me it *was* absurd to spend that much on a sweater.) I know how maddeningly pernickety he can be: I remember him crouched for hours as a boy over his amazingly detailed battlefields, over the maps he made of them: one reason, perhaps, why he is so good at designing websites. (A job that is even more of a mystery to me than he is, but which had its uses in my own battles with the Internet, much to his irritation: he did not like being used by any parent, he said.) I know some people take to him passionately, more than most people ever took to me. I know others dislike him as intensely – maybe they've disliked me as much but I've never bothered to notice that. But what do I really know of what goes on in his head as he hurtles like all of us to his inevitable end; locked within the short, comic, tragic, often dirty often brutish – mentally if not physically – ludicrous spans of our mortal lives?

I am tired now. Too tired to talk any more. 'Shall I come again tomorrow?' asks my son. I nod. 'Cool' he says, a word that never ceases to surprise me, emerging so unselfconsciously from his anything but teenage mouth. And then he's gone. And I am left wondering why I did have children. WHY? It was extraordinary really. The only reason I can imagine my embarking on such a project, leaving aside all the social pressures, was some passionate need to replace the aborted child of my lover. And if others followed it was because that seemed in some perverse way, less trouble, less intimate you might say, than simply raising one.

What I can say is that I was driven, throughout, by a fierce determination never to let my life - full from the beginning of matters I could not control: an unknown father, a disappearing mother, a married lover, much older than myself, an unsought abortion – slip from my grasp again.

It might sound odd, given my personal life: four marriages, my various affairs, long or short: given my professional one, given what's happened in my life-time to the publishing world, to say that till recently I *have* kept my life within my grasp, but so I have, pretty much. I reared my children as best I knew how and they obliged me by doing much as they should, apart from my youngest daughter's teenage rampages, none of these too unexpected, let alone unlikely. I kept my domestic life in order even if the state of my house might not have impressed a Morningside housewife. I did my job well – more than well: in doing so I made quite as many authors happy as I made others unhappy. (What can be better controlled than a book, come to think of it, even a book, like so many of mine, about that all too uncontrollable matter war - how many of those have there been in my lifetime? – more wars than I can remember, let alone count.) Books and their subject alike I controlled through contracts, editing processes, design, publicity. Until, in the end, all effort, arguments, all unruly subject matter had been corralled between carefully designed, inviting covers. If I hadn't always controlled sales figures to my liking it wasn't for want of trying.

What I did with authors – and with wars – making decisions here, dealing with the fall-out of both failure and success, there, so it was with the fall-out of my own private life. I kept my figure and my looks as far as possible. I survived, well, if not always happily, break-ups and vicissitudes; when one lover went out of the door I went out and looked for another, by whatever means available: self-contained and independent I might be but I did not much like living alone, let alone chastely; the only real gap after the too early death of the husband I'd loved and that only lasted a year or so. And all this I achieved through times when other things fell into decline, even chaos, political, financial, military. The legacy of the two world wars imposing itself still, crises erupted, conflicts broke out, empires rocketed apart, walls went up and down, regimes rose and fell, recessions came and went, AIDs decimated gays and Africans especially, drugs and alcohol became ever more socially prevalent and divisive. All of which had their impact: but for me, personal control trumped the lot. Or it did up to the mid-nineties, when my publishing career – like publishing - began to slip from my grasp.

'No,' I said firmly, when instructed by a senior salesman to take on the ghost-written memoirs of a self-styled military adventurer, some of it verging on pornography. And that led to my golden handshake, more or less, and much fluff from managers about my illustrious career. My illness appeared for the first time, not long after.

I did my best. I survived the illness, at first. I set up a small publishing house, to continue publishing the kind of books I thought worth publishing. When that too was taken over, I turned editorial adviser and freelance editor, working from home for as long as I could. That was when I began exploiting my son's internet skills – before then, apart from email, I'd been able to rely on secretaries and researchers.

So it was post 9/11, in the new Millennium, that I learned to web-surf, to Google; a programme I used ever more for my own entertainment as well as information. I also encountered the dating website on which I found The Husband, my final beloved.

When we first exchanged emails, he sounded more interested in my publishing skills than he was in me. He'd written what he hoped was a book of popular science about his ants and asked if I'd help him with it. But when I informed him, as nicely as I could, that his book did not read like popular science, nor ever would, he did not seem the least fazed. He even invited me out for a drink.

'You're not my type at all,' I said, sternly, as he nursed his pint and I my glass of Lagavulin, without ice. (I'd insisted on a pub that knew about single malts)

'You're not mine,' he agreed with a bemused but cheerful grin. 'Does it matter?'

'It might,' I said cautiously. I assessed his sagging suit, his unashamed beard and belly, his reasonable teeth, sighed, knocked back the rest of my glass and held it out for a refill and added 'On the other hand it might not. So what the hell?' And so it was, sooner rather than later, that we got together.

His appearance in my life had one unexpected effect. It emboldened me sufficiently to Google Nate for the first time – something that previously I'd never dared to. He had a large number of entries; he'd held many academic posts, written many books. Wikipedia even told me about his private life; how he had been married to the same woman since he was twenty-six – she was not only Jewish but an heiress; her father had founded an internationally famous chain of food stores, that from a back street in Brooklyn now covered the world. (No wonder he could afford to take a room in the Randolph, just for the pleasure of fucking me, I thought.) He had four children. One daughter was married to an Englishman and lived in London.

That was, I think, the first time I used Wikipedia for such a personal reason. Though I used it a good deal more once the cancer again kicked in. The first time I fell ill, in the early nineties, I had not bothered to research my illness. Much too busy at work to help the medical profession do their job I had done what I was told to, apart from climbing out of bed very soon after my lumpectomy and heading straight back to my desk. I went through radiotherapy without taking a single whole day off.

'Aren't you brave,' ventured one colleague, less frightened of me than most.

I had just arrived back from a lengthy and tedious session at the hospital. 'Not the least. Just bored,' I said.

'You shouldn't consider yourself cured,' said my oncologist when he signed me off. 'No one should consider themselves cured of cancer. Keep an eye on yourself and get in touch with me any time if you've the slightest worry.'

'I'll bear it in mind,' I said. I assented, at the same time, to yearly mammograms. In the early noughties, a year after the new Husband and I had got together, one of these turned up another cancerous lump. This time they insisted on a mastectomy and I agreed. The Husband did not seem the least upset, at least not on his own behalf. I put that down to his being more interested in my money than in my retaining my bodily parts, but that's probably just being cynical. He was very tender to me throughout.

'Don't worry,' I said. 'I've been here before. All I've got to do is put up with stuff for a bit.'

And so it was in the beginning. I even enjoyed my relative idleness and used the internet still more for amusement and information. I researched my Husband's speciality, ants, for instance, discovering them to be even more bellicose than I thought – 'the tribes of men,' I read 'and the tribes of ants are not unalike in the native combativeness that animates them.' And so forth. The main difference being that ants carry their weapons on their bodies: when I taxed my Husband with this, he showed little interest; his work relates more to the chemical ingredients of ants' complex social organisation, that is the hormones that lie behind it, or something like that.

I also began a satirical novel. On the basis of 'write from what you know', it was about a woman who worked in the House of Commons and who, on an official visit to some minor commonwealth country with a party of MPs, had inadvertently triggered a war between this country and another minor commonwealth country, then found herself in hiding there and reporting back to the British Press like a female, civil service version of William Boot. Mindful of my experience in publicising books, of the value of stirring interest well in advance, I set up a website with the help of my not very willing son and started a blog on which I reported my very slow progress, sexing it up a little with hilarious – or not so hilarious -stories about life as a breast cancer patient. In all such ways I regained control of my professional and private lives: at least I felt I had.

CHAPTER TWENTY-SIX

Don't think in all this that I forgot the one aspect of my life that has never been in my control: the great hole at the heart of it - of me – relating to my genetic parentage. In which hole lurked somewhere the whereabouts of my lost – maybe long dead - mother; in which, more disturbing still, lurked my unknown father; the parents I had been seeking all my life: not that I did much about it through my busiest years. I had no time to investigate such difficult matters I told myself: it is equally possible I did not dare to. And anyway, how could I, where would I start? There weren't any adoption papers. As for my birth certificate, my adoptive father's name was on it, as my father.

It was at boarding school following my father's holiday bombshell that I had first begun to reflect on such matters. I daresay the jibes or sympathy around my absent mother and my inability to confess my ignorance about the man who had engendered me - let alone to confess that the father who delivered me to school and fetched me back was not that father - was part of the reason. But who had fathered me? Where was he now? And where was the mother who'd fled from me - was it to rejoin him? – was it really because she couldn't stand me? - this insinuation was something I couldn't quite dismiss. Do all adopted children feel as lost as I did? Probably. These days, of course, they are allowed to ask questions, even encouraged to ask questions, but I'd never been encouraged to, quite the reverse, despite having people very close to me, not just trap-mouthed adoption workers, who knew the answers, but whom I could not – dared not – question, except in passing. Silence the culture I was brought up in, breaking it was as unthinkable as dropping my knickers in public.

In my case too – and I expect that it is true of many adopted children – I was inhibited by the guilt I felt towards the father who brought me up; any attempt to find out my true parentage seemed like a statement that I didn't love him enough even though I did love him, despite being exasperated by him, as I increasingly was. The second thing inhibiting questions, more particular to me, was the pain I knew he felt in all matters related to my mother.

(There was Patty of course; though she did drop the odd hint, she, too, batted all questions away throughout my childhood. After

I married, I rarely saw her, anyway, my father having moved away from the village with his new wife, my stepmother.)

In some respects, I came at school to enjoy the thought of my mysterious origins - *oh meines papas*. I did not, like my fellow pupils, have to put up with the mundane reality of their plump – or skinny - mothers with unflattering tastes in hats, their often balding fathers, some of them with pot-bellies, some of them already stooping and looking much older than my adoptive father, quite possibly as a result of the wartime experiences that weren't talked about except in the best-selling books that sat on my father's shelves and that I read sneakily lying behind the sofa: not that I dreamed of identifying the heroes I encountered in such books with the far from glamorous-seeming fathers of my contemporaries. Whereas I could look at my equally unglamorous father, wire-framed spectacles, receding hair and all and know that this wasn't the whole of my truth: that out there somewhere in the real world was my flighty, beautiful, barely remembered mother, whom I saw as ageless and much more beautiful than any of those other mothers. More interesting still, out there, too, stood the unknown figure of my father: *her* 'Latin lover'; *my* French father. Who couldn't really have ravished her in a tent, he couldn't have been a Sheik, there were no tents in Paris: in retrospect I'm not quite sure where any of that came from. Most likely it was from my old nanny who read old film magazines when she wasn't gutting *Nursery World* and who had one day shown me a picture of Rudolf Valentino.

My fantasies had moved on by the time Patty dropped the hint that fitted them best. All the books I'd read about heroic French resistance to the brutal Germans, about the activities of spies like Odette, had made the myth of the Latin Lover seem less interesting than the myths I'd started inventing about my mother's heroism: how she had really run away to join SOE and be a spy: how she'd been caught and had died refusing to give up secrets of her fellow spies. My real father meantime had turned into a famous writer or famous soldier or famous anything else you can name, who had died of love when he had heard about her fate: or who might even have shared it for all I knew. What Patty did– I doubt if such an outcome had occurred to her -was flesh out this particular myth, making it seem, to me, all the more certain because I'd thought of it for myself. I'd heard her referring to my mother as 'the Bolter' – she was talking to my father at the time. She instantly withdrew that name seeing the look on his face. And seeing the bewilderment on mine once she'd realised that I had been listening to what she said.

I tackled her later. 'Who's the Bolter?' I asked.

'Oh just someone in a book who ran away because she was too young really to know how to bring up a child. Like your mother.' Patty said.

'Well I knew *that*. I've always known *that*. It's the one thing Daddy's ever told me. What book?'

That had been my introduction to Nancy Mitford. I was about fourteen at the time: Patty must have thought I was old enough for this brand of English humour. I read all the Mitford books in due course but the one that meant most to me was *The Pursuit of Love*: my mother was the Bolter, of course, the mother who kept running away. But much more interesting and rather less disturbing was Fabrice, resistance hero and aristocratic French lover of the Bolter's niece, father of her child; I adopted him as *my* father, at once. To his story I appended one of my own: the story of my mother joining SOE, the British spying group. Because she would, of course, have spoken fluent French after her months in Paris and the affair with the Frenchman, her ur-Fabrice during which I had been conceived. Perhaps they'd even died, protecting each other in their Gestapo prison.

My heroic parents: what a comfort it was to imagine that. It made me feel less abandoned, after all.

My fantasies of parenthood may have faded as I aged (even if my liking for Nancy Mitford's books did not: I still rate her above her literary contemporaries like Elizabeth Bowen whose works, about women of my mother's generation, more or less, or a bit older in some cases, I also devoured at one point in my life, looking for clues to my mother's nature – and wished I hadn't: much preferring the outwardly comic version to the fine-tuned, bitchier, hair-splitting if wondrous sensibilities with which these more obviously literary writers dissected their vapid not to say vaporous characters. Throughout my publishing career I have avoided editing fiction for that reason: in particular I've avoided fiction written by and about women.) But this did not stop me asking questions. The only time I ceased to be plagued by restless reflections was in bed with some man or other, peace that never lasted very long.

Over my years of work all my myths had faded, of course; though I still assumed I was half French the thoughts grew more melancholy than fantastic. In part I wanted to know the truth of me; in part, glad to be so continually busy, I resisted. I kept shut, mostly, the doors to the innermost part of myself where the doubts, the lacks, the questions lived.

My first flirtations with cancer aroused them all over again. I even rang up Patty but she wouldn't talk to me; not about this; she sounded very old and unlike herself – 'just let sleeping dogs lie,' she said; and then more fondly. 'Come and see me, Joey. It was a shame your father ever left the village.'

'Wasn't it,' I said. - till then I'd barely even told myself how much I minded his sweeping me away from the parent that the village had represented all through my growing-up. I would have liked to see Patty, but after the way she brushed aside my questions I could not bring myself to do so. I did not even tell her that I'd been ill.

I determined to confront my father. But before I could do that my stepmother died unexpectedly, and when I went to see him he looked so old and unhappy that I relented. 'She was such a good woman, Jo,' he said, 'She truly loved me. But I couldn't love her as much as I loved your mother. I always felt bad about it.'

It was the most nakedly, confessional statement I ever heard him make: as if old age was cracking open the culture of stoicism, softening his stiff upper lip. Perhaps if I'd asked my questions then he'd have given me at least some answers. But I couldn't ask such questions, how could I? I was too locked into silence myself, and also too affected by his sadness. I was also, I think, embarrassed to hear him talk like that.

So I did not ask my questions. From time to time I made desultory attempts at searching – I went once to look for my mother's death in registry archives, in vain. I had nothing to go on: nothing.

The one thing I knew for certain was that I been conceived in Paris: making my father indeed, most likely, French. On the other hand, 1938 after the Anschluss and the Spanish Civil War, with Mussolini in Rome and Hitler in Berlin, with Europe swarming with refugees – mostly the intellectuals at this stage - he could equally have been Spanish or Italian: he could have been Jewish: not only refugees but many foreign students went to study at the Sorbonne, I thought, remembering the love of my life. He could have been English. There were plenty of Englishmen with ancestry which made them look Mediterranean; the Scottish Islands and the West Country, for instance, were full of the descendents of sailors washed-up from the Spanish armada, piratical-looking to this day. He could even have been Austrian or German for all I knew.

Maybe not knowing was for the best, I thought. Since adopted children had been allowed to follow-up their parentage there were plenty who found it a dispiriting experience and wished they hadn't. But I could never be quite certain, not in the middle of the night, the times I felt most benighted of myself, without safe shell or cover. Perhaps all my men were a means of papering myself over. I daresay I went on to the dating site to find someone to paper me over yet again; but I did better than that, I found the Husband and for the time being was happy enough for the questions to ease, to fade once more into the background.

My scientist husband himself brought them back to the surface. When I told him about my breast cancer, he said 'You know they've discovered some of the genes behind that.'

'Of course I know,' I said. 'I've done my research.'

'Is there anyone else in your family?'

'Not on my bloody mother's side as far as I know. But what the hell do I know about my father's?'

I had wondered. I must say, when I'd been asked that question at the time of my diagnosis. In the midst of my immediate terror I'd dismissed it as one danger too many. It couldn't make any difference to my treatment, after all, either then or in the future, if the bloody thing came back.

And then this: about six months before my father died, a year after he had moved into the home he hated so. (I'd been asked accusingly by one doctor why I couldn't take him to live with me - my dad wouldn't hear of it, to my guilty relief. 'I'm not having any daughter of mine wipe my bottom' was how he put it, old age taking him far more outspoken than he used to be about his bodily functions, just as it did me: he said the same to my dutiful stepdaughter when she too offered him a home). In the March of that year I went to see *Hamlet* for the first time.

When I saw the production listed, I'd thought that with a name like mine I really was about time; that I should see this play just once.

I told the Husband – we were living together but not yet married. 'Must we?' he groaned.

'A black guy from the Wire is playing Hamlet,' I said, to encourage him.

'That might be interesting, I suppose,' he agreed.

And so we went to see Hamlet. And I returned to Ophelia. And the kaleidoscope pattern in which my old life seemed set, shifted, whirled round and fell into something that I did not for a long time recognise as a pattern. Bring out the yellow flags.

CHAPTER TWENTY-SEVEN

The actor who played Ophelia in this production, like the one who played Hamlet, was a well-known television turned film actor, but the series in which she made her name- a science fiction series - was not the kind we usually watched, even though the Husband and I had sat through all kinds of unlikely programmes – for me - of an evening. (Umpteen scientific documentaries for instance, until I got tired of my Husband's fulminations against scientific inaccuracies and diverted him to programmes like *Poirot* or *Midsomer Murders*: time-wasting stuff I thought then, but entertaining just the same, and these days strangely soothing, the way they tie death up in neat packages: I wish I could despatch my own in such satisfactory ways.) The actor – my actor –had appeared in episodes of both these series before she became famous. I recognised her face by now, despite having never properly taken her in. I did know that more recently she had starred in several films, and begun appearing in gossip columns. For someone who'd never acted live on stage before the reviews of her Ophelia were surprisingly good: better than those for her Hamlet for sure.

Throughout the performance something about her – something about her gestures, her voice – especially after she'd begun to play mad - nagged at me. When we left the theatre later my Husband said: 'you know who Ophelia reminded me? You,' he said. Adding hastily – with all his experience of handling students he knew how to be crudely tactful – 'but I expect that when you were that age you were prettier.'

'Thank you,' I said. 'Oh thanks.'

I wasn't feeling very well next morning: maybe it was the first intimations that my illness would renew itself in due course. But I put it down to the fact that we'd eaten late, after the show. Having picked snails for my starter, I'd been so filled with nostalgia I'd drunk too much of the rather good claret we'd ordered, then heard myself saying –much to my annoyance – 'you know about snails – they remind me of the love of my life?' And I'd ended telling my

Husband the whole story: the first time in my life I'd told it to anyone. This might have been due to the claret; or it might, just, have been a sign of how genuinely fond I was of this man; of how safe I felt with him, even if he wasn't the sort of man who brought the waiters running in the rather smart restaurant we'd chosen. Indeed it was me to whom they offered the claret to taste and me who summoned one of them to bring us the bill and me to whom they presented it: I had taken too many writers and agents out in my time not to play the man. The Husband did not mind: he laughed if anything and made out he preferred it. It was another reason why I felt able to confide in him.

Not feeling very well I lingered over my laptop next morning, reluctant to get to my novel (I felt far more sympathetic to my authors these days than I had been when I was bullying them to deliver their manuscripts on time.) I trawled instead through the press, did the odd easy crossword. And then, still reluctant to get to work, I found myself googling the name of the actress who played Ophelia and who, my Husband said, had reminded him of me. I was astonished by the number of entries; apart from her own website, there were several fan sites, film sites listing her parts in countless television programmes and films I hadn't seen or even heard of, newspaper interviews with her, newspaper reports about her succession of high profile boyfriends, her stalker, about her being photographed drunk – once -by the paparazzi.

I trawled though this stuff briefly before settling on Wikipedia.

Now I've noticed how once you've put the right word into any search programme, a knot of unknowing unravels; a thread's unfolding reveals the next twist in the labyrinth and the next and the next until you are brought to the Minotaur at the labyrinth's heart. It led, at last, in this case, to the Minotaur that lurked – had always lurked - at the centre of my life.

I could have stopped unravelling that thread. I didn't have to go right to the centre of *my* labyrinth; I didn't need to, I told myself, sternly: it was stale old history now. But once I'd started I could not stop. Maybe I was never meant to: the Minotaur had been waiting patiently all this time, knowing I would reach him eventually; would I be a maiden he could slay and devour, or a female Theseus, who'd end up slaying him?

Personal life, the second section in the Wikipedia article was headed. She'd been born in London and was the granddaughter of the judge whose surname she bore. The most famous part played by the actress in of her grandmother's family, generations back, had been Ophelia. Her grandmother had been named Ophelia in consequence and as it was, too, her own second name: she'd always hoped, one day, to play the part herself. She had succeeded. (How quickly Wikipedia picked things up, I thought. Did the people who amended these articles – amateurs all – have nothing better to do?)

I should have stopped then – it felt already as though funeral marches were stepping through my head. But I did not stop. I googled the judge; a famous judge it turned out – he'd once been in the forefront of the campaign against capital punishment (had my father been against capital punishment I wondered – and to my astonishment found I did not know.) The questions about my father diverted me briefly from my efforts. But when I turned back to the screen I found the judge, too, in Wikipedia, but nothing about his personal life, nothing whatever about his wife, Ophelia.

I should – I could have given up then. But I did not. I googled the actress again. (I'm tired of being politically correct and calling her 'an actor.' She is an actress. That will do.) This time I pulled down an interview with her featured in the Observer Review, just before Hamlet opened; what did she feel like appearing on live the stage for the first time, was she nervous? And so forth.

Of course she was nervous: she said. But she was heartened by the memory of her ancestor, she was encouraged by her grandmother, the other Ophelia. She had always, as a child, been very close to her grandmother, closer than to her mother really; she admired her so much, she'd had such an interesting life. She was a divorced woman, for one thing, – a rare thing in her day – who, during the war, had run away from her boring first husband, joined the WAAC and become a driver to her grandfather, in something very hush hush, probably MI5. They'd fallen in love and married as soon as she'd managed to get a divorce from her boring husband: the actress's lawyer grandfather had even been prepared to have his name put through the courts as an adulterer, which was a big thing then, but it hadn't harmed his career in more enlightened days. (Apart from wanting to ban capital punishment, he'd campaigned for the reform of divorce law. But then he would, wouldn't he, I thought, sourly, reading this.) 'My grandparents have always been my inspiration,' the actress insisted. The interviewer had had great difficulty in diverting actress Ophelia from gay divorcee Ophelia and her ex-secret service husband; I wondered that this had not been edited out.

I only skimmed the rest of the article: about the actress's career, about her not very original views on Hamlet in general, and playing Ophelia in general. Afterwards I turned my laptop off and sat with my hands in my lap.

Then, very slowly, reluctantly, but unable to prevent myself, I went to my bookcase and pulled out my nineties edition of Who's Who: the actress's grandfather would, most likely, have been alive then.

I was right. For there it was: the judge's full professional life, including, latterly a knighthood. And also, more briefly, his private one. Married: Mrs Ophelia – and my own surname – 1946. 3 s, one d, my half siblings presumably. And almost at the bottom of the piece his interests: the theatre, cricket, golf. (So he had something else in common with my father, I thought, as well as his wife.) At the very bottom of the entry was an address in London, SW1.

I thought of my father: who had always kept this from me. How I could confront him with such a revelation, now? He was an old man, frail and unhappy. And whatever he'd done had been just as much done to him. Even so, it did not stop me hating him in this moment, hating my mother too for abandoning me. My hate for my father was mitigated, only a little, by the blithe description of him as my mother's first 'boring' husband. That aroused almost as much fury on his behalf.

I rang Patty. How old she sounded was my first thought, hearing her voice, but that didn't make me sorry for her; not one bit. 'Jo?' she said recognising my voice the moment I spoke.

I did not even ask how she was: 'I want some information from you, Patty, *now*,' I said. She didn't need telling what information I wanted. I wondered if she'd been waiting for something like this all these years. We said the word 'mother' almost simultaneously.

'Oh God,' she said. 'You've found out.'

'How can I get hold of her?'

She prevaricated. 'Jo, is this such a good idea?'

'You're still in touch with her, aren't you?'

'Not much these days... because.... Jo, she was my oldest friend.'

I ignored the 'was'. It did not say that my mother was dead.

'And she was - *is* - my mother, much as you both seemed to have chosen to forget the fact.'

'No one forgot that fact,' she said. 'But now, after such a time,.... Jo, it's too late; your making contact is a jolly bad idea: believe me.'

This in Patty's old voice was as defensive as she could ever sound. How old was Patty now – late eighties? - she was older than my mother I knew: but my mother by now would be in her eighties too. My mother, mother of five: who had not mothered me since I was three. Oh what lies it all was... 'What a tangled web we weave,' etc etc. They never talk about the wretched insect trapped in the middle of the web: me. Whose own carefully woven life web – mine - was being ripped apart at this very minute, with yet more rippings to come. (Had I known *that* would I have gone on with this? God only knows.)

'And my father knew?'

'Of course. He - well, all of us - thought it was better you stayed with him, didn't get confused. You were so fond of him, you two were so very close. No one wanted to get in the way of that.'

'No? How kind of you,' I said. In a voice colder than ice I insisted. And then. 'Are you saying she asked to have me back at some point? I want my mother's telephone number. Now.'

There was a long silence; I could almost hear the crack in it of years and time; 'please' I said, my voice this time not as cold as I'd have liked. And then cold again, but desperate. 'Why did no one ever tell me?' And then again, polite, yet still more frigid. 'Give me her number.'

She prevaricated still; 'Jo, I'm not sure that's such a good idea. She is so very old now...'

'Not as old as you. And I'm no spring chicken myself, am I? Give me her number Patty, please.'

My voice broke a little, to my fury. And maybe it was the plea in that which made her acquiesce suddenly. She gave me the number and the address – the address in SW1. Then she said,

'I'm not sure she'll speak on the phone, Jo.'

209

'Then I'll have to go and see her, won't I?' I said.

Patty sighed. 'I suppose you must if you must. But be careful, darling. Don't expect too much.'

'What can I expect after all this time. What have I to lose?' I asked.

Patty said. 'Be kind to your mother. She's not a well woman these days and I'm not quite sure how she is. I haven't spoken to her in a while. She took umbridge. She told me not to ring her again.'

'Has she got cancer?' I asked, bleakly, wondering if my own ailment was another legacy from my mother: on top of all the years of loss.

'No. Why do you ask? Have you had it?' The doctor's wife – or rather widow by this point - had picked this up at once.'

'Of course not," I lied. Thinking, well I can't blame dear Mummy for that anyway. But I still did.

'Well that's alright, at least,' said Patty. Adding – 'and is your life well in other ways?'

'Pretty much,' I said. 'I'm trying to write a novel.' I don't know why I told her that and anyway it was the end of my novel: nor did I ever blog another word. How could fiction compete? How could I blog this?

That was the last time I spoke to Patty, my old friend, my surrogate mother and as I now felt my betrayer. It was a year or more before she died and I half regret not getting in touch with her again. But I half do not regret it, either: I knew the full extent of her betrayal now and everything reaches its end.

CHAPTER TWENTY-EIGHT

In all the control I'd asserted over my life, only this one thing had been truly beyond me; the full content of my DNA. My ignorance, if you think of it, negated all the rest of that carefully created control; turned safety into illusion. Maybe my ignorance was precisely why I needed to control my life so tightly. Maybe keeping myself working so hard was a way of not allowing myself time to think about it, let alone time to look.

Seeking identity through your ancestry is, of course, fashionable these days, practically a disease: an infectious one moreover. I did contract it once, very briefly, enough to spend that morning among the countless others clattering through steel-edged registers in an office somewhere off the Strand, looking for my mother's death. The session was so fruitless, so dispiriting it made it feel like a disease not worth catching. When my children pressed me for information –as they did after I'd let drop in a careless moment that their grandfather wasn't their real grandfather - I refused to discuss the matter. Even now I know everything, and wished I didn't, I still haven't told anyone my father's name, not the Husband, not my son, for all that it was his internet advice put me years later on to the means of finding it out. (My children must be told of course, eventually: I owe them that, given the mutation I carry and which I may have passed onto them. I have set it all out in a codicil attached to my will for them to see when I am dead.)

Perhaps I'd always suspected that the truth might be disturbing: as it turned out it was, even more disturbing than most: not that my codicil says anything about *that*. Perhaps that's why I'd convinced myself – when I thought about it, which wasn't often – that I did not, did NOT, want to open *that* intolerable can of worms. No longer an editor I don't have to edit out such clichés, thank god: 'can of worms' really is the best expression here: - somehow I always knew it *was* one. Maybe this explains– I'm only half-joking – my visceral disgust at those open cans beside anglers sitting on river or canal backs, the contents writhing in their all-too fleshy way.

'Are you an angler, Peter,' I ask my nurse next morning, as he unhooks me from my drip, checks, adjusts it then hooks us up again.

'Whatever made you think of that? Why I should be?'

'I'm wandering,' I say. 'Can't you see how bonkers I'm getting. I'm dying – my brain is dying - in case you hadn't noticed.'

'Self-pity doesn't become you, dear,' he says, taking the covers back to reveal my grossly swollen belly.

'You're joking. What other kind can I have now?'

'Don't you see all the abused children on television?'

'Not if I can help it.'

'Well I suppose I can't blame you for that, dear. Are you in pain today?'

'No more than usual. Though I do feel weaker and weaker.'

He sighs now, more tenderly. 'I'm afraid that's how it goes,'

'How much longer, Peter?'

'Ask the doctors, It's their job to answer awkward questions. My job is to make you as comfortable as I can.'

'Which you do, Peter, mostly,' I say, gratefully, 'except when you say nasty things to me. You still haven't said. *Did* you go fishing as a child?'

'Sometimes. But I didn't like hooking the worms. I thought it might hurt them. You can see I was a natural for some kind of medical profession, can't you.'

'Did you ever catch a fish?' '

'Once or twice. But I threw them back.'

'What a saint you sound like, Peter. A latter-day St Francis.'

'I have to be a saint to deal with the likes of you, dear, foul mouth and all.'

'You can talk, Peter.'

'Can I? Though, I must say, dear, that if my fiancée could hear us sometimes, her precious hair wouldn't curl any more.'

I laugh, partly to hide the fact he is hurting me a little now, not that he or anyone can help it the way I am, partly because I am pretty sure he doesn't mean the hair on her head. I also know Peter well enough to know that when he starts talking about his fiancée he's getting tired of banter. In certain respects, I know him better, it occurs to me now, than I know the Husband, let alone my son.

Just as Peter knows *me* better than they do, at least in bodily respects.

'When are you bringing her into see me?' I ask. 'You promised you would.'

'Tomorrow?' he says, to my surprise. 'She gets off early tomorrow.'

'Fine. I'll look forward to it,' I say. But I am thinking that the hurry is because he knows I haven't got too much time left. It is not such an unwelcome thought as it might have been a week or two back.

Peter has finished his ministrations. He's writing on the chart he's unhooked from the bottom of his bed. When he has re-hooked it, replaced the blue ballpoint in his jacket pocket, he smiles at me slightly, blows a very slight – and in his relation to me, let alone my low condition - slightly inappropriate kiss, and then, his hands occupied by his tray of utensils, uses his elbow to push down the door handle, wiggles his bum the way he has to shove it open and floats out of the room, the thistledown look of it – how could such a chunky man be so light on his feet? – belied only by the meaty clunk of the door behind him.

He has left me, as always, feeling slightly, if temporarily better: the sign of a good nurse, I daresay. I guess I'm lucky, at least in him.

I suppose the time has come for me to relive to myself what my Internet researches led to.

I don't want to in the least. All I want when the Husband leaves – I've apologised for being vicious but the atmosphere between us has not dissipated, quite – is to sleep and sleep and sleep. I beg the night sister for a sleeping pill – yet another one -which seeing how restless I am and after phoning the duty doctor she allows me, at last, if reluctantly.

It works at first. I fall asleep and when I wake - I think I wake –I find myself on a sleepy mental walk through the village of my childhood – past Mrs Cosgrave's sweetshop, past the sword waving general, past the butcher's shop where our next door neighbour works, as far as the drapers and the ironmonger, confronting each other at a genteel angle - 'knickers versus nails,' Patty used to say - and opposite them, beyond the few parked

213

upright cars all with their running boards, the newly painted sign of the George and Dragon, fiery dragon, sword waving knight watching over me as I sit drinking shandy alongside my father (I'm old enough by now, obviously, to be allowed a little beer mixed in with my fizzy lemonade). But then by some circuitous route, I have left such safe places far behind. I've reached the local slum with its garbage-strewn courtyard and skinny dogs, the underside of the village that everyone tries to pretend does not exist; and there looming over what is by now a morphine-fuelled nightmare I see my father's face blown up enormously, baring its teeth and hissing out the word: *unclean*'. Still worse, strung from a rickety balcony, the picture of Ophelia has come to life: she floats down the filthy stream that leads from slum to duckpond screaming silently and festooned with dead flowers

I don't usually seek advice, not in my private life. (In my professional life I was always willing to listen to sensible suggestions: sometimes I sought them out.) One of the things that would, otherwise, have maddened me about my final husband – we had married very recently -was his reluctance to offer advice of any kind, even when asked for it. But I did ask for it on the question of seeking out my mother: I could not bear to be solely responsible for such an action. I told him what Patty said - her advice against visiting my mother. 'Should I go or not?' I asked. 'Does it matter who my parents are, what my mother is? Do I need to know who fucked her to make me? Does any of it matter?'

It was the evening. We'd opened a bottle of wine; in due course we opened another. I don't think alcohol was that good for someone with my genetically acquired condition, but what the hell? And if our discussion grew ever more verbose and ever more heated, what the hell, again?

The Husband, glass in hand, offered me his considered thoughts on genetic matters – including parentage - of course he did, he was always willing to talk about such things. In this case discourse might be a better way of putting it; that way I guess, he could distance himself from such awkward questions. None of it had much to do with me, let alone with the dilemma I confronted, panic-stricken: I *was* panic-stricken. And perhaps he was too, I'm thinking. This was heavy stuff for a man who as he often said had never wanted children himself, though he'd made an excellent grandfather to children to whom he bore no genetic relationship whatever, my grandchildren, that is: a much better grandfather than I was a grandmother; they adored him, called him PaPa: oh how sweet.

He told me – yet again – about the selfish gene: about worker ants and drone bees foregoing their own chances to reproduce, assisting their breeding queens instead, to the benefit of their mutual genes. (In all cases, forgive me, I reproduce only a crude, layman's version of what he said.) He told me how ostriches protect themselves against predators by massing together and putting the young ostriches most closely related to them in the safest place at the centre of flock or herd: he ended by telling me – this was new, to me - about some study reproduced in different parts of the world where human volunteers had to hold an uncomfortable position for as long as they could, informed that for each minute they endured someone of their choosing would receive a small reward. In every case, wherever the study was held, the closer they were related to the beneficiary the longer the volunteers were willing to endure their discomfort.

'How interesting,' I said sarcastically, hoping to stem his flow, though of course it had its uses, keeping us from the central, dangerous point.

I don't think he heard me. He was onto his ants by now: tribes of ferocious warrior ants defending their territory against tribes of other ferocious warrior ants: all for the benefit of their own genes: of course. Ripping the heads off their genetic enemies, their bodies apart. Charming creatures, ants, I told him. But no more charming I guess than the German Volk gassing Jewish non-people, Rwanda Hutus hacking to death their Tutsi neighbours – designated as cockroaches, conveniently- or Bosnian Serbs massacring Bosnian Muslims or Irish Catholics bombing Irish protestants, or Israeli planes dowsing Gazan civilians in white phosphorous. What a horrible world we live in. What stopped me wanting to die this very minute and get out of it?

This I didn't say. I pointed out instead that a lot of these visceral enemies shared the same genes - Jews and Arabs were Semites all, Bosnian Serbs and Bosnian Muslims were Serbs genetically or was it Slavs? And he said that of course human society – as if I didn't know – was more complicated than animal ones. (Too right, I thought: competing human tribes could be cultural –football hooligans – West Ham versus Tottenham Hotspurs – they could be compass points – north versus south, east versus west – they could be class wars – proles versus bourgeoisie – they could be professions – journalists compared to bankers– they could be black kids from one grotty South London housing estate versus black kids from another. Hamlet himself, come to think of it, had speared through several fellow Danes in the course of that regrettable play.)

'Oh god,' I said, at last, viciously. 'Spare me. Who would think' I went, on sourly, 'that all you bloody biologists' – 'geneticists' he amended with a pained expressions – 'have cracked genetic codes, unravelled DNA, mapped the entire human genome. And to what affect? What has it done to stop tribes bashing each other to pieces in the name of their genes, their Kith and Kin. The Falklands, dear Mrs Thatcher's war.' I said, 'was all about Kith and Kin wasn't it? So much for the scientifically, genetically well-informed twentieth century. And it doesn't look to me like the twenty-first century is shaping up to be any better. How does it look to you?'

The Husband sighed. 'Biologists, let alone geneticists, aren't politicians.' ('Oh no', I muttered.) 'Did I tell you there are some researchers who have found the gene that creates aggression in soldier ants and replaced it with one that turns them into foragers. Would you want them to do the same with humans?'

'So we've got down to genetic engineering now? If all of us were busy foraging would there be enough to go around, wouldn't the ones who developed aggression do better than the rest? Welcome to a scientific vicious circle. Bully for you.'

'That's putting it much too crudely,' he said in a pained voice, taking a packet of cigarettes out of his pocket, looking at it longingly and putting it back in again.

'Too bad, I *am* crude. Crude, rough or approximate will do nicely for me. You know I'm not a scientist.'

'All too well,' he smirked. It looked like a smirk to me.

'To hell with science. How did we get to this? What I wanted what I needed from you, dear husband, was not a scientific exposition, not this once. Maybe you can turn your mighty mind to my problem. What should I do, *now*?'

'About what?'

'About my mother, fuck you.'

'I was only trying to look at things objectively,' he said crossly. He went on a bit more then- I can hear his flat northern voice in my head, even now, a deep reverberant voice, not much varying in depth, but I'm getting too tired to reproduce the rest of what he said, exactly, there was far too much of it and it was too complicated for me even at the time. Didn't I know we were all products of our chance, coincidence, that none of us would have been born if our parents had not happened on each other, and though you can explain at lot of that by environment, geography, that doesn't explain everything or everyone. Etc.

'The stranger across the crowded room?' I said satirically. He did not pick up the reference, of course. Not even when I said angrily. 'My parentage isn't any fucking musical. It was just something that happened.'

'Exactly,' he said, smugly. 'Chance. Contiguity. People happening to be in the same place at the same time. Plus lust. Chemical attraction. A beautiful girl. And the little matter of sperm and egg.'

My mother was beautiful, I thought, desperately. Anyone might have wanted to fuck her. Anyone of a million men in Paris at that time of upheaval, anyone of the right age – and attraction – my father would have had to be attracted her, if only in passing: would have had to be persuasive -or made her very drunk. (Unless he had raped her, but I doubted this: such truths come out.) 'Shut up, will you. Just tell me what to do.'

But he still shrugged; he wouldn't: he couldn't. And in the end we had the worst row we have ever had. I threw my glass of red wine over him and he went out. I howled and howled all by myself. And then I made my own decision; as probably I had to. And when I woke up in the morning, hung-over but sober, to find the Husband back in our bed besides me, his beard reeking sourly of red wine, I still hadn't changed my mind.

CHAPTER TWENTY-NINE

The day after my genetics lesson, with or without the Husband's blessing I checked my mother's address in my London A to Z: her street turned out to lead into Belgrave Square - very fancy, I thought. Judges obviously earn a great deal more than clerks in the House of Commons. (It annoyed me, absurdly, that my mother's first husband, my adopted father, could never have afforded such an address even had he wanted it; he didn't. He'd preferred living in the country himself.) I then got on the bus with my bus pass, got off at Hyde Park Corner, and walked along Grosvenor Place to the end of her street, within sight of Belgrave Square – all the houses in streets and square alike of the plump, pompous, porticoed kind, built for equally plump mid Victorian families. They reminded me of my late-lamented publisher boss who had always sworn that his aristocratic wife's great grandfather, as a young man, had shot snipe in Belgrave Square, when it was still a swamp; what had they done with the swamp, I wondered?

I did not assay this portico, did not knock at the door. But assuming she was at home this was still as near to my mother as I'd been to my since I was three years old. (If she was as sick as Patty had implied, she was likely to be at home.)

Back at our flat, I picked up the phone at last and rang her number. It rang for a long time; I did not hang up but let it keep on ringing. At last a voice came on the line.

'Yes? Can I help you?' it asked, briskly. It could not have been my mother's voice. It was far too young and firm and, had, besides, a very faint London accent.

'Can I speak to Mrs, I mean Lady - ' I pronounced, with reluctance, the surname that belonged to my father's usurper.

'I'm afraid she's not available,' the voice said.
'When will she be available?'
'Lady Ophelia does not care to speak on the telephone.'
'Then can I come and see her?'
'Who am I speaking to?'
'Tell her it's her daughter,' I said.
'Ianthe?' the voice said. 'I'm sorry, Ianthe, I didn't recognise your voice.'

Ianthe, I thought, must be the half-sister I was never likely to meet: the mother of the actress who'd played Ophelia and gushed about her grandmother, our mother.

'Not Ianthe,' I said. 'Jo: her *eldest* daughter. The one she abandoned. She hasn't seen me for a long time. Could you ask her if she will see me now?'

There was a long silence. The voice hesitated, was less brisk than before. 'I'd have to ask. If she's having a good day. But if you really are her daughter…'

'Of course I'm her bloody daughter,' I said violently, 'why would I say I was if I wasn't?'

'No,' the voice said, still sounding very unsure.

'Tell her Jo. Otherwise known as Jane Ophelia.'

'Give me your number. I'll ask her on a good day. And I'll call you back,' the voice said.

'You'd better.'

'I'll call you back.'

The line went dead. I held the phone out, uncertainly, not sure if the voice would ring back, or if I was going to have to turn up at that street in Belgravia and hammer on the door till someone let me in. I would give it a week I thought.

But I did not have to wait a week. Three days later the phone rang and when I picked it up the voice now brisk again said. 'Am I speaking to Jo?'

'Yes,'

'You are invited to tea tomorrow. But I do warn you if it's a bad day for your mother, your visit will have to be postponed.'

'Alright,' I said. And did not know if I was glad or sorry; or even if I would have liked the visit to be cancelled for good.

There seems to be no getting away from it. As if he's heard my inner Ancient Mariner from right across London, the Husband himself brings up the subject of my parentage this evening: I suppose the questions hurry along because there's so little time left for me to answer them. Plus he does know that my illness is genetic and does have some concern for my children, in his professional way I daresay.

'Let's watch telly,' I say, to divert him from the matter. But as luck would have it he tunes into a documentary about adopted children looking for their birth parents. One thing I shall not miss, dead, is all these reality documentaries about what used to be considered private family matters. "Letting it all hang out" is not my cricket bag exactly, as my father would have said. Fortunately it's not my Husband's either, so we turn the television off. But not before he's picked the subject up yet again and run with it – another bloody cliché, but who cares, and actually he doesn't run, but creeps with it, tentatively - as we lie together, below the blank screen.

'Mind your own business,' I say viciously, in monster mode – oh I've been called a monster often; by my children, by my authors – when I've dropped them; by my colleagues from time to time. And by my lovers of course. But this beloved has never called me a monster, and I wish now that I hadn't briefly sounded like one. He looks quite crushed, for him; I think my dying is getting to him more than ever. His suit needs cleaning, his beard is almost raggedy and smells a bit like slightly rancid bacon when he kisses me goodbye. And of course he doesn't know the full truth of things (no one does, except myself and Patty who doesn't count any more, because she's dead. Her heart gave out during a yoga class, not long after my father died; a very appropriate death for her, somehow, if traumatic for her fellow pupils, let alone her yoga teacher). He could not begin to guess, I suspect, he's an innocent boy at heart, why finding-out who my father was had, for me, been so especially traumatic.

I don't quite know what I was expecting from the meeting with my mother. I'd tried not to imagine it in advance –why anticipate possible horror? But it wasn't quite a horror after all, no more than seeing your mother for the first time since you were three was bound to be a horror to a woman in her sixties as I was. The worst thing was that when I saw her I felt about as much connection as I would have to done to a dead haddock. And I never had liked eating fish.

I went to the house. I climbed the steps. I rang the bell. And at first no one answered – or I thought they didn't, not recognising the little whisper of a voice from somewhere below my feet as any sort of response. The whisper got louder. Then, painfully, louder still, an agonised squawk. I looked down, into the basement, and saw the door open.

'Is it you who's coming to tea?' the figure standing there asked. 'Come down. I'm waiting. It's nearly five o'clock. I've been waiting for a long time.'

'So have I,' I said. And I turned back, down the official steps, survived some rather less salubrious ones and was ushered into a basement kitchen that reminded me of the basement kitchen in house where I grew up besides the village green – it was as well I was reminded of something because my mother I recognised not at all. She'd turned her back as I came down the steps, led me in without shutting the door behind us – I had to do that – it stuck I had to heave at it – whereupon she sat me down at a vast wooden table in the middle of the room. Then she sat down herself, a stranger, on the opposite side of the table, in front of a dresser that reached up to the low ceiling, crowded with cups, plates, bowls, glasses, also postcards, letters, bills stuck on hooks – they looked like bills: there wasn't a spare inch. On one end of the table stood a glass vase full of sweet peas, some of them half dead: I could smell the evasive scent of the live ones from where I was sitting. Nearer, between us, were two cracked plates held together with little wire clamps like the cup out of which my father used to drink his morning tea, the cup my stepmother had thrown out as a health hazard. One plate held two large and crudely cut sandwiches, cucumber it looked like, and the other three vividly pink cakes decorated with silver balls. There were two unmatched cups, two plates, and a teapot covered in one of those retro knitted tea cosies, made like a crinoline lady. Next to it was a metal jug of milk, a bowl of lump sugar complete with tarnished sugar tongs, and a little bowl on top of which sat a metal tea strainer with the odd tea-leaf stuck to it, leaves that might have been there for a long time.

'Tea-time? she said, staring at me. 'How do you do?' She sounded like Celia Johnson in Brief Encounter: I hadn't heard anyone speak like that *since* I last saw Brief Encounter. Even my father who said things like *or*fully or *Or*stria had muted the accent a little.

'Very well, thank you,' I replied, staring back at her avidly, very angry suddenly, my anger only slightly mitigated by curiosity on the one hand, unwelcome pity on the other. It was a shock to realise that she must be more or less the same age as Mr C, our war-damaged lodger, though of course she had to be. She had whitish hair fixed in the manner of women of her generation, permed fifties fashion till it had become thin and faint. She had lips painted a harsh red and cheeks powdered pale. She had astonishingly blue eyes for an old woman, the irises black rimmed, eyes that my younger daughter had inherited; obviously I must have one blue allele to have passed this on to her (my knowledge of genetics may be crude, but after my years of being around a scientist I did know that.) She looked extraordinary, my mother; old yes, very, thin, but not the least bent – no arthritis there, obviously, or osteoporosis: I was not going to inherit such things from her, should I live long enough. She was even, curiously, if grotesquely, pretty. I could not have expected that, beautiful as I knew she had been in her youth; hadn't I seen those two pictures after all, the only ones I ever had? The one where she was a girl on the Broads, her hair as tousled as the hair of Peter Blake's Ophelia: the other one with me in her arms, the slanted hat on her head, the fox-fur round her neck, showing its pointed teeth. She showed *her* teeth to me now, in a polite smile. They seemed mostly her own, the result of expensive dentistry I daresay, more expensive than my father's, most of whose teeth had not been his own by the end. She wore a pair of heavy pearl earrings, clipped onto her un-pierced lobes: it made my similarly shaped earlobes feel sore just looking at them. She wore pearls round her neck and a fine white blouse with short sleeves above a red tweed skirt meant to be tight I think, but as I'd noted following her in, very loose on her narrow flanks. On top she wore a black apron, decorated with a pair of luscious red lips, under which was written in large red letters, *MMM.... DELICIOUS*. On her feet- I could not see them now, they were tucked under the table -she wore a pair of tatty slippers, edged by pink nylon fur that was both mangy and dirty.

'Bad feet,' she'd apologised, seeing me look at them. 'Bunions. No shoes any more. Not very smart I know.' She said it again now. 'Bad feet you know. Pretty bad form, I know. Slippers. When I've got a guest. How do you do?'

I was no longer sure what to expect next: except possibly, looking at the table, an offer of tea – 'how do you like yours, Jo?' something like that. But the offer did not come. She did not say anything. And I was left looking round a kitchen straight out of Mrs Tiggywinkle with its crowded dresser, its ancient Rayburn stove, hung with drying tea-towels, the wooden airer slung from the roof alongside a row of battered saucepans and frying pans suspended from hooks. I had a sudden painful memory of my father sitting on my bed each night and dutifully ploughing his way through every single one of the Beatrice Potter books because that's what he thought children should have. (I did not like to tell him that Beatrix Potter bored me stiff. I've appreciated her much more as an adult, when reading the books – my own old copies – just as dutifully to my children: they liked them much better than I had done at their age, oddly enough.)

Overhead, outside, I heard footsteps; when I craned my neck and looked up out through the window, I saw feet passing on the pavement above our heads. From the house above us I could hear something that sounded like a Hoover buzzing away: from nearer came the drip, drip of a tap, and the sound of water running in a pipe. It was like being underground, or even under water, given the pervading smell of damp. Maybe the Belgrave Square swamp had never been quite banished; maybe this was not so much Mrs Tiggywinkle's house, after all, but more like Jeremy Fisher's. (My children particularly liked Jeremy Fisher. They'd run around screaming with laughter and chanting 'all slippy-sloppy in the back passage,' as if, unlike me in my more innocent childhood, they'd caught the scatological sense.)

My mother might have read my thoughts. She was saying, very politely, like someone at a cocktail party, 'I've got five children, you know. One of them I haven't seen for a long time. My children had ponies and went to boarding school. Frightfully good for them, boarding school. Did you go to boarding school?'

'Yes,' I said. What else could I do except go along with this?

'Jolly good. How many children have you got? Did they go to boarding school.'

'Yes,' I said. 'I've got three children,' I added.

'I've got *five* grandchildren.'

I saw my chance.' Actually, if you add my three, you've got eight.'

'Gosh! Have I really?' she said, clapping her hands. '*Eight* grandchildren. Oh how lovely. Thank you so much. Thank you so *very* much.'

'One of them went to Australia,' I told her after a long silence during which she looked at me blankly, her head tipped to one side.

'Australia? That's a long way away. What did she do that for? Didn't she like it here?'

'Probably not,' I said. Tired of playing along with this polite not to say vapid, not to say irrelevant tea party talk, I asked, staring at her hard –she still did not move her head - 'Do you remember Jo?' Then I stated, very loudly 'I'm *Jane Ophelia. Your eldest daughter.* Do you remember me? I remember you.'

She clapped again. '*My* name's Ophelia. What a coincidence,'

'Jo. Your eldest child,' I was insisting. 'The last thing I remember about you I was three and you were wiping my bottom. And we went to the market with Patty and I saw a calf with shit all down its back and I said 'poor little calf it hasn't got a mummy to wipe its bottom and you thought I was very cute or something. At least *you* did. I'm not so sure about Patty.'

Oh my god I thought, what could I be talking about? I'd almost heard my voice turning into a twee child's voice. What was I thinking of, I wasn't in control here at all. She was. My mother. But how could this caricature, this creature, be my mother?

She smiled ever more broadly now, showing her so well-preserved and pointed teeth. 'Patty,' she said. Of course -Patty -my best friend. I remember Patty. She doesn't ring up any more. Why not? Is she dead?'

'Not yet,' I said.

I watched my mother, if she was my mother, I feared she might be, reach down into the pocket of her apron now and pull out an exquisite little enamelled cigarette box and a cheap lighter, the kind they give out free in tobacconists – my husband had been using an identical one just last night; except that his was orange. My mother's lighter was green.

'Cigarette?' she asked politely, flicking the box open. 'Do have one of mine.'

'No thanks,' I said. 'I don't smoke. What else do you remember about from Patty? Do you remember the village, do you remember my father, your husband? Do you remember *me*? Jo?' (Why was asking? At this moment I almost hoped she didn't.)

My mother had lit her cigarette expertly. She controlled it with fancy gestures as if she was smoking it in a holder, taking neat little puffs, blowing smoke at me across the table. Suddenly there came into my head a play I'd seen once called 'Sport of My Mad Mother.' All this was definitely the sport of *my* mad mother and I was the sport. Of course.

'What else do you remember from when I was, little apart from Patty?' I tried again.

'I remember Jo, of course, my little girl. I called her after me. My name is Ophelia, you know. I remember the village – those Mr Jenners, weren't they taxi drivers? – one was very fat and one was very thin. And Mrs Cosgrave, the rude woman in the sweetshop, I hated Mrs Cosgrave, she disapproved of me, I know she disapproved of me. She was always trying to feed Joey extra sweets, boiled sweets, caramels, humbugs, I didn't like that one little bit. And Leslie the boy next door, the butcher's boy he was always trying to look up my skirts, and Mrs Green his mother she was always drunk. And Mis Evendon, the ironmonger with a face like a prune and hair like metal. And the two Misses Luckin, the ugly one and the pretty one. They were all so tedious, such a joke. And then the Churchill family coming to church on Sundays everybody kowtowing to them, even my husband and he should know better he worked with people like that. And then my husband – oh my husband, he was so boring, *'Are you feeling feak and weeble today, Ophelia, what can I get you.'* He was the biggest joke of all.'

I was outraged. I might laugh at my father sometimes, he might have driven me mad, but no one else was allowed to say so. How dare she? At the same time, I thought: there's not much wrong with her long-term memory, is there? Sod her. I was ruthless, determined to exploit that. But while I was looking for the right words in which to do so, there were footsteps outside the door at the back of the room. It opened; a head appeared round it, a remarkably square head with hair cropped short, showing little ears from which hung ear-rings with what looked like Buddhist symbols on them, yin and yang. Below the head I could see the top of a black apron identical to my mother's. *MMM...DELICIOUS.*

Had they bought a job lot I wondered? Or maybe one of my half-siblings had; the half-siblings who probably did not know I existed, whom I would never meet: for it did not seem the least likely that we would all, suddenly, start playing happy families. I had no intention of going to our mother's funeral for sure.

'OK then, Phelie', the head said in the same voice as the one that answered the telephone most likely though I couldn't be sure. Its eyes cast a hasty glance in my direction, but did not seem interested in me much,

My mother looked round, vaguely and then smiled, but without enthusiasm.

'Oh. You,' she said.

'Everything's OK? Insisted the voice. 'Remember, Phelie, just the one cigarette.'

Blowing a cloud of smoke towards her my mother said, 'Oh yes. Spiffing. We're having such a wizard chinwag about the old days, aren't we…?' she fumbled for my name, gave up and said 'aren't we, darling?'

'We do seem to be,' I agreed.

'Good oh. That's alright then. If you need anything' – this might have been intended for me as much as for my mother; the head was looking at me directly for the first time … 'I'm only upstairs; all you need to do is call.'

She took her head away and then put it back, looking at me for a second time, rather more lengthily. Was she trying to see if she could recognise my mother in me, or me in my mother? I doubted if she would manage it. I hoped that she would not.

'Apologies for the kitchen entertainment,' she was saying now, more chattily. 'But your mother doesn't like the drawing-room upstairs. She thinks all the people in the street are looking at her, don't you, Phelie?'

My mother shuddered. 'They throw stones. They're bound to throw stones. They're jealous. People always want to throw stones at me,' she said.

'It's fine in the kitchen. If there's a problem, I'll call,' I added, dismissively.

The head nodded and withdrew: the door squeaked and rattled to a close. When the footsteps on the stairs had faded away, I turned back to my mother and asked, coldly - very coldly – You thought

226

my father a bore, did you? This *bore* as you called him married you didn't he, when you were expecting me? What would you have done if he hadn't? And who was it brought me up when you ran off? Bolted.'

My mother looked blank. Too much time had passed, obviously, since what she'd said before the housekeeper or carer, whatever she was, had interrupted us. Her cigarette had burned down right down by now. She took the stub out of her mouth, stared at it bemusedly – the filter was marked with lipstick, I noted- then reached up the table and drowned it in the vase of sweet peas, its little hiss of protest speeding back down the scrubbed white wood towards us.

'Now, what were we talking about?' she asked brightly.

'My father. Your first husband, your cousin the one who called such a bore, who married you because you were pregnant with me. I'm Jo,' I said. 'Jane Ophelia, your daughter. Don't you remember?

My mother looked not only bewildered now, she looked appalled. She rubbed her eyes and wrinkled them up. Her mouth turned down like a child's, her nose grew red like the nose on Peter Blake's Ophelia. A tear ran down her cheek, channelling her coating of face powder. 'Why are you being so unkind, Jane Ophelia? If you *are* her, Jo, Jane Ophelia, not just pretending.' How strange, I thought. Suddenly she does know who I am. She really does. She remembers everything. We are sitting here, mother and daughter, for the first time in more than 60 years.

My mother was wailing now, tears pouring down her face. 'I loved you. I wrote so many letters, but you never answered. I wanted to have you back to live with me when we got married. But your father wouldn't have it. He wouldn't. He wanted you all to himself.'

This information turned me first cold, then hot. Was she telling the truth? Could she be?

I took a deep breath. I tried to calm the heat and cold that had turned into unstoppable trembling and after a minute, deadpan coming as ever to my rescue, succeeded, more or less.

'I never saw any letters,' I said. Because I hadn't: not at the time they'd been sent. I didn't add, though I wanted to; *you knew where*

I was: you could have come to fetch me if you really wanted. Why didn't you?

'Didn't you?' she said. 'No letters? How very odd? What kind of letters were they,' she asked after a minute. 'Why are we talking about letters? Do I know you?'

I was no longer prepared to excuse her anything, however demented she was. 'Do you remember my real father?' I asked. 'The one you met in Paris?'

'Your father? Who was your father? Who are *you*? But of course I remember Jo's father. Hamlet, I called him; it was a joke. I was Ophelia you see. I was intact when I met him. I loved him so much. I fell in love with him. He was so handsome and so sad. I couldn't bear it. I had to comfort him. I was intact before then.'

'How should I my true love know from another one,' I sang, my sotto voce kind and unkind both, the words making me think of my lover even now, in our madhouse; but what had he to do with this? She must have heard me. 'My true love,' she said. And then – more tears ran down: her powdery face was all smeared, blurred, 'He went away. I couldn't find him any more. I couldn't tell him about my baby.'

She was begging me now -'what did you just sing, Joey? Sing it again.'

I shook my head. I wasn't going to sing again, not to her. I saw her reach up her hand, pull off, quite viciously, one of her pearl earrings leaving a bright red mark on her earlobe – a fine, curved ear-lobe I noted, just like mine. She placed it on the table and stared at it for a long minute. And then she looked down at herself and said, in her society voice, it really was horribly like Celia Johnson's: a voice altogether from the past. 'Oh dear, how rude of me. Look at me, inviting you to tea and still wearing my apron,' and she pulled at the red, red mouth and MMM...DELICIOUS, hauled, pulled the apron right over her head and threw it on the floor behind – but not before using it to wipe her face, wipe her tears away, smearing and blurring everything, lipstick, powder, tears still more. She did not look pretty any longer; she just looked grotesque.

The white blouse she wore underneath the apron was very clean and neat and flimsy. The abruptness with which she'd removed it had pulled open two of her buttons, exposing a withered cleavage that had suffered only from age, not from the activities of any surgeon, confirming that she was not to blame for my illness, at least. Her arms were very white, the white skin on the outside shrivelled like a leaf off a tree, the white skin on the inside so translucent the blue veins stood out clearly.

Leaning her smeary face across the table, she cried 'oh *dear*: your tea. What a dreadful hostess I am.' She tried for my name; gave up. 'I am so sorry, darling.' She removed the crinoline lady, picked up the pot, with the other hand pulled one cup towards her. I watched her tilt the pot over, her hands trembling as an unsteady stream of liquid fell from the spout, most of it falling into the cup, surprisingly, only a little landing in the saucer. She put the pot down at last, pushed the cup towards me across the table, the tea slopping everywhere, and said. 'How do you take it? Milk? Sugar? And do take a sandwich, won't you? They're cucumber, you know. Super.'

I did not take one. And nor did she. Instead she opened the cigarette box still lying besides her, and with a defiant look at me, the look of a naughty child, took out another cigarette. 'Cigarette?' she asked politely. 'You *are* old enough now to smoke aren't you? *Do* have one of mine.'

'No thank you,' I said, equally politely. More urgently, even desperately, I asked. 'Do you still remember my – Jo's - father's name?'

'Of course I do: he was Hamlet. He was so very sad, because he couldn't see his family, because he said they might be killed. My true love. Hamlet.'

'Not that name. The other one. His real name.'

I expected her to look puzzled and prevaricate. But she did not prevaricate. She leaned across the table as if confiding in me and whispered 'Jo's father's name you mean?'

'Of course, my father's name,' I insisted. 'Paris? You remember?'

'Whose father? Jo's? *You* can't be Jo. You're an old woman. Who are you?'

'I'm younger than you, *Mummy*. Who was he?'

She leaned back. 'Oh yes. Paris,' she said. 'Hamlet.'

His real name,' I insisted again.

'How can you be my Joey? You're so *old*? Are you going to throw something at me, like the people outside?'

'I might want to, ' I said. 'But I won't.'

She was cringing away from me now. I found this disgusting: for a moment I truly did find it so. And then suddenly, looking at her, it was as if she dissolved, as if I dissolved - around us, below us, a blackness was swallowing us both up. What was I doing here – why had I wanted to stare into this mirror of myself, that was not myself, that I should not have had anything to do with? Was entering this house the greatest mistake of my mistaken life? Blue eyes; smudged lips – smeared fragile skin – the eyes, the lips, puffing on the cigarette, that ancient skin advancing towards me over the table. The mouth opening -the cigarette removed–
'Joey?... why are you so old? Joey? How can you be my baby?'

All I could do now was groan, in sorrow, for both of us – for those wasted years of trying – and failing - to show her how it, motherhood, should be done. All I could do was gawp as she advanced on me, unable to get up and run, as much as I wanted to. And it was too late anyway. This war was lost, as thoroughly as those many wars I had copy-edited for my old boss and edited for the boss who was myself; in which, despite the flags and parades that ended them, I'd never discerned any real victors, not in the long run, only losers; always.

My mother put the cigarette back in her mouth. She puffed out into my darkness another vaporous chain of smoke. And then she leaned over the table still further, as close as she could get, closer and closer no matter how I shrank back – I might have shrunk back – or maybe I did not; maybe I leaned closer too, unable to stop myself being dragged ever deeper into the grief she represented. Out of the corner of my eye I saw the door opening behind her; peering round it the face of the carer with the square head and the omega and alpha, yin and yang earrings. And as she smiled her professional smile, I learned at last, in the tremulous voice of my long-lost mother, Hamlet's real name.

CHAPTER THIRTY

In one way I was a good mother; my absolute determination that my children were not going to grow up as I did, not knowing who their parents were. My children were going to know and be around both their parents throughout their childhood, whether these parents were adequate or not – I repeated this to their father during the difficult discussions at the time of our separation.

It was one reason I stayed with him as long as I did, most likely, till long after it must have been obvious, even to him, that we brought out the worst each other. And also one reason I stayed faithful to him for most of if not all those years - not that between work and parenthood, I had much time to be unfaithful, except when I started travelling, then I did receive a proposition or two. But I was too exhausted usually to take up such offers, even if I fancied the man who was making them, which wasn't often.

Of course, in need of comfort, I had succumbed by the time we did split up, as I confessed during those same difficult – not to say painful discussions. I knew that he'd suspected it: he'd accused me of infidelity long before I fell into bed with someone for the first time, following the party *for the end of the world as we knew it* in December 1973 which he'd refused to go to: *might as well be hung for a sheep as a lamb,* I'd thought. To which confession he'd responded with a degree of priggishness that wasn't entirely unlike him, but that surprised me just the same. 'As for me,' he said, 'I have been entirely faithful. As I promised during our wedding service. Or maybe you don't remember.' This made me want to laugh, predictably, if also quite unreasonably. But I could not laugh, not when I wanted, equally, to cry: the two impulses cancelling each other out, I looked at him, blankly. 'Well done you,' I think I said, but only under my breath.

The breakup wasn't all my fault; it rarely is. We were two people who should never have married in the first place, as both my best friends knew, though they didn't say. How could they say? In those reticent times, we never criticised each other's boyfriends: If they had done so I wouldn't have listened. At the same time, my determination that my children were not going to lose either of us in consequence made me willing to take the blame, unwilling to fight with their father over any of the arrangements we were making. I'd seen one of my author's children forced to take sides between their parents, two going off with one and two with the other; this was not going to happen to my children, no matter what.

I told him that I would accept any terms, provided it meant the children remained close to both of us. I even invoked my own lack of visible parents as the reason for my feeling so strongly: this was a subject I had rarely, if ever, raised with him before. (It was lucky I hadn't told him Patty's name for my mother: 'like mother, like daughter,' would have been far too crude a way, for him, of suggesting that I was 'a Bolter' too, but he would have used it against me in some way.) All he did say, stiffly, was 'Perhaps you should have thought of them before.' But at least he did not seriously deny me, except by declining to support me in any way at all: not that he needed to, my income was more than enough. This went to the extent of providing very little even for the children when they stayed at my house. Also, though he had previously resisted any idea of them going to boarding school, he advocated it now. This suited me, too, if I did have to come up with some of the fees. (My father helped out here. He'd always been disappointed by my disdain of boarding-schools.)
It was not that my husband was mean at heart, or the least vindictive by nature. But he was very hurt and very angry and I thought he had the right to be, so was quite prepared to acquiesce, provided the children were free during the holidays to move to and fro between us as they liked. Nor did we ever argue about Christmas or birthdays or holiday arrangements. Quite often we got together like normal parents until the children themselves pronounced this crazy not to say a complete sham. In all other respects, they spent their childhood, post divorce, shuttling between our not very far apart houses and grew up as close to both of us as they needed to - inasmuch as any of them could be close to me, the lousy mother, the mother of wire not cloth who worked for a living instead of staying at home, who could not grit her teeth and stay within the marriage, no matter what, as I would have had to a generation or two back. Even her father's refusal to let our

elder daughter move in with him and his new wife fulltime as she requested once when especially angry with me did not seem to make too much difference.

In this at least I could be – I was - a good mother.

Peter brought his fiancé in to see me today. She was not at all what I was expecting. Fastidious as he'd always appeared, I'd assumed – I think – that any girl he liked would be neat, even elegant, have a good figure, be nicely dressed, if not necessarily pretty.

Admittedly the girl wore her hospital uniform under her duffle coat – but a duffle coat? – *that* surprised me to start with; as did the clumpy shoes, the bulky figure, the shock of tightly curled hair which framed her face: this young woman did not bother to use straighteners for sure. She had a big mouth, plump and rosy cheeks, freckles across her nose, slightly crooked teeth and sandy eyebrows. She looked slightly butch to my eyes. For all the surprise, I liked the look of her, but that is not quite my point. What I could not do, hard as I tried, hard as they tried, bumping up against each other, grinding hips, giggling in each other's faces, was see them as a couple.

In between the giggles and bumps and grinds the girl was eying me with a clearly professional eye: even without the hospital overall beneath her duffle coat, I would have known she was a nurse. She glanced at Peter more soberly now: I was almost expecting them to start a consultation. But instead she came over and took my hand and said in a Glasgow accent –'I'm so glad to meet you. Peter talks about you more than a wee bit.'

'Does he tell you about all his patients?'

'No.'

'Do you tell him about yours?'

'Only the interesting ones. Interesting in a medical sense,' she added hastily, blushing in a way that accentuated her freckles.

'Tina should have been a doctor,' Peter interjected here. 'She knows more about medicine than any of them.'

He seemed a different person to the one I thought I knew, or at least the one that operated in this hospital room. His voice not the least camp, he seemed almost subservient. No, that's not the right word: he was not subservient, just not quite in charge.

'So I'm an interesting case, am I? Is that how Peter described me?'

'Not exactly,' she said. And laughed out loud, making me like her more than ever.

'What she means,' said Peter, sounding more like himself, 'What she means is that I described you as a foul-mouth old virago…'

'But a good laugh often –like FUN,' Tina corrected him, sounding almost embarrassed. 'Is Peter always so rude?'

'I don't think I've ever been described as FUN before,' I said, drily. I added, because it was true and I was glad of the chance to say it. 'Peter's a good nurse.'

'Thank you for the encomium, dear,' he said, in his most camp voice. At this his girlfriend burst out laughing revealing the full crookedness of her teeth – one at the back had a gold filling, I noticed, the glint of which seemed to add to her merriment.

'When are you two getting married?' I asked abruptly, tired of this.

They looked at each other. 'Ask her,' Peter said.

'Ask him,' she said crossly.

'What she means,' Peter said, 'Is that we can't decide whether to spend our money on a fancy wedding or a fancy honeymoon. She wants the fancy wedding. I'm for the honeymoon. What do you think?'

But I was not going to involve myself in their arguments, and, anyway, I was much too tired to care.

'It's been lovely to meet you, Tina,' I said in the warm but dismissive tones I might have used to an author I'd decided not to publish. 'Good luck with all of this.'

They *were* nurses. Both their faces returned suddenly to concerned, professional mode. Wondering vaguely if Tina was as good a nurse as Peter, I was taken aback, almost shocked, when she leaned over and kissed me on the cheek, saying, 'We have to go, you're tired.' She smelled of ether, shampoo and toothpaste: it felt strange. Peter did not kiss me, thank god. His face was almost embarrassed, yet proud at the same time. He looked back at me as they went out of the door, bumping hips again, and waved an airy hand, 'See you in the morning, dear.'

'If I survive the night,' I said.

'You'll survive this night.'

The Husband visits then, briefly, looking half dead himself. He's followed by Jen, apologising for visiting so late. She finds me still watching – half-watching – the programme he had left on, about some MPs sent to live in tower blocks among their poorer constituents.

It was hard to know which side was more baffled and appalled: the still – to me – meaty-looking MPs of whatever party or the council tenants, even if MPs and tenants did contrive some jolly parties together with wine paid for by the MPs, who were, in theory, being forced to live on the same limited benefits as their fellow tenants. One MP had refused to don the tracksuits handed out to make him and the others look more like everyone else on the estates (how patronising, I thought, was that?) He continued to march about in his own neatly creased chinos, plus checked shirt, tie, highly polished leather shoes, and talked about cricket to the Indian newsagent, from whom he tried in vain, to acquire copies of the Daily Telegraph. He reminded me – but only a little - of my Times reading father, someone I would rather not think about just now, but whom cannot help thinking about just the same. 'My father would be turning in his grave over the MPs expenses scandal,' I said. 'He'd think parliament has gone to the dogs since his day. Probably he'd blame Margaret Thatcher. He blamed her for most things.'

'Didn't the place make him cynical even then?' Jen asks.

'Maybe. Up to a point,' I say remembering the minister he may or may not have found fucking a secretary on his desk. 'And as you know he was capable of the odd treachery of his own,' I add viciously. (Jen was the only person apart from my Husband whom I'd told about my father keeping my mother from me.) Staring at the stained concrete towers rearing up on the screen behind an MP in earnest discussion with a council tenant, I try to change the subject. 'In the 70's,' I say - the weary pair have taken to pacing agitatedly round an expanse of equally weary-looking grass littered with what looked like sweet papers and dog shit and bearing a large notice saying NO BALL GAMES –on which the camera suddenly zooms in. 'In the 70's, we all had the happy idea that inequality had diminished, was diminishing, the rich not so rich and the poor not so poor, that in such respects our bit of the world was putting itself to rights. But now look at it. It's obscene, all private schools, SUV's and Filipino maids, the rich in gated palaces, the poor beating each other up. It's worse than the thirties, pretty much. And that's not to mention the worse horrors in Africa, not to mention global warming, blah, blah, blah.'

I lie silently for a moment. At last I hear myself saying, but only to myself. 'Progress isn't always progressive. Nostalgia need not always be retrogressive.' Then I add, more loudly, 'Thank god I'm dying. I've had enough.'

Jen does not grimace at the word 'dying' the way others might. But with her dark, liquid, slightly protuberant eyes she gazes at me still more intently. Her hair tied back in a severe knot, she looks older than I'm used to, huddling a hairy sweater about her despite the warmth of a hospital room. 'It's bloody cold outside,' she says. 'And it's supposed to be nearly summer.' And then she adds in a voice so soft I could hardly hear her. 'I'm sorry. So sorry.' She does not say what she is sorry about, my death, my pain, the world. It could have been anything. And suddenly I do not care about the state of the world, awful as it is: I feel my face crumpling, embarrassingly, tears welling up in my eyes for the rejected baffled child that I had been, all those years back, for my children, my grandchildren, everyone.

'Turn the telly off,' I say. 'Turn the bloody telly off.' So she does – blanking out an MP now lying face down, despairing, on the dismal lawn and leaving me with the feeling that this is, most likely, the last TV programme I'll ever see.

Coincidence; chaos; chance – how about this for your theory of pure chance; people who happened to be in the French capital at the same time as millions of other people, and who happened to frequent certain cheap left bank cafes the way the young did and always have done, who happened to be in the same café one night and whose eyes had met across the crowded room. Etc, etc. Which was all supposition, of course; except I that did know that my father liked left bank student cafes and liked picking up beautiful girls. As I also knew that my mother was both beautiful and wild enough to escape the family she was staying with, who were supposed to protect her virtue: and that my father was a long way from home, sick with worry about his family every time he opened a newspaper – and lonely. And that he liked beautiful girls. But then what man doesn't, heterosexual or gay?

My mother even threw in the name of the café: this I hadn't asked. I hadn't asked what she'd been drinking the evening she met my father for the first time, either. But she told me that too. 'It was absinthe, I think, darling? Wasn't it? Weren't we all drinking it that night?' 'How the hell would I know?' I said. Then she said something about a painter she'd flirted with who'd wanted to paint her – God, mother spare me some of the clichés. I was thinking: if only she had gone home with the painter. I'd look quite different, I'd be a different person altogether. But so what?

For it wasn't just a matter of one chance, one coincidence: there was this much worse one; the one I couldn't begin to tell The Husband. I had given him the simple information that I had once – by chance again – heard my father lecturing; but I acknowledged nothing else. It's just possible, I think, that this chance, this coincidence, might even have silenced, might even have appalled him had I revealed it, whether he admitted the fact or not.

It wasn't that such coincidences don't happen. Long separated brothers and sisters have met on dating websites, at parties, on communal camping trips. Mothers are treated in hospital by their unknown children. Fathers encounter offspring they never knew they had on the other side of the world. We've – I've - all heard of coincidences like this, equally far-fetched. Yet these coincidences did not affect me, why should I give them more than a passing thought? What I did reflect on obsessively, distractedly, was *my* turn of fate, of chance. That my mother had slept with a man in Paris, at a time when Europe was in turmoil. That a professor had come to teach in Oxford, as eminent professors do, given some visiting chair or other. That I had been in Oxford at the time and that, in all innocence, I had gone to hear him, the way I went to hear many professors, visiting or incumbent. And that when we had seen each other, across that crowded room, we had come together, drawn perhaps by our shared genes that I'd not known of till recently and that my father never did. Or maybe not: maybe we'd have fancied each other, no matter. All the rest is silence; all the rest is beyond knowing. Except for *Bring out the yellow flags*: and the words, *unclean, unclean.*

This was the real oddity. My father, Nathan Rubenstein, and I had broken a taboo laid down by almost every society that ever was, except possibly the Egyptian - and look what happened to the offspring of incestuous Pharaohs? At the same time we were innocent: when we loved each other the way we did, we had not known what we were doing. He, my true, genetic father, was the only one of my actual or surrogate parents who had not lied to me over years, all the years of my life so far. It was not he who had let me grow up thinking my mother did not want me, when actually she *had* wanted me, in the end. (My feeling that my mother, even pre-dementia, had been on the positive side of flaky, that I was most likely better off with my adoptive father, is not the point.) What this father did to me, unlike what Eric Gill did to *his* daughters, was in absolute ignorance – and not paedophilic in the least. Even his impregnating me was more unlucky than careless. All those years ago, in Paris, he had done what lusty young men do when they get the chance, especially sad and lonely young men: he had fucked a willing young woman and gone away too soon to know the consequence. And all those years ago in Oxford, with her happy connivance he'd fucked another young woman, me; who, just like her mother, had not told him of the consequence either.

In which case, given that I was equally innocent why did I feel still guiltier than the un-parents who had deceived me? Because I did feel guilty. This bore no relation to rationality, though I had taken it for granted before that I *was* rational.

I've always been as cool, for instance, about ethics, as about religious beliefs and opinion. Oh sure I believe in protecting children, being nice to your neighbours, especially the grannies, in not hurting anyone gratuitously, even, in theory, in sharing out belongings, donating to Oxfam, cutting your coat in half, etc – I never went so far as inviting beggars and slum children into my house, but then who does, except the saintly. And saintly I was not. In short, believing in basic decency, I shunned extremes: most religious tenets seemed to me extreme, one way or another.

But maybe deep in all of us, in our fundamentally atavistic hearts, there is a point which order is no more, turns into a disorder beyond any that even someone as calm, controlled and as rational as I was – as I assumed I was - can countenance, let alone control. Before all this I had not known what my moral bounds were exactly, where the limits lay: but then I found that whatever these limits were, I had, inadvertently, breached them. Definitely I had breached them.

Fact: I had fucked and been fucked by my father. And what was worse I had enjoyed it and could still feel an erotic frisson if I wasn't careful, even though mixed with guilt and disgust these days. What difference did it make that I had not known he was my father, any more than he had known I was his daughter? None at all.

Fact: I had not only been fucked by my father, I had been made pregnant by him, despite all the care he took.

Fact: that baby had been my very own brother or sister. Would have been, too, its own uncle or aunt.

Fact: I had aborted it. Which was a crime in those days as well as a mortal sin.

Fact: my father had rubbed his seminal fluid tenderly all over my still almost adolescent abdomen – *come rub it on my belly like guava jelly* - the same fluid that holds all human life and genes. Which in this particular case had engendered not only me, complete with the diseased gene that is killing me, but our incestuous, inbred baby: which I had then had scraped away in a clinic in Harley Street, London W1.

Who says the war that brought my father together with my mother and then with me, the effects of which had driven my mother away from me, who says it had ever ended? Any more than it had ended for the man in the basement, driven mad by Dunkirk (who, my husband says. has been taken to hospital now and may even be dead before me. I hope so.)

It felt as if some atavistic Aunt Ada Doom was leaping merrily inside me, jumping up, and out into the world, shouting 'something nasty in the woodshed,' and pointing at me. At the nasty thing in the woodshed, that is. ME.

I felt it the more because I still could not quite deny the pleasure of fucking and being fucked by my father. I went on being shaken by the most erotic of erotic memories. But how could I dare do that? It was MY FATHER did all these impossible, delightful things to me, He was taboo. I was taboo. All of it was taboo: I should, therefore, be shut out of society, beyond my tribe and never allowed back in. *Wave yellow flag*. Keep on waving.

Perhaps it was all my ancestors speaking through me too: genetics, yet again. The Protestant divines on the one hand – for them, if anything could lead to hell fire incest would; let alone abortion. As for the rabbis on the other side (oh god all those pogroms I had to see as part of me, even before Hitler -and the Holocaust which was also part of me, whether I liked it or not – I didn't like) as for the rabbis, what my father and I did together, even avoiding as we did my menstrual blood, would be thought of, I suspected, as the essence of non-kosher: liable to send us to that Jewish hell, called, what was it? Sheol. Not that I knew much about rabbinical ethics, let alone rabbinical ideas of hell.

One thing certain was that neither my children nor I were the safe little Englanders I'd imagined, products only of our offshore island and, possibly, its next-door neighbour. Now our past went beyond Europe, connected to some of its most fearsome history. Recognising myself as Nate's daughter meant seeing exile, pogrom, genocide locked into my genes and my children's whether I liked it or not: something they would discover in the codicil attached to my will. But at least I did not have to tell them that my eldest child was not only her father's daughter but his grandchild. *Be thankful for small mercies* my father – my adoptive father - used to say. He never said anything about big ones.

What a fuss I was making, part of me could not help thinking. Being made pregnant by one's father was not after all such an uncommon event, men - some men - being what they are: and many of those so made pregnant suffered a good deal more than I did. I had enjoyed myself: I had not known how very much I shouldn't have done what I was doing, let alone have enjoyed it. I wasn't raped and abused. I was over the age of consent and a more than willing partner.

This knowledge didn't help in the slightest. It just made me feel more abject, guiltier than ever. It was as if in finding out who I was at last, parentally speaking, I had lost who I thought I was in all other respects and could see no means whatever of getting that familiar, rational, deadpan person back. I thought of Jocasta when she discovered *her* innocent incest–with her son in this case - but no less outside her moral order than my incest with my father was outside what I'd never reckoned on before as mine, but obviously was. Maybe I, too, should have taken out my eyes with a hatpin and hung myself from the ceiling; there were moments in my madness when I felt I should do something as drastic. But I lacked both the courage and the conviction. What would have been the point? And besides, coming from an age with much less certain moral boundaries, allowed to forgive itself more readily, I could afford to be pragmatic about forgiving myself. Yet I did not forgive myself.

At the same time I was not angry with myself – or with Nate. The person I was angry with for years, up till the time of his death and after for a while was my adoptive father.

For quite a long while, my poor guiltless husband - The Husband - became surrogate for both my fathers: my guilty – deceiving – adoptive father, my innocently guilty incestuous one. After I'd learned the truth I could not even allow him in my bed, let alone touch me, let alone make love; not for months and months. Poor man. I'm not sure why he stood by me then, but stay by me he did, through all this agony, even though he did not know the precise reason for the worst of the agony. I put him off – I explained it as my rage at the adopted father for having kept my mother from me, for Patty for concealing the truth of what had happened to her, of who my father was, for all those long years. I could not bear to tell him the worst of it. It was none of his business and, besides, I felt too dirty and ashamed.

One day I try to find Nate himself. I go onto the internet, Google the campus of the University of California where he'd been professor, most likely still was emeritus professor: indeed there his name was and his email address which I copy into my address book, but then do nothing about it. How to start such an email? Hi, remember me, remember your little English lover, remember the Randolph hotel? But suppose he too is demented, suppose even if he isn't someone else fields his emails, a secretary for instance? I could just write very formally asking him to get in touch with me, making out I was a former student from his time in England. But then he wouldn't remember me as student, maybe the name Jo would mean nothing. Maybe he has forgotten me after all this time, I was just one of many such conquests.

I went on for days like this: even weeks. And then I read his obituary in the Guardian, and realised it was all too late, anyway.

On my deathbed, now, I take refuge once again in memories of my childhood when all was so innocent: at least for me. That way I can for a while put aside my anger with my adoptive father that I thought had been quenched after his death, but which has come back now in full force. Intense as that anger is it seems a simpler emotion, more easily put aside than my pity and fury with my demented mother, my guilty yet still erotic memory of love with my genetic father.

I have begun having headaches: appalling headaches. Peter, my Husband, my son, even Jen on one visit, have had to sit besides me holding wet cloths to my head to help me bear it. Doctors come in and out. They are discussing options, but not with me; obviously I am thought beyond it.

I retreat from the room once more, mentally, and return to the village where I grew up, roaming its streets, buying food in its shops – the butcher's, the baker's on the green opposite our house; the International Stores, Peggy and Maureen, the sugar that came, damp, in a blue sugar bag. I play again in the sandpit with golden-haired Maureen (*Shall I go, shall I tarry?*) I sit in my father's kitchen with Patty and the merry Mrs Watts. I have Sunday lunch in Patty's polished dining-room served by the cook who reminds me of Patty's bad-tempered corgi dog. I play in Patty's stream with Patty's son, both of us wearing his worn-out school corduroy shorts, held up belts with little snake clasps – oh how I loved those little snake clasps, the black plimsolls we put on our feet, much more than I loved my girls' clothes, the smocked dresses, the polished Clarks' sandals, the Fair Isle twinsets and cardigans, the pleated woollen skirts that I had to wear for best. How I cling to the memory of my pre-pubertal, virgin self in shorts, aertex shirt, snake clasp belt, trying to catch minnows in that muddy stream so different from Ophelia's stream in the picture on the wall of my night nursery. These days – in fact ever since I learned the truth - I have felt more in common with that drifting helpless Ophelia than I did with Peter Blake's sturdier Ophelia. I wish I didn't.

At one moment I even take myself back to picking blackberries with Aunt Anne, to cutting up meat in her clean, bleak, horrible old kitchen.

At another I am drinking sherry with that other mentor, my former headmistress while she alludes, in mere passing, to my love life.

What I do not do any more, in memory, is wander round the Houses of Parliament with all their fake gothickry. They remind me too much of the fake gothickry of the Randolph Hotel where I had been fucked by my very own father. And that memory – apart from the erotic frissons that still refuse to stay away entirely – I have returned to avoiding; even though the effort of avoiding it makes my head ache more than ever.

CHAPTER THIRTY-ONE

At some point my elder daughter turns up to see me. When exactly I cannot tell, things are becoming ever more confused. But it must have been an evening when my headaches are less active: I would not have felt strong enough otherwise for the extraordinary conversation – extraordinary for us - that ensues.

I do not see her enter the room. I open my eyes to find her sitting there, in the low green chair. I've been expecting Jen: am ashamed to find myself slightly disappointed at the sight of my elder daughter. I smile especially widely - I think I do - to make up for my un-motherly disappointment.

'Hi, mum.' She says. 'How's things?' It's a superfluous question, of course. But then she's always been less perceptive than her younger brother. This, combined with my own impatience and reluctance to acknowledge anything beyond my nose – a process too liable to complicate matters, I always thought - caused difficulties between us from the moment she ceased to be the smiling, easy, doted-on baby, turned into a fractious toddler, then an anxious, rather whiny little girl, then a querulous and insecure big one. Of all my children, unfortunately for her, she is the one who, like me, tries to hold everything tightly to herself. Not least, though she has lived all these years within the pressures of a mixed marriage, we've never talked about any problems she might have encountered. To make things still more complicated she appears to have inherited her father's lack of humour: irony flies straight over her head.

She starts telling me about worries around her oldest child – a boy: I think for a moment she is daring to mention some effect of his darker skin: but actually it's his reluctance to revise properly for his GCSE's: his general teenage recalcitrance. She is of the generation that has always been allowed to admit openly and loudly their difficulties with their children from the minute they are born; in particular how boring it can be raising your own children, hands on. Even when she was trying to show how much better a mother she was than me she never denied she found life round toddlers trying. One of her school contemporaries has made a career out of *her* boredom, producing books, doing surveys, writing articles in various newspapers. My former firm publishes

244

an otherwise excellent short story writer some of whose effusions investigate, more artfully, the same thing.

My generation never dared to be so honest. Such feelings making us feel like failures as mothers, we did not know that almost all of us had them. Had Bowlby not told us we'd be failing if we palmed off our children on cloth mothers let alone on wire ones: if we were not ever present, ever-loving mothers? Were we not informed by local Tory councillors that nurseries and nursery schools were only for inadequate, that is to say lazy – or worse still – unnatural mothers? What was the matter with *me* that could I barely spend an hour round my one and two year olds before wanting to eat myself? How was it I did not care about what they and I had such fights about – what knickers they would wear today; what plates they would eat off? (Though I knew - I think I knew – that these conflicts were a necessary part of something I once saw called their 'establishment of selfhood', it did not make them any less tedious.) Of course I'd partly solved that problem by employing first mothers' helps and later on au pairs and going off to my job. But it did not stop me feeling guilty. At the same time inhibitions about expressing my boredom as a mother also inhibited me from admitting to myself, let alone others, the many things that did delight me about my children.

'Children can be a pain,' I say now. 'It's the nature of them.'

She looks at me accusingly. 'And you should know? You were never around.'

She checks herself, glancing at me almost guiltily. Even in this friendly lamplight, I must look like death, I think.

I am less kind. I do not spare her. 'Meaning I went out to work. And you never have done.'

'No,' she said. 'I never wanted to. Not really.' But she sounds less reproachful suddenly. And then she says, to my surprise. 'You know what, though. These days I envy you. Not in seeing so little of us as we grew up, I wouldn't have missed for the world *my* kids growing up,' she adds hastily. She's not going to let me off that easily.

She pauses. I am expected to ask what she's envious of, I suppose. Riled by the implied criticisms I am almost too tired to oblige her. But in the end, half pitying her for finding it so hard to admit that there is, after all, some limit to the ideal she's always

placed so unblushingly in front of me, I hear myself asking.
'Why?'

'I'm just thinking I'd like a job again, The kids don't need me in the same way. The house is empty most of the day in term-time and I'm not fond of housework.'

'Go out and get a job,' I say. 'Why don't you?'

'It's not that we need the money,' she says defensively.

'Of course not,' I say.

Then she bursts out, fiddling with her hands, pulling her hair, taking one of her ear-rings out and rolling it around in her fingers, 'What job? Who's going to employ me after all these years? I can't just go back into publicity work, the culture is quite different, as for technology …I can use a laptop of course, but even so, who'll want me? Anyway,' she says, bitterly, 'you have to be young and pretty for jobs like that and look at me, nearer 50 than 40. I might as well give up and go for a till at Tesco.'

It's seeing your children heading into and beyond middle age I think to myself now, looking at her almost with love, that really makes you realise you're old. Forget the sick and dying bit. Old, old, old is what it's all about.

It's many years since I've felt an urge to comfort this particular daughter, but I do so now. She throws at me a look that's almost imploring – I think it's imploring – but if so, she instantly thinks better of it. She looks with astonishment at the ear-ring she's holding, replaces it, rearranges herself on the green plastic leather, sits up straight.

'What's my son-in-law say?' I ask.

'Oh he just says I could do voluntary work. Or help out in his office. As if. But that's not earning my own money.' This last comes out as a near wail, for all her straight back, folded hands, resolute expression.

How weird, I think. I've spent all these years feeling inadequate as a mother compared to this daughter and here she is admitting more or less that she feels inadequate in the face of me. I feel too tired to deal with this information now. And anyway, what can I do about it, the whole thing is intractable, such things always are, always were, always have been.

'And on top of that,' she cries finally, 'Of top of that, Milly' – Milly is her cute youngest – 'came home in tears yesterday. She's being bullied, called Darky by some horrible child at her school. I could kill her.'

'I would have killed anybody who did something like that to you,' I say. And as I say this, knew that it was true. I would have done.

'It'll blow over,' my daughter assures me then, hurriedly, as if regretting this admission. 'Her teacher's onto it. And I suppose we've been lucky really, not to have had lots more stuff like that.'

'I suppose you have,' I say. 'Give her a kiss from me, will you.'

'Yes,' my daughter says. We sit in reflective, mournful silence, for a while.

'Do you know,' I say, at last. 'I wasn't sure I wanted children till you arrived. I just went along with the idea, because that's what we all did then. But then when you came - the first few weeks of your life - I just sat and gazed at you in wonder. You were so perfect, every last scrap of you. I didn't much care for the sore breasts and leaking tits, but watching your tight face while you were sucking on me felt - miraculous. I know I wasn't the greatest of mothers, but I'd like you to know that.'

She looks at me silently. I cannot tell what her face says, she is as unreadable as ever: another way she takes after me. To break this dangerous silence, to reassure her that the rosy picture of motherhood I'd offered wasn't so unlike the image she had always carried –she'd been, after all, a child who sometimes tried to break my typewriter because of the competition it represented – I add, smiling, 'I read the whole of Bleak House while I was feeding you. Afterwards I started on War and Peace. But I didn't get very far with that.'

My attempt to ease things merely exhausts me.

'Who doesn't think they're a lousy mother sometimes. You're not unique,' she says sharply.

'I never said I was.' While responding to her censorious tone, I find myself unwilling – and too weary- for a reversion to our usual low-level warfare. Humbly I indicate my spouted cup. 'I feel parched. Could you help me have a drink.'

She becomes all guilty concern. 'Oh god, mum, I'm wearing you out. I shouldn't be talking about me. These aren't your problems.'

'Probably not, given my circumstances,' I say as she advances on me, wishing that elder daughter could sometimes be a little less upright, less virtuous. She is all virtue now, filling the cup from the water jug with its plastic lid, putting her arm round my back, lifting me a little, holding the spout to my dry lips. I can see the lines round her mouth with its cover of discreet lipstick. I can see the equally discreet mascara applied to her lashes and the lines about her eyes (my close vision is still much better than that of most people of my age; much good it does me). She smells of shampoo and some slight scent more like aftershave than scent, a bit too pungent to my nose. One earring brushing my cheeks quite sweetly as she bends ever closer, I find myself full of loving pity for my first child, with her signs of age. All too soon she'd be finding herself where I am.

'*Look on my works ye mighty and despair,*' I murmur not quite to myself as she straightens up.

She frowns. 'Come again? Who brought you those?' she asks, replacing the spouted cup on the bedside locker. She indicates yet another bunch of violets bought by Jen. 'I thought you didn't want any of us bringing you flowers.'

I wasn't so tactless as to name Jen. 'An old publishing friend who didn't know not to. And these are small enough to be tolerable.'

'I suppose,' she says. She is looking at her watch. 'I'd better be going. It's after half-past nine and I said I'd be back by ten.'

'Is it that late?' By the lamplight I should have known, but day folds into night these evenings, all too seamlessly.

She gathers up her suede jacket, her expensive designer bag. She bends over me once again and kisses me lightly.

'No point in saying look after yourself, I suppose,' she says briskly. 'But do.'

'I will,' I promise, pointless as it is. As she holds the door open, she looks back.

'Don't forget the kiss for Milly,' I say. 'I won't,' she replies. 'Good luck,' I add. I don't know if she even hears. But she lifts one hand, crooks her fingers at me in a semblance of wave and goes out. The night nurse appears almost immediately. I'm made ready for sleep

Did she believe me I lie wondering, sleepily, when I told her how besotted with her I'd been when she was newborn? This was true of all my children: there's something about new babies that always affected me, hard-boiled as I think I am. I don't just mean their absolute helplessness: I mean the way they belong to outer space; the limbs that flail at nothing, the eyes that shift at nothing, seem to be looking at something lost in their own heads; their mouths, their faces, ever wincing and grimacing: the blinking little life at the top of their head where the bone has not yet sealed over – the fontanel. Things I'd contemplated for minutes on end sometimes in my first newborn daughter as she slept besides me in a little iron cot in that ward in central London.

I have not thought about the ward in many years. But it comes into my mind now very clearly. Dating from the nineteenth century it had high-ceilings, tiled walls and signs over each bed denoting the name of the philanthropist who'd endowed it – Alderman Mrs Wilkes in my case. I think it was the only place I have ever found myself willingly subsumed within a world of women: we were all subsumed there most likely: our shared space not just the ward itself, but a space of physical discomfort – pain – and at the same time a wondrous and almost idolatrous worship of a kind none of us can ever have felt before: all of us as I remember were having our first babies. It was a world that separated us from our husbands and not just spatially. How could they understand what we felt – even though these were their children? Certainly they couldn't share what we women did: our intense if brief friendships, our irritation with some of our fellows, our amusement or astonishment at others. Our babies.

What I did not know, of course, was if any of them shared the panic I felt along with the besotted love, the euphoria; the panic I've tried to pretend all my life I did not have – that I have only just – too late - succeeded in banishing; how to be a mother, a proper mother, when I had only the barest memory – and maybe no memory at all – of being mothered myself?

Not all of us were middle-class escapees from the obstetric conventions of the time. Several patients were local women, who arrived in this maternity ward because it was the nearest: none of these as far as I could tell had attended our classes. Among them was the nurse in the bed next to me: I could not stand the woman nor could anybody else. She moaned continually about her terrible labour, the pain she was still in. In betweenwhiles she'd snatch her baby up, kissing him fervently and announcing to the entire ward 'these will be the first lips he's ever kissed,' a statement that quenched, briefly my passion for my own daughter.

There was a beautiful woman on the other side of the ward, an actress, I think, who smiled at all of us, grimaced at the nurse as I did, but hardly spoke. She had an equally beautiful, equally long-limbed black husband - maybe they were not actors but dancers - who came faithfully every night, inspected his son gravely, picked him up and cradled him for a while, but spent the rest of the visit, sitting on the bed, very close to his wife with his arm round her, both of them whispering to each other. The first mixed-race couple I'd ever come across, I was reminded of them, years later, by my daughter's family. Seeming to belong to a world whose glamour I could not dream of, their beauty made me so ache with pleasure and longing I resented all the more the overtly racist comments of the little fat girl two beds along whose equally young husband – possibly just boyfriend - tried to get in bed with her, without even bothering to draw the curtains round. He was chased out every time by scandalised nurses. They banned him from visiting in the end.

The bed between these two contained an enormous, black-haired, black-eyed and very jolly Cypriot woman, who ran a café in Covent Garden with her husband. He used to appear every night and sit besides her beaming with pride at his tiny black-haired son. With his huge moustache – how it must have tickled the baby when he kissed it - he looked like one of the Balkan peasants on buses in Jerusalem that I saw many years later. He knew a little English but his wife hardly seemed to speak any. We did know, however, how deeply the intimate exposures of childbirth offended her Turkish modesty: outraged little shrieks and giggles emerged unceasingly from behind her closed curtains one night after an equally blushing young Scots houseman had advanced between them, clutching a large torch, to search for a couple of stitches lost somewhere in or around her fleshy vagina.

I was still laughing we all were – even she was –when visiting time came round and our husbands appeared. I tried to explain the joke to my husband, but he couldn't see it: he didn't seem interested. But then, to my memory, there was little room for men in the ward's maternal space. It enfolded all of us women for that little time, and what space it made for husbands closed up as soon as they'd gone. I assumed my husband's lack of interest was another sign of distances between us: in this case, I suspect, I was quite unfair.

I, too, had soon left the ward behind. Giving birth to my subsequent children in very different environments I'd quite forgotten it. Only now, lying on my deathbed, woozily drifting into morphine assisted sleep, do I find myself back there, laughing. What happened to these women? – to their children? Are all of them still alive, I wonder? There's no reason why they shouldn't be, I'm not that old after all.

The doctors have conferred to a purpose. This morning I wake from a sleep more like coma, my head still aching, to see a hospital porter standing by my bed with a gurney, covered in a clean white sheet.

Peter and a junior doctor are standing next to the porter. 'We're taking you down for a scan,' the doctor says, bending over me closely, as if he thinks I am deaf as well as dozy. 'We want to see what's going on in your head, then we might find a way to ease those headaches of yours.'

'I don't want any more treatment,' I say, weakly. 'I've had enough.'

The doctor glances at Peter, then back at me. 'Oh this is just palliative care,' he says. 'Don't worry. It would be nothing much. Perhaps just a session or two of radio-therapy depending on what we find.'

He looks worried, tired, and very young, years younger than my son. This doesn't stop him making me feel like the child.

I say nothing. Between Peter and the hospital porter I am somehow, plus drip, catheter and everything manoeuvred onto the gurney, then wheeled like a parcel down endless green hospital corridors, the walls lined with cheerful prints and black-and-white photographs of the hospital in times gone by. Weak as I am, I make an effort to look about me. It's probably the last journey I'll take, alive; such a little journey yet such a big one.

I am wheeled at last into a big white room and parked there, close to some white humming machinery. It makes me remember my final exit from home, in a wheel chair that time, taken into the street and left in a parking space behind the ambulance, while the paramedics in their green jackets, with big fluorescent yellow stripes on, prepared it for my entrance. I had thought: *well here I am, parked, literally. I might as well just be a car.* And then: *no, not a car, a carriage without horses. A car has an engine at least, I have no engine any more or barely. I'm being taken to the dump.*' Adding to myself thinking of the private wing I was going to. *A very expensive dump. But a dump for all that.*

These days, of course, I am still weaker, too weak for even a wheelchair. So weak it's an effort to move my still aching head.

Peter doesn't usually stay with me during such expeditions. But he is there now holding my hand while we wait for the machine. The whole business seems pointless to me, so near death. I think it might seem pointless to Peter too, though he repeats the medical mantra. 'If we can see what's going on, we might be able to relieve that pain in some way.'

I groan. 'And here I am thinking you've come up with some miracle cure.'

He grimaces, 'darling that's what you all want. What we all want.'

'It's called die, death.' I say. 'Some hope. It's called get real.'

He smiles at me and squeezes my hand. 'How's Tina?' I ask. 'Still arguing' he says, fondly enough, I think. But at that moment they are ready for me. I am manoeuvred again, my head in a white tunnel that hums all round me as the scan is done.

The doctor returns afterwards. 'I'm afraid there are more tumours. In your brain this time. A few sessions of radio-therapy should ease the pain.'

'So I won't hurt any more I'll just go gaga.' I say. And then ever more weakly I beg him, beg him, 'no more treatment. No more treatment. *Please.*'

I do not feel myself being wheeled back to the room. I fall into something near coma, from which I wake sometimes to blinding, articulate clarity. How much longer now? How long?

Even without treatment my headache eases a little. Now the end is so near I feel much more peaceful. My anger receding, I know that I do not want to die angry, not with either father, not with the innocently guilty incestuous one, not even with the treacherous adoptive one. No more do I want to die angry with myself. I find myself clinging instead, very gently and quietly, to the safer memories of my adopted father in which betrayal only figures in ways, I can try – I need - to understand.

Once again in my near-coma, I disinter the decent, Trabi-like old father. Who had kept my mother from me, true, and hidden all her letters in his desk – hadn't he realised I'd find them when he was dead? And what was I to make of that? Knowing he had lied to me, not directly so much as in his silences, I used to think at times that he'd hidden the letters out of obstinacy or lack of imagination or jealousy or vengeance against his still adored ex-wife: all of which fed my anger: I have never been a very forgiving woman. Yet now I am able to think again, more kindly, that it was because he loved me so much, because he could not bear to lose me as well as my mother. Such loving had little to do with genetics, in his case. I was, after all, genetically, just his first cousin once removed.

But my father defied genetics, in many respects. He defied his tribe the way humans are able to, unlike animals. Not just voting in his old age to allow women into the Marylebone County Cricket Club, but, much more significantly, fleeing for home years earlier after less than one week of a visit to friends of my stepmother in South Africa, so appalled was he by the 'whites only' signs he saw all around him. Just the same – Bertie Wooster, Lord Jim, a left over Henty boy hero, whatever you like to call him – he would have gone willingly, gladly to die for his country, fighting the hellish Nazi Volk, had he been allowed to.

I think, too, of political philosophy, my real father's cricket bag. Forget Hobbes and the bleak pessimism to which I've been drawn sometimes: the brutality of men, needing to be contained by tyrants, seemed apt enough. Forget slippery Machiavelli whether he's telling princes what to do or warning citizens what to look out. Take instead quintessentially English John Locke who believed in reason and decency, in a system of law that invites you to behave decently but does not prescribe the behaviour as long as it *is* decent. *Negative freedom* Nate had told me that was called. I've never read much Locke – he's far too long-winded for me, unlike Hobbes. But I recognise his humanity: just as I recognise the humanity in my far from philosophical, adoptive father.

Years ago I found in Locke's journals a description of a very old woman called Alice George: the warmth of the passage, its close observation of the old woman, the equality in which she and Locke confront each other will do very well. This is a passage I know by heart almost, because it reminds me of my father's equally English decency: reminds me once more of his heading, arm in arm with the red-nosed, sometimes rather drunken widow from next door, for a drink in the Grasshopper Pub.

She goes upright with a staff in her hand. I saw her stoop once without resting upon anything, taking up once a pot and at another time her glove from the ground. Her hearing is very good and her smelling so quick that as she came near me she said I smelled very sweet, I having a pair of new gloves on that were not strong scented.....She has as comely a face as ever I saw any old woman have and old age has made her neither deformed or decrepit.

Now I do not think people are responsible for their cancers. Nor do I think – there's been a book about this recently – that people with cancer should 'think positively.' Cancer is cancer. Sometimes, as in my case, it is a death sentence – how can you be positive about that? Especially when, as in my case, a little genetic information might have saved my life. So the oncologist told me when I confessed my lately acquired knowledge of my Ashkenazi Jewish heritage: told him my grandmother had died of breast cancer in Berlin before the war. Of course I didn't know for sure that my father's family carried the Ashkenazi BRCA1 gene, but it seemed likely: and equally likely that my father had passed it onto me. 'Had I known all that, years ago,' the oncologist said, 'I'd have insisted on giving you an oophorectomy, wiping out your ovaries. Survivors of breast cancer with your genes have a more than 30% chance of getting ovarian cancer, just as you have. In fact I did offer it, I seem to remember. But on the basis of what I knew about you then, I didn't insist.'

'Maybe I wouldn't have let you do an oophorectomy even in that case,' I said.

'With those odds you'd have been a fool not to let me,' he said.

I liked my oncologist – he was neither glamorous nor handsome and had a tendency to be pedantic but he was a very nice man who listened to what I had to say and never put me down, though he might have been tempted to sometimes. Of course he had more time for me as a private patient, but I suspected he was just as nice if more hurried with his NHS patients.

'Well at least there's no arthritis or diabetes or high blood pressure in my family, as far as I know,' I said. 'Things could be much worse. I might have inherited Huntingdon's Chorea and been demented years already. And at least I'm not going to live long enough to inherit dementia from my mother.'

'There is at least that,' he said, doubtfully.

'Yes.' I said. But I was also thinking that, most likely, in the long run, nothing could have helped me, even had I known the truth in time and let him whip away my guilty breast, my most likely guilty ovaries. The bloody thing had been bound to get me in the end, hadn't it? Yet for all my refusal to admit the psychosomatic aspects of my disease – it was bred in my body, for God's sake - I do not think it was entire coincidence that it wasn't until I learned the full truth of my parentage, till I learned my father's refusal to let my mother near me, that the cancer really began its raging; it, all the cancers, all the little tumours rampaging within me, my own dear little lumps, inherited from my Jewish grandmother, that have led me here, to this room, to my approaching death.

I'd seen my mother's letters of course before then. But what had they told me? Nothing much. They said things like; *I'm in London*: or *'I'm working hard:* or *I saw ducks in the park today.'* None of which meant more to me than the repeated phrases. *I miss you.* Or: *See you soon, darling. Lots of love, mummy, xxxxx.*

Nor, until I found her, had the full extent of my father's betrayal had became clear. I did not know which of them I'd been angrier with at that time. Was it with my adopted father – why did he keep the letters all those years if he'd been keeping me from my mother in every other respect? Or was it with my unsatisfactory mother whose effusions I'd thrown in the dustbin, anyway, some time back? Because she can't have missed me, if she really had, she would have come back to find me, no matter what. I would have come back for *my* children: I think I would. But she never had. If I forgive her now, if I forgive him, the forgiveness has been hard won.

I hear voices now. I open my eyes to see Jen standing besides me; and beyond her another figure one I never expected to see in this life again. My Australian daughter.

'So your window opened: well done darling,' I say meanly – and then I add, because it is true. 'I'm so glad you made it in time. I am so very glad.'

'So am I,' my daughter says. 'Though I wish I didn't have to see you quite like this. You look terrible.' My Aussie daughter never did mince her words. Yet her eyes, I see, are full of tears.

'So do you. Join the club,' I say, closing my own. I add tartly, 'Dying isn't a beauty treatment, you know.' But I'm glad she's so direct. I realise I've missed that. Neither my elder daughter or my son spoke so openly, in that she is more like me: or at least like the person I might have turned into had I, too, ended up in Australia.

I hear Jen say, sounding both embarrassed and astonished – but then she'd never had much experience of real mothers and daughters. 'I'd better leave you two alone.' 'It's up to you,' and then 'no, maybe it would be best,' I hear my daughter answer. Though there was never overt jealousy between my surrogate daughter and my genetic ones I am sure there is some on the genetic side, if not on Jen's. The coolness in my Aussie daughter's voice confirms it, I daresay. It was hard for both her and her elder sister to understand why I was so much closer to someone of their own age – or so it must have seemed to them. But there are different kinds of closeness and they were, are, my true daughters, after all, whatever our differences.

I am glad all over again that Aussie daughter is here. I am even grateful. Jen goes out of the room – this is the last time I will see her. Aussie daughter draws up the green chair and sits close beside me, holding my hand and almost crying. I drift off again into what is this time the sweetest of sweet comas. And when I return from it – god knows when – it might have been hours or even days later - she has gone.

CHAPTER THIRTY-TWO

My story is quite done now: both Mariner and wedding guest have been relieved of duty. Though I cannot say what's happened to the albatross – if there was one – I am more resigned these days: I do not scream against death any longer. Travelling much more gently into my good night I have even come to accept it, more or less, begin to find myself half welcoming what is to come. I've lost the energy to protest, in any case; my pain has eased if not disappeared altogether. I spend more and more time in my state of coma or semi-coma - or so I hear them say, my family, the doctors coming and going: I am no longer able to reckon such things for myself. In all events, the world will soon be going on without me in its same old appalling way, added to now by global warming, by nuclear proliferation. Mankind, still as bellicose as the Husband's ants, seems to have learned no lessons; the fallout from new wars appears quite as bad as the fallout from the old ones that affected all my generation, my parents' generation. Wars may end, leaders sign their formal treaties, but in the informal heads of informal people there are no such treaties: the wars go on.

The Husband was watching some news programme last night on the television slanted above my head– he thought I was asleep but I wasn't, quite: I heard the presenters discussing the numbers of ex-servicemen in prison, survivors of Northern Irish troubles, Bosnia, Iraq, Afghanistan who suffering from post traumatic stress could not manage normal life. And this was not to mention I thought as I lay there all the civilians wounded, lost, bereaved by what had happened, whose sufferings too would echo down through the generations: all the people weeping for their dead seventy, eighty, nearly ninety years on, just like my poor father.

As for the guilt and horror aroused by the revelations of my parentage it has vanished, more or less: resignation to death, seems to have resigned me besides to who and what I was. I think with love of both my fathers, the guilty and the guiltless, neither of them like Hamlet whatever my mother thought, the two of us saddled with a name which had less to do with me, I think, than with her.

Un-Ophelia is me, pretty much, I've decided: thinking with pity – and a little love - of the true Ophelia who was and is my mother, a mother both guilty and guiltless just like my fathers: at the same time a much more conventional woman altogether than I used to imagine, growing up. I compared the demented woman I'd met with the lovely, madcap mother I once dreamed of– how else could I bear the thought of her having run away and left me? I compared both these new and the old images with the images of my morally – and yes intellectually – weightier, adoptive father: a man staid as staid, yet so much more truly romantic at heart than she was. I have even begun to compare all these images with myself, to think of myself, of all my past selves, in particular my young one, with a tenderness mixed with a certain amount of contempt. If I am in some respects still guilty, if I remain incorrigible, I can begin to forgive myself, too: I do, a bit.

   Little as it should matter now – little as I know it does - I even find myself proud still, in small ways, of some things in my life: of the many books I published, the authors I saw through to success, of the children I reared, of my grandchildren. Even, disgracefully, I remember with pleasure as well as shame at least some of my sexual adventures. Guilt has not in the end trumped everything, the way at one time I thought it would. Nor has anger trumped everything: what is the point in dying angry? – maybe anger – rage – fury - is what hellfire is about. I'm not the only fallible person around, I have realised; the sins of my many parents were far from mortal. In face of my coming dissolution, though the music is still atonal rather than harmonic, though the kaleidoscope is turning yet again - I can almost hear its sibilant clatter - the pieces are falling into shape. Dark and ever darker as it is, they form a true, a recognisable pattern. The dominant colour could be love, to my surprise: where did *that* come from? And can I believe it? I am not sure. But I'd like to.

   Life might be, it *is*, nasty, brutish and short – for many: for some it's far, far worse than that. Yet if you're lucky – or have the eyes to see them – it's also full of wonders. If the essence of holiness is to renounce such wonders, long before the end, then I'd sooner renounce holiness: I'm pretty sure I just did.

And so we arrive at DEATH. Something that terrifies us all and always has done: *timor mortis conturbat me.* Driven by our genes, we might be, just like animals, but unlike animals – ants know how to kill, they get killed but that's all there is to it - we think about it: we know what to expect.

It's not just the basic machinery, the body - sturdy bones, short legs, brown eyes, small feet, left-handedness, a reasonable brain, in my case - that dies. Along with it goes human archaeology, its equivalent of pottery shards and metal pieces: the body's history in the world. They seem trivial mostly: included among my shards and pieces are the sound of my father's quacking razor and a passion for snails in garlic butter: a pin number based on a former husband's birth date (the much regretted dead one: maybe I should have replaced it with his date of death): a preference for coffee made in an aluminium Italian espresso pot, once lovingly tended by the husband who ran off with the sexy widow in the next chateau, but left his coffee pot behind. There was also a fondness for opera aroused by my first husband– *Voi che Sapete*, I hear – and *Vissi d'arte e amore* – and the splurge of orchestral light when Janacek's three hundred year old heroine at last accepts her death – all mixed up disconcertingly with idiot tunes played round the house by my children – *Chirpy Chirpy Cheep Cheep* – *Sugar Sugar,* joined recently by *Mama says,* sung at a school concert by my talented eldest granddaughter –turning up in my head at unwanted moments, along with snatches of the poetry (*I met a traveller from an antique land…..Much have I travelled in the realms of gold…*) introduced to me by the quasi-lesbian headmistress and rooted in the brain ever since: a swathe of Somerset landscape in which I holidayed, sweetly, for once, with my children; the smell of goat from goodness knows where or when. Trivial, yes, all of it: but not *just* trivial. Such mental artefacts dug from deep-laid strata within the brain and senses of the human site sum up – summon up - whole eras of enjoyed or suffered life. I grieve for their passing, at least as much as I grieve the passing of my already near departed body. But pass they will. Sic transit. *Mama says*

My final conversation with Peter my favourite nurse, my final brief flash of lucidity and coherence in the oncoming dark, goes like this. I am pretty much comatose when he walks into the room, but not as comatose as he imagines when he starts talking; he's not having the conversation with himself as I rather assume he thinks. Though maybe he is having with it himself, maybe I am having it with *myself*, maybe I imagine this conversation altogether from the depths of my near dark.

'We have decided to get married in September,' he is saying. 'But we still can't quite agree, Tina and I, on how to spend our money. I'd still prefer the fancy honeymoon.'

'I've a feeling' I hear myself drawling out – I think I do - 'that you're going to get the fancy wedding.'

Peter sighs. 'Oh the honeymoon. Florida, I'd thought. But not if we have the fancy wedding.'

Lifting myself up into my last spurt of consciousness – if it is consciousness - I say, 'I've never been to Florida. But I'm with you on preferring the honeymoons: I've had several.' (*There you go, Jane Ophelia, boastful to the last about the entirely trivial. Look on my works yet mighty and despair.*)

'Ooh naughty,' he sounds appreciative. 'And there I was, silly me, thinking you were asleep.'

'I'm not dead yet, only nearly. Sorry, nurse.'

'Oh I know you're not dead yet, dear; your vital signs haven't given up on you entirely.'

'Well that's something to be thankful for,' I say. 'I heard somewhere that life is the sum of the functions by which it is resisted.'

'That's not entirely too clever for me, dear, but very nearly,' he says disapprovingly.

'For me too, 'I say with a sigh. 'And on the subject of honeymoons, I can tell you that I didn't always bother with the wedding.'

'Still naughtier,' he says. 'Well, I certainly was wrong when I thought you were asleep.'

'Will you invite my ghost to your wedding, Peter?' I ask, ever drowsier, coming from some place farther and farther away.

'Of course, dear. I'll send an invitation via the angels,' he says, checking my catheter, my drip, all the paraphernalia which keeps me alive more or less, though not for much longer.

For a moment I am annoyed he assumes my death so readily. But of course he's right: by now I am sinking, deep, deep, deep. 'Will you come to my dead wedding?' I seem to be asking. But maybe I do not ask aloud, maybe, by now, I cannot. And maybe, had he heard me he would not have understood, anyway, what I meant by '*my dead wedding*'.

If this was the conversation, truly, it was my last: with Peter or anyone. I am now sunken deep within my final coma. I hear people talking round me, hear every word they say, but cannot make any answers. I cannot even see the speakers any longer. I'll never know whether Peter and his fiancée spend their money on their wedding or on their honeymoon. I'll never know how my husband will spend the fortune I leave him – or how long his overweight and smoking habit will let him stay alive – or if my eldest daughter will find herself a job. I will never know what happens in the Archers – not that I've ever cared, unlike some, what happens in the Archers. The saddest thing about death, I think, is all the stories you'll never hear to the end. Although they are the same stories probably as all the stories ever. How many stories are there in the world? Not many.

My son comes now and lays his head on my breast and howls, quietly, 'Don't die, mum, I need you,' he wails. In a little while, he admits that his wife is about to leave him. This is the story I'm most sad not to be able to follow: that and the story of his pot-smoking son Jakey. I'd like to see him recover from his grief - I think he will recover, my son is tough in his head, like me: I'm not so sure about Jakey. But I'm glad he feels able to tell me, even if he thinks I cannot hear a word he says. And I'm glad he needs me – and can admit he needs me- glad I can offer just a little comfort - he seems to find it a comfort – in the warmth of the remaining breast on which he lies. I know that he knows that I love him: that is something for both of us. As is the fact that he loves me.

My daughters come and go too; the Australian one has obviously found herself quite a big window, as big or bigger than the one in my nursery that shattered when the rocket fell. I even seem to hear her crying again. I think I hear her. While the Husband sits besides me, holding my hand, except when he needs a pee or something to eat – he always tells me where he's going, as if he knows that I can still hear or at least hopes so. Sometimes he leaves me alone, tactfully, with one or other or all of my children.

My breath grows more and more laboured: comes less and less frequently. On an instant it will be ceasing altogether. Shall I have another instant of breathless consciousness I wonder? I don't know. I only know that very shortly Jo - or Jane Ophelia – or un-Ophelia -unlike my mother I did not go mad, I never fell in love with a melancholy boy, only a melancholy man – very shortly, this not always satisfactory person will reach her end. A real end: I do not believe in an afterlife. I do believe this body of mine is all there is: that the rest really is silence and the determined, the useful, busyness of worms.

There was a lady all skin and bone,
And such a lady was never known.
It happened on a holiday
The lady went to church to pray.

And when she came unto the stile,
She tarried there a little while,
And when she came unto the door,
She tarried there a little more.

And when she came unto the aisle,
She wore a sad and a woeful smile.
She'd come a long and a weary mile,
Her sin and sorrow to beguile.

And she walked up, and she walked down,
And spied a dead man upon the ground.
And from his nose unto his chin,
The worms crept out, and the worms crept in.

And the lady to the sexton said,
Shall I be so when I am dead?
And the sexton to the lady said,
You'll be the same when you are dead!

Anon

Acknowledgments

I have to thank first my two main editors: Joanna Goldsworthy, who wrestled with the earliest drafts and got me to bring a coherent one out of them. And Gillian Stern who helped me transform that draft still further.

I also have to thank friends who read the book in various drafts and made useful comments. Ruth Fainlight, helped remove much dross and made a very crucial suggestion for improving the final draft. Judith Elliott and Judith Vidal Hall both read the book at an earlier stage and made invaluable comments. I'm grateful to all of them, as I'm also grateful to my agents past and present, Deborah Owen and Clare Conville, both of whom have struggled over the years, sometimes thanklessly, on my behalf.

Thanks too to Meinrad Craighead in whose wonderful studio and still more wonderful backyard in Albuquerque the name Ophelia first swam into my head.

And thanks, finally, above all, to David Macfarland, who lived amiably through all the not always good-tempered birthing struggles from then on in.

Printed in Great Britain
by Amazon.co.uk, Ltd.,
Marston Gate.